BREAK THE CHUTE

Stefanie K. Steck

BREAK THE CHUTE

ISBN (paperback): 979-8-9866169-7-1

Edited by: Caitlin Lengerich and Jenn Lockwood.

Proofread by Vee Troy

Book Cover by EverAfter Cover Design

Character Art by Erika Plum

Chapter headers and scene breaks designed with CanvaPro

First Edition 2026

For the eleven-year-old me who wanted to be an author more than any-thing. You did it. You wrote a book you love, and that reminded you of your dream. Now...don't let it go. If you do...pick up this book again and remember.

Note from the Author

Break the Chute is a contemporary romance that handles mature themes. This book is intended for 18+ readers as explicit sexual scenes are detailed on page. It deals with topics that have taken research, such as rodeo terminology, day to day life of a bull rider, magazine and photography workplace and history on rodeo facts. Even with research, creative liberties were taken. Content warnings that could be triggering to some readers include alcoholism including potential relapse, abusive parent and spousal abuse (told on page through a memory), emotional trauma, rodeo injury, and mistreatment in the workplace. I hope I have handled these with care. Your mental health come first, and please take care of yourself. Thank you for picking up *Break the Chute*, I hope you love it as much as I do.

Rodeo 101

*B*reak the Chute is very rodeo heavy, and follows the main characters as they travel to different rodeos over the western circuits. The characters talk about the rodeo on a daily basis—including historical facts, acronyms and how the events are scored. One of my favorite things were the historic aspects of their conversations. Those facts were researched and are accurate to the rodeo. It also mentions real people who are competing, or have competed in the rodeo. Shad Mayfield, Joyce Loomis, JB Mauney, TJ Grey and Stetson Wright just name a few. For your enjoyment, here's a cheat sheet of rodeo facts:

NFR—National Finals Rodeo. Held every December in Las Vegas Nevada by the PRCA. The top fifteen cowboys/cowgirls with the highest standings from each event compete over ten days to earn the world title.

PRCA—Professional Rodeo Cowboy Association. The oldest and largest professional rodeo sanction.

PBR—Professional Bull Riders, Inc. Largest bull riding league in the world, sanctioning numerous events across various countries.

Slack Event—Extension of the main rodeo event, mainly happening before the actual rodeo begins. Most commonly used for timed events (tie down, team roping, barrel racing and steer wrestling).

Chute—Or 'Bucking Chute' is a specialized, narrow corridor designed to hold bulls and broncs before the event to get the animal positioned for the cowboy.

Standings—In the rodeo, the success is based off the amount of money earned. Cowboys/Cowgirls pay attention to how much they have earned in the PRCA Standings to compete in the NFR. Only the top fifteen in standings go to the NFR in December.

How a bull ride is scored—Bull riding is based on the performance of the rider and the bull, with a total score of 100 points, 50 points for the rider, 50 points for the bull. Four judges look at the cowboy's ability to control the situation as well as their body position throughout the duration of the ride. The bull is judged by speed and power with which he is attempting to buck the cowboy off. A good score is considered to be at or over 75 points.

Qualified ride—when the ride lasts for a total of eight seconds. The clock starts when the bulls shoulders breaks the gate and ends when the riders hand comes out of the rope, touches the ground, or touches the bull with their free hand.

No score—happens when the rider fails to meet the criteria for scoring. If the rider touches the bull with his free hands or falls off the bull before the eight second mark.

Miss Rodeo America—Pageant competition that exists for the purpose of selected a young woman to be the spokesperson for the rodeo. Applicants must have rodeo knowledge, past and present, and have skill in horseman ship.

CHAPTER ONE
Emersyn

"Nope." I glowered at my computer screen. "That sucks."

Grasping the mouse between my fingers, I raised the lighting on the photo once again. The shadow under the bull came into better lighting, but now the cowboy looked like a black blob, and the crowd behind him was nothing more than patches of washed-out color. My eyes fluttered closed, complete with a growl of frustration. Who the hell took this photo and thought it was good enough to come to me for editing? Running my fingers through my blonde hair, I looked at the top of the computer screen, searching for the photographer's name.

"Jenna..." I grumbled, hunching my shoulders. "Learn how to use the exposure...you're a photographer. You have a degree. You're the head of the department. I swear you know this stuff." Pouncing on the mouse with more rage than necessary, I went to the side of the program and tried to fix this photo. It could be a great shot. The bull was midair, right after breaking from the chute, and the cowboy had his back arched, his arm high above his head. The bones of the photo were there, but it was going to take some time to spruce up, and—lucky me—it was my job to get it to *Rodeo Way's* standards.

When I applied for the job at an up-and-coming online rodeo publication, my hope was to use my actual degree in journalism, but after a few years of being assistants to multiple higher ups, Morgan Pennel—the Editor in Chief at *Rodeo Way*—discovered that photography was my minor. When the publication began to grow, I got a promotion to digital editor—editing photos, not actually taking them. I enjoyed my job the majority of the time. It actually helped me feel like I was a part of the rodeo instead of stuck behind a desk—but I missed the dirt. I missed being a part of that world in more ways than one and being given photos that didn't capture the sport in all its glory...only made me wish I could start all over again somehow.

"Nope." I heaved a sigh. "Too bright. Now not bright enough...okay..." I twisted my head, looking at the side of my monitor. "Maybe it's the screen?" I pushed the menu button with such force that my colleagues could most likely hear the click from their offices.

"I thought we agreed that getting mad at your computer doesn't, in fact, help the photo become any better."

The voice that came from my office door was the only thing that could bring a smile to my face in the midst of frustration. I felt a grin tug on my lips, and I tilted my head to see my best friend, Luca, coming into view behind my monitor. He stood with his ankles crossed and arms folded, his shoulder resting on the door frame, with one eyebrow raised so high it hid behind his wavy dark hair.

"You would be acting the same way if you saw these photos," I quipped, pointing at my screen.

"Good thing I don't edit photos, because yeah"—he pushed himself off the door frame—"I would have been fired a long time ago. Come on." He cocked his head. "You need a break."

"A break," I parroted. "It's only ten—oh." I slumped in my chair. "You mean it's time for the meeting?"

He spun on his heel and raised a finger in the air. "Bingo. I bet you she's gonna hand out some new assignments today. I have a few approved, but one left hanging in the air."

"One assignment that hasn't been approved? That's not like you."

Luca shrugged his shoulder. "It'll get approved. No doubt in my mind. Just *you* watch."

Shaking my head at him, I grabbed my iPad and took one last glance at the photo on my computer screen. Giving it one last glare, I snarled, "I'll be back for you," before heading out of my office into the hustle that was *Rodeo Way* Magazine.

Ever since I was a kid, I had been immersed in the rodeo world. My father was a cowboy, a header in team roping, taking him and his heeler all the way to the National Final Rodeo. My mother was former Miss Rodeo America and coached stunt riders who performed during major rodeos. I, of course, followed in her footsteps and loved every single minute of it. I performed on the backs of multiple horses, doing stunts even my mother wouldn't dare to do, and made my way to my own Miss Rodeo America pageant. When I lost, I found another way to be a part of the rodeo—photography.

Getting a degree in journalism and photography seemed like my best bet to bring people into the world and let them experience it through my eyes. It seemed perfect, traveling to rodeos weekend after weekend to capture everything...if only it had worked out that way.

Rodeo Way was a brand-new online magazine when I first came on, and in the seven years I'd been here, we'd grown exponentially. What was once a small little office building with a team of ten became a building with fifty people working on different projects at a time. Journalists would travel to rodeos, sending back their articles to be edited for features. Photographers were able to fill the walls with their photos of the NFR, cowboys holding up their buckles after their wins, ranches and landscapes scattered in between them.

Being around people who loved the sport just as much as I did...that was what made this entire life shift worth it.

Luca waited for me at the door frame of the conference room, opening his arm as I passed him stepping over the threshold. The moment he was behind me, both of his hands hit my shoulders, pushing half his weight onto me before he joined the other travel coordinators on the opposite side of the table. He gave me a quick wink as he took his seat. Sliding in next to the other editors, I opened my iPad to a blank document, knowing that all meetings Morgan Pennel held had some form of assignment change to them, ready for any note taking she may need.

Right as the white blank sheet filled the screen, a notification banner dropped down. *Ty Grant scores 79 in Texas...see the video here,* and I swiped it up and away.

"Filing that away in your memory, Emersyn?"

The voice that filtered next to me caused only a slight chuckle. "You know it, Sterling."

The head of the editing department, who also happened to be my ex, Sterling Krass, slid into the chair next to me, dropping his own iPad on the table. His blond hair was perfectly styled, not a strand out of place, even after he ran his hand through it. He knew he was good looking, and he sure as hell flaunted it.

"What's Ty's average this year?" he asked, settling back into his seat, rocking it back and forth.

I shook my head, not really wanting to answer him. I wasn't sure if he was teasing me about my rodeo stat knowledge or truly wanting to know the answer. I knew it, of course. Ty was doing really well this year in the Professional Bull Riding League and Professional Rodeo Cowboys Association, but Sterling didn't need to know I knew that fact.

Morgan came in moments later, thankfully saving me from having to answer him. I gave Luca one last glance, and he returned my smile with a thumbs up and even cheesier smile. I laughed and turned my attention to Morgan at the head of the table, her fingertips touching the wood lightly.

"Good morning, everyone," she began, her smile spreading across her face. "We're all here and on time. Perfect."

I gave the room one last glance, noticing everyone sitting with their respective groups. To my left were my fellow digital editors, Gavin and Lucy, and next to them, Jenna headed up the photography department. To my right, Sterling started the row of editors, then the travel coordinators, where Luca made himself comfortable, and every feature writer, staff writer...all their assistants surrounding the edge of the room. Somehow, it seemed that every employee was jammed into this one room.

"We have a long list of rodeos to add to our docket. The PRCA website has them listed through November, and I simply can't believe how many rodeos have been added to the line-up. This year is going to be big, so after a board meeting, we have divvied up assignments and...well...get ready. I have an idea that is going to turn *Rodeo Way* into what it was meant to be."

Morgan's voice carried through the room as everyone moved to set up their own tablets or notepads. The only one who wasn't moving—I noticed—was Luca. I tapped my iPad to life, not taking my eyes off of my friend as he leaned back in his chair and crossed his arms. He popped his tongue in his cheek and gave me a wink. I narrowed my eyes at him but turned back to Morgan, who began spouting off all the different pieces that would be going into *Rodeo Way's* September issue.

Rodeo Way had just ventured out into print, printing four issues a year: winter, spring, summer, and fall. Summer was always the biggest one, releasing in May and staying on shelves until September. The fall issue mainly covered the summer round-up and had predictions for the NFR, but Morgan wanted to start something new—features. A different cowboy or cowgirl from the summer, and her idea seemed pretty straightforward. I could see the writers shifting in their chairs, most likely itching to know who was going to be chosen for the first feature to hit *Rodeo Way* this fall.

"Now, who can tell me..." Morgan trailed off, her eyes darting around the room. "Who is leading the boards in the PBR and PRCA right now?"

The room grew quiet, and all eyes turned to me. Everyone knew I was the one who had *The Cowboy Channel* on as background noise when I was at home. Everyone knew that I was the one who studied the standings each night and followed the top fifteen year after year. I followed the rodeo like some people followed college football or March Madness. I knew every cowboy, every cowgirl, every horse and bull in the Professional Rodeo Cowboy Association and Professional Bull Rider standings. You could ask me anything—and I could give you the answer. Sterling wasn't wrong when he said I was filing that notification about Ty Grant away in my brain, but Ty Grant wasn't the bull rider I had been watching.

Letting out a small, breathy laugh, I answered, "Oakes Ashford."

I felt a finger tap on my temple, and I spun to look at Sterling, who cocked me a grin with his finger still aimed at my forehead. I scoffed and lowered his hand down, brushing off the flirting moment Sterling was attempting to pull off. Sterling and I had started within days of each other. There was attraction, there was flirting, and there was...a lot more than that. And even though we had been broken up for years, Sterling's flirtatious personality still acted like we were still together.

I turned back to Morgan, ignoring the smirk spread across Sterling's face. "Oakes is leading the board with earnings of $197,187 as of Friday night. He's basically taking the world by storm."

Even though Oakes had been riding for years, he finally became a well-known name when he won the world championship five years ago...then proceeded to win three years in a row. No matter what, he would get a qualified ride. Oakes would always...*always*...give you a show. The last few years, he came in second or third, congratulating the new champion, but you could see it on his face—he wanted that title back. He trained vigorously. He rode whenever he could, sticking to the western circuits only, proving that it didn't matter how far the cowboy traveled or where they rode. All that mattered was how much money they racked up, and this year, Oakes Ashford was well on his way to getting what he wanted.

Morgan smiled at me, her eyebrows raising slightly before she inhaled, her entire body oozing with dominance. "I've had the opportunity to meet Mr. Ashford earlier this year, and I feel he would be a great cowboy to be our first feature. The plan is to shadow him for his summer run, travel with him, and truly break him open. Learn what makes Oakes Ashford tick."

"That may be harder than you think," I piped in. "All I've been able to find is his stats."

"That's why I think he would be perfect." Morgan pointed at me. "No one really knows who he is. I say it's about time we find out. I sat down with Luca—"

I shot my attention towards my friend, who only wiggled his eyebrows at me.

"—and we have his entire summer schedule. We're looking at close to forty rodeos, and we have just the person to make this feature everything it could be, exactly what *Rodeo Way* is all about."

Morgan looked around the room, and the silence grew heavy. Morgan loved to build out any tension, and the gleam in her eye told me she was relishing in this. I shook my head and scribbled on my iPad. It was only then that I noticed my new assignment section hadn't been filled yet.

"Well..." Justin, one of the lead journalists, leaned forward in his seat, his elbows hitting hard on the table. "You gonna tell us or keep dragging it out?"

"Emersyn Flynn."

Morgan's voice made my eyes shoot up.

"Wait, what?" I asked, dropping my stylus on the screen. "Me?"

"You have a journalism and photography degree, so...I want you to work on this project. The article will be due in July, and Sterling"—Morgan gestured to Sterling, who reached up and patted my shoulder—"has already agreed to be your editor on this feature. I would like you to work on your own photos, since you can take them and turn them into works of art—"

"Wait, Morgan," I waved my hand in front of me. "You want me, a digital editor, to go out on the field to follow Oakes Ashford around for the summer? Me?"

"It makes the most sense, if you think about it." Luca shrugged across the table.

My eyes met his but then darted to the other writers around the table, and to my surprise, they all seemed to agree. No one seemed shocked that I was picked for this new idea Morgan conjured up.

"I haven't written in years," I stammered. "I haven't really taken a photo in years."

"You have made some of the most washed-out photos to look like a masterpiece. How many pieces hang on these walls that you've edited?" Her eyebrow rose.

"Edited," I corrected her, "not taken. The credit goes to Jenna, or Hank, or—"

Morgan waved me off, continuing as if I didn't even speak. "I've read your past work, and I've always been impressed with your knowledge. When Luca suggested your name, it felt right. And when Sterling came on, it all seemed to fit. I have no doubt that you will be able to bring something amazing to the issue."

I bit the inside of my lip, my gaze locked in on Morgan.

"What do you say?" she beamed.

"I can't believe you hesitated." Luca flopped down on the small chair across from my desk after the meeting, his smile wide as he rested his head in his hands.

I gave him a slight glare, but ultimately, it turned to a smile. "I can't believe you kept this from me." I tapped on my keyboard, bringing my screen back to life with Jenna's photo that, at this point, I had no interest in saving. I shrunk it down and opened a Google tab.

"I wanted it to be a surprise. You deserve to be in the field, and come on...who better to follow Oakes Ashford around?" He opened his arms, leaning his chair back on two legs. "Morgan was all on board when I suggested you."

My fingers buzzed over my keyboard. *Oakes Ashford.*

"Are you Googling?" Luca chuckled, his chair hitting the carpet with a thump. "You know everything there is to know. Why are you Googling?"

"I know his stats." I looked up at Luca through my lashes, keeping my chin down. "If I go on this assignment—"

"You are. No *if.* You already agreed."

"I need to know *him.*"

"That's the purpose of the assignment." Luca moved, leaning forward and snatching my keyboard from me, sliding it over to him. Some days, I missed the wired keyboard. "Stop Googling. This isn't going to be just about his rodeo stats and how the man is making bull riding seem so easy. It's going to be the entire summer. Numerous cities. Almost forty rodeos—I think thirty-eight in total."

"And Justin or Val couldn't handle thirty-eight rodeos?"

"How many rodeos did you go to when you were Miss Rodeo Wyoming?" He raised a brow.

I pursed my lips and thought. My reign as Miss Rodeo Wyoming was one of the best years of my life...one I wouldn't soon forget. "More than thirty-eight," I admitted.

"Exactly. You can write the article, take and edit your own photos, all while working around the rodeos. His schedule is mainly Wednesdays through Sundays, so at least you'll have a few days off to, you know, really get to know him. Morgan is set that you are the one who can figure out who Oakes Ashford really is."

"He's a pretty private person," I said softly, leaning back into my chair.

"Well..." Luca sat up straight, rubbing his palms along his thighs. "Now's the time to get to know him. And that's what Morgan wants."

"Okay, Morgan wants it, but is that what Oakes is going to be expecting?"

Luca's jaw tensed, and I heaved a sigh. I met Luca on day one of being hired at *Rodeo Way*, and since then, he and I had become glued at the hip. I probably would have dated him instead of Sterling if I were his type. I knew him more than anyone...and he wasn't telling me something.

"What?" I asked him, a groan filling the space between us. "What aren't you telling me?"

He let out a breath. "I haven't personally talked to him."

"Hold on." I raised a hand, palm facing him. "What do you mean *you haven't personally talked to him?*"

"I've talk to his agent," he sighed, defending himself. "Morgan met him once, but all this coordinating has been with his agent, Drew Manning.

He's a nice guy and has pretty much assured us Oakes would be up for this."

"So..." I raised an eyebrow. "Are you saying he hasn't even agreed? Morgan said—"

"That he seemed like the perfect cowboy for this project."

"None of this is set in stone?"

"It's...painted..." Luca twisted his lips at his analogy, probably hoping it was so off balance, it would work. "...on stone...with watercolor."

"Meaning..." I urged him on.

"It could get washed away, but I'm ninety-seven percent certain the man is up for this."

"Ninety-seven percent?"

Luca nodded.

I pursed my lips. "And what happens if I get there and he's not?"

"Then you get to attend a few rodeos and write about them. You know...what you want to do."

"I hate you."

"No, you don't. And you're excited about this. I can see it." Luca smirked.

I narrowed my eyes, shaking my head at him.

I was excited. This was exactly what I wanted when I took this job at *Rodeo Way*. To be back on the dirt, taking photos, writing about the sport I was so passionate about. But a small part of me was wondering *why now? What had I done to earn this assignment?* But even with the small flutter of doubt that ran through my mind, the spark of knowing I was going to be traveling again, that I was going to meet and photograph Oakes Ashford...

"I'm excited," I admitted.

"As you should be. Oakes is trying to get his title back. I'm pretty sure he will do it even if it means breaking his privacy for a few months. Think of ways to break down that barrier and figure him out."

"Ha, nice pun." I chuckled at Luca.

He gave me his signature smile, right before it faded and his finger rose as he pointed at me. "No. Googling."

I held up my hands in surrender. "No Googling. I need to finish Jenna's photo, though." I leaned over my desk and grabbed my keyboard from him, sliding it back to where it belonged in front of my computer. "I need to...how did Morgan say it? Make it a masterpiece. Go."

Luca waggled his eyebrows before standing up. "You love me!" he shouted over his shoulder before exiting my office, leaving me alone with my Google search on Oakes Ashford still open.

To: manning.drew@pbragency.com
bcc: M.Pennel@rodeowaymag.com
From: E.Flynn@rodeowaymag.com
Subject: Rodeo Way Feature with O. Ashford.
Date: May 12th: 4:37 PM

Mr. Manning,

Hello! My name is Emersyn Flynn, digital editor at *Rodeo Way Magazine*, and I am happy to inform you that I will be traveling to Arizona on Saturday, June 6th for the Flagstaff Rodeo. The plan from there is to travel alongside Mr. Ashford as he makes his way to the NFR. The Editor in Chief of *Rodeo Way Magazine*, Morgan Pennel, and my events coordinator, Luca Magana, gave me all of Mr. Ashford's summer rodeos, and I am looking forward to seeing him ride. My goal for this article for *Rodeo Way Magazine* is to see who Mr. Ashford really is, what makes him thrive, and show the rodeo world just how he is going to make it to the NFR this year to reclaim his title.

Seeing as Mr. Ashford drives to most of his events, I will be traveling by car to Flagstaff, and I plan on following him to each event, but we can plan out specifics. I want to really see how he travels and lives during the summer—dip

my toes into his routine. I have set up my travel
arrangements, so no need to worry about that.

    Looking forward to hearing from you. Thank you
again and see you soon!

    Emersyn Flynn
    Digital Editor - Rodeo Way Magazine
    Denver, CO

To: E.Flynn@rodeowaymag.com
From: manning.drew@pbragency.com
Subject: REPLY Rodeo Way Feature with O. Ash-
    ford.
Date: May 13th: 9:48 AM

    Emersyn,

    Perfect. We are really excited about this too.
See you on June 6th in Arizona.

    Drew Manning
    Lead Agent - Bull Wing Agency

CHAPTER TWO
Emersyn

<u>Oakes Ashford Schedule June-August</u>

June 6th: Flagstaff, Arizona – Flagstaff Pro Rodeo

June 7th: Price, Utah – Black Diamond Rodeo

June 11th: Eagle, Idaho – Eagle Round Up

June 13th-14th: Vernal, Utah – Dinosaur Round Up Rodeo

June 15th: Bell, Montana – 66th Annual Belt

June 16th: Nampa, Idaho – Snake River Run

June 17th: Fallon, Nevada – Fallon's 3C's

June 19th: Reno, Nevada – Xtreme Bulls

June 20th-28th: Reno, Nevada – Reno Rodeo

June 30th: Cody, Wyoming – Xtreme Bulls

July 1st: Cody, Wyoming – Cody Stampede

July 3rd: West Jordan, Utah – Western Stampede

July 4th-5th: Oakley, Utah – Independence Day Rodeo

July 7th: Oakley, Utah – Xtreme Bulls

July 8th: Casper, Wyoming – Central Wyoming Fair

July 9th: Nephi, Utah – Ute Stampede

July 10th: Laramie, Wyoming – Jubilee Days Xtreme Bulls

July 11th-12th: Nephi, Utah – Ute Stampede

July 13th-18th: OFF – Training, Alpine Ridge, Idaho

July 19th-21st: Ogden, Utah – Pioneer Days

July 22nd-24th: Salt Lake City, Utah – Days of 47 Gold Buckle Tour

July 25th: Cheyenne, Wyoming – Frontier Days Xtreme Bulls

July 26th-27th: Cheyenne, Wyoming – Frontier Days

July 28th-29th: Riverton, Wyoming – Wind River Rodeo

July 31st: Sidney, Montana – Richland County Fair

August 2nd: Mesquite, Texas – Mesquite Championship

"And that's how it's done, that's how you ride a bull, and that's how you get the check at the end of the night."

The announcer's voice from my laptop pulled my attention away from the schedule I held in my hands, and I looked at the right moment to see Oakes Ashford yank his helmet from his head after a ride earlier this year. I had already seen all his rides, but for some reason, I decided this was the best research to do before heading to Flagstaff in the morning.

The past two weeks since I'd gotten this new assignment had been muffled in the best possible way. I finished up my project with Jenna, reminding her to try to set the exposure in her camera correctly, because damn that was a hard photo to edit. But once that was over, I was shoved into multiple meetings to prep me for the trip, given numerous interview questions they wanted me to answer, and had one too many sit-downs with Sterling and Morgan. All the ins and outs were settled. My Toyota

Corolla—which Morgan reluctantly agreed to let me drive—was packed to the brim with everything that I would need for my eight-week excursion, and Luca was set to make sure my plants didn't die.

Basically, I was ready to go. Just one more sleep and this new adventure would begin. And my mind still couldn't wrap around the fact that it was happening. Morgan only boosted my confidence, telling me there was no one else who was suited for the job, that she knew I could pull it off. Just glancing at the photos I had taken that hung around my small apartment was proof enough that I could. I was good at capturing the sport. I was good at writing about it. This was my next big step.

Breaking away from Oakes's victory interview, I focused back on the schedule. Luca wasn't kidding. The number of rodeos Oakes had planned for these next eight weeks were going to be gruesome, especially the Wyoming, Utah, Wyoming, Utah leg. Back and forth, back and forth. But once again, Luca was right. This was the same kind of schedule I was used to, thanks to years in the rodeo royalty. This was a typical schedule for Miss Rodeo Wyoming, so no wonder why he threw my name in the hat.

The next video began to play, and I watched as Oakes wrapped his hand, wiggled his hips on top of the bull, and gave the nod. Oakes made it the eight seconds, jumping off the bull and instantly taking off his helmet. He raised his arms in the air, giving the crowd a fist pump before running his free hand through his long brown hair. Even through his button-down shirt, you could see his biceps flex as he pumped his fist over and over. He was definitely built, and by the looks of it, he didn't mind showing off. He was scruffy, the only bull rider I saw with a full beard on his face, his hair wild from the helmet. He wore flashy chaps and a protective vest covered in sponsor patches. Even his boots were noticeable.

Oakes knew what he was doing for sure.

And he knew he did it well.

Dropping the schedule to focus on my 'research,' I arched my back and fumbled with my unruly blonde hair, forcing it into a messy bun. Oakes smiled for the camera again, biting his tongue and pumping a fist at the cameraman that stood on the other side of the gate. The crowd was still going crazy, even though he was off the screen.

Running my fingers over the mouse pad, I shrunk the YouTube video, looking at my Google search. Maybe if I looked at it again...it would give me something else.

Other than his past rides and his current stats, there was nothing on Oakes—as I expected. I found out that he grew up in Wyoming, but not where. He had a brother, but I couldn't find his age or name. There was nothing on his parents or any inkling as to what his childhood was like. No wife. No kids. No nothing. The only information on Oakes was his age (31), his weight (198 pounds), his most recent earnings, and that his eyes were the most gorgeous shade of brown I'd ever seen.

Not that it mattered in the slightest what his eyes looked like.

If I had to guess, Oakes Ashford grew up completely different than I did. We were both from Wyoming, so at least we had that in common, but I could see Oakes being raised in a bigger city, one where there was a rodeo on every corner for him to ride and practice. He would need a CrossFit gym and a place to run and train for his career, which was unlike the town I grew up in.

Me? I was raised in a no-name town in Wyoming, the population barely reaching four digits. My high school graduating class had eighty-two kids; the year under me had less. Not that I paid attention to that, because my adolescent years were spent being dragged from pageant to pageant, to hairstylist to horse trainer. I rarely spent time with kids I grew up with. I had a few friends in school, but they knew my schedule was crazy. We never 'hung out' outside of the normal school hours.

Thanks to my mother, I entered the rodeo royalty world at full steam. Becoming Miss Rodeo America was all I wanted; it was all I could think about. It happened in spurts, first becoming the Rodeo Queen for my high school, carrying the American flag in almost every rodeo they held, then moving to our small town royalty ranks. The next big win, one step closer to Miss Rodeo Wyoming, was winning Miss Rodeo Laramie the year after I graduated. That was another year of rodeo after rodeo, and then when I won Wyoming, that was my entire life. Nothing would compare to that. Earning the title of Miss Rodeo Wyoming got me a full ride to the University of Wyoming, a truck and horse trailer to use for the year, and an entire year full of rodeos and adventure. It was one step closer to my ultimate dream of Miss Rodeo America.

But then the pressure to win sunk in, and suddenly...I didn't want it. I mean, I *wanted* it, but I didn't *want* it—and yes, it is two different things. I was beginning to question what holding that title would give me. I already had the Wyoming experience, and I had the scholarship. What more was to it? But I went with the motions, and once I was at the NFR, on the Miss Rodeo America stage, butterflies zooming through my entire body as they announced winners...I was relieved when my name was called out as fourth attendant. I didn't win. I wasn't going to be known in the rodeo world. And I was relieved.

With how private Oakes stayed, I could imagine maybe we had that in common. We didn't want our personal lives blasted everywhere. We just wanted to love the rodeo. One quick Google search and I could bring up information on anyone I wanted. When my name was Googled, you could find where I went to school, the performances I'd done trick riding showed up on YouTube, and my pageant history came up, but that was it. When I typed in Oakes's name for the millionth time, the only new information I got was '*Wyoming native Oakes Ashford scores 91 in Gladewater.*'

I hummed. "A ninety-one." I let a 'woo-ee' loose, even though there was no one to hear me—unless you counted my plants, which I didn't.

My eyes glued on yet again another video, I reached for my phone, muscle memory taking over as I opened my texts.

Me

Pop quiz, what's the highest score right now in bull riding?

The cloud of dots danced, and I grinned.

Luca

I believe it's Oakes Ashford with a 94.

Me

Correct. Pop quiz. Who holds the world record for bull riding?

Luca

Pop quiz. Who was the first barrel racer champion?

Me

Joyce Loomis. Answer my question or you fail.

Luca

José Vitor Leme, 97 points…on Wooppa…2021, you knew that. Why are you testing me?

Me

I just saw Oakes got a 91 in Texas.

Luca

Stop. Googling.

Shouldn't you be packing anyway?

Me

My car is packed and ready to go. I leave in the morning.

Luca

What time?

Me

Early, I have to get into Flagstaff by eight, and that's a ten-hour drive.

Luca

Can your car make it? Want to take my SUV? I can drive…what's his name while you're gone.

Me

His name is Franz, and he will make it just fine, but thanks for the offer. I have an audiobook ready to go and many podcasts ready to keep me company.

Luca

If you're sure. I wish I could go with you. You need your trusty travel coordinator on the road with you in case something changes.

Me

Just keep in contact. I'm sure the next eight weeks are going to go so fast you won't even miss me at the office.

Luca

Pop quiz.

I shook my head, laughing to only my plants again, but still responded.

Me

Go.

Luca

Who won All Around in 2024?

Me

Easy. Shad Mayfield. You should think of harder questions.

Luca

Challenge accepted.

To: E.Flynn@rodeowaymag.com
From: L.Managa@rodeowaymag.com
Subject: Per Diem - Hotel Accommodation
Date: June 3rd: 3:00 PM

Your first per diem has been sent to your account. It should cover gas, food, and the next few hotel stays. Make sure you keep track of everything. Every. Single. Penny. Your first hotel reservation in Flagstaff is attached, but keep in mind…Oakes can change his schedule at the drop of a hat. Don't get used to high-end hotels.

    L

To: L.Managa@rodeowaymag.com
From: E.Flynn@rodeowaymag.com
Subject: REPLY: Per Diem - Hotel Accommodation
Date: June 3rd: 3:05 PM

I see the per diem—so far, thirty-six bucks for gas. And you know I really don't care where I stay…I'm not *that* high maintenance. We could camp for all I care.

    Emersyn Flynn
    Digital Editor - Rodeo Way Magazine
    Denver, CO

To: E.Flynn@rodeowaymag.com
From: L.Managa@rodeowaymag.com
Subject: REPLY: REPLY: Per Diem - Hotel Accom-
modation
Date: June 3rd: 3:07 PM

Drew said Oakes camps sometimes, but you make sure you stay in hotels. Pretty sure *Rodeo Way* doesn't want their new feature writer sleeping on the ground.

   L

Chapter Three
Oakes

"Hell no. Absolutely not. I refuse." I stormed past my agent, not wanting to look Drew in the eye for fear of punching him in the face.

I needed the man, so punching him probably wasn't the best idea.

"Oakes..." Drew made the O and A in my name last longer than necessary. "This will be good for you. It will get your name out there."

"My name is already out there. I don't need some reporter following me around like a puppy!" I shouted over my shoulder. I could hear Drew's footsteps as he attempted to keep up with me, but I was determined to get away from him.

He had suggested this to me a while back. He even introduced me to the Editor in Chief of this up-and-coming magazine—a trick during a gathering I was also tricked into going to. I was a bull rider, so I had to show my face sometimes, but not all the time like Drew seemed to think. I rode bulls, said a few words at the end when I won (which, I *always* won), gathered my check, and then headed to the next rodeo. That was what I wanted to do.

What I didn't want was a shadow for the entire summer.

I had rodeo after rodeo lined up, spanning all across the western circuits. It was going to be intense and hard...and a reporter was just going to slow me down.

"Technically, she's not a reporter."

That made me stop and turn to him.

"Excuse me?"

"I talked to Luca, one of the travel coordinators. She's an editor; this will be her first field job." Drew gave me his agent smile, the one that showed all his teeth, and his eyes forced a gleam.

I raised a single brow and took one step toward him. "So, you're telling me that an editor...not a reporter...is going to be shadowing me for the summer? Drew, I can't be babysitting someone who doesn't know their way around an arena."

"She works for a rodeo magazine, Oakes. I'm assuming she knows her way around an arena."

"Drew." I pinched the bridge of my nose with my thumb and forefinger. "Telling me she works for a rodeo magazine and knows her way around the arena is basically saying you know your way around, and..." I looked him up and down. Drew was wearing gray slacks, shiny shoes, and a light-blue button-up shirt. He was only missing the blazer to complete the ensemble. His curly blonde hair was slicked back, a small curl fighting to break free near the nape of his neck. I raised a brow at him. The only reason why he was an agent and even close to the sport was because his father started Bull Wing Agency, and he took it over. He knew the basic gist and how to get me scheduled, but other than that... "Sorry, man, you don't know anything about a rodeo arena."

Drew scoffed. "I know enough. But this girl…I've heard some great things about her from Luca—"

"Who?" I pinched my brow.

"Come on, Oakes, pay attention," Drew groaned, and I swear he resisted the urge to snap in my face. "The travel coordinator at *R W.* He knows her and says she's the perfect candidate for the job. So, yes, Oakes, she's going to be shadowing you this summer. She knows what she's doing."

"Have *you* looked into her?" I gave him a pointed look, one that told him he better tell me what I wanted to hear. That he did his research, that this girl was going to be worth the summer and my time.

Drew's vacant expression told me everything I needed to know.

"You haven't," I answered for him.

"Luca seems trustworthy, and he trusts Morgan, and Morgan trusts her staff."

"So, you're putting trust in her?"

Drew nodded. "I'm telling you, Oakes, she's going to be just what you need."

"I don't *need* anything."

I turned my back on him again, making my way to my truck, not even letting him get another word in before flinging open the driver's side door and climbing inside, slamming the world out.

Someone over the chute knocked on my helmet as I made sure my right hand was tight on the bull, the heat from the friction still radiating through my palm. The beast below me bucked, telling me exactly how mad he was. I dug my spur in his side. *Show me what you got.*

I could hear the song blaring in the background, Jon Bon Jovi—they always played him when I got on the bull. *It's my life....it's now or never...*and the announcer began to talk me up. Like always, I drowned the noise out, my entire focus going on my hand placement and the raging bull that was determined to kick me off. Once my hand was secure, I moved my hips, raising my left arm in the air. I closed my eyes and took one deep breath before I opened them and gave the nod.

The chute opened, and the bull jumped out, moving right, then left, then right again, forcing me to move in all directions with him. He was a jumper, and I could hear each and every grunt he let out. A smile spread across my lips, a laugh following. My heart was pounding, the adrenaline pumping through my veins. I loved this feeling and grew to crave it. These eight seconds on the bull were the moments I lived for. I was addicted to the thrill. Without these eight seconds, I would be on my family's farm, most likely hating every moment of the day. Here...right now...I was alive.

It's my life...

The buzzer blew off in the distance, and I loosened my hand on the bull, jumping off of him, landing on my feet as always. The bull fighters came running, guiding the bull out of the arena, and me...

I tore off my helmet, my long hair flying from it as I finally allowed my ears to open, taking in the crowd as they cheered.

"And with that, Oakes gives us our first qualified ride!" the announcer bellowed. "Oakes Ashford bringing the head with an eiiighty-eiiiight point five!"

88.5.

I gave the crowd a fist bump, gaining another cheer before my walk turned into a jog, heading right back to the chute. I tossed my helmet on the metal floor and climbed up and over. The buzz that was still flowing freely through me began to die down as the next rider began to mount his chosen bull.

Letting out a puff of air, I ran my hand through my hair, leaning over to pick up my helmet.

"88!" I heard someone scream. "And the first qualified ride. You're taking home a check tonight, Ashford."

I smiled at the man, not quite sure of his name. "Damn straight," I answered.

"Oakes!" Drew's voice carried over the crowd, and as much as he stood out, he was not easy to find amongst all the cowboys. "Bringing the big money tonight!" I finally found him, and he slapped my back.

Drew normally didn't stick around. If multiple clients of his were in the same arena, he would, but seeing as I was the only one here that he represented...*fuck*, he must really want to finish our conversation from earlier.

"Glad you stuck around, but...can this wait until after I get my check and a drink in me?" I asked as I tugged to loosen my vest.

"She's here, and I want you to meet her." He wiggled his eyebrows.

My hands froze at the hem of my vest, and slowly I turned to look at my agent. "She's here? Now?" I questioned. "I haven't even agreed to it yet. They couldn't have waited until I was done?"

"Man up, Oakes, and meet the gal."

I narrowed my eyes at him, and he mimicked my glare. Eventually, one of us would fold, and that—unfortunately—was me. "Fine," I grumbled. "I'll meet her, but I still won't agree to anything." I yanked my glove from my hand, shooting a finger in his direction.

"Well, then..." I heard from behind me, and I swear, my heart stopped. "I made that drive for nothing, then, if you haven't agreed. That was some ride, Mr. Ashford."

I knew that voice. I never thought I'd hear that voice again. That was a voice that followed me everywhere I went. That was the voice I heard ring through my head every time I mounted the bull: *Don't let one ride define your future.* It was the voice of the woman I would never, ever forget, and I knew the moment I looked into her eyes, I'd be a goner.

"Oakes, I'd like you to meet..." Drew's voice was barely an echo in my mind as I finally turned from him to the voice and saw her. My stomach flipped. "Emersyn Flynn with *Rodeo Way Magazine.*"

I swallowed as my gaze finally met Emersyn's. The stunning shade of blue that I remembered from that night, that was still etched in my mind, was still just as vibrant. Her hair was wavy, pulled back into a tight ponytail, and longer than I remembered. Her features had changed slightly, aged—liked mine—but that only amplified her beauty. And her smile...God, her smile...it still brought me to my knees. How long had it been? Sixteen years...and my stomach was still turning into knots.

I knew I should say something. I should probably stick out my hand and shake it, like any other normal person would. *Emersyn, it's you. I can't believe it...* But I stood there. Frozen. Looking at *this* woman who I never thought I'd see again, who gave me more strength than she knew. How did I even begin to talk to her? What could I say to her, to basically thank her for all of this?

"How long was your drive, Miss Flynn?" Drew turned to her in my silence.

Emersyn broke my eye contact and turned to Drew. "A little over ten hours. I stopped a few times."

"You drove here?" I finally stammered, my voice breaking as if I had never spoken before. Emersyn turned back to me and smiled, and I could feel the breath leave my lungs.

She nodded, her cheeks flushing a light tint of pink as her shoulders rose with her breath. "I prefer a road trip versus a plane ride. I've been all over the country, but this has been the best destination. It's a pleasure to meet you, Mr. Ashford." She smiled. "I've been following your stats all year—well…"—she let out a nervous laugh—"since your first NFR win, really."

"Really?" I parroted the word, my own voice groggy, as if a frog had weaseled its way in there.

Words, Oakes…use your words.

"Yeah, that was an impressive rookie season. One of the best I've seen."

I chuckled, feeling the confidence seeping back into my bloodstream. "I was barely a rookie when I was at my first NFR."

Emersyn's eyes widened, and her breath caught. "Oh, right, I know, but…that's when I noticed you."

I narrowed my eyes, confusion sweeping across me. Did she not know I was here because of her? "Notice me? You don't—"

"I didn't mean it like that," she stopped me. "I just meant, it was really impressive, really memorable. If someone didn't notice you, that would be a bigger issue." Her voice shook, a nervous laugh filling the space between us until she cleared her throat and lightly licked her lips. "Anyway, I'm excited you've agreed to let me shadow you to write this article, really get to know who Oakes Ashford is."

"Technically," I chimed in, "I haven't agreed to anything just yet." I smiled, knowing full well that I was in this now. There was no way I could say no to this. Not after all these years. Did she feel this too? Was her stomach bucking just as wild as mine was? "I was just talking—"

"Oh, yes, I know. Luca let me know that this whole thing was 'painted in watercolor.'" She let out another nervous laugh. "But I'm sure once everything is worked out, you will. I'd love to sit and talk—figure out the ins and outs of this assignment."

"I know just the place. Oakes?" Drew lightly touched Emersyn's shoulder and gave me a backward glance. "What do you say to Northern Pine?"

Emersyn turned toward Drew, and his smile beamed as she responded, carrying the conversation forward. I could hear Emersyn's voice becoming stronger with each word, the nerves that were there seconds before seeming to filter away as she concentrated on Drew as they walked down the hall toward the exit.

Watching her, it dawned on me.

Emersyn Flynn—the woman I had loved since I was fifteen years old—had no idea who I was.

Mom
88 – great ride!
Oakes
Thanks, Ma.
Hayes
88?? Come on bro.
Oakes
Shove it.

Chapter Four
Emersyn

I'm going to blame the fact that Oakes looked extremely different in person than he did on screen for my very unprofessional first impression. I couldn't get over the fact that he was here in front of me, that I was here *finally* doing what I dreamed of doing.

So why was it that the first thing I did was turn into a fangirl and seemingly forget that I was here on an assignment?

Oakes was taller than I expected, over six feet at least, the top of my head barely meeting his shoulders. His lean body could be seen even through his protective gear, and when he began to remove his vest and chaps, his forearms flexed, and his shoulders tensed, making him seem more intimidating than he probably was. His hair was gorgeous, tousled from his helmet, the perfect length, in my opinion, with his well-kept beard. It was hard not to look at him, hard not to lose all sense of words when it came to him. But his eyes... His eyes were what really caught me.

Those brown eyes that were ten times more captivating in real life versus the television or computer screen—specks of light brown hidden there that, for some reason, were the only thing I could concentrate on—were boring right into me.

I tried to focus on Drew, keeping the conversation professional once we sat down, starting with the basic information that Morgan drilled into my head, but I could feel Oakes's eyes on me. And that was *all* I could feel.

Heat rushed to my cheeks as I forced myself to ignore him.

He sat relaxed in his chair across from me, one arm resting on his knee, the other leaning onto the table with his fingers lightly gliding up and down his glass. He was silent, stoic to the point where no one would be able to tell you what was going through his mind. The only parts of him that moved were his chest with each rising breath and his fingers, seeming to follow the rhythm. In, out, up, down, repeat.

"I take it you've seen Oakes's schedule. I sent it over to the travel coordinator." Drew sat forward in his seat. "I think it's close to forty rodeos."

"Yes, I did. Luca sent it my way when I was given the assignment. It's going to be quite the summer." I shifted in my seat, bending to get my iPad to pull up his schedule. "The plan is for me to follow until Cheyenne. Then, I'll be out of your hair." I tapped on the document and positioned my iPad so Drew and I could review any details.

"Perfect, so that's seven...eight weeks?" Drew confirmed, counting down the list of rodeos.

"Which is perfect, I think. I'm really excited to get back to the dirt. It's been a while since I've been—"

"Hold on." Oakes's voice brought me back to his attention. His fingers were raised, eyes narrowed on me. "You haven't been to a rodeo in how long?"

"Longer than I'd like to admit." I inhaled, placing my hands on my lap. "Rodeos were—"

"How long is longer than you like to admit?" Oakes cut me off.

I met his gaze and swallowed. Biting the inside of my lip, I thought. My last rodeo was...so long ago. "Probably ten years."

Oakes's eyes widened. "Ten years?" he repeated. "You work for a rodeo magazine...and you don't go to rodeos?"

"I'm a digital editor, Mr. Ashford. Most of my work takes place behind a screen."

"Morgan was telling me you went to school for journalism?" Drew asked, and I broke contact with Oakes.

Smiling, I nodded. "That's right, at the University of Wyoming. Major in journalism and communication, minor in photography."

"That's not what I expected," Oakes mumbled, his fingers returning to his glass as his chin dipped. The brim of his hat shadowed his face from my view.

I flinched. "I'm sorry, Mr. Ashford, but what did you expect?" I asked, my tone a little harder than I intended.

Oakes raised his eyes. "Not journalism."

"I wanted to find a way to be back in the rodeo world without being on the dirt. Writing about it, taking photos...that was my way of still experiencing it after my time ended," I defended myself, keeping my voice as calm and professional as I could when, in the back of my head, I wanted to scream at him. I didn't need my career path questioned...again.

"Your time?" He raised a brow.

The flutters from meeting him earlier vanished as I looked at him. I straightened my shoulders, ignoring the imposter syndrome that he was creating, to keep it from seeping into my veins.

"I've spent plenty of time on and off the dirt," I finally answered.

"With all due respect..." He shifted in his seat. "What makes you—a digital editor with a degree in journalism who hasn't been on the dirt in ten years—think you're the best for this job? Before I agree to anything and you and my agent plan out my entire summer...tell me what makes you the most qualified for this? The rodeo arena is organized chaos, and I'm headed to big events. Xtreme Bulls, PRCA Rodeos, which means weeks on the road. I'm not sure if this is anyplace for a digital editor. Why should I trust you?"

No place for an editor?

I held my breath and reminded myself to remain professional.

"Mr. Ashford—"

"Oakes," he corrected me.

I narrowed my eyes at him, hoping it stung like I was hoping it would. "I'm sorry, *Oakes*, but I can assure you I'm more than a digital editor. I've been on the dirt more than concrete. I was Miss Rodeo Wyoming. I was in the NFR arena before you were. I've carried the flag at multiple rodeos and have performed numerous tricks and stunts, because believe it or not, I know how to maneuver a horse better than anyone at *Rodeo Way*. I know how the dirt feels under my boots. I know how it feels under my horse's hooves. I've ridden so many horses, yet I know them all by name. I know *your* stats inside and out, and I can tell you who is most likely going to head to the top fifteen this December—like you, *Oakes*." I felt the twinge of confidence flow through me as I held his gaze. I had this. I *so* had this. "Rodeo for me is more than my favorite sport; it's my life. My boss is finally just seeing that. So, yes, I *am* the right person for this job."

Oakes gave me a crooked grin, one tip of his lips raising just slightly enough to add a bit of wrinkles around his eye.

"Okay." His smile grew, and his low, gruff voice as he said that one single word had a smart of...familiarity.

"Okay?" I parroted.

"Okay, you can follow me this summer. I agree to"—he waved his hand around the table—"whatever this is. But you gotta keep up, Miss Flynn."

"If I have to call you Oakes, you have to call me—"

"Emersyn," Oakes finished my sentence.

"Well," Drew laughed, "you won him over faster than I thought you would. I got worried there for a second, Oakes."

"No need to worry," he said, his eyes still locked on mine. "Just tell me how this is going to work. You said you're driving. You plan on following me?"

"Yes," I said, sliding my iPad toward me, sitting up just a little straighter. "I have my entire trip planned, down to the gas mileage, to stay in budget. I will be contacting Luca, and he'll set up hotels for me, and—"

"What kind of car do you drive?" he cut me off.

"A Toyota," I answered smugly.

He twisted his lips and nodded.

"As I was saying, Luca will be updating my nightly stays, and when you don't have events, I'll stay out of your hair. I'll use that time to—"

"You don't have to stay out of my hair." Once again, Oakes cut me off. Was this man going to let me finish a sentence? "I'm sure we can find something productive to do while we're not at events. Those days are mostly filled with traveling."

I took a sharp breath. "I'm aware of how much traveling goes into a summer."

"From your royalty days?" he asked, a hint of sarcasm behind his smile.

All expressions left my face, and as toneless as possible, I replied, "Yes. I traveled a lot during my reign. Some days, I was wanted at two rodeos a day. I understand the travel aspects of it. But..." I heaved a sigh. "I'll be in my own car, and you in yours—out of your hair," I reiterated.

"How will you get anything done, then?"

"Oakes." Drew chastised Oakes like a father would a son, earning Oakes's attention and smirk.

Taking a deep, boosting breath, I answered him. "I have interview questions that we will do. I'll be editing and working behind the scenes. I can assure you..." *Did I already say that phrase?* Why did I have to keep assuring him…or was I trying to assure myself? I cleared my throat. "I'll have plenty to do when we aren't together."

He raised his brow. "You said something earlier…" he trailed off, his voice leaving a chill in the air. "'Show who Oakes Ashford really is.' So far, you've gone over schedules with Drew, but…what's your goal with this article? What do you want to accomplish? Why me?" Once again, his stoic eyes met mine, and I felt a chill race up my spine.

"No one really knows about you, Oakes, other than your name. We want to see what you do."

"I ride bulls," he deadpanned. "You know that. You said you knew my stats…"

"You do more than that."

He nodded and leaned forward in his seat, his elbows coming up to the table. "I ride bulls, I take the check, and then I do it all over again. That, Emersyn, is what I do."

"I think what Emersyn is meaning"—Drew leaned forward—"is the magazine wants an in-depth insight."

"Exactly," I agreed with Drew, giving him a silent gesture with my palm. "We want to know what makes you tick."

"I'm not sure how much *more* in depth I can be. You saw my schedule." He pointed to my iPad. "This summer is jam packed."

"I'll find a way." I felt my lips turn into a smile, confidence beginning to creep through me.

I would find a way, no matter what. This right here was what I wanted to do. All I had to do was prove I could do it—no matter how hard Oakes was seeming to make it.

"We want to see how you train. So, I will be accompanying you to Idaho when you take the break. We want to see your routine in front of the chute. We want to see your self-care regimens. We want to know who you are." I mimicked his posture, setting my own elbows in front of me, raising the same brow he had high to the brim of his hat. A power move maybe? But Oakes caught on, and he rewarded me with a grin.

"Let me ask you, Emersyn," he said, and his voice was like butter when he said my name, and that only caused the spark of familiarity that was there earlier to reignite. I felt like I knew this voice, knew the way he said certain words. His accent wasn't one I'd forget...but then again, how many videos of him did I watch in preparation for this? "Did you Google me?"

I nodded. "I did."

"What did you find?"

"Not much. Your stats. Your age. Your weight. I know you're from Wyoming. I know you have a brother. And I know you are a private man."

"And there's a reason for that." He held my stare.

"I understand completely." I held his.

"I don't want anything to be in this magazine that may tarnish that."

"I can promise you, Oakes, I—more than anyone—understand the value of a personal life. I won't put anything in this article that you don't want me to. I will keep your private life just that. Private."

"So, your 'in-depth' article"—he used his fingers to air quote—"won't be as in-depth as you want."

"No, but..." I sighed. "I'm confident I can give *Rodeo Way* the article they're wanting, all the while keeping it at a level you are comfortable with." I could feel the weight in my words, the promise I was giving him, and the look on his face—the way his grin turned into a full-fledged smile—told me I'd gained his trust. This was going to work.

The space between us grew heavy as Oakes and I studied each other. It felt like hours passed before, finally, Oakes spoke.

"I'm assuming there's a contract I have to sign?" he asked, relaxing back into his chair, his fingers returning to his pint, once again following the ins and outs of his breaths.

"There is." I smiled, reaching down to my bag where the written contract sat, slightly astonished that I managed to pull this off without looking like I had no idea what I was doing.

To: E.Flynn@rodeowaymag.com
From: M.Pennel@rodeowaymag.com
Subject: Arrival?
Date: June 7th: 9:02 AM

Emersyn, checking in on your arrival.

I want updates on the article as you go, including photos to be sent for approval and full interviews. Sterling will choose the answers we feel best hit the vibe/flow of what we are looking for and send them back to you after reviewing. Sterling has come up with new questions for your first interview with Oakes. Please follow and return answers by June 15th.

Looking forward to your updates.

Morgan Pennel
Editor in Chief - Rodeo Way Magazine
Denver, CO

CHAPTER FIVE

Emersyn

Have you met him yet? Saw him get that 88!

Just got back to my hotel.

And??

He's very stoic. Hasn't said much - only agreed that I can follow him. Contract signed and with Drew. He's going to fax it over to Morgan in the morning.

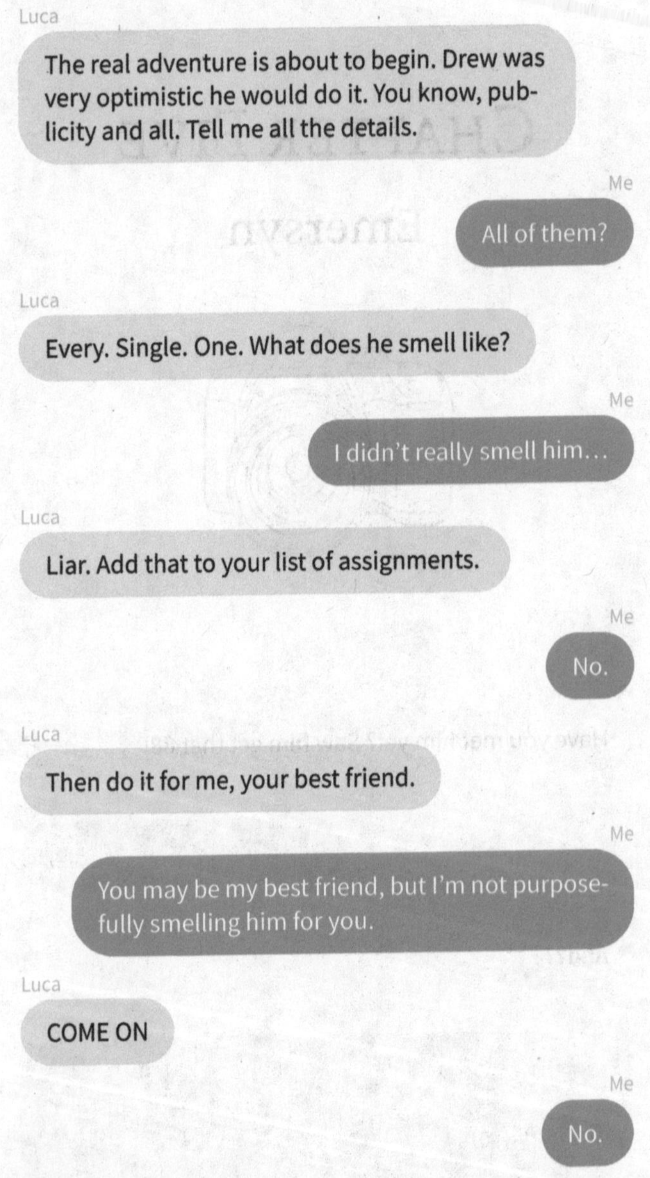

I should have taken Luca's warning about hotel accommodations more seriously. Waking up in the hotel suite he had booked for me was heavenly, and it occurred to me in the middle of my shower that, from here on out, for eight weeks, it was whatever was nearest to Oakes's events.

I woke up early, the drive today in the background of my mind, but I packed slowly, everything that happened the night before in the foreground of my mind. The contract that was signed, the promise that was made. *I, more than anyone, understand the value of a personal life.*

That was true. I did value my privacy—one of the many reasons why I didn't want to win Miss Rodeo America—but I still had an article to deliver.

For being a more 'in-depth' article, Oakes set parameters to make it not in depth at all. The questions that Sterling had sent over were ones I knew Oakes wasn't going to want to answer.

What was your childhood like?

What was your first rodeo?

What's something you can pinpoint as the turning point in your life to say 'this is it'?

How did you fall in love with the rodeo?

Out of the fifty questions he sent, I could see Oakes answering maybe five. I'd start there then slowly ease him into the others. He could tell me about his love for rodeo without telling me about his childhood.

After reading Morgan's email and Sterling's interview questions, I did yet another quick Google search on Oakes, his name popping up right away when the O hit the search bar, meaning I had Googled him one too many times. I don't know why I thought information on him would magically appear overnight, but when I found the same information as before, my stomach dropped.

He seemed so different in person than the celebrating man I was used to seeing on TV. And then there was that familiarity that, for some reason, I couldn't shake. My mind began to go through all the possible scenarios where I could have met him before. Rodeos where I was a flag girl? That was a good one. The NFR? No, that couldn't be it. I thought I would have remembered meeting someone like him. Maybe a small rodeo in Wyoming—the one where I was crowned Miss Rodeo Wyoming, perhaps? There were a lot of people at that one, and I talked to so many cowboys.

His eyes just held that feeling that I had seen them before. The specks of light brown tangled in with the dark, the way they bore into me...

My phone buzzed on the bedside table, pulling me from my stupor. A number I didn't recognize flashed on the screen, but since the words 'Potential Spam' weren't underneath them, I gave it a chance.

"Hello, this is Emersyn," I answered, shoving my phone between my ear and shoulder.

"Emersyn! It's Drew!"

"Oh." I lifted my chin, grabbing my phone before it fell to the floor. "Hi, I'm just packing up."

"I just needed to check in, let you know that Oakes will be there soon to help you pack up your things and then head off to Price for the next ride." I could practically hear Drew's smile through the phone.

"I'm actually pretty much packed. Will you tell Oakes I'll meet him in the lobby?" I glanced at my watch, a text from Luca appearing on the small screen.

Luca

Your hotel in Price is booked.

"Yeah, sure thing, I'm calling him right after I hang up with you."

"The contract got sent over?"

"Just got the confirmation code. I'm heading back to Texas today, but I'll see you the next go around. Save my number—keep it for when Oakes is giving you a hard time." Drew let out a small chuckle.

"I'm sure I can handle him."

"No doubt in my mind you can. He can be a bit of an ass sometimes, so please save my number. I also have Luca's contact to make this easy for everyone. It was great to meet you, and I'll talk to you again. This will be good for him—I know it. Talk to you soon!"

Before I could say anything in response, he was gone, and my phone screen went black.

I left the hotel room, surprised when I saw Oakes standing in the lobby with his arms folded across his toned chest. He was dressed differently than yesterday. No long-sleeve button-down with the sleeves rolled up. No sponsor patches, no chaps. Just a simple t-shirt, Wrangler jeans, boots, and a tan hat that showed the ends of his hair, wild underneath it. He looked...good. I stopped and met his gaze for a brief moment, his eyebrows perking up when he saw me.

He dropped his arms and made his way toward me, not once breaking eye contact.

"Morning," he said softly.

"Good morning," I replied, reaching out to grab my suitcase handle, only to be stopped by his hand when he snatched it up.

"I got this. You go check out, and I'll meet you out by your car?"

"Sure, thank you. I..." I looked him up and down once more. "I appreciate it. I'm the blue Toyota Corolla."

He held out a hand. "Can I have your key? I'll pack this up for you."

Willingly, I handed over my key, thanking him once more. He gave me a nod and left, rolling my suitcase behind him. I went through the motions and left, catching sight of Oakes's truck first. A deep-blue Chevy Silverado with a bull rider, mid-jump, painted on the side of the bed. I could see the small *OA* on the bull rider's chaps, but if you didn't follow the rodeo, you would have zero clue as to what you were looking at. But this was Oakes's way of telling the world who was behind that wheel.

But even though his truck was right there, he was nowhere near it. Nor was it parked near my Toyota. There was a newer Corolla parked there, and I grimaced. Did he think...

Turning down the parking lot to look at *my* Toyota, I tightened my lips when I saw Oakes leaning on the trunk, my suitcase still by his boots, his arms folded and face completely hidden by the brim of his hat. Taking a deep breath, I took the walk toward him.

"What the hell is this?" he asked once I was closer to him, unfolding his arm to place a palm on my car.

"My car," I responded, giving him a smile.

"This car?" Oakes repeated.

I hummed, giving him a nod.

"This piece of junk got you here from Colorado?"

I nodded again. "He did, and he's not a piece of junk. He's a classic."

"Emersyn." He rubbed his forehead. "He?" he repeated, clearly exasperated. He took a breath through rounded lips and lifted his gaze. "What year is this, and how many miles does it have on it?"

"2004. He's almost to three hundred thousand..."

"So pretty much it's life expectancy?"

"He has a few more years left in him," I retorted.

"Emersyn," he sighed my name again, and I couldn't help but like the way it sounded. "I can't have you drive this across the western circuits. What would happen if it goes out on us? It could easily overheat."

Us?

"It got me here with no problem."

"How often do you change the oil?"

"I—"

"How many miles does it get to the gallon?"

"It—"

"When was the last time all the fluids were changed? When were the tires rotated, or the spark plugs changed out? Have you gotten a new battery recently?" He took a step forward.

"I changed—"

"Do you have the tools to fix *him* in case something happens? Do you know how to change a tire if needed? Hell, do you have a spare tire?"

"If you'd let me talk," I stopped him, taking a step forward. "I keep up on oil changes and tire rotations. The spark plugs were changed when he hit two hundred and fifty thousand. The battery is new. I have a tool kit in the trunk with the spare, which yes, I know how to change. I am not useless, Oakes." I fought the urge to jab him in the chest. "This car got me through my last three years in high school. I moved to Colorado in it, and I'm sure he can go on the road all summer long."

"You may trust it, but I don't, even if you say it's up to date." He pushed himself off the trunk. "Come on, you'll ride with me."

My jaw dropped. "What? And leave my car here?"

"No, Drew is still in town. I'm sure he can help us arrange a tow to my training site in Idaho. I'll reach out to Cash and see if they have roo—"

"Hold on. You're going to board my car in Idaho for the summer?"

Oakes reached out for my suitcase. "I would feel better about you riding with me in my truck. I don't want to babysit you and your car on the road."

"You're not babysitting me." I could feel the anger boil in my veins. Did he really think he was *babysitting* me? Even after I felt like I proved that I could indeed handle a rodeo arena and keep his life just that—his. "My car will—"

"Emersyn, just please..." His chin raised in the air as he stopped, his shoulders slumping. "Your car is close to its life expectancy. Toyotas are great, yes, but if this thing really has close to 300,000 miles on it...and we are going to be putting at least 20,000 on it this summer, it won't get you home to Colorado at the end. I'll call Cash and see if he's willing to store it for free, and when we go to Idaho for my training, you can drive it to Utah for the rodeo there. Then, we'll go to Cheyenne, and then you'll drive back to Colorado. You'll get three thousand miles, tops, added to that 300K."

I kept my arms folded, staying near my cute little Toyota, taking in his words. It made sense...he made sense. The anger that had risen with his stupid *babysit* comment was still boiling as I looked over my shoulder at all the things I had piled in my backseat. And finally, I sighed, giving in to defeat. Looked like our arrangement just changed.

"Do you have room for all my things?" I asked him, dropping my hands to my hips.

"I have a truck and an empty horse trailer. Yeah...I got room." He smiled then, and those brown eyes flashed. "I'll pull up, and we can move your stuff over, and then I'll call Drew."

"Don't think the babysitting comment is going to blow over," I called after him. His head shook, and I swear I heard a light laugh come from him. I turned back to my little Toyota. "Well...I guess I'll see you in Idaho."

CHAPTER SIX
Oakes

I had options here.

I could give in and tell Emersyn everything. Let her know exactly who I was and what she meant to me. It sure as hell would make more sense as to why I wanted her to ride with me, probably making this entire thing easier too. Or...I could do the complete opposite and sit in silence, let things build up until, ultimately, the chute would break, and the bull would be raging.

Obviously, I went with the latter.

And as she sat beside me in the cab of my truck, her sweet scent of vanilla and brown sugar filling the entire space between us, her eyes focused on her iPad...I just let the silence build.

Mentally, I was beating myself up for it. She was here. In my truck. Willingly spending her summer with me. She'd been on my mind since that homecoming rodeo my sophomore year—the night I fell head over heels in love with her—and now, here she was. And I was acting like a complete idiot. No, not idiot. A complete asshole.

Gripping the steering wheel until my knuckles turned white, I glared at the scar on my left hand. I couldn't help but wonder if she were to see it, would she remember me then? Knowing how much she had done in the past sixteen years, I doubted it.

I'd watched her—of course I did. How could I not? She stole all my focus. I was there when she won Miss Rodeo Wyoming. I was there in the stands at the NFR when she lost Miss Rodeo America. I watched her flourish through it all...the ups and the downs. The few interactions we had during those sixteen years were enough to be etched in my brain, but to her, I was just another face. And I was too chicken shit to reach out.

Then, after Miss Rodeo America, she basically disappeared from the rodeo scene—except that one year, ten years ago. It was hard to believe that was her last time on the dirt, which also happened to be my first year riding a bull. She carried the flag during the cowboy prayer and national anthem, then she floated in between the events, being just as ravishing as I remember her being. It was a shock, seeing her, and all the memories and feelings came rushing back. And I still couldn't find it in me to approach her. By then, I had a new name and stayed completely away from social media...it was easier just to keep her as a memory.

But now...

She was here.

She was *here*.

And I was still chicken shit.

It wasn't like I was waiting for her the entire sixteen years, pining like some lovesick teenager. I had girlfriends. I had one-night stands. But none of them amounted to Emersyn, and I never had her to really know they didn't. I just knew that no one ever would.

I flexed my hand, the scar stretching with the skin, a slight pain radiating through to the tips of my fingers. It was a good thing I only needed one hand to ride bulls.

That was what she always said...right?

"Drew just texted me," Emersyn broke the silence, pulling me from my thought spiral. Giving her a small side-eye, I didn't respond. "He said my car has been loaded up and is on its way to..." Furrowing her brow, she brought her iPad to life once more. "Alpine Ridge, Idaho."

I nodded once. "Hartwell Hills Ranch," I stated. "That's where I train."

"Hartwell? As in Rhett Hartwell? Wyatt Hartwell?" Emersyn's voice rose. "You're friends with them?"

I gave her a grin before turning my attention back to the road. "I wouldn't say friends. I just rent out their arena every now and then. Cash more than the Hartwells."

"Cash Callahan. I heard he retired to Idaho—wasn't sure where."

"You really do know your shit, don't you?" I raised a brow and looked at her for a millisecond.

"I know more about Rhett than Wyatt; their names are well-known. And Cash...well, he could have been huge if he didn't get into his accident. Like I said, rodeo is kinda my thing."

"Miss Rodeo Wyoming." I flashed a cocky grin, one that normally would be taken as flirting, but the look on Emersyn's face told me she took it as anything but. Instead of erasing the grin, I made it wider, knowing very well I looked like the cocky asshole I was.

Emersyn let out a small huff. Risking a glance, I noticed her cheeks blush.

"You really don't like that fact, do you?" she asked, turning to me.

"Why wouldn't I like that fact? Rodeo queens are more than a pretty face."

"We're a lot more than a pretty face. Do you realize how much we need to know?"

"I don't," I admitted, glancing at her from the corner of my eye.

"A lot. So..."—she dropped her iPad to her lap—"I'd appreciate it if you stop making me feel less than because I was a rodeo queen."

Well...shit.

"That..." I clenched my teeth. "That wasn't my intention." I swallowed.

"You know, this may be easier if we aren't purposefully rude to each other. The entire plan changed once you got me in this truck, so"—she inhaled—"now that we truly are stuck with each other until your training, can we pretend to be invested in this? No more snide remarks, no more gruff exterior—"

"Who's to say it's just an exterior?"

"I think it is. You're a bull rider, so you have to come off as tough, but I would really like to not see the asshole you've shown."

"I'll rein in my asshole side. I'll be invested." I sighed, giving in to her.

If only she knew I was already invested in her...since the moment I saw her again.

"That's all I ask. I really can write; it's what I went to school for after Wyoming. My way of still being a part of it."

"Makes sense. There's more to rodeo than the events. Did your rodeo obsession start with the pageant side?"

"Obsession is a strong word, but no," she replied stiffly. "My dad was a team roper, a header, and my mom was in the pageant world. That's how they met. The rodeo and I have been two peas in a pod since I was a baby."

"When did you learn to ride?" I asked, itching to keep the sound alive, to loosen her up. Most of these small facts I knew, but hearing her say them was filling my senses.

"I was on a horse before I could walk. Then the real training started when I was about..."—she scrunched her nose, a deep hum coming from her throat—"seven, I think. My mom wanted me to follow in her footsteps."

"She must be proud."

"I'd like to think so, but..." She shifted, moving her fingers to brush a piece of hair from her face. "I'm not the center of the article. You are. So, tell me, Oakes..." The way she enunciated my name made me raise a brow and turn to look at her. "When did you ride your first horse?"

I forced that brow to go higher. "This isn't a scheduled interview time?"

"No." She plopped back into her seat. "This is...we are in a car, and for some reason, you don't have music playing, so we're talking. When did you first ride a horse?"

I heaved a sigh. "Before I could walk," I said, repeating her words to her. Vague enough, but true enough.

"And the first bull you rode?"

Taking a deep breath, I swallowed. "I was around twenty or so."

"And I take it you fell in love with the sport?"

The sport isn't the only thing I fell in love with...

"I guess that's true." The memory of when I was on a bull for the first time hit me like a ton of bricks. I was scared shitless, but I lasted the eight seconds. And once my feet hit the ground, and I watched the fighters wrangle the bull back into the pen, I knew that was it for me. And the soft words from years before echoed in my mind—*nothing will stop you*—and nothing ever did.

"And here we are, years later, and you're leading the charts."

"Gotta get those checks."

"That's not all you're in it for." She cocked her head, raising a single brow. "There has to be more."

"It's my income. It's my job, so...you can dig all you want, but...that's really all it is."

"But you love it."

"I wouldn't do it if I didn't love it," I admitted.

That comment got a small smile from Emersyn as she leaned her head back on the headrest. The cab of the truck grew quiet again, and the only sound was the soft in and out of Emersyn's breath. I was half tempted to turn the radio on, maybe a podcast or a book, but the other half of me—the louder part—kept it quiet, hoping...praying...that she would keep the conversation going.

And just like that, the powers that be answered my prayer.

"Pop quiz."

I furrowed my brow and turned to her. "Now we're in school?"

"It's a thing my friend and I do. I want to test what you know about rodeo."

I let out a laugh. "I know a lot."

"Okay, then, pop quiz. When was the first recorded rodeo in history?" Emersyn shifted in her seat then, her back to the window as she faced me. She ran a hand through her hair, bringing it forward to rest on her shoulder.

My breath hitched, and I held it for two...three...four...eight seconds before letting the air loose from my lungs. A flash of a memory from sixteen years ago, watching as she did the same move with her hair while she held onto my hand, her words sinking into my mind.

I inhaled sharply before answering, "Colorado, 1864."

"Where in Colorado?" Her eyes narrowed.

"Deer Trail," I answered confidently, leaning over slightly to wiggle my eyebrows at her.

A 'huh' filtered through the air, disbelief hanging on the sound. "Didn't think you would know that one. Ok...question two—"

"How many questions are there?"

"Pay attention. When was the PRCA founded?"

"You sure you're not asking me about the PBR?"

"Fine." She rolled her eyes slightly. "When was the PRCA *and* the PBR founded?"

I chuckled. "The PRCA was founded in 1945, the PBR in 1992."

"Question three—"

"Make it a hard one," I teased.

"Okay, smart ass, when was the first Miss Rodeo America Pageant held, and who won?"

I hated to admit she had me there. I could spout off facts about rodeo history, useless facts that no one really needed to know. Wanna know how to strap a bull for a ride? I can teach you how to do that. Do you, for some reason, need to know the events that were held at the first rodeo? I knew that too. But ask me anything about Miss Rodeo America, and I was a lost cause.

After a few beats of silence, Emersyn folded her arms and leaned her shoulder against the seat. "1955, Casper, Wyoming. And Marilyn Scott was the reigning queen for 1955 and 1956."

I nodded, taking that name and ingraining it in my memory. "Marilyn Scott," I repeated. "Got it."

The pop-quiz segment lasted the remainder of the drive, the questions turning from history of the rodeo to more pageant things, but it was light, and it was...fun. Normally, my drives to the next event were silent, me going through who was going to be there, when Drew would decide to call, and what bulls were going to be there to pull. But with Emersyn, she took the stress that came with going to a new arena away, simply by asking me pop quiz questions, not even making fun of me or teasing when I got an answer wrong. She knew more than I gave her credit for, that was for sure, because when I started asking the questions—and I asked the most random questions I could think of—she never got one wrong.

"Final question," I asked her as I rounded the corner into the arena. "What was my score on my first qualified ride this year?"

I shifted the truck in part, my eyes meeting hers.

"Arizona, you scored an 87."

I began to nod, but Emersyn's voice stopped me.

"But it's kind of a trick question."

I furrowed my brow, grabbing my hat off the dashboard and shoving it on my head. "How so? That's the right answer. Arizona, 87…"

"You always get a qualified ride." She opened the door. "My research for this was watching every single one of your rides, and every single one qualified. That's no easy feat, Oakes. Not many cowboys have done that, so yeah, it was kind of a trick question."

She jumped from the truck, her blonde hair bouncing as her feet hit the ground. She turned to shut the door, the only part of her that was visible was her torso up. She gave me a cheeky smile, earning her one in return.

"Smartass," I mumbled moments before she shut the door.

Drew

How was the first leg?

Oakes

You mean the three hours of constant questions…it was ok.

Drew

Don't be an ass. Talk to you after the ride.

CHAPTER SEVEN
Oakes

"What is that?" I jerked my chin in Emersyn's direction as I pulled my glove on.

She changed once we checked into the motel for the evening, donning jeans, a button-down denim shirt, and a hat covering her wavy hair as it tumbled down her shoulders. The best part of her ensemble was her boots. Deep brown with a bit of shine to them, no doubt ones she wore during her pageant days. Just seeing her put my stomach into knots. She was even more gorgeous than I remembered, than I thought.

Even if I closed my eyes, I could still see her all those years ago. Blonde hair styled to a T, stiff and unmoving under her hat, makeup covering her natural beauty with eyeshadow matching any outfit she was wearing, her eyes having a bit of fear behind them. Her hair had been brighter then, but now, the blonde seemed to fade into almost a lighter brown. The thought passed my mind that this was possibly her natural color, from before she dyed it to fit into the Miss Rodeo America mold. Her blue eyes sparkled just the same, and the blush on her cheeks seemed to be her, not makeup.

This was the real her I was seeing, and she was right—she belonged in the rodeo arena.

Emersyn looked down and then slowly raised her eyes to me. "It's a camera."

"I can see it's a camera, but why do you have it?" I shoved on my glove once more.

"To...take...pictures..." Emersyn said, a question hanging in her voice.

"But you're the writer. Shouldn't someone else be taking the photos for you?" I cocked a brow, tipping the corner of my lip up.

Her smile grew then, her eyes dancing as she raised the camera to her eye. Her finger moved, the faint 'click' sound of the camera traveling even in the loud backend of the arena.

"I told you. Journalism major, photography minor. This assignment is all mine from the photos to the article." She looked at the camera in her hands. "Handsome."

Ignoring the little jolt that flashed through me after hearing Emersyn call me handsome, I cleared my throat. "I don't remember photos being a part of the deal."

"Oakes, did you even pay attention during the dinner last night?"

"I paid attention," I grunted as I tugged on my other glove.

"It's in the contract," she added.

"Is it?"

Her expression dropped. "Having your photo taken is nothing new. You're aired on screen for every rodeo." She dropped her camera to her waist, the strap around her neck keeping it secure as she popped her hip. "I'm taking photos, editing them, and sending them off to *Rodeo Way.*"

I shook my head. "All right, whatever you need."

Closing her eyes and giving me a slow, satisfied nod, she hummed. "Thank you. Now"—she raised her camera again—"smile."

I didn't smile.

"What are your plans while I'm out there?" I asked her, taking a step forward. Grabbing my helmet, I shoved it under my arm, knowing my ride was coming up. So far, there had yet to be a qualified ride. The announcers were already shouting my name, expecting a show.

"I was going to see if I can get close to the chute when you ride, but I can focus on behind-the-scenes stuff if you'd rather."

I raised a brow. "The chute is fine."

Emersyn rewarded me with a smile, and I felt my lips tug in return.

"And after my ride?"

"My editor sent me over some basic questions to get out of the way, then...time to edit and start my article."

"Ashford, come saddle up!" I heard a hand yell, catching my attention away from Emersyn.

"Saddle up?" Emersyn chuckled, parroting his words.

"Well, come on, then." I nodded toward the chutes. "This has to get you some good photos."

Emersyn smiled and jogged slightly to catch up to me, following me onto the metal grate and up the stairs to the chutes. I had pulled Wired Max—one of the toughest bulls I've seen this year. His horns curled up to the side, reminding me of some mythical creature, and his black skin only made him look more devilish. He was already bucking in the chute when I came up, strapping on my helmet.

"Oh, good," I chuckled. "He's already pissed."

"He's not very fond of the tight space." The same hand laughed, then his gaze went to Emersyn, eyeing her up and down. "Who's this?"

"Emersyn Flynn, *Rodeo Way*." She held out her hand for him to shake, and as expected, he ignored it.

"My shadow this summer. She's cleared to be here, taking photos and such for an article. Gotta get her up close and personal." I hoisted myself up and over the gate, my thighs resting on Wired Max. The second he felt my weight, he jolted in the chute. "Easy, boy," I murmured to him, as if it would make a difference. "You'll be able to buck me off soon enough."

I slipped my right fingers into the bull rope. Wired Max let out a huff as I began to pull and tug on my fingers and straps. From the corner of my eye, I could see Emersyn with her camera raised to her eye, moving and twisting her body in all directions, just trying to get a good shot of me in the chute. Wired Max jolted again, and I saw Emersyn flinch slightly, just enough that I could see her shoulders shake with a breath. I closed my eyes and let out a puff of air, suddenly wishing my helmet had less vision capabilities than it did. I needed to focus on this bull—not the woman on the gate.

The small voice in the back of my head was repeating over and over: *She doesn't need to be here. She can be in the stands. She'll get a better view, a better shot, from farther away. It's dangerous back here.* And no matter how hard I tried to focus on the beast I was currently sitting on, the only thing that consumed my mind was the fact that Emersyn was right there. Bulls could get crazy. They jumped. They kicked. They put all their force into the person—which at the moment was me—and getting them off. Wired Max wasn't the only bull getting angry...but he was the one closest to Emersyn.

Stop.

I tried to drown out that voice.

I looked at her one last time, her face still hidden by the camera.

She knows what she's doing.

Focus. On. The. Bull.

Jon Bon Jovi started blasting through the speakers as the announcers began to really hype me up. I could hear the cheers again, the screams and whoops coming from all angles. *It's my life...*

That's right, Jon...it's now or never...

Digging my spurs into Max's sides, he jostled around, and I felt my entire body shift. I...fumbled? No. No, I didn't fumble. He was just strong.

Gripping onto the bull rope as tight as I could, I closed my eyes, raised my left hand, took a puff of air through my lips, and nodded.

Metal clanged as the chute opened...

One, two, three...

Damn, he was strong. Wired really fit for his name. Left, right, left. Up, down, back up again. Force flying through him.

Where's Emersyn?

I tried to turn my head, my focus going from the bull to...

Shit.

Four...five...six...

Fuck.

It happened faster than I liked to admit. My glove slipped, the skin of my hand suddenly becoming cold in the air after sweating in the glove, and my body flew to the right when Wired Max flew to the left.

I stumbled, my knees hitting the ground, the dirt flying up around me. I ignored the pain I could feel in my knee. I had felt worse. Plus, I really couldn't think about that now. Not with an angry bull on the loose. Adrenaline flowed through my body, and I felt my heart rate pick up, beating faster, almost as if it wanted away from the bull too, as if it wanted free from my chest. In an instant, I was on my feet, ignoring the sharp, shooting pain that hit my knee that spread down my calf, twisting my torso to see where Wired Max was. Behind me, still bucking, still just was wired, the bull fighters trying their hardest to get him to where he had to go. His crazed eyes met mine...and I ran.

```
To: E.Flynn@rodeowaymag.com
From: L.Managa@rodeowaymag.com
Subject: O. Ashford Photos
Date: June 7th: 10:08 PM
```

Emersyn,

Thanks for the photos, some are great…some are…well, what happened? You're editing, right?

L


```
To: L.Managa@rodeowaymag.com
From: E.Flynn@rodeowaymag.com
Subject: REPLY: O. Ashford Photos
Date: June 7th: 10:11 PM
```

I'm editing already. I plan to edit all my photos. Sterling doesn't need to edit photos, just the article. I have to send him over everything. Just had to share the raw moment. I'll send them to Morgan when they are ready to go. Not quite sure what happened. It was…intense.

Emersyn Flynn
Digital Editor - Rodeo Way Magazine
Denver, CO

Chapter Eight
Emersyn

No matter how many times I looked at the photos, they didn't get any easier. At first, he had the same expression as he always did, his focus seeming to be one hundred percent on the bull under him. He was in his element, and seeing him in the moment was way more exhilarating than I thought it would be. I caught a photo, a slight sense of pride slicing through me when I saw how I captured it, of him glancing up at me once more before he settled himself onto the bull.

The next photo was him giving the nod, then the chute opening, then the start of his ride. Something seemed off. I had seen way too many of his rides to know his normal posture when he was on the bull. His body was more fluid, one with the bull in a way. But here—on this bull—his body was stiff, and his heels weren't in the right place. Oakes and the bull were two separate beings. That bull wanted him off.

Oakes was acting differently.

And I was willing to bet anything it was because of me.

After the ride, he limped off the dirt and straight to his truck, his head hung low. I followed quickly, catching up to him right as he turned the engine on. I climbed in the passenger seat, and we drove in silence all the way to the motel. Accidents like this happened in rodeos; they weren't rare—in fact, quite the opposite. Oakes *always* qualifying was rare. As far as I knew, he was one of the only bull riders to get those eight seconds every. Single. Time. And the fact that he didn't qualify, but limped off the dirt, was enough to crash his ego really fast. And it showed.

At the peak of my rodeo days, I had seen so many accidents and talked to so many riders after them. They were easy to boost back up, bouncing back from a fall so fast you would never even guess they fell. You would never know they were hurt. Hell, I'd seen hands smashed by a hoof. I'd seen shoulders dislocated. I'd seen riders take entire years off to recover. I'd seen early retirements. I'd seen so much...

But never—*never*—with Oakes.

He slammed the truck in park and, in a flash, was out of the cab. I, once again, followed slowly, unsure of what to do with him. He wasn't a 'hold his hand and tell him he's got this' kind of guy, but I didn't want him to stew either. He mumbled a goodnight and then disappeared into the room next to mine. If I followed him, he would most likely shove me away. It took everything in me to ignore that urge to care for him, to just shower and change for bed.

If only my mind was that strong *to* ignore it.

So, I simply sat in my bed, going over the photos I had taken, reliving the moment over and over again. I caught the moment when he flew through the air, the way the bull turned and zeroed in on Oakes. In the next photo, Oakes was on the ground, his feet apart, knees bent, dirt flying around his boots, telling me he landed with more force than I thought.

I bit my bottom lip and looked at the shared wall of our motel rooms. He limped the entire way to the truck, to the room, and now...I'd bet him his next paycheck he wasn't taking care of his new injury the way he should be.

Stretching to the nightstand, I grabbed my phone, tapping on that little green text bubble.

Me

> Can I have Oakes's number?

It didn't take long before those dots began to dance.

Drew

> Is he giving you a hard time already?

Me

> Did you not see his ride? I just want to make sure he's ok.

Drew

> I didn't…here…keep me updated.

Seconds after Drew sent over Oakes's number, I pulled up a new thread.

Me

> Hey, it's Emersyn—just checking in. Are you ok?

A few moments passed, no dancing dots. No answer. Nothing.

Me

> Oakes, please let me know you're ok.

I stared at the screen. Nothing.

"Stubborn ass," I grumbled, tossing my phone down on my bed. It was only a few steps before I was at his door, knocking loud enough to wake the rest of the motel. "Oakes, open up!" I shouted, knocking again.

Seconds later, the door opened, Oakes's tall body standing in the frame, towering over me. His hair was wet, fresh from the shower, but his eyes looked broken. He leaned against the door frame, his left wrist resting on his forehead.

"I'm fine," he mumbled.

He looked anything but fine.

I folded my arms and glared at him. "How's the leg?" I looked down at his legs; his right leg held most of his weight.

"Fine. I've been in worse accidents." Pushing himself off the frame, he turned, silently giving me permission to follow. His room was lightly lit, unlike mine, which had almost every light on. Oakes seemed comfortable with the soft glow of the desk lamp.

His chaps laid on the spare bed, his boots toppled over next to his sponsor-clad vest. The covers on his chosen bed were pulled down, which gave me a twinge of guilt that maybe he was already settled for the night. Seeing him sit on the end of the bed, keeping his left leg straight, kicked that guilt right out of me.

"Knee or ankle?" I asked, my arms still folded as I stared him down.

"Knee." He rubbed his left knee, his fingers lightly squeezing it.

"Did you ice it?"

He let out a soft groan. "No ice." He huffed.

"Dear God, Oakes..." I quickly turned, grabbing the ice bucket on my way out of the motel, purposefully leaving the door open. I stomped down the concrete path right to the ice machine, filling up the bucket as much as I could before slamming the cover down and stomping right back to his room. Oakes was right where I left him, one single eyebrow raised as he watched me. "You're an idiot."

Using a plastic bag, I poured some ice in and wrapped a towel around it, reaching out my arm to hand it to him. He looked at the white makeshift ice pack and then at me, seeming to ruminate about it before finally giving in and grabbing the ice. He placed it on his knee and slumped his shoulders all in one motion.

"It's not as bad as it looks," he said, his voice gravelly. "I've had worse injuries."

"Still." I folded my arms over my chest, only then having it occur to me that I was in my pajamas, a tank and night shorts, which was more exposure than I really wanted at the moment. I swallowed, tightening my arms over my waist. "You don't want it to swell."

"I didn't land that hard."

"Stop acting tough. It's okay to admit you need ice."

With a slight eyeroll, Oakes raised his chin to look at me. "Thanks." His voice was soft as he said the word.

"You're welcome." Heaving a sigh, I dropped my arms. "Do you have any ibuprofen?"

"I took some just before you violently knocked on my door." A ghost of a smile spread across his lips, those brown eyes showing some of the flash they would before a ride.

I couldn't help but return the grin. "I didn't violently knock."

Oakes chuckled, situating himself on his bed so that the ice could rest on his knee while he lay back on the mattress. "Yeah, you did."

"I...did. Fine. Maybe answer your texts next time, and I won't have to come over here so"—I held up my hands to air quote—"violently."

He shook his head, that deep chuckle turning into a laugh that vibrated through his chest. "Noted."

I watched him, taking note of how his breathing slowed and a calm feeling took over him. His chest rose and fell, relaxation finally seeming to spread through his body. I could easily sit on the bed with him, make sure the ice was settled just right over his knee, make sure the pillow was propped in just the right position, just...make sure he wasn't alone. What did he do when he was hurt during rides? Did he just...take care of himself? Probably. He probably didn't want—or need—me here.

"Okay, well, I'll see you in the morning?" I hesitated, trying to force my body to make its way toward the door instead of just standing here, convincing myself that I could be something he needed in the moment.

"Sorry I ruined your interview time," he said, his voice muffled by his arms now covering his eyes.

My lips twisted, my eyes darting from the door to Oakes. "You didn't. We have a few hours in the car tomorrow. I can ask the questions *Rodeo Way* sent over then."

"Or"—he lowered his forearm—"we can get some out of the way now. I won't be falling asleep until that ibuprofen kicks in." Our eyes linked for a second before he lifted his arm back over his eyes.

"Now?" I pointed at the floor, even though I knew he wasn't seeing my gesture.

He nodded. "Why not? Who knows, it may help me fall asleep."

"Okay, I'll go get my phone and iPad. I'll…" I took one last look at him before turning to the door, forcing myself not to do a double-take. "I'll be right back."

Texts from Luca and Drew were waiting for me when I picked up my devices, Luca asking about Oakes's injury, Drew asking about if he answered my text. A couple quick *He's finally icing it* and *No, he didn't, but I got him to open his door* replies, and I made the few steps back to Oakes's room, finding him in the exact same position I left him in. I pulled the desk chair out and brought my iPad back to life, the photo I was editing before still open in Lightroom. I swiped it away as quickly as I could, pulling up my first set of interview questions.

"Saw that photo." He groaned.

I scrunched my nose and gave him a sideways glance, mumbling a quick 'sorry' so low he probably couldn't even hear it. Clearing my throat, I read the first question and jumped right into it.

"Where did you grow up?" I asked, turning to fully look at him.

He let out a long, drawn-out breath, silence filling the space only for a brief moment.

"Wyoming," he answered.

"I know that," I admitted. "Where in Wyoming?"

"The middle."

"As in?"

Another sigh. "Close to Casper."

Typing the answer into the form, I raised my brows. I can accept that answer. At least, it gave me an idea.

Oakes Ashford Interview One:

Where did you grow up: Oakes grew up outside of Casper, Wyoming.

Next question. "Tell me a little about your family," I said, my fingers still going on the tiny keyboard.

"It's me, my mom, and my brother."

Describe your family: Oakes lives with his mother, brother, and…

"Your dad?"

"He's gone."

I stopped typing, turning to look at him still lying down, his hands on his chest with his eyes closed. "I'm sorry to hear that, Oakes."

"I don't want to talk about it."

I swallowed, taking his cue to move on, and turned back to my computer. The next few questions focused on childhood—things like *Are you close to your family? Where did you attend high school? Describe yourself as a teenager, were you reckless or well behaved?*—all of which I knew I probably couldn't get him to answer. So, I picked the one that seemed the easiest. "Did you know you always wanted to ride bulls in the rodeo?"

"No. At first, I wanted to do bareback."

Did you always want to ride bulls? : Surprisingly, Oakes hasn't always wanted to ride bulls. His first event was bareback.

"Wait, seriously?" I paused, looking at the words I had just typed on my screen. I couldn't see Oakes doing anything other than bulls.

"Yeah. Bulls were the furthest thing from my mind."

"But...you're a natural at it." I twisted in the chair, facing him. His arms rose in the air, only to flop by his sides. He turned his head to me.

"It took a lot of training to get to where I am now."

"Why go from bareback to bulls?"

A pregnant silence filled the room as he turned his attention back to the ceiling. Only his steady breaths could be heard, my ears soon filling with that silent hum. But I waited for him to answer.

After a moment, I spoke. "Oakes?"

"Someone encouraged me to ride bulls when I was a kid. I guess I wanted to prove to them I could do it." He pushed himself up on his elbows, his eyes grasping mine. The connection was deep—raw, almost—as he stared me down. Shivers ran up my spine as he took a deep breath. "I almost quit a long time ago. That one person gave me the courage and helped me believe I could do it, and I hear their voice every time I get on the back of a bull."

The expression he gave me was one I had never—ever—seen before. His eyes were heavy on me, as if they carried a part of the story he wasn't saying. A small blush rose to his cheeks under his beard, and his eyes softened. He was letting me in, saying something personal that no one else knew. I felt the heat rise in my chest with anticipation. His gaze never faltered from mine as we both waited in the silence. Finally, I cleared my throat.

"Was it your dad?" I asked, a small smile forming on my lips. "You said he was gone, but did he have any influence on your career path?"

The corners of his eyes twitched slightly, but no answer came. Finally, he sighed and looked at the ice on his knee. He grabbed it and placed it on the bed next to him. "Twenty minutes on, twenty minutes off. That's what they say, right? Next question."

"Yeah, sure." Twisting, I grabbed my iPad and placed it on my lap, keeping my body to him. *First topic to stay away from—his father.* I swallowed and scanned the questions again, starting to type the next one out before I cleared my throat. "Best part about the event?"

Oakes's demeanor changed as he let out a breath of air through rounded lips.

"It's thrilling," he answered, raising a brow. "I never know what bull I'm going to pull, and sure, I can see their past rides, but I never know how the bull is going to act with me. And some are angry."

"Do you ever get nervous when you pull a bull's name? Like tonight, when you pulled Wired Max, what went through your head?" My fingers circled the keyboard, grazing across them until, finally, I lowered the iPad's cover. It sat closed on my lap, the interview questions all but forgotten.

He took a deep breath. "I just thought it would be like any other ride. I honestly love it when they jolt around in the chute—tells me it's going to be a fun time—but tonight..." He paused, his eyes narrowing. "Tonight was different."

"Why?"

"My head wasn't in it."

"Why?" I asked again, finding myself wanting the answer more for *me* than *Rodeo Way*.

He shrugged his shoulder. "Couldn't tell ya," was his only response. "Shit happens, and tonight...shit happened."

"But you always qualify," I urged, trying to sound more supportive than not.

"Yeah, well...gotta fumble sometimes, right?"

"Right," I parroted.

"All that matters is that you get up, don't let the shattered bones stop you." His eyes met mine again. "Sure, I'm upset I didn't qualify. I only get a hundred rides to put toward the NFR, and this one had some good prize money, but...there's tomorrow's ride. So tonight, I will wallow in self-pity, ice my knee, thanks to you, and then get back on the fucking bull."

"Would you have gotten ice if I hadn't come over?"

He let out a laugh. "Eventually, but I'll admit it wouldn't have been for a while."

"You're welcome." I gave him a smile, one that got me one in return. A genuine, sweet smile. Not the flashy one I saw on TV, not the one he gave to the camera. This one...I was going to keep. I felt the heat rise in my chest again, the moment of weakness where he was becoming more of himself, not the bull rider. "Are you up for a few more questions?"

Oakes scoffed and grabbed the ice pack, plopping it back on his knee even though it had only been a few minutes, not the twenty he advised just moments ago. "Hit me."

To: m.pennel@rodeowaymag.com, s.krass@rodeoway
 mag.com
From: E.Flynn@rodeowaymag.com
Subject: Interview one - part one
Date: June 8th: 7:45 AM

Morgan and Sterling,

I understand these aren't due for a few days, but I was able to get some time in with Oakes last night and asked a few of these questions—however, a lot of them I know he won't answer. He is very set on keeping his life the way it is. He's agreed to open up a little, but when it comes to questions on his family and childhood, he won't answer them. I respect that, and as much as I appreciate these templates, I think I want to act on my own here and get to know him. As we were talking last night, he said some amazing things that I can't stop thinking about. I've highlighted those in the document, and I think those will be great quotes for the article. I guess you can say I want to go rogue here, if you'll let me. I think I can get more from him than the standard questions, and with your permission, I'd like to try this. I'll still send interview questions and pieces to you by the deadlines.

Also attached are the photos from last night's ride. He hurt his knee, but the recovery should be quick—all a part of the job. He'll be back on the bull for sure.

Emersyn Flynn
Digital Editor - Rodeo Way Magazine
Denver, CO

Chapter Nine
Emersyn

My phone almost took a nosedive off the small end table as it buzzed, and buzzed...and buzzed. Notification after notification came flying in at the same time, and the death glare I was shooting it wasn't going to make them stop.

Morgan

> We need a quick chat. Are you available?

> I want to know more on this 'going rogue' idea of yours...we need to discuss it ASAP.

Luca

> Morgan's on one this morning—just be warned.

Morgan

> Meeting in ten. Conference with you, me, and Sterling. Talk soon. Ten minutes.

Jumping to Luca's text thread, I swiped it open.

Me

> Apparently. Meeting in ten? Are you going to be available for that?

Luca

> I'm just the coordinator for your travel. I'm sure if Morgan wants me to hop on, I can, but it's not on my schedule.

Me

> I sent her an email a few minutes ago. Impromptu meeting apparently!

Luca

> She must have really loved your email.

Ten minutes later, I set my phone up on speaker, propped on the tissue box on the small desk, my iPad ready to go just like at any work meeting. The shrill ring and vibration of my phone sent it tumbling over, landing on the desk with a thump. I swiped the call button and cleared my throat.

"Good morning, Morgan," I answered, fumbling to set my phone back up, only to give up and set it down on the desk, burying my head in my palms, thanking the Lord she couldn't see me.

"Hey, Em," Sterling's voice came through first, and even though I couldn't see him, I could hear his smile. "How's Utah?" he asked, his voice sure and steady, just like in the office.

"Chilly, if I'm honest." I glanced out the window just in time to see Oakes appear on the grassy knoll right in front of the motel. He ran his hand through his hair, looked from left to right, and began to stretch. Wearing just gym shorts and a wrap around his knee, he twisted his torso and began to jog. Even though he was running at a slower pace, no doubt catering to his knee, I could still see every muscle in his calf flex with each and every step he took.

"Em?" Sterling's voice called over the phone.

"Huh?" I twisted my head back to my phone. "Yes, sorry."

"I asked the temperature."

I slapped my palm to my forehead and took one last glance outside, Oakes getting smaller and smaller in the distance. "It, uh..." I inhaled, pulling myself back. "Well, last night was colder at the rodeo, but I haven't been outside yet today. I just saw Oakes go for a run, so it must be nice."

"A run after hurting his knee. Damn—"

"He's tough."

"Yeah, you would know." Sterling chuckled.

"Ah, Sterling!" I heard Morgan's faint voice come over the speaker. "Thank you for getting the call started."

"No problem. Emersyn is here."

"Hi, Morgan," I said, standing to pull the shades closed so the disappearing Oakes could stay just that. "I take it you got my email?"

"Yes!" she shouted, her enthusiasm seeping through the speaker. "And the photos. I'm sorry to hear about Oakes's injury last night."

"Emersyn said he's on a run, so I'm assuming he's perfectly okay." Sterling's voice was more faded, and I could picture the two of them in Morgan's office, Sterling pivoted in the chair on the opposite side of the desk, Morgan settling into her larger leather chair. "Her exact words were 'He's tough.'"

"He's a bull rider; he has to be. Now, I know you probably have a busy day—"

I opened the schedule on my screen, Morgan still talking in the background.

"—but I wanted to touch base on this idea of yours. Going rogue. Why do you think Mr. Ashford won't answer any of the predetermined questions, and what exactly do you plan to do?"

"Oakes made it very clear he wants to keep things professional, so I had to find another way to get these in-depth questions answered. If the question is geared toward his childhood, I skipped it, seeing as he instantly shot me down when asking about his father. That's a sensitive subject for him, and I'd rather keep that off the table."

"Do you know his father?" Sterling asked.

I shook my head, even though I knew they couldn't see me. "I don't."

Sterling let out a deep hum, and I swear I could picture his chin tipping up, his eyes narrowing. I've seen the look before on plenty of dates together—that sound always meant he didn't believe something. I brushed it off, straightening my back to boost my esteem.

"He did mention his mother and brother, but when I asked about his dad, his response was he didn't want to talk about it. So—again, Morgan—I feel it's best if I stay away from topics that include his childhood." I brought up my document I started last night, keeping his schedule off to the side. "When I asked about the rodeo, that was when he talked more. When I asked questions that weren't on the sheet, he willingly answered. I think I need to discover who he is on my own...not these predetermined questions."

"I did research on those questions, things I felt Oakes's fans would want to know," Sterling added.

"Which is great, and I appreciate it, but isn't it normally up to the journalist how their article is formatted and what is included? I have no issues with you giving me suggestions, but if I'm writing this, then I think I should be the sole brain on it."

Damn. Who was this girl, and how could I get her to stick around? Normally, if something was told to me...for example, Sterling will give you these predetermined questions and you will report to us...I just let it happen. I did whatever my bosses wanted me to do. But, let me be real here, I had to take this over if I wanted anything to come of it. This was where I wanted to be, what I wanted to do, and I was going to take it over.

"Emersyn," Morgan's voice was stern, and I waited to be reprimanded. I inhaled, closed my eyes and prepared for her to argue. "I completely agree with you."

My shoulders fell, and a heavy breath let loose. "You do?" I asked, trying to force my voice to sound clear and precise without the shake that I knew was there.

"I do. I love this idea, and I think Sterling is on the same page."

"I can be," was his answer.

"This can be an even better way to get the article we want. Maybe instead of interview questions that people have read over and over on multiple cowboys, you can give us something different. Give us a story and not an interview. Get to know Oakes, talk to him, and deliver what you feel would be the best for *Rodeo Way*."

Sterling's hum echoed once again. "That actually sounds intriguing. I like it. It will be a fun piece to edit. Become his friend, get all those secrets out of him, and discover who he is."

Become his friend, get all his secrets out of him...discover who he is?

What were they wanting?

"I'm sorry, you want me to trick him?" I asked, blinking my eyes, trying to wrap my brain around that sentence.

"Not trick, *per se...*" Sterling drew out his words.

"Just get to know him," Morgan stepped in. "There's nothing wrong with getting to know who Oakes is. That's what we want, isn't it?"

"*Rodeo Way* isn't a tabloid. I don't want to deceive Oakes into giving me this information on himself. I'll only put things in the article that I promised him I would."

"Which we will respect, and the last thing I want is for *Rodeo Way* to turn into a gossip magazine. I've worked too hard to get that title attached to it." Morgan's voice became demanding, harsh—pure authority.

Rodeo Way was hers...so sadly...

"I understand what you are saying. I'm just asking for your trust when it comes to this article. I promise you I'll deliver what you want."

"If you do..." Morgan paused. "I can see more for you in the future. I know you don't particularly care for your position, but, Emersyn, if you can provide an article that we are all proud of, I can see you moving to journalist."

"I'm sorry...you...what?" I stammered, trying to get what she said clear in my head.

"Justin is leaving at the end of the summer. They are giving us one last article for the September issue, and then they are moving to Alaska—which means a journalism position will be open. If you follow through, if you provide what we want, that position is yours, Emersyn."

Holy. Fucking. Shit.

"Seriously?"

"Seriously. We've been keeping a close eye on you, and I've always been impressed with your writing. I trust you with this project. Go. Rogue."

My entire body shook, and I had to cover my mouth to force my excitement to stay in my chest, even though I wanted to shout it to the world that I could finally—*finally*—do exactly what I wanted to do.

I lowered my hand and inhaled, strong and smooth. "I promise you, Morgan, I won't let you down."

"I know you won't. Keep sending updates and the photos. They're perfect, and we all love seeing them. Enjoy your time, Emersyn."

"Bye, Em," Sterling called. "I look forward to your next round of edits."

"Thank you...we'll talk soon."

The *vroop* on my phone signaled the call was over, and I wasted no time in snatching it up.

Me

Holy. Fucking. Shit.

My fingers shook as I typed, but Luca's little text bubble chimed up.

Luca

What??

Me

I think Morgan just offered me a promotion.

Luca

To....

Me

If I pull this article off, I'll take Justin's spot. Journalist.

Luca

Holy. Fucking. Shit.

I showered in shock. I did my hair in shock. I basically spent the rest of the morning in shock over the potential of *this* becoming my life. Writing, taking photos, capturing every single moment I could. Finally back on the dirt. Finally doing what I've been wanting to do since I graduated college.

Trying not to think about this possibility too hard, I tried to pour my focus into the photos from the rodeo. I had the next few days to think on the article and how to make it all sync up. The next event wasn't for three days, and seeing as it was here in Utah, I felt like I had all the time in the world to get this done, get everything set up for success. Set me up for—

The loud bang on my door pulled me from the photo, my hand still on the mouse, causing the lighting to darken on the photo. I let out a small groan and turned toward the motel door.

"Emersyn," Oakes's voice was faint through the door. "It's me."

I stood, my hand already outstretched for the handle. Opening it to see Oakes sent another shock through me—a completely different kind of shock. His hair was slicked back from his hand just moments before, and those brown eyes were anything but tired. His cheeks were flushed, his still bare chest moving up and down heavily with each breath.

"Good morning." He gave me a tilted smile, only showing part of his teeth. I was certain that if he was clean shaven, he'd have a dimple there.

I narrowed my eyes and glanced at my watch. "It's only ten-thirty..." I leaned against the door. "How was your run?"

"Great." His smile widened. "I just wanted to check in. We don't leave for Idaho for a few days, and I didn't know what you have planned..."

I gestured to the desk where my laptop sat open, the still-too-dark photo on the screen. "Editing photos."

He huffed. "That one—"

"We're not gonna judge my work off of that photo." I left the entryway, closing the laptop.

"Ha, sure." He put his hands on his waist. "There's a diner down the road. Would you like to go get a bigger breakfast? My treat?"

"That actually sounds great. I haven't eaten yet today."

"Give me twenty." His eyebrows bounced once before his body turned back toward his room, but he gave me one last glance as he unlocked his door and vanished inside.

The small café in town was the best local diner we could have found. It had the small-town charm you found in movies, and the smell of coffee wafted through the air. Oakes sat across from me, ordering the largest breakfast he could, his plate filled with eggs, bacon, sausage, and hash-browns. And when I was handed my scone and side of bacon, he raised his eyebrow at me.

"Big breakfast," he repeated from earlier. "This is supposed to be a big breakfast, not a snack."

"This is not a snack." I shot him a teasing glare. "Plus, I guarantee you my stomach isn't as big as yours." I eyed his plate, judging every piece of food that sat in front of him. "How much do you eat?"

"Enough. Protein mainly. Less carbs." Oakes looked at my scone with an equal amount of judgment. "At least you ordered bacon, so I can't taunt you too much."

I laughed, sticking my fork in my scone. "Protein and high-intensity training, is that the secret to qualified rides?"

"High-intensity training for sure, but my diet is my choice." His eyes met mine as he popped a piece of sausage in his mouth, giving me a grin once his mouth was closed.

"What does Oakes Ashford's workout look like?"

"Jump rope, pull ups, sit ups, cardio. If a CrossFit gym is accessible. I go there. Like you said, high intensity. Today, I just stuck to a jog, since I'm nursing the knee, but if I wasn't, I probably would have gone to the CrossFit gym I noticed down the road."

I could feel his leg straighten out under the table, his calf brushing mine for a second before he put it back down.

"How is the knee?"

"Ninety-eight percent better—thanks to you, I guess, for the ice."

"You're welcome. Just don't skip leg day." I brought my fork to my lips, grasping the scone with my teeth and raising my eyebrows at him.

Become his friend, get all those secrets out, discover who he is.

A chill shot through my spine at just the memory of Sterling's words. I tightened my lips, beginning to regret coming to breakfast with Oakes. This wasn't an interview—this was just breakfast.

Oakes laughed, a quick shake to his head. "I'll never skip leg day—lunges, squats, and IT-band stretches—but today, a nice jog was all I needed."

"Luca, my friend, he goes to one of those big commercial gyms. Back day, leg day, arm day. All the days." I took another bite of my scone.

"All the days," Oakes repeated. "I mainly focus on my core and legs, especially after hurting my knee."

"What other kinds of injuries have you gotten?"

Oakes tilted his head. "I didn't know this was another interview." A corner of his lips twitched as his gaze focused on me, his tongue popping into his cheek.

I bit on my bottom lip again, wondering if this man could read my mind. "It's not," I replied.

He hummed, his expression saying he didn't quite believe me. I didn't believe myself either. A pit began to grow in my stomach.

"You don't have to answer anything you don't want to," I added, grabbing my coffee mug and lifting it to my lips, hoping the width would hide the embarrassment in my cheeks.

"No, it's okay." His grin skewed, and the knot that was forming in my stomach loosened. "I've had a few back injuries...my shoulders take a lot of it sometimes...my knees, of course. I've pulled hamstrings and other muscles that I've had to baby for a few days. When I was first riding"—he paused and looked at the table, flexing his left hand—"I fell and hurt my neck."

"Oof," I grunted. "Most riders don't come back from that."

"I'm not most riders," he said softer, leaning forward. I leaned toward him too, as if he was offering me a secret, and I was itching to take it. "Like

I said, Emmy, the more I care for my body, the less time it takes for me to recover from injuries."

Emmy.

Did he really just call me Emmy?

And did I just really like it?

"True," I said just as quietly as he had, a slight shake to my voice. "You definitely aren't like most riders."

His eyebrows bounced once as he leaned back into the booth. "What about you? What training did you do for Miss Rodeo America?"

I scoffed. "As much as I hate to admit this, it was mainly weight control."

He gave me a disapproving look but kept silent, waiting for me to keep going.

"I lifted weights; I did cardio. Some leg days, but mainly it was diets and making sure my weight was steady. It helped with stunt riding too."

"I forgot you performed stunts," Oakes said as he took a sip from his coffee. I furrowed my brow, trying to remember any of our conversations where I mentioned that tidbit about myself to him. "You shouted that very loudly when we met, remember? When you, uh"—he coughed, completely avoiding eye contact—"were calling me out for saying you didn't belong in a rodeo arena."

I clenched my teeth. "I'm sorry about that. It was unprofessional."

"What was unprofessional was me assuming you were just a blonde who didn't know shit about rodeos or bull riding or"—he met my gaze—"stunt riding."

I gave him a soft chuckle. "I don't really tell that to people. They expect me to do a handstand on my horse as she's running around the arena."

"Can you?"

"Pfft." I waved him off. "Of course I can."

Oakes rested his elbows on the table. "Have you ever balanced on one hand before?" He raised one arm above his head, the other stretched out.

I shook my head. "Are you making fun of me?" I pinched my brows together, not giving a care in the world if he was. "Horses can run up to thirty miles an hour, maybe not in a rodeo arena, but I'd like to see you do that."

"Maybe." He smiled, that same glint in his eyes reappearing. "Maybe one day you'll get to see that from me. It can't be that hard. Easier than riding a bull."

I barked out a laugh. "Oh, that's rich. We'll bet on it." I held out a hand for him to shake. "At the end of the summer, I'll ride a bull, and you'll do a handstand on a horse running around the arena."

"You? On a bull?"

"Bring it."

Oakes grabbed my hand, and we shook, the warmth of his palm radiating up to my elbow and shoulder...right into my chest.

CHAPTER TEN
Emersyn

Four days in a small town in Utah was more than enough for me, spending the majority of my time at the tiny desk in the motel, plugging away at the hundreds of photos I had from the one rodeo we had been to. I had picked the best ones right off the bat and edited them to *Rodeo Way's* standard, sending them first to Luca, for a hype call, and then off to Morgan for approval.

Once those were done, I opened a fresh document and began to outline my article. With new parameters and a promotion on the line, the blank document sitting in front of me was a little bit intimidating. I gave myself a pep talk, repeating in my head over and over again that I could give them what they wanted. I could write a story without breaking my word to Oakes. All it took was a little more observation. I could pick up details about him without even talking to him, weaving those small facts into the article.

Like his routine. Watching him for four days, I was able to set my clock to his habits. He woke up early, always stretched in the grassy field in front of the motel, and then either went on a jog or to the gym, sometimes both. He would be gone for a few hours but return in time to shower, rest a little, and then knock on my door for lunch. Even if I declined, telling him I was too busy or trying to focus, he wouldn't take no for an answer. We'd eat, shoot each other more pop quiz questions to test our knowledge, and then go back to our own things. It was easy with him. It all seemed so easy.

Oakes called Drew daily, and the phone call either had him smiling and laughing or pacing with a scowl. Other phone calls or text messages had him smiling wider, a genuine one that wasn't meant for anyone to see, but with my desk facing the window, those moments were hard to miss.

I wanted to know who was making him react that way. In the week I had been with him, I hadn't seen him interact with anyone except Drew and me, keeping mainly to himself. But those moments of happiness and joy were there. And for some reason, I wanted more of them. I wanted to break him out and laugh with him, smile with him, and know more than the bull rider. I found myself, despite the article looming over my head, wanting to know him. So much so that staying in my room just watching him was getting harder, and that blank document was still blank.

Needless to say, when he knocked on my door early one morning, grabbing my suitcase to throw in his truck, I was ready to move to the next city. The eight-hour drive to Eagle, Idaho was nothing in comparison to other drives I'd done, and more time with Oakes was—for me—an amazing thing, but once we got to Idaho and he went to check in, I changed my clothes, donned my black hat, curls, and boots...and did what I loved to do.

Taking photos. So many photos.

I broke away from Oakes, finding bareback riders, mutton busters, tie-down and team ropers—any event that I could—asking them if I could capture their rides, their moments. And every single one agreed with enthusiasm. Even if they didn't qualify or if they broke the barrier, they came to me to check out the photos, each one leaving with a smile and handing me their information.

"Please send that my way. I'd love to keep it," one tie-down roper said to me, squeezing my shoulder.

"Of course! I do need you to sign a—" I started, twisting my torso before he was completely out of the area.

"I'll sign whatever you need, doll." He winked at me. "I'll find you after; don't go too far. You're with Ashford, right?"

I gave him a nod and a smile. "I am! Thank you!"

I glanced back at the photo. His hands were in the air, the calf was on the ground, and I caught his smile. The perfect shot.

A thrill washed over my body, my spine tingling as I began to flip through the photos. I took each and every one of these. I didn't just edit them. I didn't see them second-hand. *My* boots were in the dirt, on the metal grate. *My* heart was in these photos. *My* heart was here.

And this was all in my reach.

"What are you smiling at?" Oakes's gruff voice came up from behind me, his frame appearing moments later at my side, closer than he's ever been before.

I tilted my body away from him but my camera toward him, showing off the photo I was admiring.

"Damn." He gripped my hand, pulling the camera closer. "Is that Turner?"

I nodded. "Yeah, I think *Rodeo Way* would love this one, don't you think?"

"Didn't know tie-down could look so good." He dropped his hand, the warmth from his fingertips falling with it. "Barrels and then bulls. You gonna join me up at the chute again?"

I met his gaze, and one brow was raised. "I think..." I took a step back, catching a hint of cologne and leather, telling myself it wasn't him I was catching scent of. "I'm going to wander tonight. You're great and all—"

"No." He gestured his hand out. "By all means, do your thing, and we'll do one of your interviews tonight."

Rubbing my lips together, I gave him a small nod. "How's the knee?"

He raised his left knee, dropping it a few times before he bounced on the balls of his feet. "Better than ever. Get some good shots. Grab a beer. Enjoy yourself."

I chuckled. "I don't think a beer is in my per diem, plus I think my boss will be upset if she finds out I was drinking on the job."

"Who says you are working? Looks to me like you are enjoying your evening, and"—he spun on his heel and waved a hand in the air—"it's on me. Tell them you're with me, and I got it."

Before I could respond, Oakes's attention was already on another cowboy, so much so he missed the blush rush in my cheeks.

"Do the designs on your chaps have meaning?" I asked, taking in Oakes's brown-and-blue chaps as we walked down the hall the following night, the sounds from the arena over us faint.

Oakes glanced down as he took a step, his helmet in one hand, gloves in the other. The Vernal, Utah sun sat on his hair, making it shine brighter than normal. He ran his hands through the mess, jerking his head to flop it off to the side.

"The OA is for my name, obviously." He lifted his left leg up, the O and A written delicately in a bucking bull, just like on his truck. "And"—he spun to walk backward, facing me—"the first year I won the NFR."

"And the cross?" I raised a brow.

"Protection." He gave me a quick smile before turning again. "You sure you want to be up on the grate again?"

The last rodeo in Idaho, I didn't spend any time on the grate with him. I caught his ride from the stands, getting some amazing shots of his form and celebrations after, but today, at this rodeo, being back by the chutes with him was exactly where I wanted to be.

Our eyes locked, and I flashed him a smile.

"Hell yeah."

After giving me a surprise wink, Oakes began to walk ahead of me, his chaps moving around his Wranglers and his spurs with each step. He moved his helmet, shoving it under his arm as he began to fumble with his gloves.

"So, tell me..." I caught up to him. "What's one thing that goes through your mind as you climb on the bull?"

"I always tell myself something I was told about sixteen years ago." He stopped to wait for me, and once his left glove was on, he moved to the right. "I tell myself that one ride doesn't define my future. That no matter what happens now, or tomorrow, or the next ride, I was meant to be on the back of this animal, and it's now or never."

"And after that one thing you say, what's your thought process?"

"I close my eyes. I breathe. I repeat those words over and over. Then...I nod. I put my entire focus into the beast underneath me, in those eight seconds. Nothing else matters. Nothing. Those eight seconds feel like an eternity. I don't even hear the crowd or the music—"

"You don't hear Bon Jovi?" I smirked.

Oakes laughed. "You know, I picked that song because of 'now or never,' the exact thing that goes through my head, so you'd think I'd be paying attention to it."

"Hey, Ashford, let's mount!" a voice shouted from behind him, but Oakes's brown gaze was locked on mine.

He bounced his eyebrows. "Get that camera ready, and try to get my face the second I give the nod."

I gripped the lens and held up my camera, giving him a nod of my own. He turned, following the man up the stairs to the chutes. I clicked a few photos, catching the perfect silhouette of Oakes as he got farther away from me and closer to the chute. It was the perfect shot for the article. I could see it. Hell, I could see this on the cover of *Rodeo Way*. His name in white print, the dark hall around him, the blue of his chaps just a glimpse as they moved.

Try to get my face the second I nod...

Running to catch up with him, I took the steps two at a time, reaching the chute just in time to watch Oakes lower himself on the bull. Jon Bon Jovi blasted through the speakers, the rodeo announcers talking up Oakes, but like Oakes was doing, I tried to block out the sounds. I focused on him just as he was focusing on the bull. I raised my camera, watching him through the lens. He created the friction on the leather, and he pulled on his fingers, the bull already moving from side to side. His shoulders were hunched, his knees were tight, and finally, he leaned back. I could see his eyes closed through the metal of his helmet as he took in a deep breath.

I close my eyes. I breathe. I repeat those words over and over.

Try to get my face the second I nod...

His eyes opened, he looked at the camera, and then gave a slight nod.

The chute opened, and the bull broke free, but I pulled my attention to the camera. The light-brown flecks in his eyes showed through the black of the helmet, his focus—for a split second—on me, and not the bull. I caught it. I caught him...right before he nodded.

"And that's how you get a qualified ride! That's how you get the check, that's how you bring home the money, and Oakes Ashford just blew right to first place tonight with an 89.5!" the announcer's Southern accent rang through the speakers as the crowd cheered.

I looked at the dirt as Oakes was jumping and waving his hands in front of the crowd before he ran back to the gate, jumping on and grabbing someone's hand. Then, he was in front of me, a smirk on his face, and those eyes...

Just as bright as in the photo...if not more.

To: e.flynn@rodeowaymag.com, s.krass@rodeowaym
  ag.com
From: m.pennel@rodeowaymag.com
Subject: Check in
Date: June 14th: 12:37 PM

Fantastic photos from Idaho and Utah. The behind-the-scenes ones are fantastic. The ones of Turner Paige are great—we will want to use those for a future issue. I just want to remind you your focus is on Mr. Ashford, so please make sure you spend the majority of the time with him. Behind-the-scenes and other riders can happen later—once you move positions.

I was speaking with Mr. Ashford's agent, and I was talking to him about a possible photo shoot here at *Rodeo Way* with our photographers. Mr. Manning is certain he can tweak his schedule so he is able to come here at the end of your time with him, but this will extend your trip. Instead of ending in Cheyenne, as originally planned, he would add Colorado to his line-up. I'll have Luca send over extended per diem for gas/food once that is all settled with Mr. Manning.

Another thing is I would like to create a chat with the key people for this assignment: you, me, Mr. Ashford, Mr. Manning, and Sterling. Once his schedule is approved, I'll create the WhatsApp chat. Please give Oakes a heads up. We want him more involved. I'll also add a meeting to your calendar once things have been finalized.

Please send over the outline of your article as soon as possible. We are trusting you.

Chat soon.

Morgan Pennel
Editor in Chief - Rodeo Way Magazine
Denver, Co

CHAPTER ELEVEN
Oakes

What I decide? What the hell was I deciding on? Narrowing my eyes, I shoved my phone in my back pocket, choosing to ignore my agent for the time being, leaving the KOA's restroom to make my way back to the campsite.

With it being warmer outside, I planned to spend a lot of the time sleeping at campsites. They cost less than motels, and with a portion of my earnings going to the farm, I needed to be frugal in some places. I didn't mind sleeping under the stars or in my truck, but I didn't know if Emersyn would. I should have talked to her before I insisted she ride with me, but at the time, I didn't think anything of it. Thankfully, she went along with it, not complaining in the slightest, just jumping from the cab to the general store, coming back with firewood for the small fire pit that sat next to the truck. She had it lit by the time I made it back to the site, a blanket spread out in front of it. If it were anyone else other than Emersyn, I would have been shocked to see a fire. I had dated some girls before who just sat and watched, but not Emersyn. Seeing her lying on the blanket in front of the fire, staring up at the stars, told me she didn't mind in the slightest to be camping. If anything, she loved being here just as much as I did.

"If only I had marshmallows and sticks, we could make smores," I chuckled, coming to a stop in front of her, folding my arms and looking down at her.

She hummed. "I bet they have some in the store."

"Want me to go check?"

Giving another sweet hum, she hit the empty blanket next to her with her hand. "Nope. You need to relax. We have another state to cross before we reach Montana tomorrow, and you decided sleeping in your truck was a good idea."

"I have a tent," I deadpanned.

"And your knee?"

"I told you, one hundred percent better. You should know by now I bounce back quickly."

"Just wasn't sure if the altitude change was going to affect it. It always did for me. Motion is the lotion." She hummed, closing her eyes. "I had an ex who said that to me when I hurt my hamstring."

"When did you hurt your hamstring?" I finally sat down next to her, deciding to ignore the comment about the ex. That was one thing I knew I could decide on.

I had watched Emersyn through the years, enough to know what she was doing with her Miss Rodeo path—but not enough to know who she was dating or what she was doing. As much as it pulled on me, I didn't *need* to know that stuff.

Hell, I was still in disbelief that she was with me, that for the past week and a half, I had her to myself for the first time since she first held my hand all those years ago.

I wouldn't admit it out loud, to myself or anyone, but I was rather enjoying having Emersyn with me. There was never a quiet moment with her. Whether we were talking about my career and her article, or random rodeo facts, having her with me made this entire summer a little less lonely than normal. Most of my time was spent alone when I was on long stretches. I had friends who would join from time to time, or when I was back home, I'd stay with my mom in Wyoming, but otherwise, it was just me.

Just the idea that I had someone here with me—someone who cared enough to build a fire or ask me about an injury that happened days ago—was enough to make me see this differently. Rodeo wasn't a solitary sport. I had to stop making it that way.

Maybe Emersyn could help me make it more.

She shifted on the blanket. "When I took my ex for a ride. He didn't believe that I did stunts, and when I tried to do one and fell, I pulled it. I had to go to physical therapy for a few weeks until it finally felt better. Motion is the lotion." Lifting her legs in the air, she mimicked riding a bike before placing her feet back on the blanket.

"It's true, though." I chuckled as I lay back, my head hitting the ground with a soft thud. I could feel the heat from her arm touch my own, the feel of her warmth spreading all the way to my chest. I closed my eyes and just...let the feeling take over me.

And damn...it was a good feeling.

"What are you going to do in the morning? I can take down the tent if you need to go on a run or find a gym?" The blanket rustled as her body moved. I opened my eyes to meet hers.

"We have a drive tomorrow. Skipping a day won't hurt anything. We'll pack up and head to Montana."

A soft hum filled the air as she closed her eyes again and turned back to the stars. I searched her face, loving the way the glow of the fire created the perfect shadows on her. Emersyn truly was the most beautiful woman I had ever seen. Her blonde hair was sprawled out, the waves cascading over the blanket, and I knew if she opened her eyes, the blue would shine just as bright. I had the urge to reach over and trace her jawline, down to her neck where her collarbone was pronounced. My fingers itched with wanting to touch her. I laced my fingers together on my stomach and turned my head to mirror her.

"Have you ever seen stars like this?" I asked, the question leaving my lips before I could stop it.

"I used to go camping all the time...well, when I was little," she said softly. "My dad was big on camping. We went almost every weekend before I started getting into pageants."

"What made you turn to pageants?"

"My mom," she sighed. "Former Miss Rodeo America...she had to have her daughter follow in her footsteps. I was a shoo-in to win. Thank God I didn't."

"You didn't want to win?"

"I did for a while, I think." I could hear the lingering question in her own voice. "But being Miss Rodeo Wyoming was tough. The traveling was ten times worse than what we're doing. There were times I would be wanted in Cheyenne and in Laramie on the same weekend. I had to make an appearance at both, so I had to show face at one and then jump in my truck and drive to the next one. A few were like that, and my poor horse tolerated it. I didn't get a chance to enjoy the rodeos."

"There are a few rides like that. Afternoon rides and then evening, a few hours apart. Ride the bull, talk if I win, and then jump in the car. Not a moment to rest before doing it all again." I turned my head to her. "Not this summer, thank God," I mumbled, parroting her.

"It takes the fun out of it," she admitted. "I loved being Miss Rodeo Wyoming, but I don't think I could have done Miss Rodeo America, traveling all over the country, my face being in photos and on TV spots...I just didn't want that. And I figured that out halfway through Miss Rodeo America."

"What did you do?" I asked softly, my curiosity piqued. She was *royalty*, but everything she was saying was not at all what I expected—just like when she told me she majored in journalism. When I said that wasn't what I expected, it was the truth. But the bigger truth was that I had no idea what I really saw her as, other than a rodeo queen. A voice for the sport, giving the cowboys the encouragement to keep going...just like she did for me.

But now, looking at her, that wasn't what she was at all.

"Well, I couldn't really drop out, so I kept going. I did my best and...God." She stopped, sitting up and twisting her back to look at me. "I haven't said this to anyone. Not even my mom."

I raised an eyebrow.

"I prayed I wouldn't win. And I didn't. My run as a rodeo queen was over, I would no longer be in the limelight, and I was...so relieved."

I turned my head. "You wanted your privacy?"

She nodded, ease settling over her. "That's why I want to make sure I help you keep yours. I don't know why you're so secretive, why there is literally nothing on you online, but I get it."

"Being a rodeo name is weird." I closed my eyes, but I could still feel hers on me, or maybe it was the heat from the fire. "People either know your name and get all worked up when they finally meet you, or they know absolutely nothing about you. Rodeo is bigger than people think, but it's not watched or studied like other sports—"

Emersyn let out a loud *ha*, cutting off my thought process. "I know the rodeo like my dentist knows college football, and trust me there are times when he gets behind talking about that stupid game."

"You're an anomaly." I opened one eye. "Pop quiz."

A small giggle filled the air, bringing a smile to my lips. "Shoot."

"Name two states where the rodeo is the official sport."

"Easy," she said, confidence filling her tone. "Texas and…" she trailed off, almost as if waiting for a drum roll, "our home state of Wyoming."

"That's right."

Emersyn lay back down next to me. "The rodeo is bigger than anyone thinks. Your name is bigger than you'd like to think. I think that's why Morgan finds you so intriguing, why she thinks you are the best for this feature. People want to know who you are."

"I'm not that interesting of a guy. I'm just the grumpy asshole bull rider."

She raised a brow, her head falling to the side, making sure I caught that brow. "I beg to differ. Oakes Ashford is a household name when it comes to the rodeo. Just like Stetson Wright, JB Mauney, TJ Grey, Shad Mayfeild—"

"I get it. I'm famous," I joked, sarcasm leaking out of me.

"You are, though. So, I want to try to let the world know you while keeping your life private. I get how important that is. I promise *Rodeo Way* isn't a tabloid, even though it may feel like that with how some of the questions are formatted, but it's not all gossip."

"I know it's not. I have a subscription."

"You do?" she said, her voice raised in question, most likely louder than she intended.

"Well, my mom does." I gave her a smirk. "I wouldn't have agreed to this if I thought you were trying to turn it into a gossip column."

Emersyn chewed on her bottom lip, her eyes searching mine as we lay silent in the dark. I could basically hear the thoughts rushing through her head. So many things she wasn't saying, so many things hidden in her eyes—and I wanted to know them all.

"Tell me more about your pageant days."

Emersyn stopped chewing on her lip to give me a soft smile, and then she began to tell me story after story of when she was a rodeo queen, and I ate up every word.

"So, she's really following you around all summer? For an article?" Ty asked, his eyes focused on Emersyn as she talked to the reigning rodeo queen. Ty was a fellow bull rider, a guy I normally had no issues talking to and spending time with after the rides, but with the way his eyes were trained on Emersyn like she was some sort of buckle bunny made me see red. "She single?"

I slowly raised my glare to him, not exactly sure of the answer. The only thing I knew for sure was Ty Grant wasn't going anywhere near Emersyn. "I think she's dating a coworker. She's mentioned a Luca a few times."

"Luca? He following you too?"

"Don't even think about it, Ty."

"What?" he laughed. "Look at her, man. And if this Luca isn't around, who's to stop her?"

"Emersyn isn't that kind of girl. I suggest you stick to your regulars." I gave him a hard pat on his shoulder, one that pretty much forced him forward.

Ty's eyes wandered right back to Emersyn, just in time to see her smile at Miss Rodeo Montana.

"She's sexy as hell," Ty murmured.

If I punched him, I couldn't ride tonight, could I? I shoved my hand in my glove, flexing my fingers until the tip of the glove hit my nail, the rough fabric distracting me from Ty. His ride was before mine. It was probably for the best I didn't give him a bloody nose. The bull could do that. So far this year, Ty and I had ridden in multiple rodeos together. He qualified at least fifty percent of his rides, but he wasn't far from the top fifteen. Now, if I were to punch him...

"What I wouldn't give," he continued, "to have her ride me like—"

"Don't you have a bull to ride?" I interrupted him. "Probably should focus on that and not the reporter."

Ty shot me a look. "Come on, man, tell me you haven't been thinking of—"

"I haven't. Now get your ass up to the chute, and stop looking at my shadow."

He smirked. "You never answered my question."

Heaving a sigh, I dropped my arms and looked at my friend—former friend if he kept this up. "What was your question?"

"She following you all summer?"

My eyes drifted to Emersyn, who now had the camera to her eyes, snapping a photo of the queen and her attendants, then snapped back to Ty.

"Yeah," I breathed.

"Remind me to have Drew get me your schedule."

Fuck. I forgot Drew was also Ty's agent.

"Speaking of Drew," I changed the subject, "two of his clients are here. I figured he would be here this ride."

Ty opened his mouth to talk, but before he could, a loud *'Oy'* reverberated through the hall.

"Ashford, Grant, get up here," a rodeo worker gained both of our attention. Ty clapped his hands in front of him, the thump from his gloves echoing through the concrete walls.

"Ready, Oakes?" he asked, rubbing his gloves together. Any faster and the fabric would burst into flame.

I gave a single nod. "Emersyn, you coming?" I shouted down the hall, getting her attention faster than expected.

She gave the queen a quick hug before turning to catch up to me. "What bull did you pull?" she asked as soon as she was within earshot.

"Red California," I answered, stepping to the side to let her walk up the stairs before me. Ty had already made it to his chute and was waiting for his turn to mount his bull. He pulled Yellowjacket, and by the looks of it, that bull was ready to buck him off. My bull stood calmly in chute four, his head hung low and his shoulders moving with each slow breath...which made my heart rate pick up slightly. Red California, or Cali as he was called by his owners, was a tough one. He had a high rating this season, and the fact that he wasn't moving at all in the chute had me worried. "Looks like I'm gonna have to kick him a little harder," I grumbled, my eyes not leaving the bull.

"What do you look for when you approach the chute?" Emersyn asked, shouting into my ear so I could hear her amongst all the noise. The announcer began to spout off stats on Ty, but my focus was on Emersyn and the bull.

I met her gaze and zeroed in on her. The feel of her eyes on mine made me want to open up about everything. Every movement, every thought, every feeling that I had while on the bull...and off, especially in her presence. "The overall movement. Some bulls are already mad; they are confined, so they're already prepared to buck. Cali here is as calm as can be. His head is low, telling me he's tired, but that may give me an advantage," I told her, pointing to the bull's head.

"How does that give you an advantage?"

"Easier to predict the way he's gonna ride. The buck may not be as fierce, but if I give him a little kick, he'll get mad. Right now, he looks comfortable in the chute, and let's be honest..." I tilted my head and gave her a smile. She smiled back. "I don't want him comfortable." Our eyes met, and fuck, it was so hard to look away.

"Because where's the fun if he's comfortable?"

"Exactly, but"—I raised a brow—"I have a feeling you knew all of this." I curled my lips in a smirk.

"Strategies bull riders have before getting on the bull, sure...but I've never actually talked to a bull rider before about it."

"Ashford, let's go!"

I somehow missed Ty's entire ride while talking to Emersyn. I kept my eyes glued on her as I pulled my helmet over my head, feeling my hair push down and touching the nape of my neck. She raised her camera and took a shot before I hoisted myself over the metal gate and lowered my body on top of Cali. He was still calm, noticing me on his back, but he didn't budge like Ty's bull had. I dug my spurs in his side, getting a grunt from his nose.

"Yeah, boy," I cooed at him. "Come on." I dug my spurs into his sides again, and he lifted his head. Tugging on my fingers once more, I took a deep breath, closed my eyes, then lowered my back, raising my arm.

And right before I gave the nod, I locked eyes with Emersyn.

Drew

Sending over the new schedule. Only changes are in August. Let me know when you get them!

Join me on WhatsApp – tap the link to accept the invite.

<u>*Oakes Ashford Schedule June 15-August 4:* **RE-VISED.**</u>

June 15: Bell, Montana – 66th Annual Belt

June 16th: Nampa, Idaho – Snake River Run

June 17th: Fallon, Nevada – Fallon's 3C's

June 19th: Reno, Nevada – Xtreme Bulls

June 20th-28th: Reno, Nevada – Reno Rodeo

June 30th: Cody, Wyoming – Xtreme Bulls

July 1st: Cody, Wyoming – Cody Stampede

July 3rd: West Jordan, Utah – Western Stampede

July 4th-5th: Oakley, Utah – Independence Day Rodeo

July 7th: Oakley, Utah – Xtreme Bulls

July 8th: Casper, Wyoming – Central Wyoming Fair

July 9th: Nephi, Utah – Ute Stampede

July 10th: Laramie, Wyoming – Jubilee Days Xtreme Bulls

July 11th-12th: Nephi, Utah – Ute Stampede

July 13th-18th: OFF – Training, Alpine Ridge, Idaho

July 19th-21st: Ogden, Utah – Pioneer Days

July 22nd-24th: Salt Lake City, Utah - Days of 47 Gold Buckle Tour

July 25th: Cheyenne, Wyoming - Frontier Days Xtreme Bulls

July 26th-27th: Cheyenne, Wyoming - Frontier Days

July 28th-29th: Riverton, Wyoming - Wind River Rodeo

~~July 31st: Sidney, Montana - Richland County Fair~~

~~August 2nd: Mesquite, Texas - Mesquite Championship~~

August 1st-2nd: Steamboat Springs, Colorado

August 4th: Rodeo Way Meeting

Got the schedule. What the fuck is WhatsApp?

CHAPTER TWELVE
Emersyn

Ty Grant scored a 79. Oakes scored an 83. That put Oakes in second for this event and Ty in fourth. But to my surprise, Ty jumped up, using Oakes's shoulders, after they both appeared in the hallway. Oakes hunched his shoulders, taking the brunt of Ty's weight as he fumbled a few steps. Ty cheered, his face beaming from the adrenaline rush.

I raised my camera to capture the moment, even if Oakes looked as if he wanted to punch Ty in the face.

The other events we'd attended so far had been one in the same. We got there, Oakes got ready, I took a few photos, Oakes rode and always got top three, he gave the crowd a small show, and we left. There was no hanging around other riders. There were no flashy smiles at the camera. Other than sticking around to get his check, there was nothing to show that Oakes had a life outside of the bull. He never really interacted much with others, other than fist bumps and celebrating after his ride.

Then I met Ty. And I couldn't tell if Oakes was enjoying his company or tolerating him. Every look Oakes gave him was filled with partial disdain, partial joy, as if he himself couldn't decide if he wanted Ty around.

The past few nights with Oakes showed me a side of him I found myself wanting more of. The soft smiles, the chuckles, and the way his eyes would light up as he talked and listened. Last night, as we camped, both lying under the stars, there was that small spark of familiarity again. The ease of opening up to him, the willingness to tell him everything. We didn't talk about him. He asked about *me*. That wasn't something that happened to me. I didn't talk about myself to others. The only one who knew me was Luca. Even Sterling, when we dated, didn't truly ask about me. Having Oakes's focus on me felt more intimate than I would think it would. And seeing him interact with a friend made the moment we had more real. It wasn't just a show; it wasn't just something he was pretending for me. Oakes wasn't as he seemed on the outside.

The two took off down the hall, and Ty had a small bop to his step. I snapped another photo.

"You meeting up tonight, Oakes?" Ty gave a wry smile as he began to walk backward, looking at Oakes.

"Where ya headed?" he asked, clearly interested in what Ty was offering up.

"Cowboy Bar." Ty grinned, his arms outstretched to his sides. "Is there anywhere else to go?"

Oakes looked over his shoulder at me, a silent question hanging in his eyes.

"Go," I pressed. "We have a motel tonight. I'll just go edit these photos and start on my article. You gave me some good stuff tonight, Mr. Ashford."

"Oh, hell no." Ty stopped, his gaze now firmly planted on me. "If Oakes is goin' out, so are you." Ty pointed at me, his cocky attitude palpable.

I scrunched my nose, my eyes turning to Oakes, hoping that he would get my silent plea like I did his. Maybe we had some sort of telepathy thing going. After a week and a half of spending nonstop time together, you'd think we would be able to read each other by now. Oakes's eyes twitched before he turned to Ty.

"I think Emersyn just wants to—"

"Nope." Ty took a step toward me, wrapping his arm around my shoulders. "Come on, we're heading different directions until I can talk to Drew. We have a ride to celebrate."

"It's not really in my budget—" I began, but Ty shut that down really fast.

"My treat." Ty winked down at me. "Plus, I can give you some dirt on Oakes here, you know...for your article."

I glanced at Oakes, who simply gave me a shoulder shrug. Leaning into Ty, I felt his energy seep into me. "I could write this off as a business dinner."

"Oh, I am so down for that." Ty smiled from ear to ear, his eyes never once faltering from mine.

"Just don't say anything stupid," Oakes grumbled, yanking off his left glove and flexing his fingers. "I already want to punch you, so watch it."

Laughing, Ty turned his back and gave us a wave. "See you both at the bar, then."

Before Oakes could run off to his truck, I lightly touched his bicep, gaining his full attention. "You okay with this?"

"He doesn't have that much dirt on me, so why not? I could use a drink. Just..." he paused and glanced down the hall to where Ty was walking away. "Don't let him flirt too much."

"I can handle a little flirting," I deadpanned, knowing exactly how bull riders—cowboys in general—were.

Oakes arched a brow. "I have no doubt you can. Ty, though...he's..." Oakes let out a chuckle. "Let's just say tonight is going to be fun."

"So, tell me," I shouted over the loud music that blasted over us, "when did you meet Oakes?"

Ty shifted in the booth, raising his arm over my head, placing it on the seat behind my back. Oakes was comfortable across from us, his eyes heavy on me as he lifted his glass to his lips, his eyebrows raised.

"Oh, we go way back," Ty chuckled.

"Ten years isn't way back," Oakes grumbled.

His reply pulled a smile to my lips. "Ten years?" I parroted.

"Dumb shit broke his wrist tripping while trying to get on a horse." Oakes turned his eyes to Ty.

"I slipped," Ty corrected, shrugging his shoulder in rebuttal. "Oakes was the one who drove me to the hospital. If it wasn't for him, I would have quit."

"That's bullshit, and you know it. You were out for two weeks and rode with a cast after that." Oakes lifted his glass, giving me a slight eyeroll.

Ty chewed on his bottom lip as his eyebrows hopped up and down. "Damn straight. I couldn't let you win the title that year."

"Neither of us won the title that year," Oakes mumbled, his eyes fluttering back to me.

"You were both at the NFR last year, right?" I remarked, sifting through the rodeo files in my mind for Ty's stats. If I could pull up a quick Google search of him, I would. My mind twitched. "Ty, you've been multiple times?"

"A few, but never got that buckle." He glared at Oakes. "Someone keeps beating me out."

"Don't look at me. I'm trying to earn it back."

"Well, let's see…" I rested my chin in my palm. "Oakes is currently second in standings, and Ty, you're—"

Shit. I didn't actually know where Ty was. I had spent weeks focusing on the bull rider across from me, and I didn't pay attention to the others. I pulled my phone from my bag, pulling up Luca's text thread.

Me
SOS

Those three dots began to dance. I knew I could count on Luca.

Luca
Yes, boss?

Me
I need all the information you can get me on Ty Grant, including standings.

Luca
Ty Grant? You mean…you don't know this?

Me
Luca, please. Let's just say it's for the article.

Luca
laughing emoji sure…I'll report back soonish. I'm out with Ethan.

Me
I'll tell you how Oakes smells.

Luca
On it.

"Emersyn?" Oakes's voice filled the silence that I so awkwardly caused. "You good?"

My eyes widened as I looked up at Oakes. He and Ty were both focused on me. "Yup, sorry, just work." I set my phone down, screen up. "So, Ty...remind me of your standings." I took the conversation back to Ty, trying to egg him on to answer the question for me.

"I'm sixteenth," Ty answered.

"You knew that." Oakes gestured his chin toward me.

My phone pinged.

Luca

> He's currently sixteenth. Did he drop? Average lately is 82.

"You dropped since I knew last," I said, glancing at Oakes before focusing on Ty.

"We won't talk about that." Ty groaned, dramatically rolling his eyes as he raised his glass to his lips.

Another ping.

Luca

> He's been to the NFR but never made top three. He was out years ago due to an injury. I swear you know this stuff.

I read his message before the banner faded, and my phone went black. My lips tugged into a smile before I turned back to the men at the table. It was then—and only then—that I noticed Oakes's expression—one eyebrow raised, the same side of his lips tilted up in a sexy smirk.

"Who are you texting?" He pointed his gaze at my phone.

I rolled my shoulders. "Luca."

"The boyfriend?" Ty asked.

I whipped my head toward Ty, my eyes wide. "No." I forced out a laugh. "Luca is not my type...nor am I his. He has a fascination with how cowboys smell, and he was just asking for an update."

My phone lit up, the banner showing me a reply from Luca.

Luca

He hails from Utah. Not married, no kids, just riding the circuits.

"Well..." Ty smiled, bringing my attention back to him. "What do I smell like?"

"Cow shit," Oakes answered.

"Excuse me?" Ty barked out a laugh.

Rolling my eyes at him, I turned back to Ty. "We're here for dirt on Oakes, remember, not your personal hygiene." I locked my phone, glancing back up as the screen went black. "So...dirt." I sighed. "Ty, I know about your broken wrist. Any broken bones from Oakes?"

"A few," Ty answered for him. "Elbow and ankle, right?"

"And hand." Oakes leaned forward, his left elbow thumping on the table. His eyes met mine as his left hand flexed, the flecks of light brown hidden within the darker shade of his irises telling a story that his mouth wasn't.

His gaze narrowed as we stared each other down, and all the sound in the bar began to muffle as my entire focus went to Oakes and those damn eyes of his.

I had been watching—observing—him for days now, knowing very well I was enjoying what I was seeing, but the way his eyes met mine just now, the way the memory of us talking by the fire ignited...in this moment, it felt like there was something else here. Something more.

More to him.

His perfect lips, his broader shoulders, his toned forearms, his chiseled chest...

His deeper voice, the soft laughter that would fill my senses, the sarcasm that hid whatever laid underneath, the want to know...*me*...

Those. Damn. Eyes.

Heat rushed through me, faster than I was anticipating, and I tightened my jaw.

What I wouldn't give to slide into that booth next to him, lean closer into his side, let his mouth reach my ear to let him tell me about every broken bone he's ever had. I would inhale him, get away from the tobacco smell that was Ty, and really truly take Oakes in for the first time. What would his voice sound like that close to me? The only time I was close to him was...

Tonight.

At the chute.

I could still feel the heat from his body close to mine. Even now, sitting across the table from him, the heat from that moment was still reverberating off my bones. I could still hear the calmness to his voice as he explained the bull, letting me in just the slightest bit to his process. It was for the article, yet it felt like it was information only for me. And his eyes—those perfect eyes—locked with me right before he gave the nod, right before the chute burst open and he gave the crowd a show.

God, why didn't I smell him then?

And why was I so suddenly obsessed with the way he smelled? That was Luca's issue, not mine. My goal was—

My phone pinged, breaking the intense stare-down that Oakes and I were currently in the middle of. Blinking, I glanced down at the banner on the screen.

Luca

You gonna tell me why you are researching another rider when you should be researching Oakes?

I cleared my throat. "Right." I locked the screen and, avoiding Oakes completely, turned back to Ty. "Elbow, ankle, hand. Which came first?" I could feel the lump in my throat, which thankfully went away with the first gulp of my drink.

"Hand," Oakes replied. "Then my elbow, which kept me out for a few months since I couldn't move my arm, and then my ankle, which—"

"Son of a bitch rode and jumped off bulls with a busted ankle." Ty's head fell back in laughter, his head banging against the wall. "His physical therapist pretty much hated him."

"She did." Oakes's face grew a smirk, which he quickly covered with his pint. "She almost fired me as a client after that."

"A broken bone wouldn't stop Oakes Ashford. I had to get the man ice for his knee." I mirrored his posture, my elbow resting on the table as I leaned in. "I take it you two travel together often? Road to the NFR and all?"

"We share an agent," Oakes muttered, giving Ty yet another glare that reeked of disdain.

"Sure. Oakes and I have spent way too much time together." Ty quirked a smile back at him, his jaw flexing on an imaginary piece of gum, which just earned him another eyeroll from Oakes.

"It was one summer, Ty," Oakes groaned.

"I'm going to start counting every time you roll your eyes." I leaned in. "It had to be fun, though?" I egg on, "Traveling with a friend? Especially someone who you're competing against?"

"No competition." Oakes shook his head slightly.

"None whatsoever."

"Says the guy constantly checking his standings."

My phone lit up, and I gave it a quick glance.

Luca

Oh Emersyn....

Ty took a long drink, wiping his lips with his sleeve. "What else you wanna know?"

"She wants to know everything." Oakes avoided my gaze as he folded his arms on the table.

"He trains in Idaho—"

"Knew that." I smiled, looking over at Oakes.

"He does more CrossFit than he probably needs to—"

"Knew that too. I can set my watch to his training schedule, and I haven't been with him that long."

"His family owns a farm—"

"Oh." I raised my brow, and my grin grew. "I didn't know that."

"Yeah, his mom runs it. She's the sweetest lady. One time, we passed through Wyoming, heading to an event, and it was too late to find a camping site or motel, so Oakes drove to the farm, and his mom welcomed us with open arms. His brother was there too. I think he'd just gotten out of rehab—"

"Pop quiz," Oakes interrupted, catching my attention. "What's Ty's average scoring?"

My brows pinched as I bit the inside of my bottom lip. "82," I answered sheepishly.

"And mine?" Oakes raised a single brow.

"85.6."

"And where is he from?"

"Hey, man, the article isn't about me." Ty leaned forward, waving his arm as if to erase the question from the table.

"Utah," I answered, ignoring Ty.

"Logan, to be exact." Ty raised his glass.

"Is he married?"

"No, you told me I couldn't let him flirt."

"If anyone is flirting at this table—" Ty began but stopped once my phone pinged again. All attention went to the screen.

Oakes's eyebrow twitched. "You may wanna tell Luca the Google search did you some good. At least it got him talking."

My jaw dropped. "I didn't..."

"I have great eyesight, and your phone screen is abnormally bright." Oakes bounced his eyebrows once, raised his glass to his lips, and leaned back in the booth. "But it looks like he was promised a smell." Oakes pointed at my phone. I looked down at the screen, seeing a new text from Luca.

Luca

Um...I was promised a smell.

I looked at Oakes, who just raised his mug to his lips for the last time, a smile being revealed when he set it down.

"What did you tell him I smelled like?" Ty asked, breaking the tension that now floated around the table.

"I told you, cow shit," Oakes repeated. "Now, if you'll excuse me..." Setting his mug on the table, Oakes slipped from the booth. "I see a dart board."

As soon as Oakes was out of earshot, I turned back to Ty. "Tobacco."

"Huh?" Ty raised a brow.

"You smell like tobacco." I picked up my phone to answer Luca.

Me

Not tonight.

Luca

You. Owe. Me.

"So," Ty said the moment my phone touched the table, "you had your boyfriend Google me?"

I heaved a sigh. "Luca is very much gay, so no...not the boyfriend." I chuckled, returning to my phone.

"So, you are very much single?" He raised a brow and leaned in closer, his nose lightly caressing my temple.

I arched my back away from Ty. Thankfully, he was a decent enough person that he got the hint and backed off—even if it was only a few inches. "Doesn't mean I'm looking for a night with anyone. Didn't you hear? Oakes said you couldn't flirt."

"Oh, I will always flirt." He gave a cheeky grin, and I could see why women would flock to him. "You're stunning; it's hard not to. Especially with how territorial Oakes was earlier."

For the second time, my jaw dropped. Oakes? Territorial? That was comical. I let out a laugh. "He's not territorial."

"Oh, he is, even now." Ty motioned his chin behind me. Following his direction, I saw Oakes pull the darts from the cork and turn his back to the board, adjusting his hat slightly on his head before his gaze met mine for the briefest moment. "I've never seen him look at anyone the way I'm seeing him look at you. But hey, you got some insight. I never knew he broke his hand. Explains the scar, though." Ty shifted away from me.

"Scar?"

"You haven't noticed it?" Ty held up his left hand. "Runs from his knuckles to his wrist. Never knew where it came from, though."

I watched as Ty drew a line on his own left hand. "No, I...haven't paid that much attention."

Ty shrugged a shoulder. "He's had it as long as I've known him. Never thought to ask him about it."

I turned back to the dart board, just in time to see Oakes aim and hit the center. He inhaled, his shoulders broad as he rolled them back. His neck moved from left to right as he aimed again and again, hitting the center each time. His concentration broke as he went to retrieve the darts, his eyes meeting mine as he made his way back the twelve feet.

It took everything in me not to shoot up and go be with him, to make that smirk...mine.

"Okay, I gotta ask..."

"No," I deadpanned, stopping Ty's thought before he could even begin to think it.

Chapter Thirteen
Oakes

Fuck.

Why the *fuck* did I think coming out with Ty was a good idea?

Why the *fuck* did I assume he had no *dirt* on me when, out of everyone... Ty knew.

Why the *fuck* couldn't he just flirt like he normally would have?

The one summer we traveled together, after he signed with Drew, we stayed one night at Mom's place. She, of course, was thrilled to meet a friend of mine—ecstatic, even. I was pushing my two lives together, and my sweet, amazing mother wanted to give Ty the experience she couldn't offer friends in high school. It was one night. One night where my brother just had to be home. One night where my dad had to come up in conversation. And now, that idiot was most likely telling—for all intents and purposes—*Rodeo Way* my entire life story.

She didn't recognize me before...but she damn well would now.

Then it would get awkward.

Why I hadn't just come clean already was beyond me. I had plenty of chances, numerous times to tell her who she was to me, that her words rang in my head before I got on the bull, that it was her I thought of daily since that rodeo so many years ago...but no. I just couldn't do that now, could I? Why? Because I was scared shitless that the second she remembered who I was, she would write the article of the century in the rodeo world—exposing who Oakes Ashford really was.

Not Oakes Ashford at all.

Fuck.

Inhaling, I held my breath and aimed at the dart board, picturing Ty's face right in the center. Bullseye.

Oakes...you're. An. Idiot.

I should just tell her. I should just end this here and now. That would be the more professional thing to do, right? Expose myself, and then maybe she would be more understanding? She already told me she would keep my private life private. Was I so worried that she would suddenly change her mind and flip the switch?

The way I saw it, *Rodeo Way* was her career, her life. Past or no past, I was simply an assignment. The moment I saw her, I didn't want to believe that she was going to be just like any other reporter I had come across, and so far, she hadn't been, but she hadn't gotten the full story with me. She knew it... She had to have it stored in the back of her mind somewhere...she just didn't recognize it. Would she turn into reporter mode the moment she found out the actual dirt?

But then she would look at me, and I could still feel the spark. I could still feel every single tingle I felt that night. If I could feel it...half of me wondered if she could too.

I dropped my head, the brim of my hat touching the nape of my neck as the soft lighting touched my face.

Pull yourself together.

"Well," the soft, sweet voice of Emersyn pulled me back down to earth, "you were definitely right about one thing...he's a flirt."

I heaved a sigh and raised my chin, meeting her blue eyes and instantly melting in them.

Who was I kidding? I'd always have a thing for Emersyn Flynn. She could twist my story however she wanted, and I'd still probably have a thing for her. Thank God I wouldn't have to see that happen. She promised me she wouldn't.

"This was tame," I admitted.

"You did promise me a fun night."

"Just like you promised Luca to tell him what I smell like." I raised a brow.

This time it was Emersyn who rolled her eyes. "He's been asking since he found out we were riding together, and well..." She lifted a shoulder. "I wanted to get Ty talking. Thought the best way would be to get him talking about himself, but—"

"That backfired."

Emersyn scoffed.

I pulled my attention back to the dart board and raised the dart. "Besides..." I let it fly, hitting the twenty. "I thought you knew everything about rodeo stats?"

"I hate to admit that I'm a little fuzzy when it comes to Ty Grant." Emersyn leaned her hip on a nearby table and folded her arms, watching as I hit the bullseye. "Too much time researching you."

Turning, I glanced around the bar, noticing Ty had already moved to the bar top, his focus on a redhead. I nodded toward the bar, not letting her comment of researching me get to my ego any more than it had.

"See. Flirt." I glanced back at Emersyn, her gaze still trained on me. Did she even look at Ty?

"Oh, he did flirt with me...after you left." Her gaze dropped, her eyebrows pinching for a moment before she blinked and pushed herself off the table. "He said you were territorial."

"Well," I scoffed, "the article is about me."

She bit her bottom lip. "It sure is. And I better go get some of these photos edited and start writing...something."

"You haven't started writing it yet?"

"You haven't given me much, but I think with tonight, I have my opener. Ty said he'd pay for my drink, so...see you in the morning?"

"Didn't you say this was a business expense?"

"It could be." She gave a sly grin, one I hadn't seen from her before. "But he offered." Raising her hand, she squeezed my shoulder once. "See you tomorrow."

I nodded once and then watched her as she said thank you to Ty and left, giving me one last look before she stepped out into the dark.

I slid into the seat next to Ty, realizing I still had three darts shoved in my palm.

"What did you tell her?" I asked, pulling Ty's shoulder away from the redhead, trying to keep my voice level.

"Oakes." He smiled, my name a laugh in his throat, and then turned back to the redhead, saying, "One second, babe." He lightly brushed his lips with hers, which sent her into a giggle. "Nothing once you left. She didn't ask."

"Come on, man."

"No, you come on. You can trust me—you know that."

My shoulders slumped, the breath getting a little easier to push through my lungs.

"But I gotta ask..." Ty placed his hand on my shoulder. "Is she the one your mom told me about? She's the girl...isn't she?"

I looked at the door to the bar, silently praying Emersyn would come back in and give me that smile. One that said she remembered me, one where I didn't have to tell her anything, and she just knew.

Sighing, figuring that wasn't going to happen, I dropped my chin. "Yeah...that's her."

"You broke your hand that night, didn't you?" Ty asked, dropping his voice lightly.

I flexed my left hand, feeling the scar stretch against the skin. I nodded. "She doesn't remember me," I added.

Ty barked out a laugh then, shifting his weight on the small stool. "Well, fuck, Oakes. No wonder why you're keeping me away. You gonna tell her?"

"Eventually."

"Better tell her soon. She's looking at you the same way you're looking at her. Now, if you'll excuse me." He turned back to the redhead, who was still blushing from his kiss.

"You gonna be in Idaho or Nevada?" I asked before he was long gone.

"Oh yeah, Drew's rearranging my schedule. Remember?"

The cool Montana air hit my skin as I stepped out of the motel room. The sun had barely risen over the mountains, creating the perfect glow for my morning run. With another insanely long drive ahead of Emersyn and me today, heading back to Idaho, I had to get my blood moving somehow. I took in a deep breath, the same air filling my lungs as I fell into the stretch.

I played my timeline out in my head.

Run—sixty minutes.

Shower—ten minutes.

Breakfast and pack—multitask fifty minutes.

On the road again in two hours.

Nine-hour drive to Nampa.

That puts us in Nampa around four. Just in time to find another motel, a place to eat, and make it to the arena with plenty of time to spare.

"No music for a run?"

Once again, Emersyn's voice came from behind me, mid-stretch. I twisted my torso, keeping my feet firmly planted on the ground. Taking her in, if my posture weren't steady, I would have fallen.

Emersyn was dressed for a run, tight capri leggings hugging her thighs and hips, a white tank showing off the curves of her waist and doing wonders for her breasts. Her hair, though in a tight ponytail, flowed over her shoulders, only bringing my attention to her collarbone and...

I cleared my throat, pulling myself away from looking at Emersyn.

"Uh...no." I coughed.

"Do you mind if I join you?"

She's looking at you the same way you're looking at her...

Ty's words rang in my head as I nodded, watching the look of...was that relief?...washing over Emersyn's expression. She jumped on the balls of her feet a few times before beginning her own pre-run stretches.

She wasn't looking at me. Was she?

Nah...

No way.

"Now"—she raised her arm over her head and bent to the side—"it's been a hot minute since I've run outdoors, so"—she rose back up—"go easy on me?"

Giving her a onceover, drinking her in as I looked at every single inch of her, clearly checking her out, I grinned.

"Try to keep up." I raised a brow at her before taking off behind her.

"Hey! Wait up!" I heard her call after me, quickly followed by the stomping of her feet.

Laughing, I slowed my pace until she was at my side. And then, the next sixty minutes were spent in silence as Emersyn and I ran side by side. The entire time, my mind was running faster than my feet as all I could think about was how she would look over at me as we ran. I could feel her gaze on me, feel the heat that radiated off of her...all while I pretended like I didn't notice.

And it was pure torture.

She's looking at you the same way you're looking at her...

Drew

Join Me on WhatsApp! Click the link below to join the conversation!

Join Me on WhatsApp! Click the link below to join the conversation!

Join Me on WhatsApp! Click the link below to join the conversation!

Oakes

I said no.

Drew

Accept the invite.

Oakes

Hell no. You gonna be in Idaho?

Drew

Accept. The. Invite. Or I'm dropping you.

Oakes

gif of Dr. Evil saying 'Riiiight'

You know how to reach me if you need me. I'm not downloading another app.

CHAPTER FOURTEEN
Emersyn

I n hindsight, I probably should have skipped the run with Oakes this morning. I had everything set up in my motel room for a morning yoga session, but then I caught him stretching out in the grass and just...couldn't stop thinking about him.

Ty got in my head last night, and as much as I hated to admit it, there was a small piece—and I'm talking a miniscule piece—of me that wanted Ty to be right. Oakes wasn't looking at me, was he? He wasn't acting territorial in any way. He had made it known since day one that he didn't want to babysit some editor. Except, he actually didn't seem to mind. The man had actually made this assignment easy. He was easy to talk to, he was fun to be around, and he was opening up more than I thought. But that didn't mean he was 'territorial.' In an attempt get my mind off the comment, and the evening in general, I went to my motel room and opened my laptop with the intention of starting the article Morgan wanted—if only the intention had stuck.

An outline to my intro was all I could really muster out.

But the more I zoomed in on photos to look at his hands, trying to catch a scar, the more where I saw him concentrated on me...where his eyes were so entirely focused on *me*...

The more Ty's words ran through my mind.

The more *Oakes* flooded my mind.

There was no way I was going to be able to complete anything when it came to Oakes.

I didn't sleep, so of course when I saw him stretching, bare chested right in front of my window, I simply couldn't help myself.

The man was beautiful when he ran. His breath pumping with each exhale, his forearms and triceps flexing...it was hard not to concentrate on him. Even harder to pretend I was focused on the run.

When we got back to the motel after an hour, I leaned against the door, my heart pumping, my mind entirely focused on Oakes. On his eyes. His back. His hands.

"Fuck..." I moaned, pushing myself off the door, stripping off my running clothes, leaving myself in just my underwear before flopping down on the bed.

I should not have been thinking about Oakes this way. I should not have been thinking about him being territorial or him wanting me in any way. I should not have been so focused on the scar on his hand, trailing down to his fingers.

His fingers. God, I wondered what they felt like?

Simply the memory of his eyes heavy on me from across the table, the way his voice sounded in my ear when he leaned in close...just thinking of Oakes being territorial, being interested in me at all, sent shivers down my spine.

Of their own volition, my fingers tickled my stomach, sending featherlight touches down my navel, to my center. I was already...*God*...so wet.

My other hand trailed up as I closed my eyes, and I pictured Oakes hovering above me. It was his hand on my clit, his hand cupping my bare breast, his moans filling the room. I could feel myself grow more aroused, just from thinking about him. My breathing picked up, and my heart began to race as I imagined my fingers becoming his. How would those callused fingers feel against my clit? Inside me? Against the peaks of my tits? Just the thought made me pinch my nipple, and a high gasp filled the room. I could just imagine the roughness of them, reacting against my soft skin, forming the perfect sensation. I wanted to feel him, all of him, but for now I could only dream...

The pressure built and built, simply by imagining what he would sound like as he whispered in my ear, urging me along, begging me to scream for him, scream *his* name. My climax hit me harder than I thought, and I moaned into the empty room, letting my orgasm ride out as my fingers slowed their rhythm. My breath heavy, heat still flush against my skin, I lay on the bed, one hand still on my center, the other cupping my own breast, the skin still sensitive, semi-shocked I didn't need my vibrator to achieve it. All I needed was Oakes. Or...simply the idea of him.

Slamming my eyes shut, I willed my libido to calm. Forcing myself to remember it was just Ty's assumptions—not fact—that Oakes was interested. One little lapse in judgment when it came to Oakes...that was it. Not canon.

So why, when I was just thinking about him, did it feel so good? In so many ways.

The shrill ring of my phone pulled me back to reality. I sat up and reached for my phone and shirt, flopping back onto the covers.

Luca's name flashed on my screen, and his face appeared after I swiped the bar, instantly thankful I remembered to put my shirt back on.

"Morning, sunshine." He smiled. "How was Ty Grant?"

I heaved a sigh, and dropped my phone on the bed, leaving Luca staring at the popcorn ceiling. "He was..." I exhaled, resting my palm on my forehead, still feeling the light sheen of sweat. "Nice."

"Mad you couldn't remember all the stats yourself?" Luca laughed.

"Luca, please..." I covered my eyes with my palm and ignored the tingle that still sat at my core. "I don't really have time for a phone call right now. We went for a run, and well...I...I need to shower."

Couldn't really tell Luca I just had an amazing orgasm while thinking about Oakes, now could I? "You forgot, didn't you?"

I dropped my hand. "Forgot what?"

"The meeting? In about four minutes?"

Fumbling, I reached for my phone, looking at Luca with wide eyes. "What. Meeting?"

"With Morgan, in..."—he pulled up his wrist to look at an invisible watch—"three minutes now."

Crap.

Shit.

Damn.

I vaguely remembered a meeting being added to my calendar. With the new changes, we had to go over the extensions and timings, and I forgot. How could I forget? I didn't forget these things.

"Shit, okay...I remember. Morgan sent me the link. I need to get dressed. See you in a few."

Before Luca could even answer, I hung up the FaceTime, tossing my phone down before rummaging in my suitcase for my dry shampoo and a decent top. Two minutes now. I had two minutes to make myself look presentable and not like I was just thinking about being fucked by Oakes.

Which I wasn't.

Satisfied with the way I looked from the waist up, I yanked my laptop from my bag and settled myself on the desk, clicking on the link Morgan had sent just in time to see Morgan, Sterling, Luca, and...Drew...on the Zoom Chat.

I shivered and smiled. "Hi, good morning," I said, giving them a wave with way too much enthusiasm. "Drew, I didn't expect you to be here."

"Hi, Miss Flynn." Drew smiled the same fleshly smile I remembered from the restaurant. "How's your morning so far?"

The first thing that went through my mind was they could see the flush that I was sure was still on my cheeks, but I smiled and simply said. "Great, thank you. I went for a run, and now I'm just waiting for Oakes so we can head to Idaho."

"Ah, yes, Nampa next and then on to Fallon. I'll be in Reno, so I'll see you there." Drew gave me a smile.

"Oh, perfect." I ran my hand through my hair and inhaled.

"Now, Emersyn," Morgan spoke up, gaining my full attention, "I'm interested in how the article is going, and we wanted to touch base with Drew and Oakes—" She paused and narrowed her eyes. "It looks like he hasn't accepted the invite for the meeting."

"Oh." I gave a nervous chuckle, knowing very well Oakes wouldn't join in on a meeting like this. He had a routine after his run or workout, and by now, he was in the middle of his shower. "He's at the gym," I lied.

Drew nodded in agreement, as if he knew that's exactly where Oakes would be. But Luca narrowed his eyes at me, and Morgan let out a long sigh.

"That's okay. We can talk about how everything is going without him. He's been sent his new schedule I'm assuming?" She raised her hand palm up to the screen.

"He has. His schedule always fluctuates, so I'm sure he's okay with it. The only thing I haven't been able to do is get him on the new chat. He doesn't want to download a new app, so my suggestion there is keeping all interactions with me or Emersyn," Drew answered her.

"That's fine. If he wants to join, he can. If not, like you said, he can get all the information from Emersyn or you. Now, I hear Emersyn has been riding with him?"

I looked over at Luca's tiny square. His eyes were wide, and I could see his jaw clenched. Then it hit me—I never actually told anyone that my travel plans had changed, not even Luca.

"Yes, he didn't approve of my car, so Drew was nice enough to have it shipped to storage, and I've been with him in his truck," I answered.

"Mr. Manning"—Luca cleared his throat—"do you know what kind of truck Mr. Ashford drives? I can adjust Emersyn's per diem to add gas and travel costs."

"Oh"—Drew waved his hand over the screen—"no need. Oakes is more than capable of providing gas and travel expenses."

"This is a business trip, Mr. Manning," Luca added.

"Please, call me Drew." Drew's smile grew, and so did Luca's.

"Drew. We are fully prepared to pay for Emersyn's travel expenses."

"Totally understand, but Oakes most likely won't allow it, so..." Drew sighed. "Let's not worry about that. Lodging and food are all Miss Flynn needs to worry about."

Luca raised a brow. "Alright, perfect. I'll email you once we're done here, and we can get her travel squared away. I'll CC you on that email, Emersyn."

I nodded.

"And now the article and photos," Sterling chimed in. "We've set up the timing to do a photo shoot. Do you know if he's agreed?"

"I haven't spoken to him about that yet, but I was assuming Drew would?" I looked at Drew.

He nodded. "I'll shoot him a text. He's used to having his photo taken, so I'm sure he won't have an issue—no." He paused stifling a laugh. "He'll hate it, but he'll do it."

"Perfect, I'll make sure that's set up. And I haven't gotten an outline yet from you, Emersyn," Sterling stated. "Just those first few interview questions, have you written more?"

"No, I haven't started yet," I hesitated.

"You haven't?"

"Well, I've only been here for ten days. I have an idea of where I am taking it, and I can get you my intro within the next few days." I sat up a little straighter. "We were able to go out last night with Oakes and another bull rider—"

"Ty," Luca stopped me, and I gave his square a glare.

"Yes, Ty Grant, and I learned about his injury history. Seeing as his song is Jon Bon Jovi, "It's my Life," I was thinking about adding the *now or never* piece to his injuries. None of them have ever seemed to stop him from riding."

"Oh," Morgan oohed, "I loved that aspect. I never noticed that was his song."

"They play it every time," Drew added. "It has the same meaning that Emersyn mentioned. Apparently, someone told him that at some point, and the song fits."

"He told me that." I smiled. "I hope I can get that story one day from him."

"Please do," Sterling said. "It would be a great way to tie in the song to the injuries and why he still rides."

"Hey, Sterling," Luca said, his face still looking down at his notepad, "are you writing the article?"

"Editing it."

"Then I think we should let Emersyn write it, yeah? If she gets the story, she gets the story."

"I have no doubt that Emersyn will get us the article we are looking for. She knows exactly what we want and what it could mean for her." Morgan smiled.

"Yes, I do." I smiled back, that lingering thought of a promotion in the back of my head.

"I really am looking forward to seeing how personal you can make this story. Like we said, truly get to know him." She pumped her fist in a 'go get it' gesture, one that was meant to hype up the writer, get them moving and ready to go.

I tightened my lips. If only she knew how personal I made it fifteen minutes ago.

I could still feel the buzz between my legs.

My back stiffened.

What the hell was wrong with me? I was on my first assignment, one that could turn my entire career around, and I was pleasuring myself picturing *Rodeo Way's* client.

My client, for all intents and purposes.

I swallowed. Hard. So hard that if I had an Adam's apple, it would have bobbed.

I held myself together for the remainder of the meeting as they went over the new timeline, adding an extra rodeo to the summer, praying Luca was taking all the notes for me, seeing as everything they said just went in one ear and out the other. I caught my name a few times, mentions of places and timelines, but other than that...

I had other things on my mind.

The meeting lasted thirty minutes, which, in my opinion, was way too long. My trip was now going to end in early August with a rodeo in Colorado. Oakes would ride, *Rodeo Way* would be there, and then it would end at the office with the dreaded photo shoot Oakes would despise. All I had to do was not think of him in any other way than a professional manner and write my damn article.

Easy, right?

I waved and said goodbye, and the second the Zoom call ended, I buried my head in my hands. First things first: no more bars. No more watching Oakes run or stretch—or do anything, for that matter. No more thinking of him in any way other than as a client. Second: I had to work.

A knock on the motel door sounded through the room, making me jolt, quickly followed by a ping on my phone.

"Emersyn, I'll be ready in about twenty minutes. Meet you by the truck?" Oakes's voice was muffled.

I looked down at myself, still in just my panties from the waist down, still reeling from everything. I definitely needed more than twenty minutes, but...I could make it work.

"Yeah, meet you there!" I shouted back, glancing at the banner that dropped down on my phone.

Luca

You gonna tell me what was going through your mind during that meeting? You were focused but...not...at the same time.

Me

Do you think Morgan noticed?

Luca

Thankfully, no. She and Drew were too into schedule changes. I'll send it your way, but fill me in??

I dragged my hand down the side of my face, landing on the back of my neck. Luca had been my best friend since we started working at the magazine. If I couldn't tell him what was going through my mind, who could I tell?

Me

Let's just say…

I began, watching the words appear on my screen as if I wasn't the one typing them. The minute I hit send, I regretted it, but I forced myself to watch as it delivered.

Me

I'm also getting interested in how Oakes smells.

Like I knew he would, a FaceTime call came through seconds after the message turned from delivered to read.

Luca

I say jump him.

Emersyn

Yeah…because that's professional.

Luca

You can be professional and still jump him.

Emersyn

Stop. He has good eyesight, according to him, and I don't need him seeing these while he's driving.

Luca

Jump.

Him.

Chapter Fifteen
Emersyn

If you look closely at Oakes Ashford's left hand...

I stopped typing to glance over at Oakes's left hand as it gripped the steering wheel. He was focused on the road, his eyes narrowed as the sun rose high in the sky. Sure enough, there was the scar.

...you'll see a scar that stretches from his knuckles to his wrist. He wears it like a badge, showing that even he knows he's in one of the most dangerous professions in the world. And Oakes lives for it. Oakes Ashford is a bull rider, and the scar on his hand shows the start of his career...

Wait.

Ty told me he had a scar, and now that I knew it was there, I saw it every time.

But I still had no idea how he got it. And if I wanted this particular intro to work, I would need to ask him eventually. A part of me wanted to reach across him and run my fingers up and down the scar, try to find the memory of it and pull it from his head to the paper. But then my mind would think about other things his hands could do, and touching him in general, and that was a whole other story I didn't want to talk to him about.

So, I chose silence over the scar.

I had stayed mostly silent since we got back on the road—for the nine hours it took to get from Vernal, Utah to Nampa, Idaho. And then at the Nampa Rodeo, I focused on photos and not talking to him. Basically, I didn't trust myself around him right now. I needed to get my head back into work mode. And thankfully, Oakes seemed to respect my silence, not even turning on the radio as I attempted to pour all my energy into the article.

Not that it was working.

Every single sound was amplified, and let's face it, the silence was killing me. I didn't want to sit in silence with the only sound being the click-clack of my keyboard. I hated that every now and then Oakes would let out a deep sigh, as if he were being tortured by the silence as well. It was completely unnerving, and I felt like it was never-ending. Normally, I thrived in silence—my noise-canceling headphones on my desk at the office were proof of that—but not here.

Not with Oakes sitting so damn close to me.

I wanted him to hum along with the radio like he was doing before.

I wanted him to talk, even if it meant asking me pop quiz questions that normally came from Luca.

I wanted him to tease me about being Miss Rodeo Wyoming or ask me about stunt riding again.

I wanted anything from him at this moment.

But no, the only sound that hung between us was *click, click, click, clickclickclickclick....*

I hit that backspace button like my life depended on it.

I wanted to groan so loud people on the space station could hear me, but instead, I let the silence win, and I bit my lip.

This wasn't working. This article wasn't working. *Nothing* was working.

Currently, sitting on my desktop was what I had begun to call my 'article islands.' Small summaries of things Oakes and I had talked about, things we had done, and interview questions all spread out haphazardly on the image of a running horse. All I needed to do was write the damn intro and piece these islands together so I could shoot something off to Morgan for approval. But every word I typed felt wrong. Felt forced. Felt like a lie.

Especially tying in his scar.

Glancing over at it again, noticing the way the silver line was raised just slightly on the back of his hand, it didn't look like it could have been given by a bull—or a riding accident in general. If you asked me, with all my medical knowledge, I'd say he sliced it with a knife—that was how clean the cut looked.

I could start with his elbow...or ankle. He clearly stated that he rode with the broken ankle despite what his physical therapist recommended. Even though there were no scars on his body from those injuries, it still had the same meaning to it. Nothing would stop Oakes Ashford from riding.

Heaving a sigh, I gave in and highlighted the entire introduction I had down and smacked that backspace button with full force. The page went blank.

"I have a question for you."

I jumped, the sound of Oakes's voice *finally* breaking the silence bringing more of a shock than I thought possible.

I hummed in response, trying to play off the fact that I just jumped from my seat.

"What did that laptop ever do to you?"

"Excuse me?" I shot him a look, my head turning so fast I could have given myself whiplash.

"You basically just murdered that backspace button a while ago, and now you are hitting it so loud it echoed in the cab." He gave me a side-eye, one brow raised to his hairline.

"It did not echo—"

"Let me guess," he interrupted. "Trying to write your article?"

Lifting my chin, my head hit the back of the headrest, and I let out that groan I had been holding in for so long, and yup, pretty sure the astronauts on the space station just looked at each other and asked 'What the…'

Oakes laughed, tilting his head back on the headrest. "That good, huh?"

"Do you want to know how hard it is to write an article? One that you know is going to be the feature article for September? One that you know they have a certain expectation for, and you promised them basically the world, and now you have to deliver it?"

"I take it it's harder than editing photographs?"

"As much as I want to write this article"—I pointed at the computer screen—"I'd much rather edit photos right now. Words are not wording." I slammed the laptop shut in frustration, one groan away from a full-on pout.

"Talk it out," he suggested, moving his right arm to lean on the center console, flexing his left hand against the steering wheel and my gaze went to the scar. "Where are you stuck?"

"You don't want to talk about this."

"Sure, I do. Talk it out."

I exhaled. "The intro."

"The intro? Already? Wow."

"And my editor wants it and an outline in his email."

"How can you write an article when it hasn't even been two weeks yet? You've only done three interview sessions with me—if you'd call them that."

"They want me to be constantly working on it. It needs to be up to the magazine's standards. The intro is what draws people to read it. It is the hook that makes you go 'I need to know more about this specific topic.' The intro is important."

"I bet. I've read plenty of *Rodeo Way* articles. If that intro isn't phenomenal, I toss the magazine." The asshole smirked, giving me a sinful side eye glace.

"Are you mocking me?"

Oakes turned to look at me, that smirk expanding to his eyes, those same eyes staring right into mine with a glint of amusement. Before he turned his attention back to the road, he chuckled, "Read me what you've got so far."

"Nothing. In case you didn't notice, I deleted it."

"Fair." He nodded. "Okay, then, what *did* you have?"

I swallowed. "Well, I was trying to tie in your scar."

His left hand opened briefly before he wrapped it around the steering wheel again. "My scar?"

"Ty pointed it out to me the other night—"

"Of course he did," he mumbled with a slight eyeroll, barely noticeable.

"And I thought it may be a good way to tie in how you ride with broken bones, how you wear it proudly like nothing can stop you from riding. Then I started thinking about how I'm not even sure if you got the scar while riding, and so I just...well, it wasn't working." Giving up again, I folded my arms and glared at the closed laptop.

Is this what imposter syndrome felt like? Not only was my mind wondering and thinking about things it shouldn't be when it came to the man next to me, but I was questioning every word I had ever written. And I mean ever. As in my entire life. I majored in journalism. I had written articles before. I had published before. I knew I could write. But this? This stupid article. I wasn't sure if it was the pressure that was hanging in the balance or the fact that I couldn't keep my mind straight at all, but it was a struggle.

If Luca were here, I could talk it out with him. Hell, I'd even take my college roommate, Tessa, who helped me through multiple papers and edits, but I couldn't very well talk this out with Oakes, now could I?

What would I even say?

I'm struggling because there is a promotion hanging over my head here. I could become a full-fledged journalist for Rodeo Way *with this article, not just a digital editor. All I have to do is dig way deep into your life and give the fans something new, something...hot.*

Nope, that wouldn't work.

I'm struggling because I can't stop thinking about your hands in more ways than just the scar...

Definitely not that.

"I got it while riding," Oakes finally answered.

"You did?"

He gave me a curt nod. "At the very beginning of my career. Day one, pretty much."

"What happened?"

"It got smashed. I was out for a while, and then, before I knew it, I was back on the bull."

"So, it didn't stop you? My intro works?"

He nodded. "Your intro works."

I watched him and studied his profile as he took deep, long breaths. He concentrated on the road in front of him, and every few moments, his palm flexed. Smiling at the fact that he offered up the information without being asked, simply to help me, I opened my computer and watched as the screen came back to life. Then, I hit that undo button, and words filled the blank page.

If you look closely at Oakes Ashford's left hand, you'll see a scar that stretches from his knuckles to his wrist. Day one of riding bulls, Oakes's left hand was smashed...

"What's after the article?" Oakes asked, stopping my typing.

"What?" I questioned, pulling my hands into fists.

"This is your first article, right? You're a digital editor? So, what's after this? More field work? More articles? Or back to editing photos?"

"Oh," I whispered. I didn't expect that question from him. "Well, the simple answer is I hope to be promoted to journalist."

"In the field? I can tell you love being here. You smile more in the arenas, and anyone can tell from your photos that you have a passion for it. My favorite is when you break away from me and take pictures of everything else. Like last night in Idaho, sure you were with me at the chute, but before that, you were everywhere. People are starting to know who you are. They can see you enjoy it."

My heart jumped slightly as heat filled my chest. "It's what I want to do. The rodeo is my life. I want to be by the chutes, or in the stands, interviewing cowboys and cowgirls, and seeing everything they do."

"So do that."

"Well, I need an income."

"You can earn a living doing that."

I barked out a laugh. "I can guarantee you I can't. Are there times when I hate my job at *Rodeo Way*? Sure." I shrugged a shoulder, even shocking myself that I let that slip. "But it's a way for me to be a part of the rodeo lifestyle while still earning a decent income."

"You could become an influencer." Oakes raised a finger from his right hand. "You could start a blog." He raised another finger. "You could become a professional photographer for Wrangler—imagine that one." He raised a third finger...and he kept spouting off ideas of how I could work with rodeos that didn't involve *Rodeo Way Magazine*.

Finally, when he had all five fingers up in front of me, I jumped, reaching out to grasp his hand in mine, folding his fingers down. His hand felt *exactly* how I imagined it. He was warm, his skin rough from years of wear and tear, and I could feel him move his fingers softly, opening his palm up for mine. I slid my own hand into his and watched as his fingers wrapped around my entire hand.

Damnit. His fingertips...

Just as callused as I imagined. I slammed my eyes shut.

"I get it," I breathed, trying to force other thoughts from percolating. "There's a lot I can do, but...I don't want to risk what I have," I admitted.

Oakes brought his hand closer to his chest, still holding onto mine, and for a brief moment, I thought he might kiss my fingers. I inhaled, a shaky breath I knew Oakes could hear.

"Wanna know what you need?" he asked, raising that damn eyebrow again.

An orgasm? From you?

"What do I need, Oakes?"

He grinned and let go of my hand, the heat still lingering.

"A day off."

I chuckled. "Yeah, I don't get one of those this summer. Neither do you."

"Bullshit." Oakes shifted in his seat. "We're playing hooky today."

"We are not."

"Sure we are."

"The next ride is Fallon. We are halfway there. We can't—"

"Emmy, we *are* playing hooky." Oakes turned to look at me, holding my stare for one, two, three...five seconds before turning back to the road.

Luca

I need you to do something for me this time.

It requires you digging on a certain agent.

Oakes's agent, to be exact…

Emersyn

Emersyn has notifications silenced

Luca

ARE YOU KIDDING ME?

You never silence notifications…you better be doing something good.

CHAPTER SIXTEEN
Oakes

"So, where are we going?" Emersyn asked as her head swiveled, no doubt trying to see if someone was following us.

"Have you ever played hooky before?" I asked, raising a brow to look over at her.

I, of course, knew the answer. Emersyn was a junior when I started high school, and when she wasn't taken out for extracurricular reasons, she was in class. She never missed a day if she didn't have to. I, on the other hand, played hooky. A lot. My friends and I would go to the next town, watch whatever movie was playing at their local theater, sneak onto a farmer's land and annoy the bulls—you know, basic things that idiot kids would do. But I had never played hooky as an adult, especially if it meant missing out on a check. And as much as going to a random field and just laying with cows sounded amazing to me, I was pretty sure Emersyn wouldn't find that as appealing.

"No," she finally mumbled, dipping her chin. "I had requirements to meet, and school was non-negotiable."

I opened my mouth to ask how she managed to pass when she was barely there, but I quickly closed it before I let anything slip.

"No requirements for us bull riders," I drawled, using the thickest Southern accent I could muster.

"I didn't mean—" She jumped, her voice shaking as her hands raised in a surrender gesture.

I laughed, "I know, I know. I'm just being an ass."

Her hands dropped as she let out a long breath. "When are you not an ass?"

From scared to feisty. I liked it. "Fair point. Granted, I've been trying to be less of one around you." I leaned toward her. "And hate to tell you, but I'm not telling you where we're going. It's a surprise."

Yeah, a surprise because I still didn't know what the hell I was doing. All I knew was the run with her the other morning wasn't enough. The rodeo with her floating around me wasn't enough. The car ride with her literally right next to me wasn't enough. I didn't want her to be pulled away from me again at this rodeo. And then with Ty and Drew both being at Reno, I wouldn't get time with her at all. Out of all the rodeos on my schedule, Fallon was an easy one to miss.

Plus, she looked stressed. She looked like she wanted to toss that computer out the window and give up.

So...hooky.

A fun night to reset both our minds.

"What rodeo is after Fallon? Reno, right? Extreme Bulls and then the Reno Rodeo. And we are in"—she tapped on the maps app in her phone—"well...close to Winnemucca. Oakes, we may as well go to Fallon."

"Nope. I know exactly where we are going."

I did not.

"There has to be a KOA or camping site between here and Reno, so if you are insistent on skipping Fallon, we can find a site and take the day. Just relax. I can work on my article, and you can"—she waved her hand in the air—"do whatever you do, and then we can—hey!"

I snatched her phone from her hand, closed the map, and quickly put it on *Do Not Disturb* before tossing it in the backseat of the cab. When I finally met her gaze, her jaw was dropped, her eyes were wide, but even with the look of shock sitting in her expression, there was a smile fighting to get out.

"No maps. No plan. We're playing hooky. We're gonna drive until we get to where I'm going, and then we can find a place to camp—but no maps. No plans. No calls or text messages. No article." I looked over at her and waggled my eyebrows. "Let loose. It will be fun."

"Fun?" Emersyn parroted, slumping in her seat slightly.

"Trust me."

Two hours later and we were still driving. My 'let loose' plan was failing miserably, especially since there was absolutely nothing to stop and see. Not even a damn lake to try to catch a fish. And with no maps to give us a clue as to what we were coming up on, it seemed our hooky adventure was just sightseeing...of dirt. Lots and lots of dirt.

I'd hand it to Emersyn, though. She had yet to plunge into the backseat for her phone. She even left her laptop at her feet. She just sat with her arms crossed, looking at the passing desert. My phone, on the other hand, was attached to the Bluetooth, so when it rang again, that marked the twelfth time Drew had tried to call me.

"You know," Emersyn said as soon as the ringing was done blaring through the speakers. "He *is* your agent, and you may want to answer his phone call before he thinks something happened to us."

"He's fine. He knows we're okay."

"What if you're a serial killer? And this playing hooky game is just a way for you to kill me?"

"Didn't we already have the serial killer talk?"

"No, I don't think so. Babysitting talk—we had that, remember? When you forced me to ride with you."

I grinned. "Oh yeah." I couldn't help but laugh. "Which reminds me, your Corolla is safe and sound at Hartwell Hills."

"I can take it after your training. With your schedule being extended, I can follow for the rest of the month. That wouldn't be an issue for me. Get out of your hair," she said, shifting her body in the seat next to me.

"We can have your car shipped to Colorado."

"Oakes," she protested.

"What, you're not enjoying this? Your first hooky in how long?"

"Ever. And yes, I'm enjoying traveling with you, but..." her torso twisted as she followed a brown sign on the road. "Did you read that?" she asked, pointing her thumb behind her shoulder, her eyes back on me.

"What? No." I looked over at her, noticing the excitement that now flooded her eyes. Over a sign? Must have been a good sign.

Her shoulders slumped. "Lake Tahoe."

"Oh yeah, I guess that is coming up."

"I've never been."

"You've never been to Tahoe?"

"Well"—she shrugged—"for rodeos, yes, but I've never been there just to see it. I'd love to take some photos, and I'm sure there is a camping site somewhere."

"That sounds perfect." I smiled.

"We don't have to go if you had something else in mind—"

"Emmy," I stopped her. "I had zero idea of what we were doing. I just knew I needed you to stop stressing." A smile tugged at my lips as I forced myself to stay focused on the road. "Let's do it. Hooky adventure number one."

"Oh, there's more than one adventure?"

"Always."

"And you don't have it planned?"

"Absolutely not."

I glanced over at her, and her lips twisted until eventually, she smiled. "Perfect."

Fifteen minutes later, I parked the truck in on an outlook facing the lake, and Emersyn took her camera over to the edge. I had seen Lake Tahoe. I had skied here before, camped, participated in multiple rodeos, and seeing Emersyn see it for the first time was now my favorite memory of the lake. She raised her camera to her eyes, flipped her hair over her shoulder, and twisted, capturing the lake from every angle. I couldn't wait to see the photos. I had no doubt they were gorgeous.

I shoved my hands in my pockets and slowly made my way over to her.

When she turned, her smile wide as her gaze met mine, even with her squinting from the sun, her eyes sparkled. Glints of blue that were made brighter thanks to the light hitting them, the rosy tint in her cheeks deepening the longer our stares were locked on each other, but...I blinked, trying to pull myself out of the trance. Reaching up slowly, I tucked a piece of hair behind her ear, tempted to leave my fingers there for as long as I could.

Sixteen years ago, when that horse shattered my hand, Emersyn's eyes were the first thing I saw when I came to from shock. Her hands were on my face, her eyes heavy on mine as she said, over and over, *'You're okay. You're okay. It's not as bad as it looks.'* Then she sat with me, holding my other hand as we waited for the ambulance.

Sixteen years ago, I decided she was the most beautiful human in all of space and time.

And now, right here, with the sun hitting her blonde hair, the wind moving it just right, those perfect blue eyes on me...my statement stood true.

Emersyn was gorgeous. Stunning. A piece of art in every single way.

And she was here with *me.*

I lowered my hand and swallowed, taking a step back from her before I did something stupid, like pull her to me and kiss her.

I cleared my throat. "There's a hiking trail off to the side. We could grab a few drinks and snacks and head up the mountain. You can get more photos."

"Sounds right up my alley." She lifted her camera strap over her head, pointing to the trail head. "This way?"

"Let me get the water bottles." But before I could turn back to the truck, Emersyn was already running toward the trail.

"How about a magnet?" Emersyn pulled my attention back to her, holding up a flat rectangle magnet that showed Lake Tahoe from the view she had taken from our hike, except the mountains were covered in snow. "We could start you a collection." She smiled, handing me the magnet.

I took it from her and flipped it over, seeing the $8.99 price tag. "You may not believe this, but I don't have anywhere to put this."

"It's a magnet. Stick it on your trailer." Yanking the magnet back from my hand, she grasped it. "If you won't buy it, I will." She spun on her heels to the other side of the small gift shop. In her hands already were a few postcards, the magnet, a shot glass and a small stuffed moose. She had looked at every shelf, touched almost every book, and even considered buying herself a necklace with a mountain range charm. I considered buying it for her, trailing my fingers over the gold chain, but I didn't know how to without her noticing. I could imagine it around her neck, sitting against her collarbone, but...I refrained.

"I won't stop you." Shoving my hands in my pockets, I grinned as I followed her to the cash register.

"And I'm sticking it on your trailer."

"Perfect place for it."

We paid for her souvenirs and headed out of the shop to take one last look at the view. It really was beautiful, a sight to see, especially with the sun setting just over the mountains, the gleam hitting the lake just right.

"Okay, I know you said no article," she began as she fumbled with her shopping bag and camera, "but go stand over by the lake. It will make for a fantastic shot."

"That I'll accept." I pointed at her once, giving her a wink, before walking to the spot, turning to look at her. I shoved my hands in my pockets, standing with my feet apart. "Imagine this pose but with my hat and chaps."

Her head tilted slightly before she shook her head. "Maybe later, but not this time, look out over the lake, but I want your profile. Just...pretend I'm not here and enjoy the view." She spun her finger in a circle and raised her camera to her eyes.

Pretend you're not here? That's impossible.

I positioned myself like she asked and inhaled. As much as I didn't care for having my photo taken, I could get used to this. This view, her concentration on me. This photo would be worth it. I heard the faint click of the camera, the shutter clicking a few times, before I moved, slowly making my way back to her as she looked at the photos. I snuck in next to her, cheek to cheek, and I looked at the photo.

Yup. I was right.

Worth it.

Lowering the camera, Emersyn flipped her hair from her shoulder and met my gaze. I could kiss her—we were that close. All it would take was one move on my part, and my lips would be on hers.

"What's next?" she asked, her voice warm and animated as the adventure started to take hold of her. It was damn near intoxicating.

"Hungry?" I raised my eyebrow.

"Starving."

After asking a few locals for recommendations while Emersyn took more photos, I found just the place to take her. I grasped her hand and guided her to the truck, her energy from the surprise almost palpable as we got closer and closer to the destination. She may not have played hooky, but I could guarantee she was enjoying herself. I could feel it. I could basically taste it.

I pulled up to the restaurant, a place named *The Thirsty Bull*. I twisted and gave her a cocky grin, raising one brow as she leaned forward in her seat.

"It's a dive bar." She hummed. "*The Thirsty Bull*?"

"Hooky adventure part two."

Her smile grew. "Do you think they have a mechanical bull?" She bounced as she opened her door, jumping out in one fluid motion.

"You want me to ride a mechanical bull?" I shouted right before the door fully closed.

Emersyn caught it before the door slammed then offered me the sexiest smile I had ever seen. I felt my heart stop just looking at her. "Sure...but I was also thinking it could be practice for when I ride a bull at the end of the summer. Remember our deal?"

She shut the door and bounced on her heels before taking off toward the entrance, her blonde hair flowing behind her as she left me at the truck. I felt my entire body twitch just watching her.

Fuck.

I was in trouble.

CHAPTER SEVENTEEN
Oakes

The minute I opened the door to the bar, the country music hit my senses at full force. Thomas Rhett singing about how he keeps several pairs of boots in his truck—I mean, what country man didn't—but damn it was loud. But with each step, you got more immersed in it with the clinks of glasses and silverware only adding to the ambiance. There were high-top tables with chairs scattered everywhere and bull skulls on the wooden walls surrounded by the neon signs of the many draft beers. And yes, near the side of the bar, protected by a short fence and foam pads, was the infamous mechanical bull. And it smelled exactly like you'd think it would.

This place was phenomenal.

Taking it in, feeling my lips form a tight smile, I scanned the room for Emersyn, who was already at the bar top. Adjusting my hat on my head, I strode up to her, watching as she leaned her entire torso on the counter, trying to get someone's attention. Her blonde hair cascaded down her shoulders, her white tank top tucked into jeans that hugged her ass, flaring out at her feet, her own cowboy boots still scuff free. She was a sight to behold, and I found myself fumbling to approach her. Nerves skirted up my stomach and into my throat. Even though I had been with this woman for days now, she still made me freeze, still not believing that she was in front of me.

Still not believing that she had no idea who I was.

She waved her arm in the air, still trying to get someone's attention, I placed my hand on the small of her back, feeling her heat.

She turned and smiled at me. "Oh good, you're here. Use your fame and get that gal's attention."

Looking down the bar top, I chuckled, seeing the bartender—a pixie cut, larger-than-life earrings, and her black shirt hugging every inch of her. Currently, she was holding the man's attention on the other end of the bar, a large smile on both of their faces.

I leaned on the bar top, my elbow resting on the wooden ledge. "Excuse me, miss!" I shouted, instantly getting her attention. She gave me a slight nod, touched the man's arm with a sweet smile, and then made her way toward us. I raised a brow and looked at Emersyn. "There you go."

"Don't flirt with her." Emersyn pointed at me.

"I won't," I muttered in her ear, my eyes trained on hers, even though she was focused somewhere else.

A laugh came from the other side of the bar as the bartender came up to us. "Thanks for looking out for me, but I can assure you he ain't looking at me. What can I get you?" She smiled at Emersyn, giving me a knowing look. *Thank God the bartender is on my side.*

"What do you have on tap?" Emersyn asked.

Emersyn ordered a simple draft, while I ordered a pint of my favorite beer and a shot of whiskey. Lord knew I needed it with the way my hand was still on Emersyn's back, with the way my thumb had slid under her belt, moving in a circle right above her ass.

"You need a shot, cowboy?" Emersyn arched away from me slightly, forcing my palm to press into her skin.

"If you plan on getting me on that bull—yes."

"Oh," she laughed. *God, her laugh*. "I'm getting you on the bull."

"Karaoke is tonight too," the bartender added as she set our drinks down in front of us.

Emersyn hummed as she took a long pull from her mug. "No. Mechanical bull, yes, but I do not sing."

I shook my head, downing my shot, feeling it burn all the way to my stomach. "I bet you could put on quite the show."

"I *could* do Carrie Underwood, 'Before He Cheats,' but I don't plan on getting that drunk. Sorry, Mr. Ashford. I will not be singing tonight."

"Oakes Ashford." The bartender leaned forward again. "I knew I recognized you. I follow your schedule, and I'm pretty sure you're supposed to be in Fallon tonight. I was pissed I was going to miss it." She smiled, and I looked down and caught sight of her name tag.

"Sorry, Natalie." I slipped my hand up Emersyn's back, finding her shoulder with ease and pulling her closer to me until she just fit in the crook of my arm. "Don't tell my agent we're skipping rodeos."

Natalie's lips pursed as a tight, knowing smile spread. "Mum's the word. You two let me know if you need anything."

"We need that bull to be warmed up." Emersyn grinned.

"I'll get to see Oakes Ashford tonight after all?" Natalie leaned toward Emersyn.

"I mean, I hope to get him on that bull, but I'm riding it first."

God...fucking...dammit.

Emersyn on that bull was going to be the death of me—I could just feel it.

It had been—what?—ten days since Emersyn first got here. Ten days of seeing her every day, imagining her in ways I probably shouldn't have been. I fell asleep thinking about her; I showered thinking about her; I ran thinking about her. And now my hand was still on her shoulder, sliding down her back once again. I tugged on her tank slightly, feeling her skin on the tip of my fingers. What I wouldn't give to see every inch of her.

I cleared my throat and removed my hand from her back. "Bull before or after food?"

Emersyn arched her back slightly and gave me a glance over her shoulder. "After." She hummed. "I am ridiculously hungry."

I cocked a grin. "Best dive-bar food coming up."

Emersyn moved, a sigh leaving her lips, and her ass hit the stool behind her. I still stood with my elbow resting on the bar top, but my entire frame centered on her. There was a slight tint of pink to her cheeks as she raised her beer to her lips, her focus on anything but me. Could she feel my gaze on her? Did she know exactly what she was doing to me? I tilted my head, hoping the change in angle would get her to look over at me, but then what? Did I kiss her right here, right now? Taste the beer on her tongue and breathe her in? Or did I just...watch?

I couldn't ever see myself not watching her.

She lowered her mug and cleared her throat, gesturing with her chin to the other side of the wall. Following her gaze, my eyes landed on the large TV mounted to the wall that I had somehow missed when we sat down. Oh yeah, I missed it because my attention was completely focused on Emersyn and only Emersyn. A bull broke free of the chute the moment my eyes caught the screen, and I held my breath.

"That's Fallon," Emersyn said, her voice hoarse. "Do you think Drew is shitting his pants right now with you not being there?"

"Would it make you feel better to know that Drew has my location?" I raised a brow and turned back to her.

Our eyes met.

"He does?"

I gave her a light nod. "It's in the contract. Since we travel so much, he keeps tabs on us, which I don't mind."

She swallowed. "I should have probably shared mine with Luca. He's probably contacting *Crime Junkie* right now for my episode. I can see it now: 'Reporter gets kidnapped by bull rider—what happens next may shock you.'" She waved her hand in the air, bringing the title to life in front of her.

"What happens next Emersyn?" I asked, lowering my tone so only she could hear...leaning in slightly to her.

I heard her breath hitch before she gave me a smile, her shoulders relaxing as she said, "I'm getting on that bull."

After our meal and another round of drinks, Emersyn held onto the fence as she watched a few employees get the large metal bull ready for her. Others gathered around to watch the small blonde girl get ready to tackle the mechanical bull. I could hear some people whispering, taking bets on how long she would last, but Emersyn just watched, studying the metal frame as she waited.

I touched the small of her back and leaned forward.

"Have you done this before?" I asked.

She took a deep breath. "Wouldn't you like to know."

"I would, actually—so I can tell you what to expect."

"I do handstands on horses. I think I can manage a fake bull." She raised her brow and glanced at me. "But"—she shrugged a shoulder—"I guess a few pointers from a professional wouldn't hurt."

"A professional?"

"Teach me your ways, oh masterful one."

With a chuckle, I slid my hand to her elbow. "Are you right or left-handed?" I asked from over her shoulder, close to her ear.

"Left," she answered softly.

Knew that.

"Alright, you're going to hold on with your right hand, your left hand in the air." I ran my fingers up her left arm.

"Dominate hand in the air. Got it," she replied with a nod.

"You may need help on the bull—"

"I can get on the bull," she stopped me, arching her back to shoot me a glare.

I cocked an eyebrow. "Use your thighs to hold on, dig your heels in, but keep your torso loose. Focus your eyes on the head of the bull, and make sure you sway with it. It's gonna move, forward, back, left, right. It's gonna spin in circles. You just have to make sure to hold on."

Her lips twisted, pressed together as she concentrated. Her tongue darted out, licking them to form a wet gloss over the red hue. Lush, plump...perfectly kissable.

"It's in your hips," I croaked, my eyes glued on her mouth.

"My hips? I thought you said my thighs." She smirked.

Blinking, I stepped behind her, grasping her hips with my palms and tugging her body to mine. I swear I heard a small gasp fall from her lungs as her ass curved perfectly into my hips. "The bull is going to move..." I began to rock my hips forward, flattening my palms to move her with me, mimicking what the bull could do. "Back...and forth..." I lowered my mouth to her ear, whispering the words. Her breath shivered as she inhaled.

I could feel Emersyn loosen as my fingers pressed into her jeans, her entire body relaxing into me as we moved. She leaned her back into my chest, tilting her head so my lips grazed the bottom of her earlobe. I could feel her heat, feel my blood rushing to my cock, her heart beating against my chest...all from a few simple touches. Blinking, I pulled my focus back to the lesson.

"You just have to hold on, watch his head, move with the bull and sway..." I swayed my hips in a circle, her own following my motion. I slid my palm to her stomach, pressing her body flush against mine as we rocked and swayed, our hips dancing as if we'd rehearsed this. We blended together, flawlessly, bringing more images to my mind than her on a bull. If I closed my eyes, I could see it. Clear as day. Her above me, moving her own hips without my hands guiding her. The epitome of perfection as she rode me—not a bull.

Fuuuck.

I inhaled, deep and slow, running the tip of my nose against her hair. "Keep your torso like liquid...and don't count."

"Don't count?" she asked, a breathy wave to her voice, looking over her shoulder toward me, a light, sexy grin her lips.

"Don't. I'll count. Once that buzzer goes off...you jump off."

Laughing, Emersyn pulled away from me to face me head on. "This is a mechanical bull, Oakes. There is no time limit. The longer the ride, the more I score, right?"

"You only gotta last the eight seconds." I leaned into her, holding her gaze for what felt like forever. Second, minutes, hours...I could stare at her for as long as she'd let me. "Then we can—"

"It's all ready for you!" the man prepping the bull shouted. "You're up."

Emersyn waggled her eyebrows once before she turned and jumped over the fence. Folding my arms, I watched as she hoisted herself up, proving me wrong as she situated herself over the bronze metal. She gripped the rope and raised her hand, wiggling her hips before she looked at me and nodded.

The bull moved slow at first but began to pick up speed as it jerked from left to right, forward and back, turning in a complete circle. All the while,

Emersyn's left hand held steady above her head, her torso moved in sync with the motions, and the smile on her face proved she had played me.

She knew exactly what she was doing.

And she was fucking amazing while she did it.

Even the crowd watching her could tell, and they cheered her on just as loud, all while I stood in shock just watching as the woman that had been on my mind for forever rode the bull as if it was nothing.

And I couldn't stop looking.

The buzzer went off at eight seconds, and the bull began to slow, and once it was completely stopped, she jumped, landing on her two feet with ease as if she had done it so many times she could be well on her way to the NFR.

With her eyes locked on me, she gave me one hell of a sexy smirk before jumping back over the fence.

"It's all in the hips, right?" Emersyn brushed her hair from her shoulder and walked past me, making her way to our table where her second order of mozzarella sticks sat waiting for her. "I believe it's your turn, *Oakes.*"

I'd said it before, and I'll say it again.

I was in trouble.

"How many times have you done that?" I asked once the shock had worn off and the buzz of touching Emersyn had died off. It wasn't gone; I could still feel myself twitch every time I looked at her, but thankfully I had that under control.

We should have called it a night, but there was no way I wanted this evening to end.

"A time or two." She cocked a shoulder. "I went to college in Wyoming, Oakes. It wasn't a Friday night if you weren't getting drunk and riding a mechanical bull."

"What's the longest you've lasted?"

"Ten...fifteen seconds, I believe."

"Damn." I fell back in my seat.

"It's not that impressive."

"If you can do fifteen on a mechanical, you may be able to last eight on a real one."

She laughed. "Well, we will find out at the end of the summer, then, won't we?"

Nodding, I couldn't help but agree. "That we will."

"So..." Emersyn folded her arms in front of her as she leaned forward on the small table. "What else for our hooky adventure?"

"Bed."

She froze.

"I mean, sleep." I waved my hand in front of us, erasing the last five seconds even though I wished I didn't have to. Bed with Emersyn...*nope.* "We can find a motel or campsite. I have an air mattress and the trailer..."

"As good as camping sounds, I really need to shower." Emersyn scrunched her nose, lifting her hands above her head to pull her hair into a messy bun that fit in her palms. It fell once she let it go, not having a hair tie to keep it up.

"Then, motel it is, I saw one as we were coming in." I stood, giving my back a stretch before I reached out a hand to her. "Shall we?"

Without hesitation, she took my hand. And without hesitation, I pulled her to me, our bodies meeting in the middle, completely flush, with only our breaths in between us. Wrapping my arm around her waist, I held her there, breathing her in, making this moment last as long as it possibly could before I had to let her go.

She let out a shaky breath of air then lifted her chin.

"Citrus," she whispered.

"Huh?"

"Your smell. Citrus and…" She stopped, a faint smile appearing on her lips. "Sunshine."

Emersyn

Citrus.

Luca

What about it?

Emersyn

Just citrus.

Luca

Oranges? Mango? Grapefruit? I know you love essential oil citrus, but I need more than that to know how to even begin to respond to this.

Emersyn

Citrus and sunshine. Use your brain, Luca. Citrus. And. Sunshine.

Luca

wide-eye emoji

CHAPTER EIGHTEEN
Emersyn

I need to know where you're going.

At least turn your location on.

You can't ignore me forever.

I'll text Drew.

It's been six hours. I'm getting nervous.

We're coming on twelve hours, Emersyn...

Emersyn, you never have your phone on DND, and the fact that you haven't answered me in almost twenty hours has me kinda freaking out.

Ok…If you don't answer in five minutes, I will be calling the police and starting a missing persons report. Keep in mind I have Oakes's schedule. I can easily find you.

Me

Damn, Luca, let a girl sleep.

Luca

YOU LIVE! Don't ever put your phone on DND again. I didn't care for that. Twenty-four hours of SILENCE, Emersyn.

Me

It was not twenty-four hours.

Squinting, I sat up in the motel bed, feeling each and every scratch of the sheets as my bare legs moved. A quick scroll on our text thread allowed me to quickly count in my head. Well, shit…maybe it had been that long. My last text to Luca was just the casual information that I, too, was interested in how Oakes smelled, and then after that, Oakes had tossed my phone in the backseat, and I hadn't seen it until we went into our separate rooms.

Yep. Separate rooms.

After being in Oakes's arms that closely, after the way his hips moved against mine, separate rooms were a must. After that little show, I had to put all my focus on the mechanical bull just to stay on. My entire body was buzzing after feeling his hands on me. And then he teased me, his thumb slipping just barely under my jeans, and the sensation of the rough pad there on my skin sent me into an internal frenzy. And once my hips were cradled in his, I could feel more than his hands, and I didn't trust myself enough to *not* do anything stupid.

Easier said than done. I clasped my hands under my chin, gripping onto the pillow, my breaths heavy as the memory went flying through my mind. The only thing that helped was shoving my AirPods in my ears, pulling the blanket over my head, and drowning out the world with white noise. That was, until Luca texted me, and Siri read me his latest message.

I may have been joking when I told Oakes he was going to contact my favorite true crime podcast, but him calling the police was not a joke and something he would most definitely do, even if it was an overreaction.

But as much as I hated to admit it...he was right. Me putting my phone on *do not disturb* was something I never ever did. Even sleep mode didn't exist for me. Just like playing hooky didn't exist for me.

But then ...I wouldn't change last night for anything.

It felt amazing to let loose for a few hours. The last time I had done anything remotely close to that was in college when my roommate, Tessa, and I met up with a few guys from school. We each took turns on the mechanical bull, and when I was the one to last the longest, it became a monthly ritual. We'd go to the same rundown bar, order the same drinks and food, sing the same songs, and then each have a turn on the bull. It was a well-known fact around the university that Emersyn Flynn was the mechanical bull champion. Then I graduated, and my life became *Rodeo Way*. Everything changed after I got hired at the magazine, and I wasn't sure I could let loose like that again.

But yesterday, the only time the article even crossed my mind was when we were at the lake, and Oakes posed for that photo. I could see it on the website, the cover of a future issue, framed and behind my desk in my new office once I got this promotion. Basically, I wanted it where I could see it every single day.

I wanted to see *him* every day.

I wanted *more* of him every day.

More time to see how he was with no one watching him. More time to see the look on his face as he concentrated. More time to hear his voice and learn all that I could about him. More time to...feel him. The memory of his hands on my hips, moving my ass against his heat, flittered again, only making those butterflies fly around like crazy, like they had the whole terrarium to explore.

But that was yesterday...

And now it was today...

And letting loose wasn't an option.

Wanting to explore whatever this was wasn't an option.

I had to focus here. I had an assignment to complete.

And I had to be in the right mindset.

We had a few hours before we set out to Reno. With Oakes performing in the Xtreme Bulls portion of the rodeo tonight, this wasn't an event he could skip—meaning he was most likely going to use the morning to prepare. There was probably a CrossFit gym nearby, and he'd go on a run around Lake Tahoe—whatever he did would be to get his head back in the game. If he was, I had to too. I could totally use this time to get out of my head. Shower, yoga, breakfast, article, then back on the road. No more thinking about Oakes's hands on my hips or the way his voice sounded in my ear, or the way his eyes met mine and made my knees weak. Because that was never going to happen and was most definitely stopping now.

But before I could accomplish any of those tasks, a knock at my door gained my full attention. I stood, giving myself a quick glance to make sure I was decent before opening the door, letting the sun soak into the room. Oakes stood there, a grin on his lips, wearing a gray t-shirt and jeans, his hands shoved in his pockets. His hair was mussed just right, his beard looked freshly trimmed, and his forearms—I inhaled, stopping my gaze from traveling any farther. His forearms looked like any other forearms, I told myself over and over again. There was nothing special about them. It was his expression. The look in his eyes, the bright smile on his face was all consuming, making me forget everything I just talked myself out of.

"Morning." He smiled.

I leaned against the door. "Good morning." I crossed my arms over my chest.

"Breakfast?" His smile grew, the question lingering on his lips.

I scrunched my brow. "You don't need to run or…"

Pulling a hand from his pocket, he waved me off. "Nope. We're still playing hooky until Reno tonight, so get dressed, and let's go get breakfast." He spun on his heel, the gravel crunching below his boot. "See you by the truck in twenty?"

I watched him walk away from me, that same buzz filling my senses.

Forty minutes later, I sat across from Oakes, my hands hugging the coffee mug, the smell exactly what I needed to get my head on straight.

"How's the hangover?" Oakes asked, lifting a brow.

"Always the gentleman," I sneered. "No hangover for me."

"Three beers and a shot of whiskey? No hangover?"

"I hold my liquor very well. Three beers are nothing."

Oakes chuckled, falling back into the booth. "How about your thighs?"

My eyes widened. In an effort to hide my blush that I knew was creeping up to my cheeks, I raised my mug. "Totally fine."

I raised my eyes, looking at Oakes through my lashes. His grin was almost sinful, which only made my stomach churn faster than it already was. I could probably make butter at this point with my stomach.

"Good to hear," he mused. "How many missed calls did you have from yesterday?"

I barked out a laugh, more comfortable with that question than the previous ones. "More than expected. Luca didn't care for the silence. You?"

"Twenty missed calls from Drew, three from my mother, one from Ty, and then one very long phone call this morning."

"With?" I raised a brow.

"Drew. Basically, next time I decide to skip a rodeo, I need to run it by him. Apparently, Fallon had big money." Oakes's eye widened as he turned to me. "Ty took the biggest check home."

"Oh, well, good for him. I hope you didn't miss out on too much."

He shook his head. "Ty took home a little over 5K, which would have been good, but..." He paused, leaning forward on the table, his eyes heavy on mine. "I don't regret the day at all. I think we both needed that."

"I think so too. I haven't had a day like that in—" The shrill ring from my phone took my attention away from Oakes. "Forever," I finished, reaching for my cell phone. A few new messages from Luca sat unread, then the one that caught my eye—my mother. "Huh?" I huffed, opening the message without thinking.

Mom

> I know you're on a field assignment—exciting, by the way—but Luca is rather worried. Please message me back.

"What?" Oakes asked after a few beats of silence.

"My mom texted me. Luca has her number and only contacts her if it's an emergency," I said as I typed out a quick response, letting her know I was safe and sound.

"Have emergencies happened often?" Oakes questioned, lifting his elbows as the waiter placed our plates in front of us. A scone and yogurt for me, with a side of bacon that Oakes insisted on, and a rather large omelet for Oakes. Normally, he would be picking up his fork and digging in, but his gaze was intense on me as he waited for my response.

I heaved a sigh. "There was one—if you can call it an emergency. Since then, Luca has kept my mom's number."

"Do you have anyone else, other than Luca, to contact? Where does your mom live?"

"I'm supposed to be the one with the questions, not you." I locked my phone and slid it back in my bag.

"Just two friends getting to know one another."

"I'll answer questions"—my smirk grew—"if you answer some."

"I answer your questions all the time."

"I don't know where your mom lives." I folded my arms, trying to pull off some sort of pouty tease. I failed. I guarantee I looked more like an annoying little sister than a friend trying to tease or a girl trying to flirt.

Dipping his chin, Oakes answered, "She lives in Wyoming. On our farm."

"You own a farm? Ty mentioned that."

"I don't. My mom does. She got it after my dad...well...after my dad left. She got the farm." He gave me a side-eye, shifting his body weight in the seat. "Now you."

"Mom and Dad are in Wyoming, still in the house I grew up in."

"Which is located in the town of..." He drew the word out as long as it could go, the F starting to sound like a hiss.

I rolled my eyes at him. "A small town—you've probably never even heard of it. The population is barely three hundred. Midwest."

Oakes nodded. "I've heard of it. Ridden in a few rodeos there."

"They do put on some amazing rodeos."

"That they do. Besides your mom and Luca, who else is on your emergency contact list?"

"Just them."

"That's hard to believe."

"Not really. Luca and I met when we started at *Rodeo Way,* and my college roommate—Tessa—she moved to California and is working for a law firm. She doesn't do rodeos; she does numbers and graphs. We keep in touch, but nothing like we used to. I haven't seen her in years. I work too much to have friends."

"Invite her to a rodeo—and Luca. Luca works for *Rodeo Way,* so he'd like it, right?"

"He loves the sport, probably just as much as I do."

"That's hard to believe. I can't imagine anyone loving the sport more than you—even me." Oakes smirked. "Pop quiz?" He raised a brow.

"You know Luca started that little game with me, right?"

He shook his head.

"He didn't believe me when I said I was full of random rodeo facts. Then he started randomly pop quizzing me, and when I got the answers right, it became a party trick. The fact that you've taken it on gives me a sense of comfort."

"You *pop quizzed* me first. I just thought it was cute, so I kept doing it. But hey..." He turned his head and smirked, that damn sexy smirk that I was growing to crave. "I'm glad it brings you comfort. So..."

I lifted my fork, turning into a statue when I caught his gaze.

"What was the emergency?"

I chuckled. "I went riding with Sterling—"

"Your editor?"

I licked my lips and nodded. "And ex-boyfriend." I looked at my scone, not wanting to see Oakes's reaction to that part. "And we went to an arena. I did a few stunts for him, and I fell off the horse. I ended up dislocating my shoulder. He had to take me to the emergency room, but he didn't contact anyone—not even Luca—so when I called my mother the next day, she panicked. I never fell off horses. Since then, Luca and my mom have been emergency contacts."

"Why didn't Sterling contact anyone?"

I shrugged. "To him, it was no big deal. I was honestly just doing it to prove to him I could, and then I fell. It was a little embarrassing."

"You had to *prove* you could?"

"Well, yeah." I raised a shoulder, the question lingering on his lips.. "It's not a skill most people have."

"And you dated him?" Oakes raised a brow, his expression radiating annoyance. "And now he's your editor?"

I nodded. "We split when I got promoted to digital editor. We didn't want there to be any favoritism happening, but we keep it amicable. No hard feelings there."

He hummed, raising a disapproving brow. "A bit concerning that he didn't contact anyone, though."

"He was there with me, and he thought that was enough."

"How long had it been since you did any stunts?"

I heaved a sigh. "Longer than I'd like to admit. Once I got my job at *Rodeo Way*, riding wasn't an option anymore. I live in the city, so I don't get to see my horse—"

"Mable? Right?"

I furrowed my brow. "Yeah, how did you know?"

He blinked, his hand quickly going to the back of his head to scratch. "You've mentioned her."

Another sigh left my lips. I did tend to talk about my horse from time to time, and the fact that he remembered made my chest swell. "She's in Wyoming, so I don't get to ride her. When Sterling found out I did stunt riding, he took me to an arena. I rode a horse I wasn't familiar with, and we took a turn too fast. It happens. But I would like to ride more. I miss it. Just like I miss being here at the rodeos."

"Why can't you ride?" he asked, his voice low and heavy, his brows furrowed as he studied me.

I bit the inside of my lip and thought. Why didn't I make time for it? Why didn't I let loose and live the way I wanted to? Simple answer—I couldn't. I could...once I got this promotion.

"*Rodeo Way* keeps me busy. I'm either behind the screen at my desk or behind the screen at home. I have rodeos and dressage competitions playing on the television as background noise, but...this is it. This is the life I've built and..." The words *I regret it* almost passed my lips, but I stopped. I took a bite of my scone, trying to keep my mind on the positive things. I was finally doing what I loved, so I had no room to complain. I finally settled on, "I do love it."

"You love this." Oakes waved his hand in a circle about our heads. "But I am curious about something."

"That's never a good way to start a change in topic, Oakes."

He smiled, a small laugh filling the space between us. "You mentioned the other day about doing this, being in the field and on the dirt...but from what you just told me...that you haven't ridden, you spend most of your time in front of a screen, but...you love it?" Oakes stabbed his omelet. "What's there to love?"

I shrugged my shoulder. "I guess..." I started, pausing when I couldn't truly find the words to say. I met Oakes's eyes and suddenly had the urge to tell him everything. I wanted to tell him about when I lost Miss Rodeo America, how the world seemed so open yet so closed off at the same time. I wanted to tell him about the time I went back to a rodeo, feeling the thrill of it all again and then losing it the second I stepped back into my office. I wanted to pour out my heart and express everything that I couldn't...but all I said was, "I have grown to love the rodeo from a different aspect. Yes, I love the arenas, and I love taking photos, but at this point, I'm just happy I get to be a part of the rodeo world somehow."

Oakes pinched his brow, seeming to take in every word. Our eye contact broke, and he returned to cutting up his omelet and me going to my scone and yogurt. The space grew quiet for a moment, making me almost think I said the wrong thing—or that somehow I disappointed him—until finally he reached across the table and placed his hand on my wrist, forcing me to look up at him. He smiled, the light-brown specks turning gold as he looked at me.

My stomach twisted, and goddamn there went those stupid butterflies again.

"Pop quiz," he whispered.

I smiled, a small tug pulling at my heartstrings.

"Okay, shoot."

"Who is the one and only cowboy to get a perfect score riding bulls? And I mean *perfect* score. 100 points. You get bonus points if you can name the year."

I smirked, narrowing my eyes as if to think. Oakes waited, his thumb grazing along my wrist. I leaned forward, the confidence in the one place I knew I could flourish returning.

"Wade Leslie. October 26, 1991."

"And you're trying to tell me that Luca loves the sport more than you? That you don't belong on the dirt? Fucking impossible."

To: E.Flynn@rodeowaymag.com
From: M.Pennel@rodeowaymag.com
Subject: Xtreme Bulls
Date: June 19th: 8:32 AM

I expect a report on Xtreme Bulls tonight after Mr. Ashford rides.

If you skip a rodeo again, Emersyn, there may be more risks to the promotion you've been offered. And if I hear from Mr. Manning that you and Mr. Ashford have veered off course again, I will be looking into a replacement for the remainder of the assignment.

Look forward to getting your Xtreme Bulls report.

Morgan Pennel
Editor in Chief - Rodeo Way Magazine
Denver, CO

Chapter Nineteen
Oakes

"**C**ome on, man, you know you're not supposed to skip events," Drew lectured.

Drew began his scolding the minute Emersyn and I pulled up to the arena, and they kept coming even after I checked in. The man was relentless, letting me know in every sense that I fucked up. I could have won that money last night. I could have taken a higher lead over everyone else, basically securing my spot in the NFR (even though we still had months to go) if I had just gone to Fallon. But even with all his lectures, even with Emersyn trying to take the blame (Drew clearly knew it wasn't her idea when she tried to tell him it was) I couldn't care less about what he thought. Because I had a day with Emersyn that I wouldn't soon forget.

"Look, man, I get it. Sometimes it's too much—"

"Do you really get it?" I cut him off.

Riding bulls...I wouldn't classify that as too much. Keeping myself from telling Emersyn every thought that passed my brain—now that was too much. Not once since breakfast did we stop talking. It took everything in me not to spill my guts to the woman. After my pop quiz question, it kept going. She'd ask me a question; I'd ask her a question.

I learned she loved sunflowers, and Mable, her horse, was still alive and well at her family's home. Her favorite book was *The Invisible Life of Addie LaRue*, though it changed regularly, and she was currently obsessing over a romance book she refused to tell me the title of—though by the way her cheeks blushed when she mentioned it, I assumed it was a relatively spicy one. When she was editing or working from home, she had rodeos on in the background. She wasn't a movie person. Her favorite food was the rolls at Texas Roadhouse—something she was deprived of while she was in her pageant days, and you couldn't get her to go to a gym to work out. No, she preferred to run in the outdoors, and living in Colorado gave her the option of trees or street runs.

She learned my favorite book was anything by Robert Jordan. I did enjoy movies, mainly suspense or thrillers, though I didn't have time to watch any of them. My childhood horse was, like hers, still alive and happy. My favorite food was steak, cooked medium rare and served with a loaded baked potato. Yes, I frequented the gym, but give me a hiking trail, and I was a happy man.

I'd never felt lighter than I did talking to her.

And here was my agent, trying to take it away.

"Yeah, I get it," he emphasized, shuddering when I gave him a glare. "You're in the limelight, you have a magazine following you around, you're wanted at major rodeos...I don't blame you for wanting to take some time off. But, Oakes—"

"I'm pretty sure they didn't miss me." I narrowed my gaze at him. "They had bigger names there."

"People went there to see *you*. You know that, right?"

"Well, then I'm sure Ty ate up the attention that he got from me being gone."

"Damn straight." Ty raised his arm from a few feet in front of us.

"See"—I motioned to him— "you did fine."

"Oakes. If you don't go to rodeos, you don't get paid." He already had two fingers up as if he were counting. I could already tell which ones were coming next, and the more the man talked, the more my blood began to boil.

"Then you don't get paid—yeah, yeah, I know the chain of events. I don't get paid. You don't get paid. I don't get into the NFR. My name fizzles out, and I become a nobody." My voice rose as I turned to glare him down. I liked Drew. He and I normally got along on a client-agent basis—sometimes I even considered him a friend—but right now, he was annoying me. Right now, that urge to punch him was back.

Drew stopped, folding his arms and raising his chin slightly, no doubt a power move. He stared me down, his jaw flexing.

"Oakes," he finally said, "like I said...I get it." I held back an eyeroll. "But next time you decide to skip an event—a rather large event—run it by me first so I can give them a heads up. Don't just disappear."

I looked at him, accepting defeat and the fact that he was, indeed, right.

"Okay, fine," I gave in. "I could have handled it differently. But," I sighed, looking over his shoulder to Emersyn, who was squatting next to the wall, her focus on her camera. "She needed the day, not me."

Drew's eyebrows pinched. "Emersyn?"

"She needed to get her mind off that damn article."

"And the best way to do that was to put your career in jeopardy?"

"Drew, you know damn well it didn't put my"—I lifted my fingers to air quote—"*career* in jeopardy. She needed it."

"Did you think about *her* career here? What did *Rodeo Way* think of her skipping out on her assignment?"

Well, shit...

I didn't think about that. Not in the slightest. I thought about clearing her head, getting her away from the computer—and her. Only her. Not the repercussions it could have on her career. What would come from this on her end? I wasn't an issue, but did I royally fuck it up for her? I stopped, held my breath for one...two...three seconds before letting loose a strong exhale.

"I don't regret it," I finally mumbled to him. "I don't think she does either."

Raising his hands in surrender, Drew lowered his chin. Looks like this was a conversation neither of us was going to win. "Okay, fine. Just next time—"

"I'll be sure to let you know."

He gave me a curt nod. "That's all I ask."

I nodded, noticing Emersyn behind Drew. She took off her hat, placing it top down on the cart next to her so she could slip the camera over her head. Once her hair was pulled from the strap and her hat was securely on her head again, she turned toward me. She smiled and raised her camera. I kept my eyes on her, watching as the camera hid her eyes for a spilt second before the vibrant blue came back into view. Her smile widened right before she turned her back.

"Oakes?"

"Hmm?" I looked back at Drew.

"I asked if you got the schedule changes."

"Yeah...yeah, I saw them."

Drew had sent over a long email right before we ditched out for the day. I lightly glanced over it, noticing a few changes to the end of the summer, but since my course for now was still the same, I brushed it off. Schedule changes happened. Rodeos were canceled; trips were adjusted. It wasn't a summer road trip without a few hiccups.

"Great, so you're on board."

"Yeah, sure. Did you send it to Emmy as well?"

"Emmy?" Drew raised a brow. "Yeah, she has it. We'll finish in Reno, then Cody, West Jordan, Oakley, Casper, Nephi—" Drew began to list off every single city I was traveling to in the next month, tallying them off with his fingers.

Ignoring him, I pulled my attention to the muffled voice of the announcer. Barrel racers were almost done, bulls next, and I was starting. I needed my gloves, my helmet, my vest...shit, I wasn't ready for this ride. And Drew was still talking.

"I need my helmet," I interrupted him, pushing past him only to come face to face with Emersyn, my helmet and vest in her arms. She tossed me my helmet, the grin she was wearing turning into a sexy smirk.

Drew's gaze went from me to Emersyn, back to me.

"I'm gonna"—he used his thumb to point behind his back—"check on Ty. See you out there, Oakes. Don't fall off."

Once Drew was out of earshot, Emersyn chuckled. "He knows you never fall off, right?" She handed me my vest and gloves, and as soon as her hands were free, she popped her hip. "Ready?"

I slipped on my vest, tugged on my gloves, traded my hat for my helmet, and mimicked her stance.

"What questions you got for me today?"

"None. I just wanna see you ride. As much fun as yesterday was, *this* is what I love to watch." She pushed my shoulder. "You're not in too much trouble, are you?"

"Nah, he's pissed, but he'll get over it." I lowered my chin, catching her gaze for a millisecond. "What about *Rodeo Way?*"

A soft grin, full of concern, appeared on her lips, but it quickly disappeared with a shake of her head and a shrug of her shoulders. "We probably shouldn't skip any rodeos again, but..." Her eyes sparkled, the concern being replaced with radiant joy. "It was worth it."

"Oh, extremely worth it." I whispered, bending down so only she could hear.

She huffed, biting her bottom lip to hide her smile. "Now go do your job so I can take some photos."

"You jinxed me," I groaned as Emersyn helped me into the hotel room.

"I did not," she grunted.

The entirety of the Reno Rodeo only proved to Drew that missing one ride didn't make a difference in my standings. Every night, I climbed the boards, and each night, Emersyn was right there with me as I did. I'd qualify, jump off the bull, give the crowd a show, and then rush to find her. She was always waiting for me, looking just as thrilled as I was. The night before the finals, I lasted the eight seconds, scored an 83, but rolled my damn ankle as I was running off the dirt. And now I was milking the fact that it slightly hurt while I walked, relishing in the feeling of Emersyn's arm around my waist.

"You're the one who said I never fall." I quirked a smile.

"A week ago! Plus"—Emersyn kicked open the door to my hotel room—"you didn't fall; you tripped over yourself. You sure you can't walk? You're a lot heavier than you look."

"Oh, I don't know." I adjusted my weight that hung over her shoulder as we walked into the dark room. "It hurts."

"Well, then, why did we come back to your room when we should have gone to the hospital?"

"Pfft." I waved a hand. "I rode with a broken ankle…"

"Oh, so"—she released my waist—"you can walk to your bed."

The sting shot up my ankle into my calf as my entire weight hit. Okay, so maybe I wasn't milking it as much as I thought.

"Shhhit," I hissed, falling on the edge of the bed.

Emersyn raised a brow, folding her arms over her chest. "Let me guess, if I don't go get ice, you won't ice it?"

I smirked, dipping my chin down to my boots.

"Oakes." She dropped her arms, her chin raising to the ceiling, clearly exasperated. "I'll go get ice, prop it up with a pillow, and then I'll run and get you a wrap."

"I have a wrap."

"Oh, good." She turned quickly, her hair flipping over her shoulders. "Then I'll be right back with ice."

"What am I gonna do after the summer?" I asked. "Who's gonna get me ice?"

With her hand on the doorknob, she tipped her head back to me. I could practically feel the eyeroll. I couldn't help but let my smirk grow. She was freaking adorable when she was annoyed. "What did you do without me before?"

"Suffered."

Finally, she smiled, letting out a small chuckle. "I can only imagine. Take off your damn boot." Then she slipped out of the room, closing the door behind her.

Doing exactly as she asked, I slowly yanked off my boot, only to see my ankle slightly swollen. I lifted it in the air, twirling it in a slow circle. The pain radiated, but it wasn't *that* bad. I'd had worse. I'd skip my run tomorrow, but I would be able to walk and ride. Reaching behind me, I grabbed a few pillows to stack on the bed. I'd just finished recreating the Leaning Tower of Pisa when Emersyn came back into the room.

"Ice." She raised the plastic bag. "Where's your wrap?"

I pointed to the duffel bag on the dresser. "Side pocket." I stood, hissing as my weight hit my ankle.

Emersyn turned, putting her hand on my shoulder. "First your knee, now your ankle. Same leg too... I need you to take better care of yourself."

"Why?" I mumbled as I scooted up on bed, plopping my ankle on the pillows. "I have you here to help take care of me."

Emersyn scoffed, dropping the plastic bag on my ankle before turning to my duffel bag. The ping from my phone forced me to shift, pulling it from my back pocket. Emersyn watched me from the corner of her eye as she rifled through my bag.

Drew

> How's the ankle?

Me

> Dandy.

"Let me guess. Drew?" Emersyn turned, my ankle wrap in her hand.

I nodded in response, watching as she messed with the bag of ice, molding it to my ankle.

"Damn, you're already swollen."

Repeating the motion from earlier, I circled my ankle. "Not much. Thanks to Nurse Emmy, it won't swell too much."

Her eyes met mine. "Do you have ibuprofen?"

I nodded. "Same pocket."

Drew's response pinged in my hand.

Drew

> I'll call the arena and pull your name tomorrow.

Me

> Fuck that. I'm not missing the finals. I can ride.

Drew

You sure?

Me

Hey, if I don't get paid, you don't get paid, remember?

"You look so serious."

I scoffed. "These things happen with bull riding. Ankles, knees, shoulders, broken bones. One injury and he's talking about pulling my name from the finals." I tossed my phone on the bed next to me.

Emersyn heaved a sigh, her fingers lightly touching my skin as she pressed into the swollen ankle. "I mean, it wouldn't be a bad idea. It wouldn't affect your standings *that* much."

I shook my head. "Did you not hear me earlier when I said I rode with a broken ankle?"

"You've mentioned that a time or two." She smiled, and my entire body shivered at the sight.

"I'll be fine in the morning. Keeping it elevated tonight, ice every twenty minutes..." I trailed off, watching as she flawlessly moved to the side of the bed.

She reached up, removing her hat, running her free hand through her hair, the soft blonde curls falling over her shoulder. Hat hair didn't plague her, fuck no—she was too gorgeous for that. Everything about her pulled at my chest. It wasn't just her hair, her outfit, the way her jeans hugged her just right, the sixteen years of longing—no. It was the fact that all the times I'd been hurt, I spent the night getting myself back in order alone. Sure, I'd forgotten the ice a time or two, but I did it alone. But tonight, she was here. Twice now she made sure I had the ice; she made sure I took the pain meds. And she was...here. Just here. Perfect.

"You're perfect, you know that?" I heard myself say before I could stop myself.

She froze, her chest heaving with each breath. "You must be going into shock from all the pain you're in. Let me get you the meds." She moved.

I sat up, making sure to keep my ankle firm on the pillow as I reached for her hand. She watched as my fingers wrapped around her palm, gently tugging her to me. Her hand in mine felt like it fit—not to sound cliché—like the perfect puzzle piece. The last time her hand was in mine was when she sat with me, giving me the inspiration I needed to be here. I wasn't sure what I was doing, what was possessing me to do this, but it was physically impossible for me to stop. I wanted to feel her near me; I wanted her to know *everything*.

"I'm not going into shock, Emmy. I'm not in that much pain." I smiled up at her, pressing my fingertips into the back of her hand. "I just...Em...you're here."

She avoided eye contact as she allowed me to pull her to the edge of the bed. Her eyes studied me, trailing from our joined hands, up my chest, to my neck, my lips. And finally, her eyes met mine. "I'm here, Oakes. I don't plan on going anywhere."

"I never—" I reached up, moving her hair from her shoulder to cradle the back of her neck. To my surprise, she let me. I could feel her skin twitch under my touch, the warmth from her veins spreading into me. "I never knew—"

Without even thinking, I pulled her to me, moving on complete instinct at this point, finally feeling complete euphoria as my mouth met hers.

CHAPTER TWENTY
Emersyn

I must have been imagining things.

Because Oakes Ashford was kissing me. He. Was. Kissing. Me.

And I could literally feel my bones melting.

His fingers laced with my hair, pulling me closer as his tongue swiped my bottom lip. I didn't even hesitate to let him in, feverishly feeling his tongue against mine in an instant, and...oh my *God*, I could stay in this kiss forever. His lips were pillowy soft as they moved in sync with mine. He had complete control here, and I moaned into his mouth as he somehow managed to kiss me deeper.

I wanted to touch him, feel more than his hands on my skin, but I was frozen. My hands sat on his legs, motionless, as he explored the nape of my neck, his thumb sliding across my jawline and down my neck to my collarbone. I wanted his lips there. I wanted his hand to move farther down. I *wanted* Oakes everywhere.

He broke the kiss, and a gasp escaped me. He kissed my jaw, that sensitive spot right below my ear, my neck, my shoulder. Then it was his turn to let out a breathy moan, which only sent me deeper into whatever I was drowning in.

"I've wanted to kiss you since the moment I saw you." His voice was light and airy, just as breathless as I felt.

"The exact moment?" I questioned, my eyes still closed as I processed that life-changing kiss.

"The"—he kissed my jawline—"Exact"—he kissed my temple—"Moment." Then he finally kissed my lips again. "It's been really...*really*...hard not to kiss you every second for the past two weeks. Every time you ask me a question, every time you smile at me, every time before a ride...*fuck*, Emmy...what the hell am I going to do when this summer is over?"

Just the summer?

Why just the summer when we could have...

Oh.

Right.

My article.

Rodeo Way.

My career.

And suddenly, I remembered why my hands were frozen, why I was letting him have complete control here.

This simply couldn't happen.

I had never felt my stomach drop so fast. Nausea waved over me, and suddenly, I was just too hot, and Oakes's hands were ice on my skin.

I cleared my throat and finally opened my eyes. His were heavy on me, searching my body as his hands moved down my arms, creating shivers that shouldn't be there in the first place.

"Well," I sighed, "I'd assume you'd go on like you were before...right?"

"Sounds fucking terrible," he sighed as he moved to me again, but before I could turn into complete mush, I arched back, removing my hands from his legs, taking that tingling feeling with me.

"You should..." I cleared my throat, trying to find the words to say that wouldn't crush every amazing thing he had just said, that he had just done. "...get some rest."

I twisted to reposition the bag of ice on his ankle, making sure it covered the swell, and then I stood.

"Emmy," Oakes breathed, his fingers still trailing my elbow to my wrist, leaving the fleeting feeling on my fingertips as I left his personal bubble.

"Make sure you take the ice off in about fifteen minutes. Here," I grabbed his phone from the bed, pointed it at his face to activate the ID, and set him an alarm. "Take it off when the alarm goes off, and then set another one for twenty minutes. If it starts to melt, text me, and I'll get you more. Stay off your feet tonight." I pointed at him, and my mind fog lifted as I went back into—what did he call it?—Nurse Emmy mode. "Keep it elevated, alright?"

He reached for me. "Emmy?"

"Text me if you need me." I gave him a solid stare, then...without any other word from him, left him in his hotel room to fend for himself, telling myself it was just a fluke—that this wasn't supposed to happen.

I watched as Oakes limped down the hall, the fringe on his chaps swaying back and forth with each clunk of his boot. It wasn't a noticeable limp, but half the people that surrounded us saw his landing last night, and they could see it just as clearly as I could. He wasn't hissing in pain anymore, but the right foot definitely hit down harder than the left.

"Are you sure you're—" I started, catching up to his side.

"Yup," he answered dutifully, not letting me finish my sentence.

"Just don't jump off the bull this time." I smiled, trying to add a joke in there.

He gave me a side-eye, a hint of a gleam there. "How else do you suggest I get off the bull, Emmy?"

Emmy...

He was still calling me Emmy.

And my stomach was still churning over it.

The wry grin I caught as he turned his attention back in front of him only amplified the feeling.

It had been almost twenty-four hours since Oakes kissed me, and I could still feel his lips on mine. I could still feel his fingers interlaced with my hair. I could feel his breath on my collarbone and his fingertips as the glided down my skin. My body was practically still buzzing from it—just the simple memory—and I was more alive than I had been in a long time.

And I wanted it again.

But stupidly—or logically—I pushed that feeling aside.

After the kiss, I tried to focus on something other than Oakes, which was hard when my assignment *was* Oakes. I edited photos, I worked on islands for my article, and then I read Morgan's email over and over again.

Letting it sink in that I had screwed up and she wasn't happy.

I had responded with a recap on his ride from the first night at Reno Xtreme Bulls—where only bull riders in the PBR came to ride and earn money toward the world PBR standing—but then she responded, asking for a report on each ride. I convinced her to let me report on Reno as a whole. Reno was the richest rodeo, lasting ten days, and Oakes was expected to win the finals. She agreed but reiterated that we had to stick to his schedule. That was our last email, and it had been a blissful week of not worrying about reporting back to her...but then he kissed me.

And life as I knew it was thrown off course.

My entire body was screaming to kiss him, jump him and make it happen again and again, recreate the zing that flowed through us.

But my brain was telling me I had so much riding on this that another kiss would screw things up more than they already were. I didn't regret the time I spent with Oakes at Lake Tahoe, but my promotion was now being dangled in front of my face.

A summer fling...a kiss...couldn't get in the way of that.

I had to focus. I had to give Morgan exactly what she asked for.

Oakes took one step up on the grate, yanking his gloves from his back pocket with one hand as the other flung his helmet forward. I stepped after him, gripping onto my camera's lens as I dipped my chin, my hat covering my view as the chutes got louder. I followed Oakes to his chute, his bull already there and waiting for him. He shoved his helmet on, giving it a knock before he worked on his gloves.

Ok...focus.

Give Morgan exactly what she wants.

"Okay, Oakes!" I shouted. "I have a few questions I can ask you tonight. Mainly about this week. Can you believe you're in the fina—"

"Emmy," Oakes stopped me, his head tilted as he looked me dead in the eyes, his voice low. "I'd rather focus tonight. No interview. If that's alright?"

I blinked a few times, a sense of rejection settling into my bones that I couldn't shake. Of course. This was a big ride. This was Reno Rodeo Finalist. Why would he want me up here with him? I rejected him last night...it was only fair he did the same in this setting.

I let out a breath of air through my lips and forced a smile. I would not make this awkward.

"Oh, totally. I'll just"—I used my thumb to point behind my shoulder—"go find a place in the stands. I bet I could get some amazing views from there."

"No, Emmy." He raised his gloved hand. "I want you here." The same hand pointed one finger down to the grate. "I need you here."

I held my breath. "But you need to focus, and I can really get some amaz—"

"Emersyn." Oakes raised a brow. "You." He pointed at me. "Here." He pointed back to the grate. "Just no questions."

I pursed my lips in a tight smile and held his stare. "No questions."

"Photos. Just photos."

I raised my camera and tilted my head, flashing a smile at him. "That I can do."

He bobbed his eyebrows at me, flashing me a smile that told me I was the only one making this awkward, then he began to jump on the balls of his feet. I raised my camera and took a few shots, loving the way his body bounced with anticipation. Keeping my camera to my eyes, I tilted to look at him.

"Hey, Oakes!" I shouted.

Still bouncing, he looked at me.

"Just...be aware of your ankle...okay?"

He gave a wink right when Jon Bon Jovi started blaring through the speakers, and the announcers began to hype him up. He climbed on the bull, created the friction with his glove and leather, and once he was situated and semi-comfortable, he nodded, and the chute flew open.

I snapped photo after photo of the bull moving left, right, twisting its body in ways I didn't think possible, all while Oakes kept his left arm steady in the air, his body moving fluidly with the bull. Once that buzzer sounded, he leapt from the bull, and my mind went to his ankle, but then I noticed how he landed. A duck and roll—a perfect execution to keep all weight off his ankle. The crowd roared when he stood, and the announcers even commented on the flawless landing. He scored an eighty-nine—the highest of the night so far and now the time to beat.

He ran to the chute and climbed his way back over the metal bars as the bull fighters wrangled the bull back in the pen. Once he came up to the grate, he used his teeth to pull his gloves off and let out a sigh.

"I'm honestly kind of glad this week is over." He heaved, his eyes filled with both excitement and exhaustion. "A few more before a break. I'm ready to get to that ranch...relax a bit in between trainings. You down for that, Emmy?" He gave me a crooked grin.

I grinned at him and felt the heat rise in my chest as I watched him breathe in and out, his shoulders rising and falling with each inhale. His hair was messy from the helmet, even his beard was sticking in all directions. There was a flush to his cheeks, and his eyes were darting from place to place. His body was leaning to the right, but there was a crocked smile to his lips, and he never looked more perfect.

What I wouldn't give to kiss him again.

And again.

If we went to that ranch with the tension and heat that was between us now, we wouldn't be relaxing in the way he—and I— needed.

Okay, time to nip this in the bud.

"Oakes," I said before I could stop myself. "Can we..." I swallowed. "Talk?"

Oakes's eyes landed on me, and he gave me a single nod, grabbing my wrist and pulling me off the grate, back to the quiet of the hallway. I timed it out in my head. There were five other riders. If they each qualified and took their time getting on the bull...

Basically, I didn't have a lot of time here.

"About last night," I began, not exactly sure how to keep going.

"I crossed a line." Oakes filled the emptiness that was growing between us. "I'm sorry. I shouldn't have kissed you. I meant what I said. That I've been wanting to since the moment I saw you. I...I would..." His head dropped, and a few breaths left his lungs, then he raised his chin, and those brown eyes I had found myself wanting to get lost in met mine. "I would kiss you right now if I could."

"I have a lot riding on this assignment, Oakes," I mumbled, closing my eyes to avoid the lust that was growing in his.

"I know, but I'd like to think this is more than an assignment to you."

I swallowed, forcing myself to look at him, I nodded. "It is. This could be life-changing, and...as..." I sighed, which sounded more like a pleasure release than relief, "amazing as last night was—"

"It was the best kiss of my life," he interrupted me, taking a step forward, and I gasped as his eyes bored into me.

"As amazing as it was," I said again, "we can't. You're—for lack of a better description—*Rodeo Ways'* client, and Morgan is already upset we veered off the schedule..."

"Do you regret it?"

"The kiss?"

"Any of it?"

I heard the crowd cheer in the background, a faint reminder that a rider was done. I heard the announcer's muffled voice call off a seventy-eight, and still with the noise and bangs from boots on rafters, Oakes's concentration was on me. I could see everything in his eyes, every moment we spent together. It was all there in the sea of brown.

Finally, I shook my head. "No. Not one minute of it."

He nodded. "I don't either."

My eyes fluttered closed as I felt him get closer to me, the heat from his breath hitting my skin just right.

"I have a job to do, Oakes. It's important to me that I do this right," I reminded him—or maybe I was reminding myself? "I need to finish this article and prove to *Rodeo Way* that I'm worth that promotion. That this is where I'm supposed to be."

Oakes raised a single brow. "So, what I'm hearing you say is...*after* the article is done"—a long muffled groan came from the crowd— "after your assignment is over and I'm no longer a client"—my heart skipped a beat—"I can kiss you again?"

I stood frozen, every sound happening around us muted as the only thing I could hear became my heartbeat. *Thump. Thump. Thump.*

Oakes took the last step that separated us, and using his thumb and forefinger, he lifted my chin. Our eyes met—more intense than ever before—and my entire body turned to Jell-O.

"That's okay," he whispered. "I'm a patient man."

His thumb swiped my bottom lip, the callus creating the most perfect friction there. He dropped his hand and took a single step back.

"Ashford!" a man called from behind us. "You're taking the night!"

Oakes gave me a smile. "You gonna get photos of this? Pretty sure I just won the Reno Rodeo."

I blinked. Once...twice...three times before I gave him a smile in return. "Wouldn't miss this moment for the world."

To: e.flynn@rodeowaymag.com, s.krass@rodeowaym
   ag.com
From: M.Spencer@rodeowaymag.com
Subject: Reno Follow Up
Date: June 29th: 8:17 AM

   Emersyn,

   Great photos and snips from Reno. Glad to see
Oakes won and that things remained according
to plan. Please send the latest developments.
Attached is a questionnaire we'd like you to
complete. We'll be watching the schedule closely.

   Please send your introduction for approval. We
want to see what you have been doing. Your due
date for the article has been pushed up. Please
have your final draft to Sterling by July 20th.
He has requested more time with it before we get
a proof ready.

   Please be more active in the WhatsApp chat.
The purpose of the chat is to communicate
expectations with our clients, but no one is
using it.

   Morgan
   Editor in Chief - Rodeo Way Magazine
   Denver, Co

Attachment:

- How did you find Idaho—Hartwell Hills—to train?

- Where did you attend high school/college?

- Are you currently dating anyone, or what do you look for in a romantic partner?

- Where do you see yourself five years from now?

- Is Oakes Ashford your real name?

CHAPTER TWENTY-ONE
Oakes

C ody, Wyoming...89.

Emersyn got that on camera, and that night, she showed me every single photo. I had seen photos of myself plenty of times, but this was different.

I wanted to pull her in my arms and thread my fingers in her hair.

West Jordan, Utah...78.

Emersyn leaned against my shoulder during the drone show, claiming it was the best view as she raised her camera to her eyes.

I wanted to trace her jawline and kiss her, deep and slow.

Oakley, Utah...76. 79. 87.

Emersyn took videos of the flag girls carrying the American flag and every sponsor flag that lit up under the fireworks, and she had a gleam to her as she told me about a story of her flag girl days.

But all I saw was the way the red and blue from the fireworks glowed in her hair.

Casper, Wyoming...85.

Nephi, Utah...90.

Then, we were back in Wyoming.

"I need to tell my mom I'm here." She smiled, pulling her phone from her back pocket. "She'll want to watch this one to see if she can catch me on camera."

"I'm normally the one on camera." I smirked.

Emersyn let out a breath through her nose and tilted her head, giving me an eyeroll. "She'll still watch, then she'll text me about it and talk about *you*," she grunted, elbowing me in the side.

I chuckled and glanced at the stands. They were jam packed, people ready for a show. It was peak rodeo season, after all. People from all over the state flocked to the stands, and every cowboy was bouncing from rodeo to rodeo to rodeo. It felt good to be back in Wyoming. This wasn't our first trip to my home state, but the time spent in Cody and Casper...my focus was elsewhere. Bull, drive, bull, drive. Zero time to think about anything else other than getting the checks. I was ready to slow down.

This particular rodeo in Laramie was the one my brother, Hayes, would always try to make it to, whether by himself or with a few of his friends...but that was when he lived in the city, years ago. Currently, I knew he was on the farm with my mom, and Mom never came to my rodeos.

It didn't bother me that she didn't. She kept up on my scores and standings, and then she would text or call to ask how things were. She'd always listen and be supportive in her own way, just being in the actual arena was still too much for her, and honestly, I didn't blame her. I used the rodeo as a way to build myself back up after what happened, the reason to keep going. To her, it was too close to the memory of the night when we almost lost everything.

And now, here in Wyoming with Emersyn, only added to the guilt that I still hadn't told her anything about who I was and what she meant to me.

That kiss—damn, I still thought about that kiss.

And the past three weeks had really tested my patience when it came to her. If all I had to do was wait until the article was over to kiss her again, to have her, then I'd wait. But should I be waiting that long to tell her everything?

I had to open up at some point. I knew the moment I told her my real name she would remember everything, that maybe everything would click and we could start fresh. No more hiding, no more longing looks. Except, I didn't want those looks to fade.

I saw them; she wasn't very discreet about it. I noticed the way she studied me getting ready, the way her eyes lingered on my hands and arms as I readied the bull. I could almost predict she was telling herself this was for her article, that she was simply doing her job in observing me, but with the way her chest would rise and how she would have to pull herself back to the camera, told me she still thought about that kiss too.

Over the past weeks, we talked. We laughed. We joked. We...flirted. We touched without realizing it. Everything was easy with her.

Telling her everything would be just as easy.

All I had to do was say, *"Emersyn...it's me...that kid from sixteen years ago...that kid that you gave confidence to...that kid who..."*

"Ashford!" I heard the hand shout my name. "Chute four!"

"You lost over there?" Emersyn said, a smile on her lips as she tilted her head away from her camera. "You look like you were thinking about something."

I raised a corner of my lips. "Yeah, I was." I cleared my throat. "You mentioning your mom made me think of my family. My brother used to come to this rodeo."

"Is he here today?" She beamed. "Do I get to meet him?"

"Nah." I shook my head and reached in my back pocket for my gloves. "Casper was closer, so if he were to come to any, it would have been that one. He's...working."

"What about your mom? Does she come to your rides? Why have I never met her?"

You have...several times. "She, uh..." I hesitated, wondering how much of this I wanted to share tonight. I wanted to tell her...just not now. This was the closest I could get: "She doesn't come to rodeos. It's too much after—" I inhaled, stopping.

Sensing my hesitation, she lightly dropped her camera and touched my bicep gently. The touch caused a zing to rush up to my chest, and I met her gaze. Understanding flashed in her blue irises, and I had to remind myself that I couldn't kiss her. Not even a small peck.

"That's too bad," she sighed. "Maybe once the article is out? I'd love to meet your family."

I raised a brow at her. "Is that a hint of something more after this assignment is done?"

She bit her bottom lip. "Don't you have to get to chute four?" She pointed her thumb over her shoulder.

I waggled my eyebrows at her, stepping away from her touch to start pulling my gloves on. "Yeah, you do too. Come on, Miss Rodeo Wyoming."

"Shh..." she hissed. "Nobody has recognized me yet, and I'd like to keep it that way," she whispered.

"Seriously?"

"Have you not noticed the hat? The hair pulled back? The way I'm dressed completely different. If I wore what I normally did here, they'd flag me instantly, and I'd rather not be noticed."

For the first time tonight, I looked at the way she was dressed: tee half-tucked into her bell-bottom jeans, her normal brown boots, and as she mentioned, her hair was in a low ponytail, her brown hat lower than it normally was. No makeup donned her face, and yet she was still the most breathtaking woman I'd ever seen.

Just tell her...right now...

Emmy... It's me. It's A—

"It's been a long time since I've been in this arena, and I really don't want to make a show of it. I'm not sure if they would, but I'm not here for that." She raised her camera. "I have a job to do...remember?"

"Got it. No more Miss Rodeo Wyoming comments." I gave her a nod.

"Thank you. Now"—she dropped her tone—"chute four." She pointed to the chutes, and I chuckled, following her instruction to head there.

Laramie, Wyoming...94.

And I didn't tell Emersyn anything.

Hayes

a 94. Damn.

Oakes

Keep watching, little bro.

Hayes

You know we watch like a hawk. You coming home after training this year?

Oakes

Can't. I got a magazine following me.

Hayes

No shit? Which one?

Oakes

Rodeo Way.

Hayes

And you're just now telling us.

Oakes

Mom knew. Not my fault if she didn't tell you.

Hayes

Damn. Why are you so special?

Oakes

Been asking myself the same thing, but you'll never guess who the reporter is.

Hayes

Who?

Oakes

Emersyn Flynn.

Hayes

Well, damn.

CHAPTER TWENTY-TWO
Emersyn

*O*akes Ashford, rising bull rider well on his way to the National Final Rodeo this year, stands at the ready, patiently waiting his turn to jump on the back of the bull and take the world by storm. With his hands on his hips, he sways, the fringe of his chaps moving with him, his helmet bobbing back and forth. What could be going through his head at this exact moment? The cheer of the crowd? The Bon Jovi song blasting in the background? Nope. Oakes is just clearing his head, breathing, telling himself the exact same words over and over as he prepares. The same words that have been repeating in his mind for the past sixteen years...

"I tell myself that one ride doesn't define my future. That no matter what happens now or tomorrow or the next ride, I was meant to be on the back of an animal, and it's now or never. I close my eyes. I breathe. I repeat those words over and over. Then...I nod. I put my entire focus into the beast underneath me. In those eight seconds, nothing else matters. Nothing."

He readies himself on the bull, making sure his right hand is secure, before he leans back, raises his left arm, and gives the nod. Once that chute opens and the bull spins, you can see Oakes Ashford in his element, doing the one thing he was meant to do over everything else.

If you look closely at his left hand, you'll see a scar stretching from his knuckles to his wrist. He wears it like a badge, showing that even he knows he's in one of the most dangerous professions in the world. The scar on his hand marks the start of his career, only reminding him that nothing can stop him, not even an inju—

"We're here."

Oakes's voice pulled me from my computer mid-sentence just in time to see the wooden archway as we drove underneath it, the rustic metal sign spreading from one side to the other, the deep-brown letters standing out against the green landscape.

I instantly closed my laptop and shifted in my seat, taking in everything for the first time since getting in the truck. The drive from Utah to a no-name town in Idaho was spent in silence for the majority of the trip. I was immersed in my article, knowing this was my time to finish it before I had to send it off. The Fourth of July craziness was over, Oakes was ready to train, and I could concentrate on my article. My plan was to finish it early, with the hopes of revising it before sending it off to Sterling, and just...relax. Especially after seeing the scenery.

"Okay, this is the most beautiful place I've ever seen." I jumped from the cab of the truck, taking in the surroundings of the ranch around me, grabbing my camera bag and swinging it over my shoulder.

"Taking pictures, Emmy?" Oakes chuckled, coming up to my side.

"Have you seen it here?" I responded.

His laugh grew, and that same flutter sparked in my belly. "I have, looking at it right now."

I had known of the Hartwell family and their ranch, but mainly I followed their rodeo stats. Rhett Hartwell had won the NFR before he retired. His brother, Wyatt, was a well-known broadcaster, and their cousin, Lachlan, had retired suddenly, never to be seen in the rodeo circuits again. This was a family that breathed rodeo, but their ranch was a whole other world. The green rolling hills flowed perfectly into the mountain backdrop with the lush colors of summer making everything more vibrant than normal. Bright-green grass with pinks and yellows popping out around the buildings brought complete magic to the area. The white stable stood out against the green, the sign above the entryway reading *Nova Luna Stables and Indoor Arena*, catching my eye as Oakes made his way inside like he owned the place.

"I can't wait to go for a ride, take some photos."

"We have all week, Emmy. Come on, let's see if anyone is in here." Oakes quickly made his way into the stables entrance.

I followed him, turning around to take everything in one more time, only to be greeted by a gorgeous dapple gray the moment I stepped into the stable. Its nostrils flared as I took a step forward.

"Well, hello, gorgeous." I smiled, reaching out to let the horse sniff my hand.

"That's Pepper," Oakes's voice came up from behind me. "She's an old gal." He reached out, scratching behind Pepper's ear.

"She's stunning." I stroked her forelock, loving the small puff of air she breathed.

"Don't let her hear you say that. It may go to her head." Gently, he placed his hand on my lower back. "Come meet Zee."

"Zee? Who's that?"

"My horse."

My eyes widened. "You board your horse here?"

He nodded, guiding me toward the other row of stalls, and I finally took in just how large this stable was. It had to have more than twenty horses in it and a few empty stalls. Not even the stables I grew up with had this many horses. It was massive.

"Well, yeah, I can't very well take him to every rodeo, now can I?"

Near the end of the row, a dark-brown horse with a white nose popped his nose out of the stall, a whine coming from him as Oakes got closer. His head began to move up and down, his lips forming what I took as a smile. He let out a huff and neigh as soon as Oakes was close, his nose brushing up against him.

"I thought you said he lived on the farm?" I smiled, loving the interaction between Oakes and his gelding. I knew that if I were to see Mable now, she'd react the same way. I felt a pinch in my chest, suddenly regretting not going to see her while we were in Wyoming. We had been there three times in the past few weeks, and I hadn't gone to see my family once. I bit my lip and looked over at Oakes.

"Nah, you assumed. I said he was alive and happy. Happy here. On the ranch. Abi spoils all the horses." Oakes reached up, giving his horse more affection than Pepper. He bobbed his head and let out an even louder neigh, which caused a chain reaction from every other horse in the stable. "We'll go out tomorrow, boy, I promise." Oakes cooed at the horse.

I inhaled.

"So, what's the plan for training?" I asked, reaching up to stroke Zee's nose.

"Ride as many bulls as I can. Ride as much as I can. Sleep as much as I can." Oakes raised a brow at me, looking at me from the corner of his eye. His lip twitched into a smile as he turned back to Zee.

"How many bulls is 'as many bulls as I can'?"

"Last time he was here…" a deep Southern drawl approached us, making both of us turn our heads. The man approached, his tawny skin covered with a sheen of sweat, a small smile on his face as he sauntered up. "I think it was every bull on site, some a few times. Guy's relentless."

"Hey, Cash." Oakes smiled, a laugh filtering through the air as he removed his hand from my back, that I didn't even realize was still there until it was gone, and made his way toward the man.

Cash Callahan, one of the top trainers in the rodeo world, grasped Oakes's hand and gave it a firm shake, both men obviously happy to see each other. I smiled, watching the exchange, keeping my hand on Zee's nose as he relished in the attention.

"They have—what?" Oakes slapped Cash's shoulder before turning back to me. "Forty bulls on site?"

"I think, but that's a question for Lach. I only know the arena schedule." Cash shoved his hands in his pockets. "You gonna introduce me?" He turned to Oakes, nudging his head in my direction.

"Emersyn, this is—"

"Cash Callahan, I'm Emersyn Flynn." I reached out my hand to him, shocked it didn't hurt or break my hand after seeing his shake with Oakes. "I'm Oakes's shadow this summer. I'm with *Rodeo Way*. Nice to meet you. I've followed your career for years."

He raised a brow. "Really? I haven't heard that in a long time."

"Pop quiz," Oakes chuckled.

It was our first *pop quiz* in weeks, and it made my stomach flip. Cocking my head, sticking a pose that said *bring it*, I stared at Oakes.

"What was Cash's average score from the year"—Oakes narrowed his eyes and looked up at the ceiling like he was trying to get the question from the rafter—"2019?"

Cash scoffed. "Like she would know a specific—"

"Average score for Cash Callahan in 2019 was 79.8. You almost made it to the NFR that year and had to retire the next."

"Well, damn." Cash let out a deep laugh. "I'm impressed. Nice to meet you, Emersyn." He turned back to Oakes, the smile still radiating, his chest basically puffing with pride. "The bunkhouse is ready for you. You're welcome to unpack. And I take it Emersyn is staying with you?"

"Sure," I said, more confident than I'd imagined.

"No," Oakes said at the same time.

We both glanced over at each other. "I mean," Oakes began, "if you wanted to find a room in town, I wouldn't be offended."

I opened my mouth the speak, but Cash beat me to it.

"Last I checked, it was all booked up," Cash stated.

"Oakes." I lightly touched his arm, the shiver touching my fingertips. "I'm fine with it if you are."

Oakes gave me a short smile, bringing his lips to my ear. "You sure?" he whispered so only I could hear.

Arching my back, I gave him a quick nod and said louder so even Cash could hear, "You're not scared by only one bed, are you?"

"There's a pull-out couch," Cash added.

"See"—I pointed to Cash—"problem solved. Mr. Callahan—"

"Nope...don't like that." Cash shook his head, turning his back. "Call me Cash."

"Cash," I corrected myself. "Could I unpack the truck into the bunkhouse?"

"Sure thing, sweetheart. Right this way. See ya soon, Oakes." Cash waved a hand in the air as he left.

"I can get a room in town. There has to be somewhere that's—"

"Cash said everything was full."

"Emmy...my patience is wearing thin."

I raised my eyebrow. His *patience* was wearing thin. I tightened my lips, forcing the grin to stay down. "What patience, Oakes?"

He took one long deep breath, and his eyes traveled to my lips.

Oh, that patience.

I'm a patient man...

"I'll sleep on the pull-out couch—"

"No, you won't."

"—and have you just pretend I'm not even here." I waved my hand in the air, erasing his comment he snuck in there.

"That's the second time you've said that to me."

"It's true. Just pretend I'm not here." I lifted my brow, turning my body to follow Cash out of the stable.

But I still heard him mutter, "Impossible."

The bunkhouse was a lot smaller than I thought it would be. It was basically one room, a couch separating the bedroom and living area, and the only doors led to the bathroom, closet, and outside. It was a cozy spot, and the Hartwells had decorated it well. From what Oakes told me, the youngest Hartwell, Wyatt, used to live here before he moved out. Now it was open to clients who rented the arena for longer stays. Like Oakes.

I made myself comfortable, using the small dresser in the living room for my clothes, and unfolded the couch. It didn't look very comfortable, but it would do. I laid a blanket out on the thin mattress and grabbed a pillow from the bed, and once it was made, I turned and fell back onto it—my spine instantly connecting with the metal bar.

"Ow..." I groaned.

"And that," I heard Oakes's voice, "is why you are not sleeping on that damn bed."

"It's not bad." I didn't move, laying my hands on my stomach. "I could fall asleep right now." I closed my eyes, hearing only his footsteps as he came close to me—five total, that was how small this place was.

"It looks pitiful."

I responded with a hum. "I'm unpacked. What's the plan?" I opened my eyes and glanced up at him. He stood with his arms folded over his chest, his legs slightly spread, and those brown eyes trained on me, his stance reminding me of the night we spent under the stars...

"I'm going to unpack and then head into town to get groceries for the week. Any requests?" He tilted his head.

"Veggies and ranch. Apples and oranges. Avocados. Spaghetti—the protein kind for you. Hamburgers and chicken."

"How about"—he dropped his arms, bending at the waist before he grabbed my wrist—"you come with me?"

"Only if you agree that I sleep on the pull-out." I let him pull me from the mattress, the metal bar digging into my spine again, and I held in my groan of pain.

"Fine."

"Then, yeah, I'll go. Let's get you unpacked."

We worked together, soft conversation flowing between us as we unpacked Oakes's suitcase. Once our suitcases were away in the closet, we left, waving to Rhett Hartwell and his daughter as we drove down the dirt road to the store. It was domestic almost, shopping with Oakes and picking out things we could make together. Lately on this trip, it had been diners and quick meals, and I would be lying to myself if I said I wasn't looking forward to this. Homecooked meals with Oakes. Waking up and falling asleep in the same space as Oakes. An entire week to ourselves. No emails from Morgan, no phone calls from Drew, no rushing to get to the next rodeo. Just us...and I could almost see it.

I just had to write this damn article first...and then...*then* it could possibly happen.

Once we got back to the ranch, I pulled my phone out to text Luca a quick update.

Me

Made it to the ranch for training week. I'm going to go hard on this article. So…would you hate me if I put my phone on DND?

Luca

Only while you're writing. How is the place? I've never been. Always wanted to go to the rodeo there.

Me

It's stunning. I'll send some photos tomorrow once I go out and explore a little bit. Plan is to get the article done so I can focus on other things.

Luca

Is that other thing Oakes?

Scoffing, I locked my phone and went to toss it on the pull-out couch—only to find Oakes sprawled out on it.

I hunched my shoulders. "We made a deal." I glowered.

"You…" he sighed, "are not sleeping on this bed."

Chapter Twenty-Three
Oakes

The pull-out couch was, by far, the worst thing I had ever attempted to sleep on. And I had slept in some weird places. The crease that formed when you folded it didn't want to be flattened. The small springs dug into my back, and no matter where I moved, they followed me. My feet hung off the edge, and the stupid oven light blinked in my eyes. The fact that Emersyn told me she would sleep here was laughable. She wouldn't have gotten any sleep on this thing. She finally relented, and I won that battle in the end.

"Oakes," Emersyn's voice fluttered through the dark. "You awake?"

"I've always wondered how someone was supposed to answer that." I shifted, looking toward the space where the queen-sized bed sat.

The studio apartment above the bunkhouse was the perfect size for one person and one person only. Spanning six hundred square feet, the apartment had a wide-open layout. The small living area and kitchen were shoved into one tiny space, and the bed was far enough away that I assumed Emersyn was fast asleep by now. It had been so quiet over there I couldn't even hear her breathing.

"You say, 'Yup, can't sleep because I insisted on taking this sad excuse for a pull-out and not the insanely comfortable bed I normally sleep in while I'm here.'" She deepened her voice, mimicking me in the best way possible.

Thank God she couldn't see my smile.

The fact that we could still joke and tease even after I kissed her senseless was a good sign. The fact that she still let me touch her at times and the way she would stare was an even better sign. But I knew if I climbed in that bed with her, I would want more than kisses, more than touches. I would want her. For the first time since we had begun this adventure, this was our first time in the same confined space overnight. When we camped, it was easy to not think about her, but in the privacy of my own hotel room, she was constantly on my mind. And now she was just feet away in a bed big enough for the two of us. I told her I was a patient man...and I still had so much to tell her before I could do more than kiss her.

And that was why I would stay right here in this bed.

When I didn't respond, I heard Emersyn heave a long sigh. "Oakes, just get your ass over here. It's a big enough bed. We're both adults."

"I'm fine here, thanks," I muttered, lacing my fingers over my bare stomach as if to shove every thought I had further down.

"Oakes. Ashford," she grumbled, and then I heard the comforter ruffle and feet gently hit the wood floor then stomp over to me. Ten steps, that was all it took until she was standing right in front of me, her arms folded over her chest, staring down at me. "Get your ass over in that bed right now. You're training and need the rest."

"Emmy—"

"Shove it and get in that bed." Raising her arm, she pointed at the bed. "Do not make me tell you again."

I held back my smile now that she could see me, but my lips twisted, and my eyebrows bounced. She just glowered.

God damn she was cute.

As much as I wanted to resist, to stay right here, the glower on her face told me she wasn't going to give up as easily as she did before. Her finger still stood, hovering in the air, pointing at the bed, and her brow raised. As soon as this woman had kids, they would get the full wrath of this look.

"Okay, fine." I held back a chuckle, trying to sound annoyed as I flipped the flimsy blanket from my torso and sat up, coming up to her just in time to see her turn and walk back to the bed.

She crawled in, pulling the covers to her chest. Not bothering to grab a shirt, I took her ten steps in seven, coming up to the opposite side of the bed, lifting the covers, and sliding my body in. Already I could feel the difference. The sheets were soft, the Memory Foam melted to my weight, and the down pillow was exactly what my head needed.

I settled, letting out a deep sigh of relief.

"Better?" Emersyn asked.

I turned to look at her, realizing our shoulders were barely touching, her body heat already making me warmer as it radiated from her into me.

Stay on your side of the bed.

"Much," I muttered. "Thank you."

Shifting, she turned her body to face me, her hand slipping under her pillow. "So," she sighed, "what's on the agenda tomorrow?"

"Ride a few bulls, strength train, and a ride."

"Are you going to ride Zee?"

I nodded. "Who else would I ride?"

"Pepper?" Emersyn smiled, the slight tease in her voice reminding me that we were okay—and that thought reminded me not to kiss her.

"Not sure if Pepper would appreciate riding bareback," I retorted.

"Bareback?" The look of shock spread across her face, her eyes widening. "You're riding bareback? I used to love riding Mable bareback. Just her and me. I felt like it helped us bond—if that makes any sense."

"It does. It's also a great way to train. Really works my legs." I turned to face her, mirroring her position. "You gonna ride tomorrow?"

"Can I?" she asked, lifting her head softly off the pillow.

"Cash's wife, Abi...she owns the stables and takes care of all the horses. I'm sure she has a calm one we can get you on." I waggled my eyebrows at her, licking my bottom lip.

"A calm one? Ha, sure. You're going to make her think I've never ridden before."

"They don't have any trick horses here, Emmy." I raised a brow.

Her lips twisted as her eyes fluttered back and forth, holding my contact. Her lips parted as a soft, sweet sigh filled the space between us, seeming to replace words that were hanging in the air. She blinked a few times before scooting closer to me still, our noses inches apart.

Licking her lips, she spoke softly. "I may regret saying this later, but out of all the people that call me Emmy...I honestly love it when you call me that."

Damn, I could kiss her right now.

"Goodnight, Emmy."

"Goodnight, Oakes."

Seven bulls in, fifty-six total seconds, and my body was feeling it.

After a while, Emersyn joined, saying her brain was starting to ache because of the words on the screen and that she needed a change of scenery. Even though Cash suggested she take a walk around the ranch and see it in all its glory, she raised her camera and replied that this was exactly where she wanted to be. Emersyn circled the indoor training arena, taking photos and talking to Abi, staying clear of the bulls. I had to give it to her—she let me focus. She didn't ask any questions. She didn't get up close and personal. She just watched.

Once that part of the day was done and the bulls were back in their pens, I went to get Zee ready for our first ride in months. Like I told Emersyn last night, riding bareback was the perfect way to strengthen my lower body, and even though I'd be sore the next day, Zee was used to riding with no saddle. He was used to my weight, used to my cues. That horse knew me inside and out, and I couldn't wait to be on his back.

I stepped in his stall, grabbing the rein and bit that hung on the inside of the gate. Zee stomped his foot, ready for a ride. The horse in the next stall bobbed her head, letting out a heavy huff.

"You wanna ride too?" I asked the Carmello horse to Zee's left.

The mare nodded her head, the bangs on her head flapping up and down.

A quick look back in the arena told me that Emersyn was still talking with Abi, the two of them smiling as they looked at the camera. What I wouldn't give to have her ride with me. Have her to myself for a few hours until the next step of training commenced.

"You wouldn't mind company, right, boy?" I asked Zee, slipping the lead around his neck, fitting the bit in his mouth. The head nod and stomp of his foot told me he didn't care in the slightest. "You're gonna love her," I told him quietly, leading him from the stall.

Instead of turning to the right to exit the stable, I led him back into the arena, catching Emersyn's and Abi's attention.

"Emmy." I smiled at her. "You gonna join me or what?"

A smile tugged at her lips. "I'd love to. Could I borrow a horse?" she asked Abi, excitement beaming off of her.

Abi gave her a quick nod. "I'll grab you a saddle."

"Actually," Emersyn stopped her, "could I ride bareback?"

CHAPTER TWENTY-FOUR
Emersyn

Riding bareback was a skill, for the rider and the horse, and thankfully, I grew up on those skills. Riding a horse bareback was easier than riding a bike for me. I could climb on any horse, get a feel for their movements almost instantly, and then before I knew it, the horse and I were one being. I loved riding bareback. It was more intimate than anything else, and Abi Callahan gave me the best horse.

Her name was North, a gorgeous Carmella that lived next to Zee, and she was more excited than I was. I gently stroked her nose, cooing as she learned my voice. I led her to the block, stepping up slowly and hoisting myself onto her back.

"Attagirl." I leaned forward, stroking her neck and mane. Kicking her forward, I felt her back move, every muscle flexing with each step. Straightening my back, I watched as Oakes grabbed Zee's mane and swung himself onto the horse's back. Zee bobbed his head and began to move the instant Oakes was settled.

Oakes gripped the reins and, in one fluid motion, kicked Zee into a run.

And I just watched in awe as Oakes moved with the horse below him, his legs putting just the right amount of pressure on Zee's sides with one hand holding the reins, the other free at his side. The gleam on Oakes's face was pure perfection, and I was suddenly heartbroken I handed my camera off to Abi and that I couldn't capture this moment in time. As amazing as Oakes was on a bull, he was absolutely brilliant on the back of a horse.

Clicking my tongue, giving North a quick kick, I pulled her into a gallop to catch up with Oakes. We ran, side by side, until we reached the mountains that framed the valley, finding a trail that led up and up.

"Follow me." Oakes waved his arm. "You gotta see the best view here." Twisting his torso, he turned to looked at me over his shoulder, giving his hat a quick adjust before turning back to the trail. "There's a ledge, and the horses can rest. Will you be able to get up without the block? I'm sure there are plenty of rocks."

Even though he wasn't facing me anymore, I could feel his smirk on his face just from the tease in his voice. It was most likely cocked to the left side, a single dimple on his cheek. It was one of his sexy smirks, one that had annoyance yet a spark of joy that came with the tease.

"Hey," I bit back, "I don't need a block to mount a horse. Trick rider, remember?"

"I dunno," he mumbled, "North is a pretty tall horse."

"Stop being a dick. I can do that fancy move just as flawless as you can."

"Fancy move?"

"You grabbed onto Zee's mane and basically flipped yourself up." *It was damn sexy,* I added in my head. He didn't need to know all my thoughts.

A laugh flew through the air. "I can only do that with Zee. Any other horse would kill me." Zee moved off to the side of the trail, forcing Oakes to duck down so he wouldn't get hit by a branch. "It's not far, so just enjoy the scenery."

And with that, the teasing was gone, and we were silent. Like he suggested, I took in my surroundings, loving the way the earth moved here. It was untouched and perfect—something I didn't see much of in Colorado anymore. The rodeos back home were hidden in the buildings, the dirt surrounded by concrete. This was the world I grew up in, the world I loved. But as we pressed on, the scenery became the least of my focus.

Oakes and Zee walked calmly in front of me, Zee sneaking a few leaves here and there as the trees grew denser. Oakes's back was straight, even as he swayed with Zee's movements. His hips flexed, his feet moved in circles, and his left arm would reach out to his side, his fingers feeling the leaves that Zee didn't manage to take. He was just as relaxed as I was, and soon, Oakes began to whistle. I focused on the tune, recognizing it instantly. A song that would play during rodeos back in high school, a classic country song.

"I love this song," I muttered under my breath, finding myself softly singing as he hummed and whistled.

After a while, time didn't matter. The only thing that did was me, Oakes, and the horses we were on, but sooner than I hoped, Oakes slowed Zee, coming to a clearing on the top of the mountain. Giving Zee a pat, he dismounted, stretched his back, and walked over to North.

"Here." He held out a hand. "Let me help." His eyes met mine, heavy with...something. I wished I could read him better. I would dissect everything that sat in that mind of his. There was still that spark of familiarity there that I had tried to ignore, but now his eyes boring into me...it struck like lighting. I had been with him for almost two months now; I knew the way he moved and spoke. I knew his smiles and the tones his voice would carry...yet those eyes. There was still so much hidden there.

Something he wasn't telling me.

Without hesitation, I reached out for him, ignoring his hand and placing both of my palms on his shoulders. Swinging my leg over, I slid from

North's back, Oakes's hands finding my waist with ease as my body went flush against his. Raising my chin, I took him in, not wanting to leave this spot, sandwiched between him and a horse. My legs ached, but I was comfortable right where I was. North had another idea. She huffed, free of the weight on her back, and made her way over to where Zee began to nibble on grass. Oakes let out a sigh, his chest rising and falling deep before he let go of my waist, taking a step back.

"You gotta see this view." He stumbled over his words, his fingers trailing down my arm to my hand, where instantly they wrapped around my palm. He pulled me toward the clearing.

And the breath left my lungs.

It was the most beautiful place I had ever seen in my entire life. The mountains cascaded as far as you could see, the greens and yellows popping out in spurts of color. I could just imagine seeing this place in the winter, with snow-capped tips, or in the fall, with the vibrant colors creating the perfect watercolor painting.

"God, I wish I had my camera," I breathed, raising my hand to cover the sun from my eyes.

"Not sure if *Rodeo Way* wants this for their article." Oakes sighed, putting his hands on his hips.

"Oh, hell no, that photo would be just for me. Just like—" I stopped myself. *The photo at Lake Tahoe.* I edited it after he had kissed me, and I couldn't find anything to change about it. It was perfection. He and I were the only ones who knew about it. I hadn't even told Luca about that photo. That photo was still mine, not for *Rodeo Way.*

"Just like what?" Oakes asked, his question pulling my attention to him. He was looking at me, not the view, his eyes not even squinting, thanks to his hat.

I shook my head. "That photo of you that I took at Lake Tahoe."

"Ah." He lifted his chin. "The staged one where I had to pretend you weren't there."

"Yeah." I looked at my boot, shoving my toe into the ground. "It's a fantastic photo. It's mine," I admitted.

"Yours?" he parroted.

Nodding, I looked back at the view. "*Rodeo Way* doesn't need everything. As much as they may want it, they don't need it."

"They don't need everything?" Oakes repeated softly. I turned to him.

"Well, they want everything. They want you. Personal life and all. But that photo...they can't have."

"They really want all the juicy stuff, don't they?" He shifted on his heels, kicking a rock that sat on the dirt.

I let out a small groan. "They do, but I'm not giving them that. I've kept the article professional, and I stuck to the guidelines we set. I do have some questions they want me to ask, but..." I inhaled, feeling my chest rise. "I haven't even read the questionnaire through all the way."

"What are some of the questions?" he asked, his brows furrowed.

I scoffed. "Well, the first one is asking if Oakes Ashford is a pseudonym. I responded and told Morgan I wouldn't be asking that question."

"Why not?"

"There are some things the world doesn't need to know, Oakes. They don't need to know where you went to high school, or where you spend your days off. They don't need to know if you're dating anyone. They don't need to know what kind of boxers you wear—"

"Boxer briefs," he cut me off, and I turned to him, my lips forming a tight, amused smile. He mimicked it. "Regular boxers are too loose in my Wranglers."

With a chuckle, I added, "I'll make sure to add that to the article."

"Okay, Emmy..." He took a step toward me, the tone in his voice carrying...intrigue? Once again, I wished I could read him better. "I'll tell you something personal about me, but I want something about you first. You tell me something that makes you...you, and I'll tell you something that has shaped me into the man I am now. But I want to know you first."

"The article isn't about me, Oakes." I tilted my head, dropping my arm and turning my back from the view.

"This isn't about the article. This is about me getting to know you, and you getting to know me because, Emmy...I really want to get to know you more. And I'd like to think that you want to get to know me more. I can see it when you look at me, so let's shove *Rodeo Way* out of the equation for one moment." He took a single step, dropping his arms. "This moment is ours, right?" I looked at him and nodded. "Then tell me something about you...that makes you...you."

What makes me...me?

Former rodeo queen.

Trick rider.

Digital editor at *Rodeo Way*.

Photographer...journalist.

Passionate about the rodeo.

But he knew all that.

Licking my lips, I thought of the one story no one really knew. The one story that has never left my memory. That had inspired me for the past decade...and in reality, I had no idea if it helped who it was meant for or if it just helped me.

But this was what made me...me.

Heaving a deep sigh, I turned to look at Oakes. "Okay. You know I come from a small town in Wyoming." He nodded. "Well, in that town, there are no homecoming dances, there's homecoming rodeos."

"Naturally."

"And my senior year, I was the Homecoming Rodeo Queen." I gave him a stupid bow. "The night of the homecoming rodeo, I did a few tricks, held the firework and flag as the national anthem was sung, stood still for the cowboy prayer, and then I stayed behind the scenes so the cowboys could have their time. I was going to do a few tricks for a show, move the barrels in for racing, so I was just waiting for my time. Saddle bronc was first, and the first kid that went lasted the eight seconds and got a hell of a reaction from the crowd—like, he was meant to do this. I didn't him. He was a few years below me, cocky but kinda nerdy—" Oakes raised his brow, a scoff leaving his nose. "But overall, he was fun, and I think he heard the crowd and wanted to give them something more. So...instead of waiting for the pick-up men, he jumped off the horse and landed with his palms in the dirt." I held my hands out in front of me, acting out how the kid landed. "And in a second—less than a second—that bucking horse landed right on his hand." I used my fist to pound on my left hand. "His hand was shattered."

Oakes stared at me, his eyes wide, not moving. His entire body turned into stone as I talked. Swallowing, I finished my story.

"He was a wreck. Obviously, his hand was flatter than a pancake." I let out a chuckle, trying to lighten the mood, hoping it would relax him. "But the rodeo had to keep going. So even though an ambulance was called, the other cowboys rode. And I sat with him. I held his hand—the one that wasn't crushed—and I talked to him. He was worried that he was never going to ride bronc again, that this was his first time riding in front of a crowd and he messed up his entire life. His career was over before it had even begun. I told him that the best thing about riding bronc...or bulls...was that you only needed one hand to hold on, that one single ride didn't end his career, that his hand would heal and I would be seeing his name on the NFR screen in a few years. I swear he took in every word, and I can still picture his eyes on me as I spoke. The crowd was still going insane behind us, but for that moment, it was me and that kid. I think about that a lot, the words that I told him, hoping that they inspired him somehow, because hell, I had inspired myself with that speech. I wish I could remember it. I should have written it down; it probably would do me some good now, but..." I stopped, trying to find the reason why this was the story that made me...me. "I didn't. Those words were for him, not me."

"What was his name?" Oakes asked in one breath, barely audible.

I shook my head. "Slade. Ashton Slade. I knew his family. His dad was a rodeo name, and they lived in our town, but...when I Google the name Slade, the only thing that comes up is his dad, who apparently is in prison now. But I watched for him. I looked for his name everywhere. I searched for him so many times, but I never found him. So...I don't know what became of him or if he ever rode again. But that makes me *me*, because it's how I got so involved in the rodeo outside of being the rodeo royalty. Before it was the pageants and the tricks, and after that, it became knowing everything about the rodeo. Names, stats, events, rules...everything. I love this sport because of that moment."

I inhaled, finishing my story with gusto. And Oakes...

Oakes just stared at me.

"What?" I asked after a beat of silence.

"You never saw him again?"

I shook my head. "No, but that's not without trying. I wish I could see him again. He wasn't even in our town when I visited. I even asked my mom about him, but she said she wasn't sure. She thinks he bought his own land somewhere and is living peacefully."

"And his...hand..." Oakes looked at the ground beneath his feet. "What happened to his hand?"

"Not sure. I was pretty busy my senior year, but I imagine it healed. He probably had to have surgery—he may even have a killer scar now and a fantastic story to tell."

"Emmy..." Oakes took the few steps that separated us, holding out his left hand to me. His eyes were heavy, concentrated, as he studied.

Breaking the contact his eyes held, I lifted my hand to his. He let our palms touch for the briefest moment before he spun his wrist, revealing the scar I'd longed to touch so many times. The scar that started at his knuckles and went to his wrist. A small, faint gasp left my lungs as I took it in.

I traced the silver line with my fingertips, feeling the high ridge of the scar, but then finally noticing little, tiny lines that branched out like a tree that decorated his hand, in the shape of an oval...or a hoof...

How had I never *ever* noticed this...

That spark...

Those eyes...

My breath stopped.

"Oh my God," I whispered.

It was...*him.*

"You changed my life that night, Emmy. I remember every single word you said. I could write it down for you if you wanted to hear it again. It flows through my mind every time I get on the bull. You told me one ride didn't define me, that one injury wouldn't set me back, and yes...I only needed one hand to hold on to *bulls.*" His voice was a whisper. "I'm where I am...because of you. You have no idea how much you mean to me, how much I've wanted to tell you that exact story for weeks now...how for the past sixteen years...I've thought of you so many times."

My heart raced, my breath uneven as I looked up at Oakes Ashford—no Ashton Slade, seeing those eyes that I loved to get lost in, remembering the moment all those years ago when I first looked into these eyes, when they were still so full of hope, so full of admiration.

"I hoped you would remember when we kissed. I wanted to tell you then—so bad—but I couldn't figure out how. How do you tell the woman you thought you'd never see again that she changed your life, that she's the reason you kept getting on that bull? How do you tell the woman who doesn't remember you that you've loved her for longer than she knows."

"Oakes..." I muttered, breath barely leaving my lungs, right before I raised up on my toes and kissed him, taking him in with everything I had in me.

CHAPTER TWENTY-FIVE

Emersyn

O akes led me into the bunkhouse, and suddenly, the small space seemed even smaller. There was a part of me that still couldn't believe that Oakes was the same boy I spoke to that night. Sixteen years ago, he was a scrawny twig, taller than me but so thin I could wrap my arm around his waist and probably hook my elbows. Now, watching him as he moved around the kitchen to get dinner started, I squinted, trying to pull a memory of that night, trying to see how much he had changed.

His shoulders were broader, his muscles more defined. His hair was scruffier, still soft now that I had the chance to run my fingers through it, but I remember it being thin and chopped short, completely hidden by his hat. Without his beard, I probably could have recognized him, but even then, he was just so different. The years of training and work he had put in to become Oakes Ashford showed with every move he made. His body had become a piece of art, a masterpiece he took time to sculpt. The only thing that was the same...now that I really truly looked at him...was his eyes.

Those eyes were still the deep shade of brown that I could get lost in. I had, a few times, over the past couple of weeks...but why had I never made the connection?

That night stuck out in my mind, always. I didn't lie when I told him it was the reason I started looking at stats and watching rodeo after rodeo. I wanted to see him again, the kid who had something terrible happen to him, who thought his riding career was over before it even began, but when his name never came up, I still paid attention to the sport that had become my entire life.

Watching him now, a small spark shot through my stomach as I realized I had watched his entire career unfold. I had watched as he never let that one injury stop him. He listened. I just never knew.

"You're staring," Oakes said, not even looking up from stove as the water boiled for the spaghetti.

I inhaled. "It's really hard not to. You're just...so..."

"Different?" He cocked his head and smiled, placing the package of opened pasta next to the pot of water.

A chuckle rose in my throat. "So...what do I call you now? Your name is Ashton. Where did you get Oakes? And Ashford?" I asked him, sliding onto the stool on the other side of the tiny kitchen peninsula that was made to only seat one.

"Ashton Oakes Slade," he answered, "My mom always called me Oakes, so when I told her I wanted a name that wouldn't be connected to my dad...she told me she wouldn't accept anything other than Oakes. Her maiden name was Ashford. She named me Ashton to honor it, so...I used Ashford to honor her. Oakes Ashford." Oakes let out a breath, keeping his focus on the stove. "I'd prefer if you still call me Oakes."

"Oakes fits you," I said sweetly, my fingers finding each other as the nerves crept into my belly.

I could still feel him everywhere. I could still taste him on my lips. I didn't mean to kiss him after discovering who he was, but when he said the words *the woman I love* I seemed to have lost control over my own body. In that moment that he called ours, it felt perfect and right, but now that we were back in this small, confined space, my thoughts were going haywire. I wanted to kiss him again, but that didn't really seem appropriate.

"Did you really Google me after that night?" he asked.

I nodded. "Almost every week."

"And you really didn't find anything?"

"I mean"—I shrugged a shoulder—"I found the article about the accident, but other than that...nothing."

"My evil plan worked, then," he muttered, a wry smile on his lips as he broke the pasta apart.

I furrowed my brow. When Oakes caught sight of my expression, he continued.

"When you Googled my real name, what came up?"

"Your dad. Roper Slade."

Roper Slade was a name that everyone knew in the rodeo world. He was a bull rider, and he would always put on a show, even if he rarely qualified. For a while, our small town in Wyoming was proud to be the home of Roper Slade. It was even on the welcome sign. But as well-known as Roper was, it was also known that he was a drunk. It was a huge thing when he got arrested. One moment, he was the big name everyone loved, and the next, he was gone—and so was his name from the signs. If my memory serves me correctly—which I was questioning it—Roper got arrested before the homecoming rodeo. Suddenly, Oakes began to make a lot more sense.

I swallowed. "I thought you said he died?"

He shook his head. "No, I said he was gone. You assumed he died. He was a waste of space, and I, for one, am glad he's rotting behind bars. Right where he belongs. I changed my name so that when you Googled Oakes

Ashford, I was a new name. Truly a rookie with no standings, no rodeo background, no drunk, abusive father to be tied to." Oakes came up to the counter, leaning his weight on his palms, leaning closer to me. "The fucker almost killed my mother the night before my accident. He beat her in front of me and my brother, her face barely recognizable once he was done. If I hadn't called 911...if he hadn't been arrested...he probably would have come after us next."

"Oakes..." I sighed, but his heavy headshake stopped me.

"I don't like to talk about it. I don't like to think about it...I only go forward. Once he was out of our lives, it got"—he scrunched his face and tilted his head from side to side—"semi better. My mom took over the farm, I got surgery on my hand, and my brother...well, Hayes...he, uh..." Dropping his chin, he heaved a long sigh. "It messed with him more than me. We both went to therapy after witnessing that, but I found a passion. Hayes didn't."

Reaching across the counter, I placed my hand over his, feeling his warmth instantly. He turned his hand, lacing his fingers around my palm, his gaze now focused on how we were joined.

"He's not a bad guy. He just didn't know how to act. He got mixed up in the wrong things and has been to rehab a few times. He lives on the farm with Mom now, helps her there. It keeps him busy and on the straight. When he needs a little more, he calls me. I can normally get him back on track, but if I can't, he has his therapist and sponsor that are always there for him. I haven't..." He trailed off, the weight of his body resting on his arms. "I haven't heard from him in a while, which is good. That means he's doing better, that he hasn't relapsed."

I took in a breath. "You don't talk about your mom. Or brother."

"And there's a reason for it. I don't want my life to take away what they've built. I don't want them in the limelight. So, name change, and I keep my past just that."

"Your past."

He nodded.

"I can just imagine how social media would react if Roper Slade's son showed up on the scene. Everyone would be waiting for me to slip. I didn't want that kind of reputation. I wanted to grow into myself, defy the odds. And I did. I didn't let one injury"—he lifted his left hand—"or two or three or four...stop me from doing what I loved to do."

I gave him a slight smile, tempted to reach out and grab his left hand and pull it to my lips and kiss his scar. "Who knows? Ty? He said something about your brother that night."

Oakes nodded. "And Drew...for legal reasons. But he agreed to keep my real name under wraps. He gets ten percent of my checks, and I send forty to my mom to help with the farm and upkeep—"

"Forty percent of your earnings go to your mom?" My eyes widened, hating the feeling of his hand slipping from mine as he turned to look at the pot of water.

"Well, yeah, keeping a farm isn't easy, especially when half the town already takes pity on you—even sixteen years later. She couldn't go get a job, and Hayes was useless there for a few years so...I did what I could. After I won my first NFR, she told me to stop sending money, but..."

"You never did."

"I don't have any debt. I don't own a house. I own my truck outright. I pay for gas, my phone, food, Zee's boarding..." Oakes listed off everything, raising his fingers in the air, each tick bringing a smile to my face. His secretive personality, the want to keep things out of *Rodeo Way*...was all to protect his family. "I don't need all that money."

I couldn't help but stare at him. "What do you need?"

He raised a single eyebrow. "Not a lot. I can tell you what I want, what I've wanted for a long...long time." He took the few steps around the counter, coming up to me with a darkened, lust-filled expression in his eyes. I guessed we were done talking about his family and his past. Using his hands to part my knees so he could step as close to me as possible, his fingertips found my skin.

"A long...long time?" I parroted.

"Ever since that night." His forefinger raised, tracing my jawline. "Sixteen years ago, I heard your voice, and since then, I've heard those words in my head so many times."

"And then?"

"And then I saw you. And I fell all over again. You were just as beautiful, just as perfect as I remembered, and right now...Emmy..." I closed my eyes and sighed, the sound coming out more like a breathy moan, as my name slipped from his lips. I loved it when he said my name like that. "I've wanted you ever since I was fifteen, and then even more when you came back into my life."

I brushed my hands up his chest to his shoulders, feeling him flex under his shirt. "I..." I stumbled, forcing the words to form, "I want you too, Oakes. More so now that I *see* you." My eyes met his. "I just..." I swallowed, pushing my fingers into his shoulders. Was this where the nerves were coming from earlier, knowing I could kiss him again, now that nothing was there between us, that *we* could possibly happen? "I just wouldn't..."

"Wouldn't what, Emmy?" He husked into my ear.

I met his gaze. "I wouldn't admit it. Forced myself not to. Thought of the job first and you second."

"Admit it," he growled. "Put this first." He cupped my face gently, his thumb tracing my bottom lip.

I kissed him, grabbing his collar to pull him to me. His tongue licked my bottom lip where I could still feel the pad of his thumb, and I opened for him instantly. I loved the way he tasted, and the way his hands found their way in my hair, deepening the kiss. He was all consuming, and I was falling into him more with each lick.

His kisses turned heady, more powerful, as his tongue danced with mine. His hands held me to him, his fingers laced in my hair and neck. Sparks flew off in every direction, blazing my entire being as if a firework were going to explode inside me. I could hear the hissing now as it rose in the air and thundered.

My hands began to trail down his chest, finding the hem of his shirt with ease, slipping to his skin and feeling his abs tighten once I made skin-to-skin contact. I had dreamed about these abs. I had dreamed about his fingers on me—more times that I cared to admit. I wondered if he ever dreamed this too. If he was enjoying this and wanting it just as much as I did.

His hand moving from my neck to my breast answered my question. He did, and when I arched into him, feeling the hardness there under his Wranglers at the same time he kneaded into me, I gasped into his mouth—the sizzle too much to bear without having more.

Oakes broke us apart, taking a deep breath as he came up for air.

"We don't have to do anything you're not comfortable with," he whispered, wrapping his arms around my waist to pull me from the stool.

Comfortable? I let out a long sigh, my mind only going to one place. I wanted everything he had to offer. I wanted his lips on me. I wanted to finally know what his fingers felt like. He was warm and solid against me and...*oh*...I was comfortable right where I was.

"What is it?" he asked, his voice heavy as he dipped his lips to my neck, kissing the hollow space there. "We could stop now."

"You're too good to be true." He raised a brow, a silent plea to egg me on. "You're amazing, and perfect, and now you're here allowing me to set the pace? You want me to be comfortable. Next thing I know, you'll tell me you're a bull rider that doesn't get fazed by the buckle bunnies." I relished in watching the smile grow on his face. "You're the bull rider that doesn't have any condoms, aren't you?"

"Oh…" He grinned. "I have condoms. It's just…" He kissed me lightly. "I just got you, Emmy, and we don't need—"

"Do you want to know how many times I've thought about your fingers on me? How many times I've desperately wanted them on my skin?"

His grin grew, and his fingers rose to once again trace my jawline. "These fingers?"

I tipped my jaw back. "God yes. Those fingers," I moaned. "I want to know what they feel like, if they are anything like I've imagined."

"Emmy…" Oakes kissed my neck, his tongue drawing a circle on my skin. "I think that can be arranged."

In an instant, he lifted me as if I weighed nothing, a squeal echoing through the room. It took him two, three, four steps until I felt the bed against my back, Oakes's hands on my thighs, sliding up until they slid under my shirt. God, already I could feel how rough his fingertips were from the time they spent in gloves. They were warm, yet they sent chills throughout my entire torso, down to my center.

"Tell me what you imagined," he said, a husk to his voice that I had never heard before.

"I want to know what they feel like." I reached for him, my hands finding his hair, lightly tugging until he was looking up at me.

"Where?" Slowly, he lifted the hem of my shirt and kissed right below my belly button. I gasped. "I won't touch you until you tell me where."

"God, Oakes, everywhere." My head hit the bed, a soft thump following.

"No…" he grumbled, and suddenly, he was above me, his lips moving as if he wasn't able to kiss every surface of me fast enough. "I need you to be specific."

"My breasts," I breathed, my voice more air than anything else. I could feel the heat rise and build in my body, and he hadn't even done anything yet. His hands hadn't even moved from my stomach. We were still fully clothed. There were so many barriers between us, and I was already coming apart. "Please…"

"Sit up," he ordered, and I obeyed, using my elbows to prop myself up. He tugged on my shirt, pulling it over my head, leaving me in my bra. It didn't even bother me that it was a plain beige bra; a part of me knew that he wouldn't care. And damn…he didn't. "*Fuuuuck,*" he groaned, taking in the sight of me. His hands moved quick, unclasping my bra, letting it fall to my waist. "You want me to touch you here," and then his hands were on me, kneading and pinching in all the right places.

"Holy shit," I gasped. "How does this feel so good?"

Oakes replaced his hands with his mouth, the warmth spreading over my nipple as his tongue lavished and licked. He pushed my shoulders down to the bed, his mouth not breaking contact with my breast, his hands still moving against me as he bit my already sensitive nipple. I tugged and pulled at the fabric of his shirt, needing and wanting more already. Getting the memo, he pulled away from me and tore his shirt over his head, tossing it to the side and raising up on his arms.

God, he was perfect. Every inch of him. I touched, running my fingers along his pecs, his abs, trailing a line down to the perfect triangle that sat right above his jeans. His stomach twitched a little, and I giggled, not believing that this perfect man was here with me. That I had somehow almost let this all go. Let him go. Just the thought now of being with anyone other than him was laughable. Oakes and I fit together, and we were dancing, our bodies contouring and blending in one fluid motion, and we still hadn't removed all of our clothes.

"You"—I worked my hands to his belt—"are wearing too many clothes."

My hands worked at his buckle, wanting to feel every piece of his body. I could see how hard he was, how much he wanted this just as much as I did. I could see it, but I wanted to feel it. My fingers brushed his boxers, but before I could get any farther, his hand wrapped around my wrist.

"I'm pretty sure I'm supposed to be touching you." He leaned down, taking my lips with his.

"I can touch a little." I sighed.

"No." He pulled me away from him. "Tell me where else."

"Oakes," I grumbled, a little mad my hands weren't on him. "You're being..." I gasped. "What's that word Ty used? Territorial."

"How can I not be? With you here, like this, for me?"

I let out a moan, loving the way his hands felt against my skin, his tongue tracing in their wake.

"You're...teasing," I said between gasps.

"Then, Emmy..." He kissed my navel. "You need to tell me where."

"My stomach," I answered, and he moved, his palm flattening against my torso and sliding down...down...down. "My ass," I breathed, arching my back to kiss him.

He rolled to the side of me, his hand keeping me on my back as his palm slipped under my shorts. His hand explored as his tongue danced with mine.

"Anywhere else?" he whispered against my lips.

"My..." I hesitated. "Oakes...touch me."

"Tell me where."

"My clit."

Then, he was there, his fingers sliding to where I most wanted him, finding my sensitive bud with ease. He moved, slow at first, making sure to listen to all my gasps and moans as his fingers moved against my skin.

"You're so wet, Emmy," I heard his voice in my ear right before I felt his lips on my neck. I shivered. "So wet for me. All for me."

His fingers danced in a circle, creating the most beautiful feeling that spread up through my core into my stomach, all the way to my chin. My breath hitched as I forced a cry to stay in, but in reality, I wanted to scream. I wanted the world to know how this felt. The rough calluses of his fingers created just the right friction against my soft core. Each move he made was a different sensation, and I couldn't...wouldn't ever...get enough of this.

"You can be loud," he whispered. "No one but me will hear you."

"God, Oakes..."

"Fuck, Emmy, you feel..." he stammered, kissing me. "I can't wait to have my cock inside of you."

"Don't tease me," I grumbled, instantly wanting him rather than his fingers.

But then, in one fluid motion, he slipped two fingers inside of me, this time causing a moan to echo through the room. Twisting, he instantly found the spot that no one else had ever been able to find, and then his thumb was on my clit, circling it still as he used his fingers to push and pull. The room began to blur and spin until the only thing that was in focus was him. His eyes were on me as his fingers moved in and out, twisting and turning, and all the while, his thumb created the most perfect friction. I could feel the pressure build, rushing to my core as I began to wither against him. Reaching out, I grasped his shoulders, our eyes making contact that I never wanted to break. So intense, so intimate I could see into him, and he no doubt could see into me.

"This is not enough. I want you," I begged, arching my back to kiss him.

"Oh no, Emmy. I'm watching. This is...you are...fuck, Emmy. Come on my fingers. Come for me, Emmy. Let me feel it." He kissed me again, the mixture of his tongue and words sending me over the edge in the most perfect way, shocks flying through my body like a current, over and over until his fingers slowed and I came down from my high, my entire body shaking with pleasure. His lips were featherlight against my neck, my collarbone, the swell of my breasts, kissing me through the motions until his fingers slipped from me.

"Now tell me," he moaned, his voice still heavy. "Was that like you imagined?"

I hummed, my heartbeat erratic, pumping through my chest. "Nothing will ever compare to that."

"Challenge accepted." Oakes grinned, kissing me once more.

CHAPTER TWENTY-SIX
Oakes

The only thing that pulled me away from Emersyn was the hiss of the boiling water hitting the glass stove top. *Shit*. I was making dinner. Emersyn's laugh filled the room as I shot up and fumbled over my own two feet to get to the kitchen. As soon as the water was contained and cleaned, and the pasta was boiling, I joined Emersyn in the bed again. She had covered up her bare chest and curled herself into a ball, her hands under the pillow. She only moved once she felt the bed dip, her arms wrapping around my waist to pull me close. My entire being hummed being this close to her.

"The pasta," she hummed, her eyes still closed.

I kissed her forehead. "I set a timer."

I could feel the soft smile spread across her lips. "Of course you did," she whispered, and then she nuzzled herself closer to me. And thank God for that timer, because in the seven minutes it took to boil the pasta, I was already drifting off.

We ate, continuing the conversation from earlier, but this time lighter. We didn't talk about my dad; we didn't talk about my brother; we just...were. The more we talked, the more I fell.

After dinner—not even caring what time it was—we showered, dressed, and climbed back into bed. Emersyn curled up to me up like it was something she had done every single night of her life. Her body covered mine like a weighted blanket, her breathing steady, grounding me. I never had issues falling asleep at night, all I needed was a few minutes to clear my head, but with Emersyn in my arms, her heartbeat in rhythm with mine, I fell asleep faster than I ever had before.

The buzzer sounded, and I jumped from the bull, dirt flinging into the air around my boots.

"I'd give that an 88," Cash snickered, leaning against the metal bars. He watched a few of the ranch hands wrangle the bull back into the pen, and once it was safely there, he pushed off, opening the gate for me to walk through.

That was the tenth bull this morning, and my body was aching in all the right places. I wanted nothing more than to go back to bed with Emersyn. Almost got away with it too, until she kissed me and pushed me out the door. Her exact words were, 'This week is for training, not sleeping.' I furrowed my brow and protested a little, practically begging her to kiss me again before making my way to the arena where Cash was waiting for me.

"That was a 90 at least," I rebutted.

"Nah, it wasn't you. It was that bull. Try a horse."

Meaning 44 of that 88 was me. The way the rodeo scored half to the cowboy's ride and half to the bull's performance was still harsh. It made sense, but I would still prefer the majority of the 88 to go to me for being able to stay on for eight seconds when the bull clearly wanted me off.

I glowered up at him. "I don't ride bronc." I hadn't since my hand got smashed. Bareback—sure. A bucking bull—no issues. But you wouldn't find me on the back of a bucking horse.

"It'll give you a break from bulls." He wasn't wrong, but it also wouldn't help me. I pulled on my glove and shook my head at him, and with a chuckle, he finally said, "Eighty seconds on the back of a bull calls for a drink, then. I bet Abs will have a cold one waiting for us in the house." Cash slapped my shoulder.

"It's eleven," I reminded him.

"A cold one, and lunch."

Cash walked ahead of me, leaving the training arena. I gathered my things sitting on the small tackle bench and then followed, catching the slight buzz coming from my phone. Digging it out of the pocket, I brought it to life, smiling once I saw several texts from Emersyn.

Emersyn

How many bulls are they taking in there?

I've counted ten...are you really riding ten bulls this morning?

Do you know how hard it is to write an article?

Especially when all I can think about is you.

Okay, okay...really now. I'm focusing.

Tweaked the intro and sent it off to Sterling just like Morgan wanted. Once I started focusing, it got easy.

But now I'm thinking about you again. Are you almost done?

My smile tugged at my lips, and even the promise of a cold beer and lunch couldn't stop me from going to her. Even with the main house in view, Cash vanishing behind a side door, I jogged toward the bunkhouse.

Emersyn was sitting cross-legged on the couch, her laptop resting in the hollow of her legs, when I burst through the door. Her head jerked up, and the moment our eyes locked, she smirked.

"I take it you got my texts?"

"Writing an article may be hard"—I unhooked my vest and dropped it to the ground with a thud—"but have you ever ridden a bull?" I took the small stride toward her, leaning down and placing my hands on either side of her head on the back of the couch.

The expression that cascaded her face only turned me on. The way her lips pursed, the way her eyes shined as a single eyebrow rose, the hint of sass that sent me right to my knees. Damn this girl could do anything, and now that I knew she was thinking of me...I'd feel my dick twitch. The dynamic completely switched between us, and I'd be damned if I would allow it to switch back. I bit my bottom lip and leaned in.

"How long did I ride that mechanical bull for?" she teased.

I took her mouth with mine, not wanting to waste another moment without tasting her. She hummed into me, leaning forward ever so slightly, deepening the already perfect kiss. I could make a comment here—it flowed through my mind more than once, *What else can you ride, baby?*—but another thought popped into my head, one that was stronger. *Savor her.* Breaking the kiss, I tightened my lips, keeping the comment in.

"You managed." I cocked an eyebrow at her, pushing myself off the couch.

"Excuse me?" Her jaw dropped.

I smirked, reaching down to grab my vest from the floor, gently placing it on a bench instead. I heard her shuffle, her feet hitting the floor and the small pats of her bare feet.

"I managed?" she parroted. I turned to look at her, and her hands were folded across her chest, her hip cocked with one leg out, giving me *that* look.

"Damn, you're cute." I smiled.

Her cheeks flushed as she dropped her gaze, but I didn't miss the sweet smile that spread across her lips. "I did more than manage." She breathed, the small gasp making it really hard to not take her right here, right now.

"How did the article go?" I asked, kicking off my boots, reaching for her belt buckle to pull her toward me the minute my feet were flat on the floor.

"Nice subject change," she began, settling into my chest, her palms sliding to the nape of my neck. "It was good. I sent a good chunk of it off to Sterling."

"Any word back from him?"

She shook her head. "Not yet. I just barely sent it. He's a decent editor, so I don't think anything will come back with red streaks or changed too much. He'll be able to tell I've put a lot into this. It helps when my subject can't leave my head."

"Well..." I pulled her closer still, her chest becoming flush with mine. "Your subject is top tier if you ask me."

With a small laugh, she raised on her tiptoes, gently pressing her lips to mine before pulling away from me. "Please tell me you got some training in? I saw a lot of bulls going into the arena."

"Ten bulls. Eighty seconds."

"You rode ten bulls? Qualified each time?"

I raised a brow and nodded.

"And what do we do now?" she asked.

"Now?" I moved my hands to her waist and pressed into her skin. "Now I plan to spend the rest of my evening right here with you."

"Sounds phenomenal, actually." She left my touch, heading back to the couch, returning to the same position as earlier.

I followed, wanting her warmth again. "Do you need anything else for your article?"

She shook her head. "Believe it or not, I think I got enough to make it what Morgan is looking for. I'm not sure why they put me on the entire summer, honestly. We can head to Colorado sooner and get that photo shoot out of the way." She leaned forward, reaching for her laptop.

Furrowing my brow, I began to unbutton my shirt, yanking it from my jeans. "Photo shoot?"

"Did you even look at the new schedule?" Emersyn questioned. "And Morgan is upset we aren't as active in the WhatsApp chat. It's mainly her and Sterling at this point. Drew pops in every now and then, and I give emoji reactions."

"Yeah, no to the group chat, but...I guess I didn't look at the schedule that closely, but I take it I already agreed to a photo shoot?" I sat down next to her, raising my leg up to rest on the couch, my arm falling behind her head, loving the way she leaned into me.

"I can take it off. I have so many photos of you anyway; it's not needed—"

"No," I stopped her, my fingers reaching out to touch her hair. "I'll go to Colorado. I'll do the stupid photo shoot."

Twisting her torso, she widened her eyes. "You're serious? You fought the article in the beginning, but you magically agree to a photo shoot? I've been so nervous to ask you. I was going to make Drew talk to you."

"Emmy." I leaned in, kissing her gently. "If it means a lot to you that I go to Colorado and stand in front of a camera, then I'll go to Colorado and stand in front of a camera. For you"—I brushed her hair from her forehead—"if you haven't guessed, I'd do pretty much anything."

I swear, I could literally see Emersyn melt on the spot. Her shoulders loosened, and a heavy sigh left her lungs.

"I don't want to force you—"

"You're not." I cupped her check. She rested into my touch, taking it with ease. "I want to."

I pulled her to me, kissing her once more. She gasped, opening up for me, and I drank her in, still not believing she was letting me kiss her over and over.

"Now," I breathed, leaning my forehead against hers and slyly pulling her computer from her lap, "put the laptop away, let's order some food, and watch a movie."

"We bought so much food, and you want to order in?"

"You've never had June's Pizza. Trust me." I brushed my lips over hers.

Her eyes fluttered open. "Sounds perfect."

Two hours later, Emersyn's head was resting on my shoulder, her knees curled up as she fit in the crook of my arm. My one hand drew circles on her bare shoulder, the other enjoying the way her fingers were laced with mine. I had stolen kisses throughout the movie she picked—oddly enough *Back to the Future 3*—but none that had turned into more. Wanting more—yes. Taking more—no. I'd let her lead this, and as badly as I wanted to feel her again, to hear those small gasps and moans again...I scoffed to myself...I was a patient man. And for her, I'd wait forever.

While Emersyn watched Marty and Doc use horses to pull the De-Lorean, my thoughts flew to everything that had happened up until this moment. Why didn't Emersyn recognize me that first day? She said I was different, but I couldn't have changed that much, could I? Emersyn's beauty only amplified. I could still see the rodeo queen that was hidden behind the thirty-four-year-old eyes, her smile was brighter—if that was even possible—and she just radiated beauty. If I tried to see myself through her eyes, I could see where the disconnect would be. Maybe I was a little too different than I was in high school.

That night my hand got crushed, I truly thought my career was over before it even began. My mom was still recovering from the beating my dad gave her, my brother was discovering drugs, and I was just trying to live as normally as I could. I entered myself in the rodeo and told myself this was it; this was my life, and my dad wasn't going to take it away from me.

Then that fucking horse landed on my fucking hand.

But then something else hit me.

I took every piece of what Emersyn said to me and used it. I centered my entire life after it. That was where the change came from. At first, I joined the rodeo to try to distract myself from what was happening. I had been training and riding bronc my entire life—that was the next step. My dad always said the arena was no place for me. And when my hand got smashed, a part of me believed him. But after Emersyn's words of encouragement, the rodeo became mine, and I returned to prove to myself that the arena was exactly where I was meant to be. So, I worked—hard—to make it my place and keep my old life out of it.

She inhaled and scooted closer, her exhale leaving her lungs in a small hum.

"Can I ask you a question...or are you too immersed in the movie?" I asked softly, resting my cheek against her hair.

"Ask away."

"How did you not recognize me?"

She lifted her head, forcing me to do the same, and our eyes met.

"I've been asking myself the same thing since I held your hand. There was always something familiar about you, but I couldn't place it. But remember"—she laid her head back down on my shoulder—"I had only really truly seen you the one time. Every other time was on a screen."

I nodded, holding onto her a little tighter. "I looked for you too, you know. I followed you. You were easier to Google, though."

She let out a small chuckle. "I was. So many events. So many rodeos. The NFR."

"I was there." I sighed. "When you lost America."

Emersyn shifted against me. "You were?"

"You never seemed upset about it—losing. I saw a few of the girls crying after the contest. Not you. You were smiling and beaming at the winner. You looked..."

"Relieved?" she suggested.

I nodded. "Yeah." She raised her eyebrows and let out a small sigh of agreement. She never wanted it. "When you first got the assignment, during that meet with Drew, you said you, more than anyone, knew what it meant to keep things private...why?"

Her head lifted again, and I felt her lips against my cheek. A warmth spread through me with that one touch, and I turned to her, kissing her softly before resting my forehead on hers.

"Halfway through the Miss Rodeo America pageant, I realized I didn't want it anymore. I didn't want to be in the limelight. I didn't want the schedule that came with it. My time as Miss Rodeo Wyoming was enough. I had the experience, and I just knew it wasn't for me. There have been times when I've gone home and they've asked me to make an appearance—"

"I was at one of those too. My first ride as Oakes Ashford...you were there."

She smiled up at me. "You were? And you didn't come up to me?"

"I was Oakes Ashford then. I was...different. A little cockier, a little grumpier...still chicken shit."

She gave my chest a light slap with the back of her palm. "Chicken shit," she muttered. "That was the last time I was asked to do something. I don't agree to anything anymore. That's why, in Laramie, when you made the Miss Rodeo comment—"

"I shouldn't have said that."

"It's fine," she assured me. "I just don't want to be recognized for that. I want to be recognized for other things now. And hopefully, this..."—she raised our hands, and her lips met my knuckles—"you. The article for *Rodeo Way* will be that for me. I feel like I'm finally getting what I've always wanted."

"You should have written that speech down. It was a good one. It would have given you strength too."

"Like I said," she sighed, moving to climb over me. "That was meant for you. Not me. I'm glad you listened to me. I'm glad it helped you become Oakes Ashford. I'm glad you took every word and became who you are today. I wouldn't be here"—she wiggled in my lap—"if you hadn't."

"What about..." I ran my hands up her back, loving the way she arched for me. "After this? After the article is done."

"I told you I have a possible promotion on the line; I just have to give them the best article I can, and then..." she trailed off.

"You'll be exactly where you want to be?" I raised a brow.

She shrugged a shoulder. "I'd like to think so. With you?"

I felt my lips twitch into a smile. *With me.*

"After the article..." my voice trailed.

"You can kiss me as much as you want."

"What about now?"

She gave me a wry grin. "I'll be done with my article before we leave this ranch, so—"

I cut her off with a kiss, taking it as I could kiss her as much as I wanted *now*, which was exactly what I planned to do.

Oakes

Are you going to be in Colorado?

Drew

If you want me there, I'll be there.

Oakes

Yeah, can you manage to get Emersyn's car shipped there for me?

Drew

Does this mean you finally agreed?

Join Me on WhatsApp! Click the link below to join the conversation!

Oakes

I said yes to the photo shoot, still no to that fucking app.

Chapter Twenty-Seven
Emersyn

"**A**nd..." I hovered the mouse over that final button—the button that would end this portion of the assignment, the button that would take the stress away from the rest of the trip. After I hit this button, my only worry was how many photographs I could take of Oakes. "...send."

That little circle whirled around on my screen, and I watched it like it was going to vanish if I blinked.

Your message has been sent.

I heaved a sigh and fell back on the couch, looking at the computer screen in shock.

It was done. My article was done.

And if you asked me...it was perfect.

I wrote the in-depth article that Morgan would eat up, all while keeping my promise to Oakes. It was the perfect balance of giving a better look into

Oakes's world and keeping it focused on his path to the NFR. I did this. I was damn proud of those ten thousand words, and the fact that they were going to jet-set my career as a journalist made me giddy. It felt like there was nowhere to go but up.

This week ended up being exactly what I needed to get this completed. No rodeos, no photos to edit, no emails or text messages from Morgan, no long car rides—just me and my laptop while Oakes trained. And every afternoon, he would come back to this small slice of heaven that had become him and me. We'd go for a ride, sit and talk while I rested against him, and every night, he'd take me in his arms and turn my world upside down. Between his kisses and his touch, the man was hitting so many sensations I didn't know existed. And we hadn't even actually given fully into each other yet. It was his hands, his lips, his voice—*him*. Just all of him. We were relishing in each other, savoring every inch, not rushing a single moment.

Licking my lips, the buzz still high in my chest, I closed my laptop and set it on the coffee table in front of me. I hit the side of my phone, the gray screen of the DND feature lighting up, a small white banner on the bottom. *Four new notifications.*

Swiping to unlock, I turned off *do not disturb* and saw the little red bubbles appear faster than I'd like.

Morgan in WhatsApp

> Remember the schedule change for Oakes, photographer has been scheduled.

> I've added it to the itinerary and sent it along.

Drew in WhatsApp

> Thanks, I'll pass the word.

Perfect. See you both then. I hope to have a final proof if Emersyn can submit her article in time for editing.

I smiled at myself. Submit I did.

Clearing my throat, I typed...

I just submitted to you and Sterling, ahead of schedule!

I see it in my inbox. Perfect. I'll get started on this ASAP.

Thanks for the extra time, Emersyn. I knew you were the right one for the job.

We had no doubt.

Can't wait to see it in Denver. Thanks.

Swiping out of the app, I went straight to my texts, pulling Luca's thread up.

We celebrating tonight?

For?

Submitted the article…and Luca, it's phenomenal.

Luca

Can I read it??

Sterling has to edit it first, then Morgan said she will have a proof. See you in Denver in a few weeks?

Luca

Where I finally get to see the elusive Drew in person. And meet Oakes.

Me

laughing emoji Yes, Oakes is coming. I can't wait for you to meet him. And Luca…I have a story for you.

Luca

wide-eyed emoji Do tell.

Me

It's more powerful in person…

As expected, a FaceTime call from Luca came through, and with a laugh, I answered. Before I could say anything, Luca's voice came through the speaker.

"Okay, we're in person." Luca's dark hair was styled to perfection, his glasses perched against his nose as he leaned back in his chair in his office. Behind him, I saw the bookcase holding framed photos and statues of bronc riders mid-buck that he had collected and the Denver skyline out his window. A small part of me missed the *Rodeo Way* office, that view that came with it, but when my gaze went from his to the rolling mountains of the ranch I was currently on, I knew there was no comparison.

"This isn't what I meant," I laughed at him. "Maybe I'll keep you in suspense until we get to Colorado."

"You fucked him." Luca's smile grew.

I could feel my cheeks turn bright red as the heat rushed there. "Well—"

"I knew it." Luca clapped his hands.

"Technically, not yet."

"What do you mean 'technically, not yet' you either have or you haven't."

"Fine, then by that logic, we haven't, but Luca...he's..." I brought my knuckles to my lips, not exactly sure why I was nervous to tell him who Oakes truly was. My smile grew under my fingers just thinking about everything that had happened over the past week here at the ranch with him, how her he was mine and only mine. I didn't want to lose that just yet by telling it to my best friend. I dropped my fingers. "He's so much more than we thought."

Luca's lips twitched in a devious smile. "You got in depth with him."

"You could say that, but—"

"So, I'm assuming you gave Morgan the article she wanted."

"I hope so, without breaking into his privacy too much. I'll tell you everything when I see you. It really is a fantastic story. Maybe while he's getting his photos taken, I can tell you, but...damn, Luca..."

"You are far gone, aren't you?"

"I wouldn't say that, but..." The heat in my face deepened. "He's really...really amazing."

"Okay, well, fuck him, and then we'll talk."

"Luca!"

"And find out something about Drew for me—"

"No." I shot him down instantly on that front. "I will not be setting you up with Oakes's agent."

"Normally I have a good read on people, but he's...I can't read him."

"Well, maybe that's because most of your communication has been through email, but Luca, I don't know if he's gay."

Luca raised a brow. "He very well could be. He's given me the look."

"All men, according to you, give you the *look*."

Luca smiled. "Well, yeah, I mean...look at me."

"I'm gonna go."

"Emersyn, wait..."

"I'm on a beautiful ranch, I've finished my article, and Oakes has a few hours left of training, I'm going to go explore with my camera."

"Emersyn!" Luca shouted, trying to get my attention, but I waved, yelled goodbye over his shouts, and ended the FaceTime.

Laughing to no one, I placed my phone face down on the coffee table, reached for my boots, grabbed my hat and camera, and left the tiny bunkhouse—with my phone and laptop—behind me.

The bunkhouse wasn't far from the stables, and the closer I got, the clearer Oakes's cheers and claps became. I peeked my head in the indoor arena, seeing him tossing his helmet over to the side, a blond man catching it with a laugh, a short brunette next to him. She clapped as the blond flipped his helmet in the air, then I noticed Cash on horseback, getting the bull back into the pen. With one glance at the clock on the wall, I saw he lasted the eight seconds, and it must have been a hell of a ride.

Not wanting to bother him, I meandered to the same horse I rode the first day we were here—North—and stroked down her nose. Her jaw moved as she chewed, the *crunch, crunch, crunch* that came with it actually soothing me.

"Hey, girl," I cooed, "wanna go for a ride?"

"Want a saddle this time?" a sweet voice came from behind me, and Abi Callahan came into view.

Swinging my camera over my shoulder, I gave her a nod. "Sure. You don't mind if I take her out, do you?"

"Not at all. I bet she'll love it. I'll open the tack for you. Her things are labeled with her name. You got it?" Abi lowered her chin, digging in her pockets for a key, jingling them the moment they were free.

"Of course, would you tell Oakes I went for a ride?"

"Sure thing. Enjoy your time." Abi smiled, opening the tack shed for me before giving me one final wave.

Sometime later, loving the fact that I wasn't paying attention to the time, North and I had explored almost every inch that we could of Hartwell Hills Ranch. I took photo after photo, capturing a teenage boy and a smaller girl with a brown-and-white cow, birds flying through the trees into the sky, a white horse enjoying a lounge in the pasture, each photo showing the beauty that was this ranch.

Maybe once I was home and could edit and develop these properly, I'd send Abi copies. I could picture them, hanging in her stables, next to the drawings her husband drew. Just the idea that someone, somewhere other than *Rodeo Way*, would hang a photo I took—not just edited, but *took*—sent my entire being into chills.

There was no doubt in my mind now. After being on the dirt for almost two months, taking photograph after photograph, seeing Oakes—and other cowboys and cowgirls—in motion, after writing that article...this was where I was supposed to be. This was exactly what I was supposed to be doing, and for the first time in a long time, this felt right. I felt right. Everything seemed so clear when I thought about it: traveling—with

Oakes, hopefully—to rodeo after rodeo, taking more photos, perfecting my skill and writing, bringing the world of rodeo to life.

Maybe I could even interview Miss Rodeos...they were so much more than a pretty face that helped kids after mutton busting. Those girls had stories to tell too, and I could be the one to tell them. There was so much I could do. That I wanted to do.

And it was all possible.

Like Oakes said the other night...I'd be exactly where I wanted to be.

A rush of emotion swept over me as my entire being came into view.

This was who Emersyn Flynn was supposed to be.

And I owed all of this to Oakes.

Making sure my camera was secure, I kicked North into a run, making my way back to the stables in no time. Abi was there with Cash, and they both watched in awe as I quickly undressed North, brushing her down with care, though with speed, giving her an apple before placing her back in her stall. I waved to them and ran—literally ran—back to the bunkhouse.

I slowed down once I reached the steps, calming the surge of energy that was brewing inside me before I opened the door and burst at the seams, most likely scaring Oakes. But when I saw him in the kitchen with his protective vest open, jeans covered in dirt, and hair messed from his helmet...the volcano all but erupted.

"I love this," I said to him, my voice barely a whisper.

He furrowed his brow. "Love what?"

"Everything about this." I held my arms out. "The rodeo, the travel, the photography..." I dropped my hands, hearing my palms hit my thighs with a slap. "Oakes..." I took a step toward him. "This is everything I've ever wanted. And I think..."—I blinked—"I *know* it's possible."

A wry grin spread across his lips. "You finished your article."

Rolling my lips, I nodded. "I finished my article."

His helmet hit the floor, and he reached out for me, his finger hooking with my belt loop. "Come here," he said right before our mouths met, and my body ignited from his all-consuming kiss.

Chapter Twenty-Eight
Emersyn

His kiss was electric, as if every other time he'd kissed me before now was child's play. Every kiss was just a tease as to what was to come. Oakes could *kiss*. He knew the exact way to hold the nape of my neck to take control, turning me in the position he wanted so he could claim me over and over. His hands knew exactly where to go to first, creating those sparks of fire that sizzled up my spine that I would rather die than extinguish.

My breath hitched as he broke the kiss, a sharp inhale filling the space between us before his lips found my neck, and his tongue began to move against my skin.

"You," I gasped, my fingers threading into his hair as he began to suck. "You weren't kidding when you said you would wait until after my article."

Oakes's tongue trailed down my neck to my collarbone, and then his eyes were on mine.

"You've been holding back," I hummed.

He hummed back, the reverberating sound filling my senses. "You have," he gasped, his eyes closed, his lips touching me reverently, "no idea."

His arms snaked around my waist, his body arching into me as I wrapped my arms around his shoulders, pulling him as close as I could. His citrusy scent enveloped me as I breathed him in, drowning in the way he tasted, in the way he made me feel.

My sex life wasn't something to write books about. My past boyfriends—Sterling included—didn't create this cosmic feeling that Oakes did. From the second night here, the first time he touched his fingers to me, when he was more focused on my pleasure than his, I knew that this was going to be something to savor. And savor we did. Each night since, he kissed my shoulders, teased my pussy, licked my nipples, and kissed me senseless. I'd touch him, I'd kiss him, I'd taste him, I'd rock against him, I'd practically beg for him—but he'd stop. He'd kiss me and then hold me tight as we both fell asleep, only to wake up and play all over again until I had to remind him that he was here for a reason.

And right now, *I* was the reason.

And I felt like I had died and gone to heaven.

My body never felt so alive as it did with his hands on me.

Oakes bent his knees, his hands gripping my ass as he lifted me off the ground. I wrapped my legs around his waist, hooking my ankles together, amazed that, in this maneuvering, our lips never left each other. The kisses were still just as hungry as they were when I first walked in the door. Frantic, heady...as if we would be torn apart at any moment.

How much time had passed since then? How long had we stayed in that small kitchen, just immersed in each other?

Could have been years, for all I cared.

As long as his lips were on me, nothing mattered.

Just him. Just us.

His hands slipped, and I hit the bed, my eyes coming to his belt buckle as he towered over me. The silver flashed, the O and A that stood over a bucking horse, the words National Finals Rodeo circling the edge, reminding me exactly who this man was. His body was built for the bull. Strong thighs, a lean back, fine lines defining each and every muscle that graced him. And this man always put on a show. Bull rider. Oakes Ashford. Ashton Slade.

My chest tightened, and I swallowed.

I gripped onto his hips, my eyes trailing from the buckle to his waist, finally up to his eyes. Those brown, tantalizing eyes. He let out a breath, and then his fingers were on me again.

"I had no idea, Emmy," he whispered, tracing my jawline with his fingers, "that it would be like this."

"Like what?" I hummed, keeping my gaze locked on his as I worked on his belt buckle and jeans, loving seeing his hard length come into view even through his boxers. Leaning in, I kissed his hip bone and the hollow space leading right to where I wanted to be.

"That..." he sighed, lifting his head back with a moan as I trailed my palm over his cock, "that it would feel like this."

"We've only just started." I smiled, my hands moving to his ass, slowly pulling his jeans from his waist. "The way I see it, you've given me so much, helped me see more than what was behind the lens or on a computer screen..." I squeezed his firm ass, grinning as he twitched under my touch. "I want this...*you*...more than anything."

"Emmy," he groaned.

"You've helped me remember why I love this, how *much* I love this. You've brought me back to life, Oakes." I heard his jeans hit the floor with a thud, and my hands worked their way up his chest, his shirt gliding over his body with ease. I hummed as I felt each and every line of his abs, each and every pulse of his blood as his breath got quicker and quicker.

His fingers tangled in my hair as my own tickled down his now bare stomach.

"I've imagined this," he husked. "You. In front of me. So many times." His hands began to play with the straps on my tank top, pulling until it was free from my jeans and slowly sliding it over my head. "Do you want to know how hard it was knowing you were in the next room, that I could have made this a reality?"

I smirked. "I probably would have let you."

"Don't tell me that," he growled, his head tipping forward to take my lips, his tongue not even giving me the chance to open up for him.

It was a territorial and dominating kiss—once again, unlike the others we've shared—and it only made me more aware of the arousal pooling at my center. I tightened my thighs to try to contain myself, but it didn't do any good as the tingles shot through me. I tugged at his briefs, feeling his cock break free, and I broke the kiss, replacing his mouth with the tip of his length.

He let out a deep moan. "Fuck, Emmy."

A bead of pre-cum hit my tongue, and I went feral. I used my tongue to swirl the tip, tasting the saltiness of him, smelling the citrus as I began to slowly bob my head. Blow jobs before were a chore, something I never really wanted to do, but this... I wasn't sure what consumed me to take him. I *wanted* to. And I could live in this moment forever. I could take him every night for the rest of my life and be blissfully happy. His moans filled the air as I took him as far as I could go, flattening my tongue to tease him more as I slowly pulled away, then brought him back in, over and over, until I could feel him quivering.

"God, you're perfect." His voice was barely a whisper in my ear as I worked him, feeling his veins rub against my tongue as I sucked and licked and savored. "Just like that, baby. Fuck, Emmy, I want to feel you. I want to taste you. I want...*fuuuuuuck.*"

Tilting my gaze, I looked up at him, and the look of pure ecstasy that painted his face was enough to send me over the edge. I could feel him throbbing around my lips, and I sucked him, my free hand reaching up to cup his balls, only adding to his pleasure—his loud groan was proof enough of that. His grip in my hair tightened, and he guided me to the right rhythm, helping me give him just what he wanted. I moaned around him, enjoying this a little too much. If this was all we did, I wouldn't complain. In fact, I'd gladly do this again.

"Are you wet for me?" he asked, opening his eyes and meeting my gaze.

I gave him a soft smile around his cock and nodded, humming in approval.

"Take off your jeans—now."

Fumbling, I did as he asked, trying not to lose the contact with him, but ultimately, his dick popped from my lips, a sensation I didn't realize I'd miss. Stepping back, he tugged at my jeans and left me in just my panties before coming back to me, his hand grasping the back of my neck. Oakes pulled me back to him, and I opened for the reward.

"Touch yourself," he demanded. "Touch yourself as I fuck your mouth."

I closed my eyes and swirled my tongue again, one hand gripping the bottom of his shaft, the other finding my clit with ease. It was all too simple to pretend they were his fingers, especially now that I knew what they felt like. The pressure built inside of me, my fingers working the bundle of nerves harder than intended as I continued to taste him. It was all too much and not enough at the same time. I wanted so much more than this. So much more than what I'd already had. The promise of something else, something real with Oakes. *Him*. I just wanted him.

"I'm...Emmy..." he breathed. "I'm going to come. Emmy, I...fuck!" he cried out.

I sucked, hollowing out my cheeks, feeling his hot release hit the back of my throat, and I moaned with him, my own orgasm sweeping through me as he throbbed against my tongue.

Oakes's fingers caressed the nape of my neck, and he pulled out of my mouth, giving me just enough time to swallow before he gripped my face and pulled me up to him, capturing the same kiss as before. He took a step forward, and we fell, my back landing on the mattress, his fingers already trailing up my side and under my bra.

"If you think I'm done with you..." he growled.

"Oh, God, I hope not." I arched my back, allowing him to unhook my bra, and the moment my tits were free, his mouth latched on. I gasped, and this time it was my turn to thread my fingers through his hair. "Ah, that feels so good. So...right."

Using his teeth, he teased my already sensitive nipples, his tongue following where he just bit.

"Touch me," I whimpered. "I don't care how, just touch me. Please."

"Emmy baby," he cooed, "you don't have to beg."

A gasp left my lungs as his hand began to travel down, first focusing on my breast, then finally my core. He played, small circles at first, laughing at the way my body reacted to his touch before he slid two fingers inside me, hitting my g-spot like he had known all along how to get there. No one else had found that spot so easily. Oakes was... Oakes was...

"God dammit," I wheezed, my thoughts blanking as his finger tapped relentlessly. "How did you—"

"You didn't think this week was just me putting this off, did you? No..." He kissed me. "I was studying. I was learning every curve, every moan, every inch of this pussy to get you right here. I know you, Emmy. I know your body. I know exactly what you want."

God. Fucking. Dammit.

"Oakes, I want you inside of me. I want you." I arched my back to him, chasing his lips as he lifted his head. "You... Are you... Can you..." I stammered, knowing he just had an orgasm. Could he again so soon? I was ready, but I didn't know if he could again so soon.

"I'll always be ready for you, Emmy. Always."

I whimpered, furrowing my brow as I met him for a kiss, just as he slipped his fingers from me and pushed himself away. I hit the bed, now feeling empty with him gone.

"I need to get—"

"Condom." I blinked. "Yes...now."

Oakes moved, almost tripping as he kicked off his jeans the rest of the way before he began to rifle through a duffel bag. I twisted, giggling as I watched him frantically pull the foil package from the bag.

"What are you giggling about?" He cocked a sexy grin, taking the few steps back to the bed. He crawled over me, and I lifted myself up on my elbows, kissing that smirk right off his lips.

"You. We didn't even get you undressed all the way. You almost tripped over your jeans."

"I had more pressing things to do than to make sure my pants were off all the way." His eyes trailed down my naked body. "Speaking of..." He sat back on his heels, his fingers hooking into my panties. Once they were off and I was bare before him, he flattened his palm and ran his hand up my entire torso, goosebumps following him in his wake. With his teeth, he opened the condom and slowly rolled it on his cock, and my mouth watered. "I still have to actually feel you..."

Crawling over me, he stilled, his eyes heavy on mine. "Let me feel you," he whispered, kissing me softly.

"Yes. Please." Running my hands up his arms, I settled there on the nape of his neck. He bored into me, his brilliant brown eyes holding so many more secrets that I couldn't wait to unveil. "Please, Oakes," I whispered, "I'm yours."

"Mine," he confirmed. Then, in one fluid motion, he was inside me, filling me so full that I wanted to cry out. He kissed my shoulder as he rocked, deeper and deeper inside of me, stretching me to my limit. I tightened, never wanting him to stop.

The frantic movements from just moments before began to slow. He rested his forehead against mine as our bodies moved seamlessly together. His thrusts that were once hard and heavy became soft and fluid, drawing out the sensation even longer, making this last as long as he could. But for me, the tenderness of it, the look in his eyes, the way his lips caressed mine... I was going to explode before we could think about making this last. Sex had never been *this* good, this...life-changing.

Oakes Ashford had officially ruined me for all men.

"God, Oakes," I moaned.

"Mine," he repeated, lifting his head, and I felt his hand slip between us, his thumb finding my clit with ease, applying the most perfect pressure with slow circles, following our pace.

"Oakes," I whimpered, "I'm not going to last—"

"Mine," he whispered into my hair.

"I'm not going to—"

Fuck, I couldn't even speak. Everything about this, about him, was too good to be true. Too good to waste. Just too...fucking...good. The pressure built and built as my center began to pulse, and every inch of my body began to scream.

"I'm going to come," I muttered.

"Come for me, Emmy. Come."

With one more thrust, my release hit me like a tidal wave, flowing from my body, starting where we were connected and roaring to my toes and fingers. My breath quickened as every inch of me shivered as he rocked me through my orgasm. Oakes buried his head in my shoulder, biting my skin as I felt him chase his own release, our heartbeats matching perfectly as he collapsed on top of me.

Moments passed as our bodies calmed, and slowly he pulled away from me, rolling off of me to my side, his face still nuzzled in the crook of my neck.

"Mine," he whispered, kissing my shoulder one final time.

Was it too early to say I loved Oakes? Because it definitely didn't feel too early. The room was dark as we lay in the bed, our bodies flush against each other, my head resting on his shoulder as his finger traced lazy circles on my skin. The only thing I could think as I looked into his eyes was how my heart raced when he was near. He made me feel warm and content, like everything I needed was right here in my arms. His gaze on me made me feel like I was the only thing he saw, that to him I was all that mattered.

We showered, ate dinner and spent the rest of the day—and night—in bed, worshiping each other until we had no stamina left. And after, we just lay with each other, lost in whatever...*this*...was.

Love?

It sure felt like it.

"Tell me what's going through your mind," I said, breaking the trance. It was a better thing to say than *I love you*.

Oakes gave me a sleepy smile. "That I can't believe I finally have you. That you're here. That you're in my arms...finally." He kissed my forehead. "I've waited sixteen years for you."

"You waited?" I pinched my brow, running my hand up his chest to cup his cheek. "What do you mean you waited?"

"I fell in love with you that night, Emmy. No one has ever amounted to you, and no one ever will."

Love. He just said *love.* Oakes *loved* me.

It took everything in me not to tell him I felt the same way. It wouldn't hurt to tell him. If anything, it would take what we were to the next step. The past few hours already proved that there was something more here; all I needed to do was tell him the exact same thing.

But I couldn't. Not just yet.

"Why didn't you say something when you saw me? You recognized me right away, didn't you?"

He nodded. "I did. And...I don't know." He sighed, lifting his other hand to rest behind his head. "I was...scared. Maybe you didn't remember that night, maybe it was nothing, maybe all I was...was an assignment. That's what it felt like at first."

"At first..." I shifted, resting my arm on his chest, my chin on my hand. "You were."

"Gee, thanks—"

I used my other hand to poke him in the side. "At *first*. But Oakes...you became so much more than that."

"When?"

I tightened my lips. "Would you believe me if I said I wasn't sure?"

He scoffed. "Yes." He kissed the tip of my nose. "I don't care when it happened. I'm just glad it did. I'm glad you see me. I'm glad you remember me. I'm fucking glad I have you."

I smiled. "You know, if you had told me, 'Hey, remember when you talked to me after the horse crushed my hand?'...I would have remembered."

He laughed, and damn...I loved his laugh. I loved his smile when he laughed. I loved everything about him when he laughed.

I loved him.

"I should have led with that when Drew introduced us then, huh?"

"Most definitely." I kissed him, a small peck on his lips. "Your eyes came back to me once it clicked. They're the same."

His eyebrows raised slightly, the curve to his lips spreading as he leaned in to kiss me again. "Yours are the same too. The same blue. The same sparkle. The same light. And Emmy..." he trailed off.

"Hmm?" I egged him on.

"I've always loved your eyes."

If I wasn't in love with him already, I was now. I melted back into him, kissing him deeply, feeling the heat rise in me again. His arms circled me, folding me into his body as he rolled me to my back, the contact of the kiss never breaking. I could feel him getting harder and myself getting wetter, and I couldn't wait to feel him inside me again.

A phone—annoyingly loud—rang on the opposite side of the studio, its echo carrying in the space.

"Who's calling? The sun isn't even up." I asked, my head hitting the pillow with a thump.

"It's mine," Oakes whispered, kissing my jaw. "It's probably Drew reminding me we have to drive to Utah today."

"Oh, I'm looking forward to this one. We're camping, right?"

"Oh, yes," he moaned, kissing me again and again. "What do you say we combine our sleeping bags?"

I giggled as the ringing faded, the room returning to silence. Oakes rubbed his nose against mine before kissing me again.

Seconds later, his phone rang again, the same shrill sound blaring.

"We're changing your ringtone," I grumbled.

Oakes smiled against me. "It must be important. A schedule change or something. I'll be right back. Don't. Move." He kissed me quick before bolting out of bed to the kitchen.

Missing his heat instantly, I yanked the comforter over my shoulders, relishing the way it was still warm from his body heat and still smelled like him. Humming, I turned on my side to watch him in all his glory when I finally noticed his expression. His eyebrows were furrowed, his eyes were concentrated, and his breathing had picked up.

Something told me it wasn't Drew on the other end of the phone.

"Oakes?" I sat up, holding the comforter to my chest. "What is it?"

"It's my mom," he replied. His voice was vacant. Lost. Hollow.

His mom.

Drew

Alright, I have Pioneer Days and Days of 47 canceled. Do you think you'll be able to make Cheyenne Frontier Days? If not , I can cancel that too.

Oakes

I'm not sure. I don't exactly know what's going on.

Drew

Have Emersyn keep me updated. She has my number. You just take care of what you need to take care of.

Oakes

Thanks, man. You can be pretty great some-times, you know.

Drew

You hired the best for a reason. Keep me updated on timeline.

Oakes

You won't be left out of the loop. Thanks for let-ting me do this.

Drew

No issue at all. Tell your mom I say hi.

Luca

Is Oakes okay?

Emersyn

Yes? No? I don't know. He's quiet.

Luca

Are you okay?

Emersyn

Besides the fact that I've fallen madly in love with him and don't know how to help him…yeah, I'm peachy.

Luca

Morgan wants me to get you home.

Emersyn

Not a chance.

Luca

Figured that's what you'd say.

Pop quiz.

Emersyn

Luca ..

Luca

Pop. Quiz.

Emersyn

Shoot.

Luca

What does Oakes Ashford smell like?

Emersyn

> Citrus. And sunshine.

Luca

Keep hold of that. Everything will work out. Keep me updated.

Emersyn

> Love you.

Luca

Love you more.

Drew in WhatsApp

There has been an emergency, and Oakes's schedule has changed. Due to the travel situation, Emersyn will be accompanying him to his home. Please don't ask any further questions.

Morgan in WhatsApp

Please give Oakes our best wishes with his emergency. We haven't seen anything about an accident since his training. I'll have Luca look into flights and get Emersyn back to Colorado. I'm sure Oakes doesn't need her there. Her article is completed.

Drew in WhatsApp

No. Oakes wants Emersyn to stay. It will be a few days, then he's back in the circuit. You won't even notice this blip.

Morgan in WhatsApp

> @Emersyn—please provide confirmation on Oakes's schedule, and we will expect reports. @Sterling—have you began editing?

Sterling in WhatsApp

> Yes, ma'am. I'd love to see where Oakes hails from. Emersyn, get photos please!

Drew in WhatsApp

> Not a chance. Please don't ask any further questions.

Emersyn in WhatsApp

> I've sent over Oakes's new schedule. I'll report back when I can. Thanks for being understanding, Morgan.

CHAPTER TWENTY-NINE
Oakes

Oakes Ashford Schedule – July 13th-August 4th

July 13th-18th: OFF – Training, Alpine Ridge, Idaho.

July 19th-21st: Ogden, Utah – Pioneer Days

July 22nd-24th: Salt Lake City, Utah – Days of 47 Gold Buckle Tour

July 25th: Cheyenne, Wyoming – Frontier Days Xtreme Bulls

July 26th-27th: Cheyenne, Wyoming – Frontier Days

July 28th-29th: Riverton, Wyoming – Wind River Rodeo

July 31st: Sidney, Montana – Richland County Fair

August 2nd: Mesquite, Texas – Mesquite Championship

August 1st-2nd: Steamboat Springs, Colorado

August 4th: Rodeo Way Meeting

My mom rarely called during the summer season. Even though I told her she could call me as much as she wanted—that I'd answer any text, any call—hearing from her was something that just didn't really happen. There were a few 'I saw your ride, proud of you' texts, or the occasional 'I told you we don't need that portion anymore, why don't you buy a house instead of sending it to me,' but even those were far and few between. She claimed it was because it helped my dad while he was on the road. That not hearing from her helped him concentrate and get the 'big checks.' In reality, it was so he wouldn't be distracted while he was fucking every buckle bunny that came his way. When I told Emersyn that my dad was a waste of space, I meant it. My hardworking mother, who raised both Hayes and me on her own while tending to a small farm, still took his words seriously to this day, even though he was well out of the picture.

So, when she called for the second time, when her name blared in the dark of the small studio, I had to answer.

And of course, it was about my fucking brother.

And I wouldn't be on the road now, fifteen minutes from my childhood home, if it wasn't for the person who held my hand like her life depended on.

I told Emersyn I'd simply call him, get him out of whatever funk he was in. There had to be a reason for his relapse. He'd gone so long without a drink—our last phone call seemed liked years ago—so what turned him to the bottle now? I could call him, sort it out, and then we'd go to Utah, stick to our plan...but Emersyn wouldn't have that.

"Oh, hell no," she scolded, waving her finger at me as she frantically gathered all of her clothes off the floor. "If your mother says you're the one he was asking for, then we go. He needs you."

So, with a kiss, I listened. We packed up the small bunkhouse, took Abi over any of the leftover groceries we had, said goodbye to Cash and Hartwell Hills, leaving Zee behind as always, and began to make the drive east instead of west. Hours later, we turned onto the dirt path that led to my farm, Emersyn's hand still in mine as her gaze traveled the scenery as we got into Midwest, Wyoming.

"I never knew we lived so close to each other." She took a deep breath, her focus completely on the landscape in front of us. "I haven't been home in a while."

"What's a while?" I asked, trying to distract myself from the fact that we were approaching my mom's house. Soon, we'd pass the wooden archway that read *Farrier Farm*. It used to be *Slade Acres*, but we changed that the second we could, using one of my first earnings to get a bigger, bolder sign for the arch. We chose the name together, and now it's a farrier station. Everyone brings their horses here to shoe, and my brother learned the trade to live up to the name. As much as I loved the sign, as much as I loved to see it...I didn't want to see it now.

"Um..." Emersyn thought. "Since I started working at *Rodeo Way*."

"You haven't been home in that long?" I raised a brow at her.

She shook her head. "When you're trying to climb the corporate ladder you don't have a lot of wiggle room for vacations."

"We can stop by and see your parents before we leave, and your horse." I raised her hand to my lips, kissing her knuckles.

She gave me a weak smile. "This is about your brother. I'll tell my mom I'm close. I can go see them, but you need to be—"

"Wherever you are," I said sternly. "My brother won't take long to sort out."

I could see Emersyn drop her chin from the corner of my eye, and when I turned to look at her, she had a single brow raised—and damn, when this woman became a mom, she would scare the crap out of her kids. I couldn't help but smile at the thought, which only made her glare stronger. But before she could open her mouth to scold me again, we passed under the wooden arch.

"Farrier Farm," I said, taking my attention from her to the land around me. "We're here."

Emersyn's brow relaxed, and she turned to look around her, her grip on my hand tightening.

"I still can't believe it was you this whole time."

I kissed her knuckles again. "Ready to meet my mom?"

She turned to look at me, that smile I loved growing on her face. "Did you tell her I was coming with you?"

"No." I motioned my head toward the small blue house that sat on the end of the dirt drive. "But she's a mom. My text said 'we're on our way,' so she knows I'm not alone. See." My smile grew when I saw my mother's petite frame grow closer, and the fear and nerves that came with being here vanished. "She's waiting."

Emersyn looked out the windshield, her smile growing once my mom came into view.

Angie Slade stood on the porch, her arms folded, her hip cocked, her boots covered in dirt and most likely manure, her brown hair pulled back into a loose ponytail. Age never seemed to take her. Sure, there were a few grays near her roots, but you could see she was a worker. Her smile grew as I pulled the truck up, parking it and giving her a small wave before grabbing my hat from the dash.

Reluctantly, I let go of Emersyn's hand, opening my door after killing the engine.

"Ashton Oakes Slade," my mom's voice carried, "I told you, you didn't have to come. I just wanted to let you know what happened."

"Great to see you too, Mama." I opened my arms and pulled her into me. The scent of cookies mixed with hay hit...and I was home. "Where's Hayes?"

"You're not going to introduce me? I raised you better than that." My mom raised a brow, nodding toward Emersyn as she climbed from the cab of the truck.

And suddenly, I felt like a dick for leaving her there. I should have opened her door for her, held her hand, and took her over to introduce her before anything else. I furrowed my brow as I watched Emersyn hesitate by the truck, clearly not at all fazed by my lack of gentlemanly attributes. My expression softened as I watched her give me my time with my mom. I didn't deserve this woman.

With a grin, I waved her over.

"You know her—or at least you should." I turned back to my mom. "I used to talk about her a lot."

Her eyes widened as she glanced over at me and then back at Emersyn. "That's not..." she trailed off, watching Emersyn walk closer. "Well, if it isn't Miss Rodeo Wyoming, Emersyn Flynn."

Emersyn smiled, giving my mom a sweet wave. "Hi, Mrs. Slade." She smiled with a sweet tone.

"Do not call me Mrs. Slade, please." My mom heaved a breath. "I watched you grow up. Mrs. Slade is too formal."

Emersyn huffed. "Angie," she corrected herself.

"Please tell me you've been to see your mama."

"Not yet, but I will. I needed to make sure Oakes got here." She came to my side, slipping her hand to my forearm.

My mom caught the gesture, and her brow raised even higher as she looked from me to Emersyn. "You finally acted on that crush of yours, I see."

Emersyn breathed out a small chuckle, and I felt her eyes on me.

"She came back into my life. I had to." I shrugged a shoulder.

"He's worth the wait." Emersyn reached up to kiss my cheek.

Noticing the smile on my mother's face, I inhaled, taking the conversation back to the sole reason I was here. "Where's Hayes?" I repeated.

My mom, not taking her eyes off me, reached out for Emersyn. "He's in the barn, fixin' shoes. You go talk to him, and I'm going to talk to Miss Rodeo." She smiled as she pulled Emersyn away from me.

Pulling her back before my mom could get her, I gave her a kiss. "Don't believe anything she says."

Emersyn laughed, kissing me again. "See you soon." Then she was dragged into the house with my mother, their voices already carrying into the house. Knowing my mom, she'd have Emersyn's entire backstory in a few hours.

My brother, Hayes—who was three years younger than me—enjoyed working with horses more than anything. After our dad was arrested, and even after therapy, he took to drugs and alcohol to cope. I threw my energy into the rodeo, having it quickly become a passion, while he numbed everything. He checked himself into rehab a few times, getting better with each one, but he was never able to stay on the right path. He lived in the city, falling in with the wrong crowds over and over again. That was, until recently. He moved in with my mom and began to work with the horses. He trained them. He took in horses who were headed for slaughter. The horses became his world, and they helped him stay sober—at least for the last two years.

When Mom's phone call told me she found him drunk in the barn, a rock dropped in my stomach. He had been doing so well the past couple of years; this had to be just a hiccup. I hoped and prayed it was a one-time thing—a slip that would get fixed. Was I terrified this was going to be more than that...take away everything he's worked for? Absolutely.

Hayes was right where my mom said he would be, hunched over with a hoof in between his knees, his arms moving as he trimmed the nails poking out. Horses were waiting in the stalls, his motorcycle propped up in between two stalls. I raised a brow at a horse trying to nip at his leather jacket that hung off the handle, then my eyes went to my brother. Where I looked like our mother—my brown hair and eyes—Hayes looked like our dad—blond hair, blue eyes, tanned skin from hours in the sun, and a lanky build that could somehow lift any weight. Hayes was built for farm work. He noticed me the second I came into his view, dropping the hoof and standing up with a long, drawn-out sigh.

"Let me guess," he started, raising his chin to the ceiling, "Mom called you."

I reached my hand out to the horse eating his jacket, gaining her attention. "Do you blame her?"

He groaned, turning his back and tossing his tool to the side. "Guess not."

"She said you were asking for me?"

"I don't remember. Sounds about right since you're the one who can always get me out of this mindset." He groaned, walking to the back of the horse, using his hand to tickle down the horse's leg. The mare lifted her leg, and Hayes took it with care.

"What happened?" I asked.

"A lot happened last night."

"Like?" I pushed, slapping my thigh, leaning my weight on his bike.

He gave me a glare, eyeing the way my foot was propped on the muffler. Hayes loved horses—he rode them constantly and cared for them better than anyone I knew—but this bike...this bike was his pride and joy. The one thing I knew he bought with his own money and didn't lose when he had lost just about everything. Catching his glare, I lowered my foot and gently got off his bike.

"I just went out with a friend," he finally answered.

"And drank?"

Hayes shot me a different look, and I saw it in his eyes that he was still feeling the night. I raised a brow and watched my brother move. He grabbed the shoe puller and reached for the horse's hoof. "I meant to only have one drink," he mumbled.

"How many did you have?"

"More than one."

"How did you get home? You rode your bike?" I gestured toward his bike.

"No." He shook his head. "Conway brought it back just a bit ago."

"So, you got home…" I trailed.

"I got an Uber. I've learned my lesson enough not to drink and drive."

"Was Conway with you? Why didn't he try to stop you? He's always been on top of that."

"Yes, he was, and he did, but I didn't listen," he snapped. "What's with the interrogation?" He dropped the horse's hoof, his puller falling to his side, hitting his leather chaps with a slap, which honestly sounded like it hurt. "I fucked up, okay? And Mom was awake when I got home. I thought I could sleep it off in the barn, but she came out and saw me. She was worried, so she called you. Trust me, I'm feeling it today, and I know where I went wrong."

"Where'd you go wrong?" I asked, my voice dropping, thinking about how, just five years ago, getting this information out of him was tough. He would deny anything and everything you shot at him, but now here he was, answering everything before I had the chance to ask it.

"Last night…or years ago?"

"Let's start with last night."

He bent to pick the hoof up again, starting to remove the shoe. Then he went into a long-winded story, telling me everything, every single detail about the night that led to him drinking. Came to find out, when someone brought up Dad, it was still a sore spot for him. And even now, years later, well into adulthood, people still liked to remind him who he came from. And Hayes didn't take to it well at all.

The entire time he talked, he worked, changing all four shoes in the time it took to tell me the story. Once the last shoe was placed, once his tools were put away, once everything that was weighing him down was out in the open, he put his hands on his hips and looked over at me.

"I'm sorry you had to come all the way out here for this," he sighed. "The second Mom told me she called you, I expected a phone call, but here you are, in the flesh." He waved his hand up and down, gesturing to my entire being.

"In the flesh. And...yeah..." I rubbed the back of my neck, pushing myself off the wall to walk toward him. "I was going to call, but Emersyn said we needed to come, and I'm glad I listened to her. You needed to get all of that out."

He nodded, his body language completely different than when I came in. Now, he was calm, his breaths easy, and his shoulders relaxed. A sense of relief came from him. "I called my therapist and sponsor. I have an appointment this afternoon."

"So...you're telling me a phone call would have sufficed?" I said, hoping he'd catch on to the edge of sarcasm that I slipped in there.

"Probably...but"—he met my gaze, taking a step forward—"it's good to see you, and it was good to get all of that out. Therapy works, AA works, but nothing beats talking to you. Thank you."

I grabbed his shoulder, pulling him into me for a hug. "I'm glad I came. And I'm glad you're okay. Just"—I pulled away—"punch someone instead of grabbing that bottle next time."

Hayes dropped his chin, a genuine laugh filling the distance. "Ah, yeah, and have you pay for bail money instead of gas getting here? Now, I have a question. Emersyn? She's here?"

I chuckled, giving his shoulder a squeeze. "Why don't you come inside and meet the woman I'm madly in love with."

Right before dinner, Hayes came out of his bedroom, just having finished his appointment with his therapist, his eyes puffy from tears. He pulled Mom into a hug, whispering to her, making her cry in turn. Then once again, he pulled me in his arms. I tried not to see this as a start-over for him, just a small hiccup, that tomorrow he would wake up just the way he was before someone made him remember the shit he went through. He knew his triggers; he knew his steps; he knew what to do. Now, I just had to trust him.

He smiled at dinner, talking to Emersyn and hanging on to her every word as she talked about my rides, even pulling out her phone to show off some of the photos she had taken. He lit up talking to her, and she was loving talking about her passion. And I just loved hearing her talk about it.

"So, what's next?" Hayes asked, leaning back into his chair, the question directed at me. "The article is turned in, so why you hanging around this guy?"

"My contract is for the summer, ending in August. I had to get the article in so the proof could be made. Now, I get to take more photos, maybe throw some more questions at this guy." She nudged me with her elbow parroting Hayes. "Maybe just,"—Emersyn gave me a side glance—"enjoy my time while I have it. As much as I like my job, I love rodeos more. So, we have a few more before we head to Colorado. I'll just embrace what I have left."

"Utah is next, right? Mom has your schedule," Hayes asked, raising a brow as he leaned on the table.

"Not that it's accurate. Drew keeps sending me all kinds of random emails that change your trip. I can't keep it straight; how do you?" My mom rolled her eyes, grasping her water glass with two hands. "He's keeping you busy, that's for sure."

"NFR bound. That's the goal, but Utah got canceled, which is fine, that won't hurt my standings. We'll head to Cheyenne after this. Then Riverton, and Montana, and then…" I glanced over at Emersyn. "Gotta get this gal back to Denver."

She gave me a tight smile. Denver was the end of the line for Emersyn and me. She'd return to her day-to-day life with *Rodeo Way*, and I'd go back to traveling alone. A conversation definitely needed to happen before we got to Denver. I wasn't ready to stop this yet. Long distance, weekend trips, phone calls, FaceTime… I didn't care how we kept it up, just as long as we did.

"Cheyenne is in, what?" Mom asked, breaking my train of thought. "Five days?"

"Yeah…the 25th." I shifted in my seat, draping my arm on the back of Emersyn's chair. "I need to tell Drew I'll make that one, He was nervous I would have to cancel. We didn't really know what to expect once we got here." I gave Hayes a quick glance, noticing the shame drape across his eyes. "I think I needed to come home anyway. It's been too long, and he understood. He says hi, by the way."

My mom nodded. "I do like him. He needs to come by more often too."

"Or…" I began, "you guys can come to Cheyenne. Drew will be there, Ty too." I grabbed my glass, gulping the water down before I could take back what I said.

When I first started riding, I asked Mom to come. She flat out told me she couldn't. It was too hard for her—and I understood. She had a copy of my schedule, and she could watch whatever ride I had, but she hadn't been on arena dirt since Dad. I never asked her to come after that, never expected her to. Looking from her to Hayes, I caught the slight hesitation on her face before she looked to Emersyn. Emersyn smiled at her, raising her brow and leaning forward lightly.

"You'll be there, Emersyn?" she asked.

"I will. Camera in hand, ready to get the perfect shot."

"Well, then"—my mom looked over to Hayes—"I don't see why not."

"I can ask Conway to watch the horses." Hayes reached in his pocket for his cell phone. "Guaranteed he'll do it."

"Seriously?" I looked at my mom.

She smiled at me. "Yeah...why not. I haven't seen you ride in a long"—she sighed—"long time. It's about time I do."

Oakes

Can you get tickets to Cheyenne? Two?

Drew

Can I get tickets? Who do you think you're talking to?

Oakes

Two.

Drew

I can get two. How's Hayes?

Oakes

He'll be okay, but I am really happy I came home. Thanks again.

My mom says hi.

CHAPTER THIRTY
Emersyn

Angie handed me a mug full of tea, the steam wafting through the air, right before she took her seat next to me on the back porch. I took it, giving her a sweet smile before turning back to the view that was Farrier Farms. Two amazing places right in a row. The sun had begun to set, the golden grass blazing to life as the few horses still grazed in the pasture. It was the perfect picturesque scene, and I was here without my camera.

Oakes and Hayes went to work, doing the nightly check on the horses, Oakes promising me he'd be fast, only to have me *and* his mother telling him to take his time with his brother. Angie pulled me into a hug after that, chuckling as she mumbled, "I knew I always liked you."

"So," Angie sighed, "when you're not digital editing or following my son around, what are you up to these days? I see your mama in the store every now and then. She tells me you're busy."

I nodded, lifting my tea to my lips to smell the chamomile. "I am," I responded. "I'm normally just..." I sighed, leaning my head back, seeing

Oakes and Hayes come from the barn, Oakes slapping his brother's shoulder. "...surrounded by concrete."

Angie hummed. "Sounds miserable."

"It wasn't," I said. "Until recently."

"You were always something to watch growing up. Always on the back of a horse, doing some trick, or off to another rodeo. When you didn't win America, I think everyone just expected you to come home." She shrugged. "You never did. What made you realize concrete walls didn't amount to this?"

I shook my head, her words at the forefront of my mind as I watched Oakes lean against the wooden fence. He and Hayes faced the sunset, their arms draped over the railing—another perfect moment I wished I could capture on film. I had the urge to go get my camera, but I stayed right where I was and soaked in the sight of Oakes and his brother instead of wasting a moment here to dig out my camera.

I breathed in deep. "Your son," I answered, saying it out loud for the first time since the realization hit me yesterday. "This assignment. Being with him at all the rodeos. Watching him train and being a part of everything again. Writing about him sparked it. I love writing about the rodeo. I love photographing it. This entire endeavor sparked that back in me. I think I forgot for a while what was important, what I loved. He helped me see this was all possible for me. If it wasn't for him, I wouldn't be sitting here. I wouldn't feel like I had clear direction," I said softly, taking a sip of my tea. "Did he tell you I didn't recognize him?"

She nodded. "He did, over a phone call earlier in the summer. We don't talk much when he's on the road, but when he called that morning, I answered. He told me all about you, how you were just the same—if not better—but had no clue who he was. And he wasn't quite sure how to tell you."

I chuckled. "It's a little embarrassing."

"Nah, honey, he's changed so much. Physically and mentally. He's always so rough around the edges; he doesn't want people to see him. He's never brought anyone back here when he visits. I've met his friend Ty and his agent, but other than that, I haven't met a single soul from his world. Oakes Ashford and Ashton Slade are two separate people, and I know what happened to us still haunts him. He wants to keep it all separate...but you..."

I glanced at her, pulling my knees to my chest.

"You see him."

I scoffed. "Now I do. After he told me who he was."

She shook her head. "You saw him that night his hand was crushed. I was—" She stopped, inhaling and taking a look at her sons. "I was in the hospital that night. I missed his ride and the accident. Hayes was the one who told me what happened. His brother was a wreck, but when Oakes came in the hospital, he was calmer than anyone. He let them assess his hand and bandage it up. He scheduled his own surgery and treatment, and then...he came to my room, and do you want to know the first thing he told me?"

I pinched my brow and tightened my lips, my gaze glued on Angie. Her eyes, the exact same as Oakes, seared into me. Oakes never confirmed that the events of his father and the rodeo were so close together, but this solidified it. He handled his hand all on his own while his mother held on for her life in the hospital. It gave that night more meaning than it already did. He was alone...except, he wasn't...not in the slightest.

"He told me, 'I fell in love tonight.' I held onto his hand and told him that if he really was in love, he needed to hold on to it, not forget that feeling, and it seems with you sitting here, he never did. He may put on a gruff exterior, he may act like a jackass sometimes"—I snorted at her remark—"but he loves you, because you've always seen him, even if you don't even remember it."

"I remember that night. I told him it was the reason why I got so into rodeo stats, having to know everything. I was always looking for him. He was always right there."

"He's the kind of guy that won't go anywhere either."

I smiled. "I sure hope not."

"Trust me, Emmy." Angie reached out and placed her hand on my forearm, and her saying my nickname sent comfort through my bones. "He loves you. He isn't going nowhere." She took a deep breath and removed her hand, standing from the chair. "Now, I set the guest room up for you and Oakes. His room still has his twin bed in it and—"

"Oh," I cut her off, moving my legs to sit up straighter. "I can find a motel, or I can sleep on the couch, or—"

"Emmy." Angie dipped her chin and raised her brow. "My son is thirty-one...you are thirty-four. I have no doubt what you two have been up to, and I do not mind you sharing a bed while you're here. The guest room is set for you, and Oakes will show you the way. Hayes and I wake up early to tend to the farm, so I'm off to bed." She touched my shoulder, giving it a light pat. "It's good to have you here. Sleep well."

I rolled my lips together, a tight smile forming, loving the way she squeezed my shoulder. "Goodnight, Angie."

To: E.Flynn@rodeowaymag.com, S.krass@rodeowaym
   ag.com
From: M.pennel@rodeowaymag.com
Subject: Reno Follow Up
Date: July 20th: 4:34 PM

Emersyn,

Update?

How is everything going with Mr. Ashford's family? Can you send a little information on it? We'd like to be in the loop. Mr. Manning is being awfully quiet as well.

Sterling says the article is great, up to par, and he's making it as polished as possible. We will have a proof in August. Be proud of yourself.

Morgan
Editor in Chief - Rodeo Way Magazine
Denver, CO

CHAPTER THIRTY-ONE
Oakes

"Make sure you say hi to Mable while you're here." Mrs. Flynn—Rebecca, as I was told to call her—gave her daughter a knowing look, the same look that Emersyn gave me just days before, and I couldn't help but chuckle.

Tonight was our last night in town, and Emersyn had all but blended in with my family. She cooked with my mom, helped Hayes with chores, letting him talk about anything and everything as they worked, even going a ride on his bike with him. And once we were ready to climb in bed for the night, she curled right up to me like it was natural. My mom and brother accepted her right away, and I was grateful to be receiving the same treatment from the Flynns while we joined them for dinner.

Rebecca and my mom had gone to school together, though they didn't run with the same friends, they knew each other and treated each other decently throughout the years. We learned that Hayes was in charge of all of their horses' shoes, and he came here so they didn't have to load them back and forth. They, not once, mentioned my dad, or where he was, or my change of name. They took to calling me Oakes just as easily as Emersyn did.

When Emersyn gave her mom the same knowing look, she reached under the table and squeezed my knee.

"I actually should ride for Oakes. We have a bet going."

"A bet?" Mr. Flynn—who, like his wife, demanded I call him Jack—raised a brow, and if he wasn't bald, it would have touched his hairline. "Watch it, Oakes, she's competitive." He pointed his fork at his daughter.

"So am I." I smiled, reaching over to give Emersyn's knee a harder squeeze. "I'll admit she has me beat on that front, though. Are you aware of how amazing your daughter is at the mechanical bull?"

Rebecca gave a smirk as her gaze turned to her daughter. "Oh, we've seen videos. Never actually *seen* her on it, though. What's this bet?"

"She bet me she would ride a bull if I did a trick on a horse."

"A handstand," Emersyn corrected.

"Technically, a handstand is a trick, so I'm tweaking it to trick," I teased, looking at Emersyn.

"Handstand. We shook on it."

"You gave him the hardest trick in the book. That took you years to master." Rebecca lifted her glass, gesturing it toward Emersyn.

"Meh, it's a piece of cake." Emersyn waved her mom off.

"I'm sure Mable will be happy to let you show Oakes how it's done." Rebecca gave me a wink.

"Well, in that case…" Emersyn scooted her chair back, the wood screeching against the flooring. "I'll go get Mable ready." Emersyn bent down to kiss my cheek before turning to leave the dining room.

I turned back to her parents. "Is she really going to do a handstand on the back of her horse?" I pointed my thumb over my shoulder, listening as the front door closed.

"Pretty sure if she had been allowed to do a stunt during Miss Rodeo America, she would have won." Rebecca stood, grabbing Emersyn's plate from across the table. "It doesn't take long for her to get Mable ready. Why don't you head out to the barn; she'll be waiting for you."

Taking the cue, I thanked them for dinner and slipped on my boots. Emersyn was in the barn, a gorgeous pitch-black horse in front of her being readied with a white saddle. White leather straps hung from each side, and the reins and lead had gold jewels, making it sparkle.

"You went all out designing this saddle, didn't ya?" I asked, coming up behind her.

Emersyn looked over her shoulder. "My mom had it made. She was big on bling."

"How did you get into trick riding? I mean, I remember you being a stunt rider in high school, but did this come before or after the Miss Rodeo pageants?" I reached up, giving the mare a pat on the nose. "You must be Mable." Mable huffed and stuck her nose into my palm.

"I did equestrian riding first, but that quickly evolved when I got bored. So...we upped the game. Pageants came after that, but all the training helped with the horsemanship category." Emersyn bent, cinching the saddle on the horse tight. Mable didn't even flinch. "Mable got me through so many competitions; she's probably excited to have this saddle on her again." She stood and slapped her palms on her thighs. "Ready, girl?"

Mable nodded her head, giving her rider a small huff.

Emersyn grabbed the lead and walked past me. "Ready for your lesson?"

Looking her up and down as she passed, thoroughly checking her out, I followed as she led Mable into a small arena I didn't notice before. Fenced off with a white metal gate, the arena had no chutes, no holding areas, no pens. It was set up for horses and horses alone, and as weird as it was to admit...it was a relief to see. This space was for Emersyn. She had seen me in my arena, and now I was going to see her in hers.

"I'll just"--I raised my boot up to the gate, leaning forward with my elbows—"watch from here."

Emersyn gave me a smirk. "Pay attention." She pointed at me before she slipped her boot in the stirrup and hoisted herself into the saddle.

She kicked Mable into a gallop right off the bat, taking a few laps around the arena, letting go of the reins to move her arms up above her head, to her side, moving in the wind. Once she seemed to find her own balance, she shifted her weight and placed her knees on the saddle. I cocked a brow as I watched her raise one leg straight behind her, the entire time Mable in a steady gallop.

"Damn..." I muttered.

With each trick, Emersyn's confidence boosted. I could see it on her face. She would hesitate for half a second before taking a deep breath, then her body would move. My jaw dropped when she used one leg to hold onto the horse, her head close to Mable's back hoof, her hair flowing freely. She grabbed Mable's tail and let the hair fall through her hand before she hoisted herself up, back into the saddle.

She cheered at herself once her weight was back in the center, raising her arms up high. The memory of that rodeo sixteen years ago, of watching her do a few tricks before the events began, hit me like déjà vu as she circled the arena. The thought of how strong and daring she was to do stunts like these, to trust her horse that much, made what I was about to do look like child's play. The routine was perfection even then, and now—decades later—she was performing the routine with ease, as if she had never stopped.

And I was completely mesmerized.

She shifted her weight again, easing Mable into a canter. She leveled her shoulders out and raised her chin, lifting her arms out to her sides. The world turned into slow motion as I watched her. I could hear her deep breath, the air coming from her lips as she exhaled, and when she opened her eyes, she had more determination, moving her body, and then, she moved as if she were underwater. Her forearms rested on the saddle, her hands clamped onto the horn, and suddenly, her legs were in the air.

"Holy fuck," I mumbled, stepping off the gate as I watched.

She held it for two, three, four...eight seconds before she flung her legs back, landing in the saddle with a look of pure excitement plastered on her face as she slowed Mable to a stop. Once Mable was trotting, Emersyn leapt off, and without even stopping, she raced toward me, her smile only growing the closer she got.

I climbed the gate, jumping over it just in time for Emersyn to jump into my arms, her legs wrapping around my waist. I held her close, feeling her body shake with adrenaline as the laughs spilled from her.

"Did you see that?" she shouted into my neck.

"I saw it, Emmy." I smiled at her, loving how every pore seeped joy, every piece of her radiated with a glow I had never seen on her before. "I can't believe you fucking did that."

"I haven't done that in years!" She moved, arching her back softly, her arms still wrapped around my neck. "I'm going to be so sore tomorrow. I was honestly worried I wouldn't be able to do that."

"You did it. It's like riding a bike." I kissed her, just a soft fleeting kiss. "I only wish I had that on camera."

"Well"—she flipped her hair off the side of her face—"I won't be doing that again, so..."

I silenced her with a kiss, a deeper one this time, tasting the sweet wine from dinner still on her lips. "You're still gonna get on a bull, right?" I whispered against her.

"You gonna do that now that you've seen it in action?"

I pinched my brow and looked behind her at Mable, who stood in the same place, her body heaving just as much as Emersyn's. There's no way in hell I could do what I just saw Emersyn and that horse do. No. Way. In. Hell.

"Maybe we need to rethink our bet."

She laughed, sending a fizz through my entire being, right before she kissed me again and again.

Rebecca and Paul were reluctant to let us leave, but they finally—with a promise of a trip sooner than a few years—gave each of us a hug and waved as we left. Emersyn's adrenaline rush had faded, her cheeks still pink and her eyes still glinting, but she was drained, I could tell. She blew her mom a kiss and leaned her head on the headrest, turning to look at me.

"Thank you," she whispered.

I raised a brow and reached for her hand. "For?"

"Just being you, being amazing, being the man I'm falling for."

I brought her hand to my lips and lightly kissed her knuckles, watching as her sleepy, sexy smile grew. I loved her. There was no doubt in my mind how I felt for Emersyn. I loved her the moment she took my hand, the moment she gave me the courage to do more, the moment I saw her walk up to me even though she had no idea who I was. There was nothing that was going to change the way I felt toward her, not even if she didn't give those words the same value I did. She was here, she was glowing...and she was mine.

Chapter Thirty-Two
Oakes

The house was dark by the time we got back. The plan was to leave for Cheyenne early, so Hayes and Mom most likely called it quits right after night check. The slack events were happening before the rodeo began, and even though I had plenty of training time at Hartwell Hills, adding a little slack wouldn't hurt. Plus, that would give Mom and Hayes time to settle in, get their bearings. And Emersyn...it would give her time to bask in the new life she was going to embrace.

Seeing her take hold of it was something to witness. She went from being unsure, her confidence only showing when she was in the arena, to bold and positive about what she wanted. Seeing her on her horse, her legs high in the air, the smile beaming on her lips...she was finding herself again, and it was nothing short of miraculous.

We linked our fingers, slowly making our way to the guest room. Wanting her in my arms more than anything, I pulled her down the hall, taking it in long strides, until I felt her tug at my arm, completely stopping me. I turned to her, raising a brow.

"Is this your room?" she whispered, her free hand pointing toward the cracked open door of my childhood bedroom.

"Yeah…" I drawled, confusion laced in my tone.

"Can we go in?" She tugged again.

"Emmy…" I sighed as I willingly let her pull me into my bedroom.

She slipped her hand from mine, her mind on one track to see who I used to be. I quietly shut the door behind us. She turned on the bedside lamp, creating the soft glow that illuminated the photos that hung on my wall. We had been here for days, and I hadn't come in here. It had the same feel to it, the same smell of hay. I scrunched my nose, knowing if I was smelling it, so was she, but Emersyn was zoned in on the photos on my wall. I still couldn't believe my mom hadn't taken my photos or posters down and turned my room into an office or stuck a treadmill in it. She kept it the same.

I leaned on the small desk, facing Emersyn as her fingers trailed over the photographs.

"This is the Oakes I remember from all those years ago." She pointed at a photo of me in a Future Farmers of America group photo, her fingers lightly touching the Oakes from so long ago. The photo featured a tall, lanky freshman; my nose way too big for my face, and I hadn't grown into my ears yet. "Maybe a little older." She gave me a wry grin before turning back to the photo.

Pushing myself off the desk, I came up behind her, wrapping my arms around her waist, loving the way her body melted into mine. "I was in eighth grade in that photo. I was a sophomore when I had my accident."

"What did you do that year after the accident?" she asked, her voice low and somber as her head tilted to my shoulder. I took in the moment, feeling her heartbeat thunder through her back.

I kissed her shoulder and then spun her in my arms to face me. She wrapped her arms around my neck, her gaze locking onto mine as she waited for the answer.

"Physical therapy on my hand, took up running and CrossFit. And then, once my hand was better, I began to ride bulls."

"You jumped right into that, didn't you? You mentioned that you wanted to do bronc; you were riding bronc that night."

"Yeah, bronc was how I started, but that was until the love of my life told me I could ride bulls one handed." I grinned at her.

"Love of your life?" she repeated, a dip to her voice. "That's not the first time you've said that."

Taking a deep breath, I let the words fall. I knew how I felt, there was no denying it. "I love you, Emersyn. I have for sixteen years. You are what keeps me moving, what makes all of this worth it. I love you with everything that I am. You have all of me, from now until you decide you're done with me."

She gasped, a small breath of air filling the space between us. "I don't think I'll ever be done. I don't think I could ever get enough of you. I've never fallen this hard, this fast... I—"

I crushed my mouth to hers, nothing gentle about the way I desired her. She gave me a small moan, her sound making my dick twitch, wanting her more and more. She didn't even have to say it, but yet...I knew she felt it. She loved me just as much as I loved her. I began to walk us back, our lips never leaving each other, until we hit the edge of my small twin bed. I fell, and just as smooth as if I were a stunt she was performing, she crawled on top of me, straddling me. Her hands grasped the nape of my neck, her lips claimed me, her tongue danced with mine, and every single nerve ending in my body ignited.

She trailed her fingers on my shoulder blades, and she trembled, letting out a breath of air that shook.

"This feels…" she sighed, her forehead leaning against mine, "…different."

An ache grew in my chest. "This feels right," I corrected her, bringing her lips to mine, cupping her face in my palms.

With a push from her palms, my back hit the bed, a small squeak coming from the frame. Emersyn smiled against my lips, a small giggle escaping her.

Trialing my fingers down her arms, I played with the hem of her shirt. "This bed is old," I commented.

"Is it going to be loud the entire time? Should we stop?"

"If you think I'm stopping, we'll move to the floor."

"We'll just be quiet," she whispered, her eyes fluttering closed the moment we kissed.

"Can you be quiet, baby? I do love your moans, your screams…especially when it's my name." I grasped the nape of her neck, my fingers pressing into her.

Emersyn shivered. "I'll whisper your name, when I'm so close only you can hear."

Shifting her hips, she rocked against me, and any amount of patience fled my body. I gripped her hips and rolled, the edge of the bed closer than I anticipated, but we stayed on the mattress, Emersyn grabbing onto the blanket to steady herself. I worked on her shirt, my hand moving on its own until her breast was in my palm. I kneaded, feeling her nipple pebble under my touch.

I loved the way her body reacted to me. I loved the way her breaths would hitch, the sound engraving into my brain. I loved the way her cheeks flushed as the heat rose in her body. I could feel the warmth spread across her, only causing the heat to rise in me. I couldn't wait to feel her clench around my cock while trying to hold in her moans and gasps.

Her hands began to fumble with my pants, working quickly, and once her hand flew down my boxers and was wrapped around my length, I moaned—a little louder than I should have. Emersyn laughed, a shaky 'shhh' vibrating with her laughter.

"We have to be quiet," she reminded me.

"I want to be inside of you. I want to feel you, every inch of—shit," I grumbled, remembering that all the protection I had was in my duffel bag. I dropped my head in the crook of her neck.

"What is it?" she asked breathlessly.

"I don't have a condom." I lifted my head. "As much as I would love for this to—"

"I'm clean, and I have an IUD."

My eyes widened. "I...uh...I...are you sure?"

She nodded, giving me a kiss. "I want you, Oakes. All of you. I trust you."

"I'm clean too. I've never not used a condom," I promised her. "If you are one hundred percent—"

"Two hundred." She smiled.

"Well, then..." I grinned. "Be quiet," I repeated, using the tips of my fingers to play with her shirt.

"Pretty sure *I* just had to remind *you* to be quiet," she laughed, tugging my shirt over my head.

It became frantic after that, the burn racing through us as our clothes flew to the floor. Once we were skin to skin, I could feel how wet she was, how perfect her pussy felt against my cock. Just the thought of having her bare sent that flame through my body, a hyper-awareness that we were so close. Kissing her to hold in her moans, I ran my hand down her side, caressing her thigh, until I was gripping my cock. Using the tip, I created small circles around her clit, teasing her ever so slightly until her moans turned to whimpers. I pressed my cock to her entrance, loving the little gasp that filtered the air. As much as I wanted to hear her little noises, the moans that sent me over the edge, we did agree to be quiet. I furrowed my brow, regretting that decision as a moan tried to escape her.

I slid inside of her, and she took all of me, her warmth enveloping me. Her head dropped to the pillow, her eyes closed tight, and I swear, she was trying her hardest not to cry out. On instinct, I reached up, using my palm to cover her mouth. The warmth of her breath hit my fingers as her eyes widened, a look of complete pleasure filling the blue orbs.

"Fuck, Emmy," I whispered in her ear, the sound of my voice making her tighten around my cock. "You feel so goddamn fantastic around me. So. Fucking. Perfect."

She hummed into my hand as I began to rock, her hips following my every motion. We moved in sync with each other, the frantic need now replaced with the want to savor this feeling. Our bodies hummed and fizzed as we chased our releases together. This was more than I had ever felt. This was...this was...*everything*. The slow, steady rhythm that combined us, making this real. *Us* real.

Releasing my own moan, another *fuck* murmured through the air, and I removed my palm to kiss her gently before raising slightly to look at her. Glistening with a light sheen of sweat, Emersyn glowed, more beautiful than ever. Our eyes locked, and the pressure began to get stronger. Stronger...*stronger*...

"I love you," she whispered, raising up to kiss me. "I love you."

"I love you," I said, pulling her to me, covering her completely, making sure my heartbeat became hers, to not only tell her but show her how much I loved her. I would never stop loving her. "I love you."

Our climaxes hit us at the same time, and we silenced our cries with a kiss as we rode through it together, our bodies twitching and buzzing as we slowly came down from the high, making it last as long as we possibly could.

CHAPTER THIRTY-THREE
Emersyn

My hands trailed down Oakes's shoulders, down his protective vest, over his sponsor patches, to his belt buckle—basically anywhere I could touch while he was dressed like this—my eyes following the path my hands took. I'd memorized his skin under my fingers, every line and crease that formed with his muscles, and even now with his vest, chaps, jeans, shirt...I could picture them. I could feel them, feel *him*.

The way I loved this man.

"You're supposed to be zipping up my vest, not undressing me with your eyes," Oakes said, his lips raising in the corner.

Lightly, I give his pec a slap. "I zipped it."

"And then felt me up." He leaned down, giving me a light kiss.

"Not much to feel up under all this, but"—I kissed him again—"I couldn't help myself."

He hummed against my lips before inhaling, standing up straight, hooking his thumbs in his chaps. He looked me up and down, obviously liking what he saw by the small grin that spread across his face. Flared-out jeans with my black boots, a tucked-in white button-down with a fringe vest over it and a black hat perched on my head, I was channeling my Miss Rodeo days, down to the wings in my hair and the confidence that came with the outfit. I loved the way I looked tonight, and I loved the way Oakes was looking at me. Leaning in to give him another kiss, he arched his back.

"You're missing your camera," he said, pinching his brow in the middle.

"Your mom has it." I gave him a wink. "I came to wish you luck and then meet your mom and Hayes in the stands."

"You've been at the chute almost every ride—"

"Almost."

"I kinda think I need you there."

"*Oakes Ashford,*" I drew out his last name, the stage name that he wore so well. "You don't need me or anyone at that chute."

"Nah." He moved, wrapping his arm around my waist. "But I like having you there."

"Ashford!" his name was called, and he turned toward the chutes. "Barrels are almost done. Get up to chute eight."

"Go." I gave him a small kiss, finding it hard to stop myself from kissing him every moment of every day. "I gotta get to the stands before you're up."

"Where you sitting?"

"With Hayes and your mom."

He gave me a slight eyeroll followed by a smile. "I meant section."

"Oh." I dipped my chin, placing my hands on his chest. "East side, I think."

"Perfect."

Then, he turned his back and jogged up the metal stairs. I watched until I couldn't see him anymore then took off the other way. The crowd was thick, but I weaved my way through, only managing to get stopped by a few cowboys that I'd been introduced to along the way. Ty was there, giving me a fist bump, the current Miss Rodeo America gave me a smile, and Drew—surprisingly—pulled me in for a quick hug.

It only took two months for me to get fully immersed back into the world I loved so much. How was I supposed to go back to *Rodeo Way* after this? Stay still in Colorado when I knew all of this was happening without me? Morgan still hadn't reached out to me about the article, other than saying it was heading for proof after it had been edited, promising me that there would be something for us to see when we were there, but other than that...nothing. I was certain the journalist job was mine. There was no way I would be content working as a digital editor anymore, and *Rodeo Way* could use more remote writers. Maybe when I got back, I'd mention it. Maybe after the feature was published, she would go for it. Luca could set my schedule, and I could lessen the budget by camping. I'd have to invest in a new car, but that wouldn't be too much. Or I could travel with Oakes. I could stay with Oakes.

Just the thought of being with him brought a smile to my face and butterflies to my stomach. This was where I was supposed to be, there was no doubt. I had been missing out on so much, seeing this world through a screen.

My boots hit the metal stairs with a clang, and my heart soared. I loved that sound. You could smell the dirt, the beers, and, even though most people hated it—but I loved it—the livestock. The screens on either side of the arena showed the barrel racer up close as she rounded the third barrel, the crowd cheering once the announcer shouted her score, then they calmed again, waiting for the rodeo clown to roll his barrel out.

"Emmy!" I heard my name through the dull roar of the crowd, looking up to see Hayes, standing up and waving his hand in the air. Hayes looked nothing like Oakes did, his blond hair flopping over his ears, his blue eyes standing out in the crowd, but his smile...his smile was the same as Oakes. "Up here!"

We weren't sitting far away from the chutes. Drew was able to get us fantastic seats, the perfect view for me to get the shot of Oakes. I shimmied my way past the people next to us and took my seat next to Angie, giving her a quick side hug as she handed over my camera.

"What chute is he at?" Hayes asked, leaning over his mom's center.

"Eight," I responded, slipping my camera strap over my head.

"When's he riding?"

"Not sure. I think he's third or fourth."

I raised my camera to my eyes, zooming in on the chutes. I could see Oakes clearly as he swayed his hips from side to side, his gaze searching the stands in front of him. The animal in the chute bucked once, gaining his attention, and a smile ripped across his face. Then Ty came into view. I clicked a photo and lowered my camera, taking a look at the candid shot between him and his friend.

"He's getting ready." I leaned in to tell Angie.

"I feel terrible I've never been here for this. The last time I saw him ride was back home, and he was so young. So different," she said, louder than normal, keeping her eyes on the chute.

I turned to her. "Which one?"

"You were there. You carried the flag." She bumped into my shoulder with hers. "Oakes may have let it slip after his ride that day that he was going to marry you one day."

I let out a small chuckle. "Did he?"

"Can confirm," Hayes said, popping a piece of popcorn in his mouth.

I smirked, pulling my camera back to my eyes. Oakes was easier to find this time, even with his helmet on, but he hadn't mounted the bull yet.

Marry Oakes?

I pursed my lips, knowing damn well if he were to ask me tonight, I'd say yes. The idea that this could be our life was a little overwhelming, but I could see it—and I wanted it.

Shoving that aside, even if my mind didn't particularly want to let go of the thought of Oakes being my husband, I turned back to Angie. "Don't feel terrible. He understood."

She gave me a soft smile. "I do love rodeos. Like you, they were one of my favorite things. It's only fitting that Oakes loves them just as much. I used to take the boys to so many events. Oakes was the most excited about them. He would jump in his boots, waiting for event after event. As soon as he was old enough, he was mutton busting and then learning to ride bronc. This was always his life. He's lucky he's found someone who loves it just as much." She turned to me, her smile growing.

I wrapped my arm around her shoulder and pulled her close. "What about you, Hayes?" I asked, leaning forward to get a better look at him.

"Watching them, sure, but"—he shook his head—"never thought it would be fun to ride a wild animal. I guess I lost interest in that after—" He stopped, swallowing and dipping his chin. He paused for a moment, then as if he didn't say anything, he raised his soda can to his lips. "I'd rather work with horses than ride them like this. Nah, this is all Oakes."

The event started, and the announcer began to talk about the bulls, '*the world's most dangerous sporting event, only the bravest men willingly get on a bull*,' and then when the music started, my entire body lurched forward.

"He's first." I cheered as Jon Bon Jovi began to blare through the speakers.

"How do you know?" Hayes asked.

I looked over at him, dumbfounded. "Do you not watch your brother's rides?" I asked sarcastically.

Hayes raised his eyebrows in question.

"It's the song, baby." Angie tapped his knee.

"He's the one to watch," the announcer's accent flooded the arena. "The million-dollar bull rider who has taken the world by storm. His only goal is to get back his title of NFR World Champion this year. The one who's never fallen off the bull" —I scrunched my nose, remembering the time we spent in the room after he hurt his knee—"the man who gets that check at the end of every night. The one. The only. Oakes. Ashford."

The crowd went wild. And I meant wild.

For two months, I had followed this man. I had spent time with him at the chutes and in different events through the western circuits, and the way this crowd screamed was unlike anything I had ever heard. Angie cupped her hands over her mouth, shouting his name. Hayes stood and fisted his arm in the air, and I raised my camera and focused on the chute.

I could see him pulling and tugging the rope, positioning his left hand just so, and I could see his back rise with each breath, and then he settled and stopped. Then...he nodded.

One. Two. Three.

The bull moved left and right and then in a complete circle.

The crowd cheered.

Four. Five. Six.

I snapped photo after photo of him and the bull, watching as their bodies moved in perfect sync with each other, his back like liquid as the bull bucked and bucked, his arm never once falling to his side.

Seven.

"And that ride!" the announcer shouted.

Eight.

The buzzer roared over the crowd, and Oakes jumped off, catching himself for only a second before running toward the gated stands. The bull fighters wrangled the bull, the cameras focused on the angry animal as it was led back into the pen, but my attention was on the man I had fallen so in love with. Even though we were many feet apart, I could still see his features clear as day.

The crowd still screamed as he removed his helmet and tossed it to the side, his unruly brown hair flying in his face. He whipped his head back, climbed up on the gate, and scanned the stands. The moment he found us, his smile spread so wide that anyone looking at him would notice it. It would light up the darkest room, and it was just for me. Leaning his body forward, he waved his hands in the air, catching the attention of the entire stadium.

"Oakes leads the night with a 95!" the announcer screamed. "It's going to be hard to beat that, but *damn* what a ride!"

Oakes mouthed something, and narrowing my eyes, I could just catch the faint movement of my name. *Emmy.*

"I think you need to go down there." Angie nudged me.

I didn't need to be told twice. I tossed my camera on her lap and shot up, making my way to him as if there was no one in between us. Everything moved so fast, and the next thing I knew, his hands were around my neck, my hat falling to the ground below me as I stepped up on the gate.

"Fuck, Emmy," he laughed in my neck.

"A 95." I pulled away from him. "Not bad, Ashford."

"I fucking love you." He smiled.

And I kissed him, hard, knowing all eyes were on us, but also finding that I didn't care at all. Let the world know that I was madly in love with this man. Let them know he was mine.

"What comes next?" I asked, resting my chin on Oakes's bare chest. His arm was wrapped around my shoulders, and he began to draw those lazy circles on my skin.

After the rodeo, the four of us went to dinner, but the minute the check was paid, Oakes and I said goodbye to his mom and brother and celebrated in our own way. We should have probably closed our eyes and gotten sleep, knowing tomorrow was another road trip, but we simply could never get enough of each other. Hands, lips, tongues…there was no part of us that we didn't explore. It wasn't until the only glow in the room was the moon that we slowed down, our bodies finally giving in to sleep. But my brain still wouldn't stop.

Oakes raised his eyebrow and looked at me. "Meaning?"

"Well…" I shifted my weight, my entire body on top of him now. Resting my chin on my fists, I took a deep breath. "Only a few more events…and then Colorado. I won't be traveling with you anymore, so…what comes next?"

"I guess I hadn't really thought about it. I just know that whatever comes next involves you."

I held back my grin. "I want you in my life too. I just would like to figure out how it's going to work. This has been the best summer of my life: you, rodeos, camping, you…" I kissed his chest. "I don't want it to stop."

"It doesn't have to."

"But my job," I shifted again. "I have a good feeling about my future there; this article is going to change so much for me. There's already a promotion on the table, a journalist job, but I had the idea today to talk to Morgan about possibly going remote."

"Remote? As in?"

"Traveling with you. Writing articles, taking photographs, working like I am now." I sighed. "But it wouldn't be an instant change."

He pinched his eyebrows, a deep inhale forcing me to rise and fall with his chest. Then, I could see the gears working in his head, his eyes studying the blank space behind me, until they finally met mine again.

"I could make Colorado home base." Oakes moved, resting his head on his hand. "I mean…I don't really have a home base. I go home from time to time, so making that shift to Colorado wouldn't make a difference. I wouldn't want to travel without you, but…we need a place to call home."

We need a place to call *home*.

My heart leapt.

"And that's Colorado?"

"That's wherever you are. You have a life in Colorado, and I won't ask you to give that up, but I do like the sound of you traveling with me, you working remotely—whether it be for *Rodeo Way* or your own thing. I want that to happen. So, what happens next?" he repeated my question, running his hands down my spine. "You and me. Long distance for a while, but we'll make that work. I'll come to you always. You and me, that's what happens next."

Although it wasn't a definite answer as to what the future held, it was the perfect start. We'd mold to fit each other's lives. We both wanted this, wanted each other, more than anything.

"I'll always want you." I sighed, pushing myself up to meet his lips. "This is the most important thing to me. It'll work."

Oakes cupped my face with his hand, drawing me close to him, deepening the kiss that was already melting my bones, that sleep that was so close seconds before fading away with each swipe of his thumb on my jawline.

This. Us. Heaven on earth. The only thing that truly mattered.

To: E.Flynn@rodeowaymag.com, S.krass@rodeowaym
   ag.com, manning.drew@pbragency.com
From: M.pennel@rodeowaymag.com
Subject: Photo shoot schedule
Date: August 2nd: 4:32 PM

Team -

Below you will find the schedule for the photo shoot with Mr. Ashford. We are looking forward to having Emersyn back in the office and seeing Mr. Ashford in person. The article that will feature Mr. Ashford is completed, and it turned out perfectly. I can see this becoming quite the buzz.

Please remind Mr. Ashford to bring two shirts, two pairs of jeans, two chaps, one protective vest, two pairs of boots, and two different colored hats.

   8 am: Arrive at *RW* building.
   8:30 am: Hair/Makeup
   9-12 pm: Photos
   1 pm: Meeting

See you on the 4th!

Morgan
Editor in Chief - Rodeo Way Magazine

Denver, CO

CHAPTER THIRTY-FOUR
Emersyn

"**P**erfect. Now, if you could hook your thumbs in your belt loop, kinda look off to the side..." Jenna, the lead photographer at *Rodeo Way*, instructed Oakes on how to stand as he begrudgingly stood in front of the brown backdrop. I could see the slight eyeroll he gave her as he followed her guidance, shifting his feet, his spurs hitting the floor with a jingle. "Great, I love it."

I stood next to Luca, watching as the photos Jenna was taking appeared on the screen in real time. She had Oakes dress like he was ready for the bull. Vest, chaps, boots, the only thing that was different was the black Stetson on his head instead of his helmet.

"He looks so thrilled," Luca leaned into me, whispering.

The first hour in the *Rodeo Way* building was hectic to say the least. Jenna met us right away, giving us a quick hello before her focus went right to the bull rider in front of her. The way his eyes widened when she said the words 'hair and makeup,' I couldn't help but laugh as she whisked him away, not even allowing him a second to give me a kiss. The man was totally out of his element here, but he did it…and did so without complaint.

The first thing I did before heading to the studio was go find Luca. He was hunched over his desk as I thought he would be, but when he saw me, he shot up, instantly dragging me from his office to the studio.

"Well, he doesn't really want to be here. He's only here because…" I whispered back, folding my arms but keeping my eyes on Oakes.

"He told you he would. Does the man ever smile?" he asked.

"Yes, he does." I bumped into him, nudging his body slightly. "And it's amazing."

"I'm just gonna say I called it."

"You didn't call anything. You just wanted to know what he smelled like."

"We didn't exactly write a romance clause into your contract, but I saw that kiss from Cheyenne."

I blushed, just thinking about it. The kiss still ran through my memory—every moment since that day in Hartwell Hills did.

It was hard not to want to be near as he took the photos, not to want to kiss him and tell him to loosen up, to make him laugh and smile like I knew he could. Instead, I stood back and tried my hardest to act professional. Luca knew I loved him, but he was still a client. And to my knowledge, dating clients or coworkers wasn't particularly welcomed. When Sterling and I started dating years ago, we had to disclose it and then sign a form stating our romantic relationship. It felt very *The Office*-esque. And seeing as Oakes and I planned to keep our relationship going after he wasn't a client anymore, I didn't feel a need to disclose anything to anyone. So back to being professional Emersyn. Oakes and I would have tonight at my place, and then the rodeo tomorrow before he was back on the road—this time without me. I was home for the time being, until I knew where my career was headed, but thankfully, I had an amazing man who was being supportive.

"Okay, great," Jenna said loudly before she walked up to Oakes. "Close ups. I just want you to stay still and look directly at the camera."

"'Cause that's not awkward or anything," Oakes grumbled, forcing me to hide a smile.

"I tell people to just imagine the camera being someone you love, someone you want to see again and again, and it makes it a little easier." She raised her camera, and I heard a click right as Oakes's gaze met mine for the briefest second before he turned back to the camera.

"I bet you one million bucks he's thinking about you," Luca whispered.

"Shh..." I shushed him, knowing full well that was exactly what Oakes was thinking about.

"Emersyn," a stiff voice pulled me from Oakes, and I turned to see Morgan. She jerked her head to the door, motioning for me to follow. I glanced back at Luca, lightly touching his arm before following my boss out of the studio.

"Morgan, hi. I was wondering when we were going to see you." I smiled.

"I just had a few things to grab, but here..." The excitement on her expression spread as she placed a hand on my shoulder, leading me farther away from the studio, handing me a copy of *Rodeo Way.*

I had held our publication in my hands multiple times, but none with a white canvas as a cover. The words floated on the blank space: *Rodeo Way: September-October 2025, Oakes Ashford: The Million Dollar Bull Rider—Ours for the Taking.* I took a heavy breath, knowing that tag was going to pull all the readers to it, but I couldn't open it.

The cover was the last thing they did, so I knew very well it was formatted and ready on the inside. My fingers were itching to move, to see my article and the photos I had taken...but I was frozen. I wanted Oakes to be here with me as we saw it come to life together.

"It's going to be our best issue yet," Morgan's voice filled my senses. "I knew you had to be the first to see it."

She led me into the same conference room where I was given this assignment, Sterling already inside sitting with his laptop open and a mug of coffee next to him. I took the seat across from him, the magazine sliding on the wood finish.

"Hey, Sterling." I nodded toward him.

He gave me a nod and his signature smile in return before leaning back in his chair, folding his arms over his chest. "Great article. I barely had to edit anything."

"Well, I thought I'd make your job a little easier. I did a few edits before sending it off."

"I had to change a few of the wordings and phrases, but other than that, it was damn good. Congrats. We knew you were the right one for the job."

"I wanted to talk specifics before Mr. Manning and Mr. Ashford get here, then we will finalize the cover and ask a few questions about the summer, but Emersyn"—Morgan placed her fingers on the counter—"I'm really impressed with this article. I love how you executed it, and all the photos you sent over only made it better. His story is exactly what I wanted."

I took a breath, knowing the words *the job is yours* were going to come flowing out of her mouth. My heart rate picked up, excitement flowing through me as I waited.

"I'd like to offer you the journalist job."

Before I could answer—which was me shouting *yes* at the top of my lungs—Morgan continued.

"Sterling has agreed to work as your editor, and each summer, we'll send you on a different feature. You'll do exactly what you did this time with a different NFR contender. And traveling with them? That was genius. You were able to really get to know Mr. Ashford, so we'll duplicate it every year. I'm sure other cowboys wouldn't mind having someone travel with them."

I listened to her and furrowed my brow. What she was offering me was something I could see myself loving: being on the road, going to rodeos, writing about what I loved... But she was missing the biggest key factor.

Oakes.

This wasn't successful because of how we executed it. It was successful because of him.

"Just for the summer?" I asked, my fingers finding the edge of the magazine.

"Summer is the prime season for rodeos, so it's the perfect time to capture this kind of story again. I want *Rodeo Way* to be known for its summer features, and you can bring them to us."

"I was hoping I could work remotely year-round," I began.

"Oh, no"—Morgan pushed her weight off the table—"during the off seasons, you'll return to digital editor, but you and Sterling will work together during the summers."

"Editing...and journalist?" I asked.

Morgan smiled, but then the conference door opening caught all of our attention.

"Mr. Manning!" Morgan shouted, raising her arms in the air to greet him. "Right on time. And Mr. Ashford."

Oakes.

I stiffened, stopping myself from reaching out for his hand. My mind was buzzing. I had gotten the offer, but not one I wanted. I could take it and still travel and see Oakes during the summers, making sure my schedule aligned with his, but just thinking about that put a strain on my thoughts. But then the memory of him calling Colorado his home base...maybe it wouldn't be too bad. It *could* work. Just like we promised last night, we'd make it work.

"You must be Mrs. Pennel," Oakes said as he pulled out the chair next to mine. Glancing over at him, I saw he had removed his vest and chaps but kept his hat firmly on his head.

"Please"—Morgan put her hand to her chest—"call me Morgan."

Relaxing into his chair, Oakes gave her a nod. Drew took the seat next to his client, unbuttoning his suit jacket as he settled, and finally, Luca took the seat next to Sterling. I wanted to send him a silent message, asking him if he knew about the job Morgan just offered me, but when Jenna came into the room, all of our attention went to her.

"How was the shoot?" I leaned in, asking Oakes, keeping as much distance as I could.

He shrugged a shoulder. "She said she got the perfect shot for the cover. She said she could do a quick *mockup*," he air quoted, "but I asked why we couldn't use one of yours for the cover."

"Show us what you have, Jenna," Morgan said, making me pull away from Oakes.

Jenna connected to the projector, which turned on behind Morgan, showing us hundreds of photos of Oakes. Close ups on his face, showcasing his gorgeous eyes, standing with his expression on the camera, his head turned, looking down. Jenna had put him in every pose she could think of, and he made every single one look just as good.

"Oh, this is going to be hard," Morgan said, looking at all the options in front of her. "Do you have the cover? Can we try a few images?"

Jenna and Morgan began to play with the cover art, trying a few images and cropping photos to fit, and I just watched—Morgan's offer still filtering through my head. Before, I was itching to sit down here and look at what I had accomplished. Now, I was just trying to get through it so I could talk to Oakes. I wanted his thoughts on it, wanted to know if it would work with us. He said he'd make Colorado a home base. We said this wasn't going to be an instant change. We knew there was going to be work. But the end result was me with him...not me with another cowboy all summer.

"I'm sorry, I just don't get why we can't use one of the photos Emmy took while we were in the field? These are great and all—it's been a while since I've had shots like these done—but Emmy got a lot of fantastic action shots." Oakes leaned forward in his chair.

"Oh, she got some amazing ones, but we've used all of those in the article. You take up seven pages, Mr. Ashford." Morgan turned, her eyes on the still-closed proof in front of me. "Take a look. The formatting is top tier."

"This it?" Oakes reached past me, sliding the white cover over to him.

"Let's see." Drew leaned in as Oakes opened the magazine. "*Ours for the Taking*, is that the name of the article, Emersyn?"

I stiffened, inhaling. Oakes, obviously sensing my sudden unease, reached under the table and gently put his hand on my knee, giving it a small squeeze. Loving his touch but reminding myself where we were, I placed my hand over his, removing it just as gently has he had placed it there. I could feel his eyes on me, but I kept my focus on the magazine.

"No, it's not. That's just the hook."

"To draw people in," Sterling added. "Pretty good if I'd say so."

"You came up with it?" Drew raised a brow.

Sterling nodded. "Yes, I was the editor on the piece."

Drew gave him a curt nod before he looked back down at the article.

Oakes had it open in front of him now, the introduction in white lettering over a full-blown photo of Oakes behind the scenes. His head was down, his chaps in movement from his gate, his hands at his sides, one carrying his helmet, the other free. They had edited it to black and white, but I remembered the moment right before he climbed the stairs to the chutes.

The first sentence caught my gaze: *Oakes Ashford, rising bull rider well on his way to the National Final Rodeo this year, stands at the ready.*

My words.

My photos.

Everything was right there.

The world grew silent as Oakes and Drew studied the magazine, flipping through the pages as they scanned the article. All the photos that I had fallen in love with were there on the page, the words flowing seamlessly with them. And Oakes, the man I loved, was reading something I created. All summer, I had watched him glow, and now he could see where I shined. My heart wanted to cry out, pull him to me, and cry on his shoulder, thanking him for this summer, but I stopped and just caught gazes with Luca. I gave him a steady smile and looked down.

I'd be a complete idiot not to take this job, even if it meant one article a year. Seeing that photo, those words...that right there made it worth it.

It will work, I told myself. *We promised it would.*

"Now, we just have a few questions before you head out, Mr. Ashford." Morgan pulled out her chair. "But first, thank you so much for agreeing to be here today."

Oakes's eyebrows were pinched, but he looked from the article up to Morgan. "I didn't have much of a choice, did I?"

"Oakes," Drew mumbled, his eyes not faltering from the magazine.

"It's alright." Morgan waved him off. "What bull rider doesn't have that gruff exterior? I'd love to hear about the summer from your point of view. Emersyn has already agreed to do this for us year after year, but we wanted to get your insight on it. What was it like having *Rodeo Way* with you for two months?"

Oakes's gaze went to me, and I could feel the heat of his stare. I didn't agree to anything yet, but I couldn't tell him that here. I had to wait until this was all over.

"If I'm being honest, it was just as rough as I thought it would be." Oakes's words caught me by surprise. I quickly turned my head to look at him, seeing him looking everywhere but at me. "Thankfully, she knew her way around an arena, her rodeo background helped, but it was distracting sometimes."

Morgan hummed. "What do you mean by that?"

Oakes didn't look at me. "I never fall off the bull. But I did, knowing she was at the chute. I was worried she'd get hurt or be in the way of another rider, so my concentration wasn't where it was supposed to be. I think if you're going to have her do this again and again, you need to instruct her to stay away from the chutes."

Morgan narrowed her eyes and nodded. "Her shots from the chutes are some of the best photos."

"Yeah, they're good for you—but not the cowboy." Oakes glared at her. "We have a job to do, and we can't worry about an editor getting hurt."

Editor? What the hell was going on? Did I misunderstand when he said he wanted me at the chutes in Cheyenne, or in Riverton, when I tried to go to the stands, but his hand tightened around mine before I could even consider leaving him there? Or in Montana when the pick-up men were smiling and loving the attention they were getting from my camera? What about last night in Steamboat, we he kissed me right before he got on the bull, telling me it was for luck? He didn't need me there, but he *wanted* me there.

My stomach began to churn as I looked up at Sterling, who sat with one eyebrow raised, his chin resting on his thumb and his finger over his lip, his attention glued on Oakes. Blinking, I slowly turned to Oakes, who was looking anywhere but at me.

"Oh, that's fantastic insight." Morgan nodded. "Do you have any other suggestions?"

"An entire summer isn't feasible." Oakes relaxed in his chair, his body shifting away from me. "A few weeks, sure, but an entire summer?" He shook his head. "No. Doesn't work. She had all of her interview questions and photos taken within a short time span. She didn't need to come to Idaho with me or on the family emergency I had. Two, three weeks tops is enough for her to get what she needs."

I glanced over him at Drew, who had closed the magazine and had his hands folded in front of him. He looked stoic, a demeanor to him I hadn't seen. Agent mode.

Morgan twisted her lips. "It would definitely help the budget too. Can you tell me what it was like having her travel with you in your truck? That was your call, right?"

"Yeah, well, her car wouldn't have made it. So that was something else I didn't have a choice on." Oakes tilted his head. "So if you're going to send her out on something again, make sure she has proper transportation."

"And her writing tactic? At first, we sent her with interview questions, but when she came up with the idea to—oh, what did she call it?" Morgan raised her chin then looked to me for clarification. I just sat stunned as I listened to this all unfold, my stomach doing somersaults, trying to make heads or tails of it. "Going rogue? She found her interview process on her own and was able to really get to know you. How was that?"

"Really get to know me?" Oakes raised a brow. "Well, she may want to be more open and honest with her clients before anything is sent off to be edited or reviewed if she's going off script."

"That's enough for today." Drew stood. "Oakes is getting upset, so before he does anything he'll regret, I say we call it a day. Mrs. Pennel, would you mind if I speak to you in your office for just a moment?"

Drew gestured to the conference door, and as if everyone could sense the tension in the room, they stood and left—except me. I was frozen next to Oakes. He stayed seated too, his breath heavy. Once we were alone, the door clicking behind Luca—who gave me a reassuring look—I turned to Oakes.

"What the hell was that?" I asked him, turning my entire body to him.

"Emersyn," he grumbled.

Emersyn? He hadn't called me Emersyn in a while. I was Emmy...his Emmy.

"*This* is your article?" he asked, the same gruff tone to his voice that he was giving Morgan, as his finger landed on the blank cover.

"Yes..." I hesitated.

"Fucking bullshit."

Chapter Thirty-Five
Oakes

My head was swimming. Emersyn had been acting off since the moment we walked into the building. She didn't give me a kiss when I was taken for the photo shoot, even though I had leaned in for one, and she wasn't taking any of my touches. I was completely thrown off by Emersyn removing my hand from her leg when I could tell she needed the support, but I tried to just write it off as her professional side. We finally opened up to each other once we weren't in front of any arenas or crowds, but then I read her article...and a rock landed in my throat.

The photos and layout, like Morgan said, were fantastic—it was meant to completely draw in the readers. But the words on the page sent a shock through me. The intro was the same, pulling in my scar from my hand to how I never give up...but then it changed. And I saw red. Rage filled me as I read each and every word on the page, and it took everything in me not to get up and storm out of the room.

Drew could tell. He saw me stiffen, and his breath was getting heavier as he read along with me. And now, Emersyn was telling me this was her article. That I had been taken and played

"You wrote this?" I asked her, trying to keep my composure.

She shook her head. "Yes, you saw me writing it daily. You were there for it. You agreed to it."

"You told them about my family, my brother. My dad." I finally looked her in the eye. "I didn't agree to that, Emersyn."

She blinked a few times and then swallowed. "I...I..."

"I thought you told me you would keep my private life—"

"Private," she interrupted. "I did."

"No, Emersyn, it's all right here. I just read it. So did Drew." I balled my fists. "The only thing you left out was the fact that we fucked."

Her body shook with shock as she stood. "Oakes, I have no idea what you're talking about. I told you I'd keep that out of it, and I didn't—"

"Oh, come on!" I shouted, standing up and reaching for the magazine. I flipped through until I found the article, hating that I loved seeing the photos she had taken of me sprawled out on the page. Once I found it, I gripped the pages, forcing them to fold as I began to read aloud, *"Oakes Ashford hails from Midwest, Wyoming, the small town where his mother, Angie, and brother, Hayes, live on their family farm that was once owned by Oakes's father—Roper Slade. Oakes has tried to stay away from the fame his father brought on, even taking on the stage name of Ashford, but he still returns home every now and then to make sure his brother's recovery from alcoholism is steady. The rodeos were what he turned to as a way of coping with his childhood trauma, which turned into a passion of his, leading him here."* I tossed the magazine on the table. "You have to be fucking kidding me, Emersyn."

She stood still, her chest moving up and down with each breath as her eyes focused on the magazine, now a crumpled mess on the table.

Was any of this real? Or was this all a ploy for her to advance in her career? The thought had crossed my mind a few times, but I always pushed it aside, blinded by the feelings I had always carried for her. And now, I was being ripped open, piece by piece, by the woman I thought I loved.

"Oakes..." she finally mumbled.

"You played me," I stated. "You 'went rogue.' Was this all a game for you? An assignment?" I rolled my eyes, remembering all the times she laughed with me and dug a little deeper each time, cracking me open like an egg. "You knew exactly who I was, didn't you? From the very beginning. Everything you told me about the story of how we met, and how you were always looking for my name, how I got you looking into rodeo stats, how it inspired your career. That was all bullshit, wasn't it?"

"Oakes, I..." She wrapped her arms around herself, tears forming in her eyes.

Fuck. It took everything in me not to pull her close to kiss those tears away. Maybe it wasn't real for her, but it was still real for—

No. It wasn't.

None of this was real.

Her body language, the way she wasn't able to answer any of my questions with confidence, proved I was right.

And fuck I hated that I was right.

Pinching my brow, I looked away from her. "I can't believe I trusted you. I can't believe I let you in and gave you everything. You got what you wanted, didn't you? This was all for your fucking career." I grabbed the magazine, anger rippling through me as I moved. My blood was boiling as I took a step toward her, handing her the ruined proof. "I don't give a fuck. Publish it. Take the job. But don't ever contact me again. I don't want to be associated with this magazine in any way after this feature."

"Oakes," she croaked, letting the magazine fall to her feet, "if you would just listen to me."

"No, Miss Flynn, I'm done. We're done here." I stormed past her. I felt the air in the room move as she spun, but I walked out of the conference room with my boots thumping every step of the way.

Fuck, I'm an asshole.

CHAPTER THIRTY-SIX
Emersyn

My breath hitched up, higher and higher, as I just stood there in the empty room, the magazine at my feet, crumpled from Oakes's tight grip on it. Was I starting to hyperventilate? Was this a panic attack? Couldn't be—I'd never had one before. I barely had time to register what he had said before he was gone. I desperately wanted to explain myself, but I didn't even know how. He was acting so mean, so disrespectful to me and my coworkers. It was like he was the Oakes from that very first meeting, not wanting anything to do with me. Nothing like how he had been the past few weeks. Nothing like the Oakes I had grown to love.

Love.

He said I played him?

The magnitude of the last five minutes hit me like a punch to the gut, and I fell to the floor, my knees hitting the magazine, forcing me to slip farther. I let out a deep, ragged breath that I couldn't even begin to control and buried my face in my hands.

What the *hell* just happened?

My hope that Oakes would be at my apartment when I returned home that night was shoved out when I walked into darkness. We had stopped by earlier to drop off my bags and make sure my Corolla was delivered safe and sound before we went to *Rodeo Way*. Oakes had driven me there, and if it weren't for Luca finding me in a puddle of my own tears in the conference room, I would have had to walk home, but thankfully, he drove me. He let me sit in silence, still processing everything as I clutched the magazine in my hands, still not having the guts to open it.

I could hear Luca come up behind me then felt his hand on my shoulder. "Welcome home, Emmy."

I inhaled. The name Emmy was never going to hit the same again.

"He really left?" I murmured, turning to look at him.

He stepped in the dark room, going straight for my lamp in the corner, flicking it on. "I saw him and Drew leave, yeah. He didn't look happy. You finally gonna tell me why I found you crying in the conference room?"

I plopped on the couch, tossing the proof copy on my coffee table, and told Luca everything, including things I promised Oakes I'd keep private. But it had made its way into the magazine, hadn't it? I didn't write those words that Oakes read aloud to me. I turned my article in before I met Angie and Hayes, and in all my research, I hadn't found their names anywhere. My parents wouldn't say anything to the magazine, and I didn't tell Luca until now. I was just so...confused. Oakes knew when I turned in my article—he had pulled me close that night. We made love that night. It was *before*... Did he forget that easily?

"I just..." I finally sighed after relaying the story to Luca. "I don't get it."

"I read your article, Emmy—"

"Don't take this the wrong way"—I leaned back into the cushion, looking at my friend—"but please don't call me Emmy anymore."

"Em? Can I call you Em?"

I nodded. Luca let out a breath.

"I read your article, Em. That was in there. You mentioned his brother, his mom, his dad...the fact that Oakes Ashford was a stage name. It wasn't hit on much, but the details were there, the in-depth things that Morgan wanted." He licked his lips and leaned forward on his elbows, looking at the article. "I don't blame the guy for being upset. I was kinda shocked you put all that in there. You told him you wouldn't."

"I didn't," I bit out. "I wouldn't. I can prove it. I have my article on my laptop. Somehow...my words got changed."

"The only people who had access to your article were you, Morgan, and Sterling, and they wouldn't jeopardize the magazine like that."

"I hate it when you make sense."

"Did you send them something after—"

"No, Luca. That's not my article." I gestured to the magazine. "And that's going to be published, with my name on it, and people are going to know about Oakes, and his reputation won't be the same."

Luca rolled his eyes. "I mean, does the guy have a great reputation? He's kind of a jerk."

"He's not. That guy you saw in there...that's not him. He's upset, and fuck, Luca..."

"Ah, so you picked up language from him."

"He has every right to be mad." I leaned my head back, staring up at my ceiling. I missed the stars. "I messed up, and I don't know what to do to fix it, and...I've lost him." I could feel the heat rise in my cheeks, the tears building until I just let them fall. "He said I played him."

Luca furrowed his brow. "What does he mean? Played him? You just didn't follow the interview prompts they gave you."

I turned to him. "No, Luca. We grew up in the same town together. We met before. I helped him when he was injured. The scar on his hand," Luca nodded. "I was there that night when it happened, and I told him not to let it stop him. I always looked for him after that but never saw his name. I was always looking for Ashton Slade...not Oakes Ashford. I didn't know he had changed it. That was how my obsession with stats came about. But I didn't recognize him. I didn't until we had a moment...and then after that moment on the mountain...I fell for him. He thinks I knew all along. He thinks I was using him for my career gain."

"But...you didn't, right? That's not you."

"I had no idea who he was, and Luca..." I shot up, going for my computer case that was still sitting by the front door. "Those aren't my words." I pulled up the article I had written and placed my computer on his lap. "Read it and tell me my article got published in that magazine."

Silence ensued for fifteen minutes while Luca read, and once he closed the laptop, his gaze met mine.

"So, I'll call Drew."

"Why? What's Drew going to do? I messed this up somehow, and now he's gone. He told me he wanted nothing to do with me after this. He thinks I betrayed him. I..." Tears formed again as I held in the words I didn't want to say. I didn't want to admit to losing him over something like this.

"Call him and send him this piece. *You* didn't mess up. Something must have happened in editing. If we send him this piece—"

"He'll just think I changed it. I know him. Once he sets his mind on something, there's no convincing him otherwise."

"So, what?" Luca placed my laptop on the coffee table. "You're just going to accept defeat?"

I bit the inside of my lip, shrugging my shoulders. "I don't think there's any way I can win him back. He's..." I took a shaky inhale. "Luca...I love him, and he's gone."

The tears broke through, and the knowledge that Oakes didn't trust me, didn't believe me, no longer loved me was enough to send me down a spiral that I couldn't see myself getting out of anytime soon. I felt so lost without him, and it had only been two months. But those two months, those moments with him in the car, the arenas, the motel rooms, his farm, under the stars...those moments became everything. And I lost it.

I bent, my head falling into Luca's lap as I cried and cried, all while my best friend let me. He rubbed my back and didn't speak. He just let me accept my defeat. And I swear, he could feel my heart breaking through my skin as he rubbed up and down, trying to calm the shuddering that came with a vengeance.

"You didn't mess up, Em," he finally whispered when my tears had stopped. "I can see why you think that, but you didn't. All I can think to do is order ice cream and pizza and watch chick flicks with you—but you don't even watch chick flicks—so how about I order a pizza, go get your favorite wine, and we watch your favorite rodeos."

I let out a soft laugh. "No rodeos for a while." I sniffed, not moving my head from his lap. "Pizza doesn't even sound good either. A shower, though..."

"Go shower. I'll find something to make, and then we can watch...something," Luca scoffed. "I'll stay here as long as you need me to."

I pulled myself to sit and looked at my friend, giving him a soft smile. I stood, heading into my shower to wash away everything that had happened over the past two months. I didn't want to accept that he was gone, but he was. I didn't want to accept that it was my fault, but it was. I needed to erase it, needed to...forget everything.

CHAPTER THIRTY-SEVEN
Emersyn

Luca fell asleep on the couch shortly after we started the baking competition show we finally agreed on. There was something about someone screaming, 'Nailed it!' that took away my own woes, so I admittedly was awake for hours upon hours of watching people fail. Once Nicole ended the last season Netflix had to offer, and the holiday ones didn't hold the same charm, I pulled myself from the couch and grabbed the magazine that kept staring at me from the coffee table. Its white cover with nothing but that stupid hook...*Oakes Ashford, Ours for the Taking*...

I snatched it up with silent force and trudged into my bedroom, feeling the weight of it in my hands. *Rodeo Way* knew how to give you a magazine. Each issue was packed full of column after column. And this was supposed to be my issue. Yet, here I was, wanting to desperately toss it out my window than do anything else with it.

I still hadn't looked at the article.

I still hadn't read it. Nothing but that first line.

And I still wished it was Oakes sleeping next to me instead of Luca on my couch.

His words still rang through my head even after I tried to erase them. And I just took it. I just stood there, not knowing what to do. He was visibly hurt. I had caused that pain—not intentionally...but this was all my fault.

Something happened with my article. Somehow, the details about his mom, his brother...his dad...were all laid out in there.

Just read it. Not much you can do until you know exactly what was changed.

Curling my legs underneath me on my bed, I finally gave in and opened the magazine. I read the intro slowly, taking in each and every word.

If you look closely at Oakes Ashford's left hand, you'll see a scar that travels from his knuckles to his wrist. The scar came from an accident on his first ride in a rodeo arena—surprisingly not on a bull. To some, a scar is just a white line on your skin, an ugly thing that's plastered for everyone to see. For Oakes Ashford...it's the drive. The horse that crushed his hand almost took away his passion, but that scar serves as a reminder for Oakes to not let one ride determine your fate, not to let one ride take away from what could be yours in the future. It's the reason he's where he is. Without that scar, there would be no Oakes Ashford, the man who has taken the rodeo and PBR world one ride at time.

This summer, I got to spend every moment with Oakes, watching him, learning him, figuring out exactly who he is and what makes him soar—and what a summer it was.

The more I read, the more mix of emotions filled my body. There were tiny changes at first, word choices, grammar fixes—the normally editing process I did on a daily basis—but then when the story shifted from Oakes to his past...my body got hot.

Luca said it was subtle, but...

They changed...everything.

The following morning, my eyes still heavy from lack of sleep, I calmly walked into *Rodeo Way*. Keeping myself composed was easier than I thought, even with the churning sensation in my stomach. I had read that article several times. I had it marked up with red pen and printed my draft up, so I could show Morgan, side by side, what happened to my article. I believed Luca when he said Morgan wouldn't jeopardize the company like this, so my mind went straight to the other person that had access to my work—Sterling. What I didn't know was how he could possibly know these details about Oakes…or why he would do this.

Passing my office, Luca's office, all the cubicles I had spent so many years in, I went straight to Morgan's corner office and lightly knocked on the open door. Raising her head, she offered me a smile.

"Emersyn, good morning, are you feeling better?" she asked, gesturing for me to come in.

Right. Luca told her I needed to leave early because I suddenly got sick. I mean, it wasn't a lie. I probably would have gotten sick if I had stayed.

"Much, thank you," I replied, taking the seat across from her. "I wanted to ask you about my article and the job offer."

"Of course. We have so many specifics to cover. Salary, dates, the next feature. Mr. Ashford made some pretty amazing points yesterday. Mr. Manning had some good suggestions as well. I was just going over your new contract." She turned back to her computer, spinning her laptop to show me the sheet she had been working on.

Job description, salary, a company car—all laid out there on the screen.

I narrowed my eyes. "What did Drew suggest?"

Morgan sighed. "Well, he was upset, but he made some valid points. As much as I loved your approach, we'll have to stick to a more"—she waved her hand in the air in front of her, as if trying to conjure the right words to use—"professional process. Stick to the interview questions, and a separate photographer for events. He asked us not to publish your article, but I was able to talk him down. As long we compensated Mr. Ashford properly, we could publish."

"No," I said, my voice steady. "I can't have you publish that article."

Morgan blinked and then gave a soft chuckle, but once she caught on that I wasn't kidding, her face went to stone. "What?"

"That's not my article. It's not what I sent you. It's my body, but it's been changed, and I have my original draft to compare." I leaned forward, placing the proof on her desk along with my draft. Her eyes narrowed as she looked at both documents in front of her. "I think Sterling added to it. He warped it somehow. It's not my article in the proof."

Morgan picked up my draft, gave it a glance, and then tossed it down on her desk. "Emersyn, that's still your article. We didn't *warp* it. No, Emersyn, we made it better."

I jerked, my eyes blinking quickly, trying to figure out what I had just heard. What *did* I just hear?

"Better?" I repeated. "Excuse me?"

"Let's get Sterling in here with us. He can explain." Morgan reached for her phone, and silence fell between us for a heartbeat, her eyes locked on mine. "Sterling," she finally said, a smile spreading across her face. How the hell can she be smiling? "Can you I have you join me in my office? Yes, now, thank you." She hung up. "He's coming, you know how close his office is. But, Emersyn, we didn't warp your words—"

"Warp?" Sterling's voice sounded in the doorway faster than I would have thought. He folded his arms and came up to the side of Morgan's desk.

"Emersyn is saying you changed her article. She used the word *warp*." Morgan gestured to the chair next to me, a silent order for Sterling to sit.

My head snapped to Sterling, who...like always...gave me his brightest smile.

"I didn't warp anything. I edited. I added. That's my job."

"You added words I didn't write. You changed my material." I gestured, open palm, to the documents. Sterling looked at Morgan's desk and let out a sigh.

"You didn't give us what we wanted," Morgan chimed in. "You gave us a bland look at what we already knew about Mr. Ashford. He's been a mystery to the PBR and PRCA. We knew there was something there, and I was hoping you would be able to get it out of him. Instead, you gave us the exact opposite of what I asked for."

"Hold on." I held up my hand, trying to stop it from shaking. "If you already knew there was something there with him, why did you send me on an assignment to get the information? Why not just publish it and turn *Rodeo Way* into a gossip piece?"

"Because that's not what *Rodeo Way* is," Morgan said, matter of fact, folding her arms across her desk.

"You were the obvious choice," Sterling remarked, his hand squeezing my shoulder as he leaned forward.

My head shot toward him, my gaze looking down at his hand. "Excuse me? What the hell does that mean? I thought Luca put my name in?"

"He did, but it was already decided before he suggested it. You were made for this project, Emersyn," Morgan added, as if stating that would completely reset my thoughts.

"You had the rodeo knowledge, you had the background—plus, you were almost Miss Rodeo America. How many rodeos have you participated in? People know your name. We figured he would be comfortable with you since you grew up together, which you kept from us, by the way."

Sterling shrugged, his hand dropping from my shoulder, his voice not once faltering.

It seems both Oakes and I got played.

"How...how did you know that?" I gaped at him. I didn't even know that until it clicked on the mountain side. How did Sterling know that?

"Information on him isn't hard to find. I found out Ashford was connected to the name Slade, then I found his yearbook photos, the articles on his dad's arrest, along with his title being stripped from him, information on his brother's rehab visits. It's all online if you know where to look. You guys grew up in the same town. You're in the yearbooks. We just put two and two together." Sterling looked me dead in the eye.

"You mean to tell us you didn't remember him?" Morgan asked, leaning forward.

I glared at her. "No. I didn't. He was a few years below me; we didn't really hang out on the weekends." I looked from her to Sterling. "And I did my research, and I never found any of that information. How did you?"

Sterling cocked a grin and raised a brow. "I know a few people."

"You've got to be kidding me," I bit out. "You're telling me that you were able to dig up all this information and then put it into my article without informing anyone and just assuming it would be a good idea? You realize that I promised Oakes that would stay out of the article."

"But he *did* tell you?" Morgan asked, her brow raising to her hairline.

She was so calm here, acting as if nothing was wrong with what was transpiring. I, on the other hand? I wanted to take Sterling by the collar and toss him aside, call out all his bullshit and force Morgan to see it wasn't right.

I just kept my glare on her. "Not that it matters. Even if he didn't, you would have put it in the article anyway."

"Oh, Emersyn, you knew what we were looking for. I could see that he would open up for you. We could see it in the earlier interviews you sent. But the article you sent—"

"Is a damn good article!" My voice began to boom as I pointed at the pile of papers on her desk. "It gives insight to what Oakes does, plus keeps his private life his—just like I promised him. And you broke that. You took his trust."

"If we 'took his trust'"—Sterling air quoted—"why is he letting us publish it?" Sterling grinned at me.

Huffing, I shifted my body to him, trying not to punch my ex-boyfriend. "If you publish it, I will sue this company. I have the proof right there." I reached forward and grabbed the magazine and my draft. "I have times as to when I sent it, and I can for sure get times as to when this was edited and printed. You took my work and changed it."

"Your work belongs to *Rodeo Way*," Sterling started. "You know that, Emmy..."

"Sterling." Morgan raised a hand, stopping him. "Emersyn, honey, that's a bit extreme, don't you think?"

I stood, shoving the documents back into my shoulder bag. "No, I don't. You went beyond the trust of your client. Oakes will even back me up, and Drew—I can't believe he agreed to let you publish it."

"Well," Sterling laughed, "it wasn't without a fight." His eyes widened as they rolled, turning back to Morgan.

"That doesn't seem wrong to you? In any way? Manipulating your staff, your clients? You say *Rodeo Way* isn't a tabloid, that it's a prestigious publication for the sport...but right now, this entire thing only shows that it's going down, and it's going to fail. The rodeo doesn't need another train for gossip to leak out, and that's exactly what you're going to be doing here. If you publish this, I will take legal action." I could hear my voice getting louder and louder, echoing off Morgan's wall.

"Emersyn, keep your voice down," Morgan said quietly, looking toward her open door.

"No, I won't. I'm beyond pissed, because not only did you take work I was proud of and ruin it, but you want me to do it again and again. That's not only going to look bad for *Rodeo Way* but the sport and cowboys in general. And you're hurting the man I love to start this process. Sterling, I thought you were more professional than this. I'm not sure what caused you to do all of this behind my back, but it only proves to me who you are. And you"—I turned to Morgan—"you're a piece of work, Morgan Pennel." She stared at me, her jaw slowly getting wider and wider. "Publish this, and I'll sue."

With one last glare at Sterling, I stormed past him into the office, where almost every single employee had their eyes on me, a silence filling the space like I had never heard before. I didn't look at anyone, I didn't stop by my office—there was nothing there I needed anyway—and I left the building, not even a glance behind my shoulder at what I just lost.

Emersyn

Oakes, I can explain everything. Please call me or text me.

I know I'm the last person you want to talk to, but I need to tell you what happened. Please call me.

I miss you so much. I love you so much. I want to fix this. Please.

Don't make me text Drew.

Okay, that was wrong, I won't do that. I just want to hear your voice. I want to let you know what happened. The article isn't getting published. I threatened to sue them if they do, and I won't hesitate to do that. That wasn't my article. Please, let me explain.

Oakes. I'm sorry. I miss you. I love you, but…I understand. If you love something, let it go, right? God, I hate that saying… I love you.

From: emmyflynn88@xmail.com

To: manning.drew@pbragency.com

Subject: Thanks.

Date: August 7th, 12:32 PM

Drew - thank you for making sure my car was transported to and from all the destinations. I'll send a check of expenses to your office. Luca has the address. Thanks again.

Please let Oakes know I'm doing everything in my power to not have that article published. I could explain until I'm blue in the face, but…it won't matter. I love him. Please let him know that.

Thank you for giving me the best summer in my entire life.

I'm so sorry.

Emersyn.

From: manning.drew@pbragency.com
To: emmyflynn88@xmail.com
Subject: REPLY: Thanks
Date: August 7th, 12:45 PM

No need to refund me. I'll send it back if you do.

Thanks, Emersyn—I'll let him know.

I know he enjoyed having you there. I've never seen that man smile that much.

Drew.

CHAPTER THIRTY-EIGHT
Emersyn

"Come on, Emersyn, I know you're in there," Luca's faint voice carried through my front door. He banged a few times, even shook the door handle. Why he didn't just use his damn key was beyond me. I just sunk deeper into my couch cushion, pulling the cozy blanket over my head.

It had been three weeks since I left *Rodeo Way*. Three weeks since I contacted a lawyer and found out I had a case if I needed to pursue it. Three weeks since I had last seen Oakes. And what was I doing? I was currently on my third rewatch of *Nailed It*, I discovered *Outlander* and *Doctor Who*, and I subscribed to Disney+, where I was quickly forming an obsession with Tom Hiddleston. I couldn't tell you the last time I washed my hair, and I was living off of DoorDash. I hadn't watched a single rodeo, hadn't paid any attention to what *Rodeo Way* was doing. Basically, I was done...with...

I heaved a sigh.

Everything.

And by the sound of Luca's pounding...he was done with me being done.

"You have a key!" I shouted.

"I'm purposefully not using it because I know you're just sitting there, so use your body and open the damn door."

Letting out a groan, I stood and shuffled to the front door, unlocking it and swinging it open. Luca stood there, his eyebrow raised.

"Glad to see you're alive," he deadpanned.

Glaring at him, I spun, leaving the door open for him, returning to my place on the couch.

"Have you done anything?" he asked, looking around the apartment. "Dishes, laundry, anything?"

Glaring at him, I blinked at took a few looks around my small apartment. The last few door dash bags were on my coffee table, surrounded by the empty food containers and plastic utensils. The dishes hadn't been touched in days...a week maybe...and blankets and dirty socks were scattered all over the floor. Raising my brow I bent at my waste at looked at myself, wearing the same leggings for the past three days, a pair of fuzzy socks and I could only imagine what state my hair was in. The curtains were drawn, the sun basically banished from my apartment. I inhaled, twisted my lips and returned my gaze to Luca.

"I'm fine," I grumbled, grabbing my remote, shoving myself back into the cocoon he so rudely made me get out of.

"When was the last time you ate?"

"Today."

"What did you eat?"

I pinched my eyebrows. "Noodles?" I replied, more of a question than a statement trying to remember if that really was what I ate last. The bag on the coffee table told me it was.

"Noodles?" he parroted.

I nodded. "Noodles & Company, mac 'n' cheese, a Rice Krispie...and a root beer."

He blinked and looked around. "Well, at least you're eating. Water consumption?'

"Could be better." I rolled my eyes, having them land directly on my Hydro Flask that stood...full...on my coffee table.

Luca, now standing with his hands on his hips like a disappointed parent, leaned down and grabbed the bottle. "Drink it."

I removed my arm from the blanket, grabbing the handle of the Hydro Flask, and took one measly sip of water, then gave him a 'happy now' look. He nodded.

I swallowed. "How's the office?" I asked hesitantly. I wanted to know what was going on, but at the same time, I couldn't care less. I had heard back from the lawyer I called, following up if I needed his representation, and I couldn't answer the ca;;. I should probably have that answer.

Luca sighed, reaching down to grab a carryout bag from the coffee table. "Wouldn't know. I quit."

If anything was going to pull me out of my rut, that was it right there. "You did not."

"I did. A lot of us did. You caused quite the scene. Come to find out it wasn't the first time they changed articles—the other journalist just didn't say anything. Funny thing, it was all Sterling's articles that were modified. Ever since he got that promotion to editor, a lot of articles got published differently."

My eyes widened. "I don't know if I want to believe that."

"Believe it."

I took a breath, relief filling my lungs. I looked up at my friend. "You didn't have to quit."

"Oh, but I did. I didn't want to work for a company like that. There're other places I can work for. You too. Lots of magazines are looking for editors or journalists. You have the experience."

"I don't want to edit photos anymore," I finally admitted to him. "And I don't know if I want to write for another magazine."

"Freelance?" Luca suggested.

"I want to travel. I want to go to rodeos and take photos. I want to experience what I did this summer every day."

"So, you're going to make that happen by moping around your house, huh?"

"I'm not moping. I'm..." I searched my brain for a word. I *was* moping. Full Bella-Swan style. There was no other way to explain it. "Fine, I'm moping. But I have every reason to. I lost my job, I lost the man I love, I lost my passion...Luca...I lost everything."

"When you lost Miss Rodeo America, did you mope?"

"No, I was relieved."

"Okay, so let's think of it this way. Be relieved that you don't have to work with Morgan or Sterling anymore. Be relieved that you can set your pace and start your own thing. Is Oakes in the picture anymore? No. But does that matter?" *Yes...* "No. He's a jerk who wrote you off without hearing what you had to say. You can pull yourself up from this, and you don't need that asshole bull rider to do it."

Mentioning that Oakes didn't matter stung more than it probably should. In the back of my head, I was still thinking of ways I could win him back, but the three weeks of silence only proved that he was holding up his *we're done* statement. As much as I wanted him back, he made it clear he didn't want me. His words still rang in my head, starting random bouts of tears that would last until I didn't have any tears left.

"You're really bad at pep talks, you know." I sniffed, holding back more tears. There couldn't be any left in me.

"No, I'm not. I'm the best. Now, get your ass in the shower, because you smell, and we can talk about this traveling freelance thing you mentioned, because hell, I'd love to do that with you."

Yet again, another thing that got my attention.

"Wait...what?"

Luca dropped his hands from his hips and raised his chin, a smirk forming on one corner of his mouth.

"You're not serious."

"About the shower? Dead serious."

"Luca."

"Shower...then we'll talk." He gave me a stern look and pointed toward the bathroom.

"We'll talk..." I stood up, the blanket dropping on the couch.

"Shower," he said again, taking my shoulders and shoving me in the bathroom.

Maybe a shower was a good idea. Changing out of my pajamas was a good idea. Braiding my hair was an even better idea. I felt refreshed—still missing that vital part of me, but refreshed nonetheless. I came out to see Luca vacuuming my living room, the dishes in the running dishwasher, and the blankets folded on the couch. I looked around the newly clean apartment and then at Luca. Stopping the vacuum, he held open his arms to me, and I instantly went to him. I let myself fall into him, loving the comfort his arms brought around me when he hugged me back.

"You smell better already." He chuckled in my hair.

Slapping his back, I pulled away from him. "Okay, fine, you were right. I need to stop moping."

"Ah we finally agree. So..." He leaned on the vacuum cleaner. "Can we talk about this freelance thing? Or do I need to clean some more?"

"It's just a idea." I turned my back to him, shaking my head, the urge to plop on the couch strong.

"That could become something, so...talk."

"Oakes mentioned it at first. I was working on the article in the truck, and he asked what came next. He threw out all these options, but none seemed plausible." I leaned up against my dining table, folding my arms over my chest.

"It's plausible. Most definitely."

"How would we even make it happen without *Rodeo Way* to back us up?"

"We would back us up."

"Luca..." I drawled.

"You said it yourself: you don't want to be an editor anymore. You don't want to work for a magazine."

"I don't. I want to be on the dirt, with the events and the cowboys. This summer was the best time I'd ever had, and I was good at it, you should have seen me. It was like a fire burning in my belly and a new passion coming out. It wasn't just for *Rodeo Way*; it was for me too." I sighed, telling myself I would not cry again. There weren't any tears left. "I thought they would see that, but—"

"No buts. Why can't we make it happen?"

"Well, for one, we need funds."

"Lucky for you, we have savings and ways to get loans."

"How would we travel?"

"Again, lucky for you, I have an SUV. I'm not afraid of camping while we're on the road."

"And how are we going to plan it?"

"Wasn't that literally my job at *Rodeo Way*? Wasn't I the one who put your entire summer itinerary together? Didn't I plan your budget, confirm every expense you had—"

"Okay, okay." I chuckled, raising my palms up in surrender.

"I can plan. I have connections with event centers and agents. You have the skills to write a blog, take photos, and manage and edit content. We could start a blog. Get freelance jobs, like you said. There are a million things we could do. The options are endless. And it wouldn't be just a summer gig; it would be year-round."

I took a deep breath. "You're serious about this?"

"I'm down if you are. Hell, I can even get us on the road as quick as next week."

"Next week?" I shouted. "Luca, I'm not..."

"Ready?" He raised a brow and took a deep breath, leaning on the table next to me. "And as amazing as that would be...we should probably start next season. Hit up a few local rodeos now, get our bearings, and then hit it harder in October."

"It's not just being ready about setting this all up. It sounds like just what I wanted with *Rodeo Way*, what I was hoping to do with the promotion. It's the..." I swallowed and looked up at my friend. Our gazes locked, concern shining through his deep blue eyes. Looking down at my bare feet, I shook my head. "It's dumb, I know."

"It's not dumb. You miss him."

"I can't cry any more."

Luca grew silent. The only sound coming from the apartment was the tick of the clock, the seconds passing slower than I wanted. I glanced into my living room, the blanket I had been using for the past three weeks now neatly folded. I could go right back over there, wrap the blanket around my shoulders, and keep going down the Tom Hiddleston-Loki rabbit hole, or I could try to start something new. Something that would—hopefully—bring back that same feeling. Maybe it wasn't Oakes that made this summer fantastic, even though, yes...he was a huge part of it...but it was the rodeos. It was the lifestyle. It was everything about it that I loved, and with what Luca was saying...I could have it again.

"What if," Luca began, crossing his ankles, "I made sure to schedule rodeos where Oakes wouldn't be."

"That's a little childish, don't you think?"

"Nah, at least until you're comfortable." He bumped my shoulder.

I licked my lips and turned back to him.

"What would we call it?"

Luca grinned. "Not sure...but I'm thinking something to do with a chute."

```
From: LucaLucaMagana@xmail.com
To: manning.drew@pbragency.com
Subject: I...have a favor to ask.
Date: August 28th: 4:32 PM
```

Hey, I have a favor. Text me. 555-8214. As soon as humanly possible.

L

Drew

What's up?

Luca

That was fast...I have an idea...but I need you.

Drew

I'm in.

CHAPTER THIRTY-NINE

Oakes

*F*our weeks later

Ty

Me and a few guys are heading out after the rodeo tomorrow night. You comin?

Me

No.

Ty

Emersyn with you still?

Me

No.

Ty

Why not?

Me
Contract ended.

Ty
So…she's single?

Me
Fuck off, Ty.

Ty
Someone's in a bad mood.

Me
I said fuck off.

Hayes
Sixty-seven??

Me
Hey, at least I qualified.

Hayes
What's going on?

Me
I don't really wanna talk about it.

Hayes
How come you're not playing the song anymore?
It was a different one last night.

Jon Bon Jovi's a good song…suits you.

When does Emersyn's article come out? We've been looking for it.

Me

Hayes…

Hayes

Alright, man…just checking in on ya.

Drew

You good?

Me

Dandy.

Drew

How's the knee?

Me

sends photo of ice bag on right knee

Drew

Riding tomorrow?

Me

Yup.

Drew

Twenty minutes on…

Me

Twenty minutes off.

"You know..." Drew followed me off the dirt, his voice carrying through the concrete tunnel. "If you'd focus, you'd stop falling off the damn bull."

"I am focusing," I growled. This had been the worst yet, and my knee throbbed with each step I took, but I wouldn't let Drew see that. I'd ice the thing every night, but it never seemed to calm down. With each land I'd take, I could just see myself getting closer to a knee replacement—or worse, having to take a year off.

"That was your fourth no score—"

"You don't need to remind me." I yanked my helmet off my head and tossed it over to him. By some miracle, he caught it. "I'm not the only one who didn't make the eight seconds. Ty fell off too. How about you go punish him."

"Punish? You think I'm punishing you?"

"What else would you call this? Torture?" I pulled my gloves off and shoved them in my back pocket before going for the string of my chaps, not once stopping to let Drew get another word in.

After the entire clusterfuck that was *Rodeo Way*, I went back home. I prepared my mom and Hayes for any backlash that may come their way. To my surprise, neither one was upset. My mom's exact words were 'We'll take it if it comes.'

If, not *when.*

When I told them what Emersyn had written, how she betrayed us, they didn't seem to want to believe me. It was hard to choke down at first too, and granted, I didn't handle it well, but I handled it.

What was even harder to get over were these lingering feelings that no matter how hard I tried, I couldn't shake them. I hated that I missed having her on the chute, I missed having her next to me in the truck, and fuck,

I missed her arms around me. I missed her kiss. I missed her taste. I just fucking missed *her*.

But she's not who you think she is, I had to remind myself over and over again.

Blocking her number and ignoring any time Drew mentioned her name was the best I could do. I just had to wipe her from my memory...every last bit. Including the words she told me sixteen years ago.

So I did.

I stopped saying them to myself before my rides.

And I could guarantee that was why I was fucking up.

Not that I'd admit it.

"I'm just trying to get your head back in the game," Drew replied, my helmet waving in the air next to him.

"I am in it."

"You're not, but whatever you say. You know, if you talked to me, we could figure this shit out."

"There is no *shit* to figure out. When are you going to stop with that?" I growled.

"When we get it figured out."

"Drew." I stopped, lifting my chin in the air. "I have it figured out. I'll focus. Now can you please stop pestering me about it."

Drew let out a puff of air, his eyes twitching as he studied me. Then, he changed the subject. "Where's the ride tomorrow?"

I inhaled, breathing in the air around me, the scents of the indoor arena hitting just right, grounding me. "Texas City," I replied, grumbling in his direction.

"Smaller turf, good. That's good."

"A smaller turf is good? The check won't be as big."

"Bigger than you're bringing in now." He tossed me my helmet, walking past me down the hall, no doubt going to check on Ty after his four-second ride.

I hadn't brought in a check in weeks. Sure, I'd had qualified rides, but since I stopped repeating Emersyn's words, none had brought in the money. If I kept going at this rate, I'd lose my NFR standing. I'd lose more than I already had.

I was back to where I was in the beginning of the summer. Nothing had truly changed...yet it felt like everything had.

I swallowed, a question pulling at the base of my throat. May as well fuck up some more. "Did it get published?"

He stopped and turned back to face me. "No. It didn't. Last I knew, Morgan was revamping." With that, he turned and kept walking down the hall.

That night, I lay in the hotel, missing the nights I could camp in the back of my truck, sleep under the stars, but now that fall was well under way and the temperature had dropped, it was back to hotels and silence. I had ice on my knee, Emersyn's stern face an image in my mind when I plopped the bag of ice on my skin, and a book laid open on my chest. But for some reason...I had a Google tab open on my phone, my thumbs moving faster than I wanted them to.

I told myself this was for closure. That seeing her face again would help me move on from everything. This wasn't because I missed her; this was because I needed to focus.

I typed her name and watched as her Miss Rodeo Wyoming photos came up, a photo of her doing a stunt on Mable. Her carrying the flag and holding fireworks high in the air. She always had a smile on her face in these older photos, the same smile she would give to me right before I kissed her, the same one I saw on her lips after I told her I loved her.

Fuck, this wasn't working.

I scrolled, seeing the past news articles that she was featured in, stopping only when I saw something new...something I wasn't expecting.

Break the Chute: with Emersyn Flynn and Luca Magana.

I shot up, a jolt of lightning flashing through my knee, my book falling off my chest as I instantly clicked on the link. A website pulled up, the background a view of a rodeo arena with Luca and Emersyn standing in the middle. Emersyn had her hip popped, her camera in hand, her smile lighting up the screen. Luca stood next to her, a brown cowboy hat on his head, his thumbs locked in his pockets.

I clicked on the links, reading about them under the *About Us* tab, looking at photos that Emersyn had taken under the *Gallery* tab, and saw a blog and podcast application.

Wanna be the first cowboy or cowgirl to be featured on Break the Chute? Accepting applications now. We will have a new feature once a month, featured on a new podcast starting soon! New blogs posted weekly – turn on your notifications to stay up to date, and make sure you follow us on our socials!

Instagram, TikTok, and YouTube were listed below, and to say I wasn't tempted to look at them would be a lie, but I refrained.

This was supposed to be a way for me to get closure. Not a way for me to miss her more. She was doing it. I wasn't sure if she had left *Rodeo Way* completely or if she was trying something new and I just happened to stumble on it, but a feeling of pride rippled through me. I was proud she was going for something she wanted, something that made her happy...but along with that was shame. Shame I was missing it, that I wasn't there for this. That I had told her I never wanted to see her again when she was the only person I wanted to see.

Locking my phone, I tossed it aside and plopped on the bed, my arm covering my eyes to block out any and all thoughts as I forced the emotions I felt climbing to fall back down.

Chapter Forty
Emersyn

"God, I missed this!" I exclaimed as I jumped from Luca's Chevy. The sun was high in the sky, even with the chilly air that came with October, but it was the perfect setting for a rodeo.

"You're welcome." Luca came up to my side, handing me my camera bag.

I gave him a laugh. "For what?"

"Making you take a shower." He gave me a wry grin and wink, his chin down as he typed out a text.

"Jerk." I nudged him with my elbow before lifting my camera bag over my shoulder.

In reality, I should be saying thank you. After that one shower, my world seemed to come together. Our new blog—and soon-to-be podcast—*Break the Chute*, already had over one hundred applicants for features and interviews, and I was simply blown away. How the word broke about our little adventure was beyond me, but I couldn't be more grateful for it. Our social media pages climbed the charts, gaining follower after follower and even catching the eyes of a few sponsors. Everyone seemed excited for our first post.

Luca worked behind the scenes, setting up rodeos for us, agreeing to any rodeo that would have us, leading up to the National Finals Rodeo in December. Our schedule was booked. I worked on photos and getting the blog set up and ready. I already had one article posted, introducing Luca and me and what our vision was for *BTC*. Then—after Luca talked me down—I sent an email to Drew, asking him if I could publish my original article on Oakes.

He emailed back faster than I thought, simply requesting he read it before publishing, and I happily sent it over. Less than an hour later, I got his response with the green light. The post went live an hour ago. *Break the Chute's* first official post was online and being seen by the world. Oakes was being seen by the world. I promised myself I wouldn't look at comments or reactions until after the event, but my phone was on fire in my back pocket, just begging to be looked at.

Our first official post. Our first official rodeo. There were a lot of firsts happening tonight, and my stomach was in knots.

"I'll go get us checked in," Luca said, his eyes still trained on his phone.

"Perfect, I'm going to go scope out the stands and chutes." I watched him, tilting my head, trying to earn his attention.

"When's the live?" he asked, biting his bottom lip as his brow furrowed, his thumbs tapping on the small screen.

"Who ya talkin' to?" I pressed, stepping forward.

His head shot up, pulling his phone to his chest. "Just checking the website for check-in info."

I raised a brow, which earned me a long sigh and eyeroll as Luca shoved his phone back in his pocket. He licked his lips. "The live? When did we say we'd start it?"

I shook my head at him. "Um...I think we agreed the bulls?" I situated my hat on my head. "Why did we say bulls?"

"Because bulls bring in the crowds." Luca tapped the rim of my hat, forcing me to situate it again. "Now, if you don't mind, I'll go get us checked in and then"—he inhaled, raising his chin high in the air—"I'm going to go sniff some cowboys."

"'Cause that's not creepy at all." I laughed, situating my camera bag on my shoulder as Luca began to walk backward away from me.

Luca pointed at me, the excitement seeping from him. "Not. At. All. Hey, pop quiz."

"Shoot."

"Whose blog post went live tonight?"

I smiled at him. "Ours did."

He winked. "*Yours* did. Go take a look around."

I chuckled, shaking my head at him before turning to take in the arena. The stands were starting to fill, the cowboys and cowgirls were checking in, and everything was just as it should be. Fumbling a little, I took my camera from the bag and removed the lens cap. I had so many photos of events; maybe the feed could use some behind-the-scenes action.

My mind was always on what kind of content I could come up with now. What kind of shot I could grab here, or what kind of video I could post on TikTok and Instagram. So far, our posts had been performing well, and my TikToks and reels were what was finding the sponsors for us. I was good at this, and I actually really enjoyed it. Not to mention, it had become a great distraction from missing a certain cowboy. Luca reassured me he wasn't going to be at this rodeo, calling it a 'small fry' for the likes of Oakes Ashford, but I would be lying to myself and everyone around if I said there wasn't a small flicker of hope that he was here...or at least near.

He wasn't performing the greatest—not that I was keeping tabs on him... Okay, I totally was, and my heart broke seeing him fall for the past four rides. As much as I hoped I would see him, I didn't want an accidental run-in to add to his losing streak. I didn't need another thing he would blame on me.

But still, with all the mistakes that had been going on the last seven weeks, he was still in the top fifteen, well on his way to the NFR, and I had no doubt in my mind he was going to get there and win back his buckle.

Break the Chute wouldn't be able to go to the NFR this year—not for lack of trying—but that was our goal for next year. Maybe then I could go up to Oakes and give him a congratulatory hug after he won his buckle back for the second time.

There were so many things on my horizon, and it all felt so right. Even if it was missing something. knew I was on the right path for me.

Music began in the distance, and the rodeo announcer's voice boomed overhead.

"As the time draws near for the Texas City Rodeo, I wanted to take a minute to tell you guys about something I think is quite amazing, and as you're coming to your seats, if you could point your eyes to the screens and check out that QR code—"

Excitement buzzing through me, I took the steps two at a time up the stands, the clink of my boots giving me that feeling of being home, and the second I could see the arena, I looked at the jumbo screen being held up by a crane. The promotional photos Luca and I had taken a month ago were on the screen, our logo and QR code at the bottom. And it hit me...this was all real.

I raised my camera and took a photo, getting the arena with the screen in the background, praying the image came out.

"We're lucky to be the first stop for a new podcast and blog that just launched today. Former Miss Rodeo Wyoming, Emersyn Flynn, and her partner in crime, Luca Magana, have teamed up to bring us a blog that hopes to encompass the beauty of the rodeo, showing off the greatest sport on the dirt in the best way they know how. I know for a fact that Emersyn and Luca are around tonight and will be meandering all night with a special live that will take place during the bull-riding event. So, if you see Emersyn or Luca, make sure you congratulate them on their new journey, and don't be shy to ask for a photo. Post it on your own socials with the hashtag '*Break the Chute does Texas*' for your chance to win—"

Drowning out the announcer's words, I lowered my camera. The few shots I was able to get were good, but there was something on the screen that formed another knot in my gut—the dreaded dying battery.

"Shit," I groaned, starting to dig in my bag for my replacement battery...which...wasn't there.

I spun, my mind now in photographer mode, to get to my back-up battery before the stands started getting even more full of spectators, taking the same metal steps two at time, trying to shove my camera in my bag at the same time. I turned the corner, my eyes darting up, my body hot from the motions...only to be frozen seconds later.

Because right in front of me...

My heart stopped, and I stopped breathing.

"Oakes," I whispered under my breath.

Chapter Forty-One
Oakes

If you look closely at Oakes Ashford's left hand...you'll see a scar.

I swallowed, staring at my phone, completely unaware of my surrounds as I read the blog post.

Of course I subscribed to her blog. I would have been an idiot not to.

I just didn't expect to see me when I opened up the email notification.

It was the shot. The shot that was just for her. It was me, standing on a mountain overlooking Lake Tahoe, hands on my hips and my profile in full view. I wasn't wearing any of my uniform—no cowboy hat, nothing to tell you I was a bull rider—yet it was the perfect photo for the article. And even as people rushed around me, my eyes were consumed by the words Emersyn had written.

They weren't what I had read at *Rodeo Way*. No...this...this was so much better.

The world became a blur as she wrote about her summer with me, how I made my own name and pushed through every little injury, telling the story of the time I hurt my knee in a way that even made me chuckle when she called me a stubborn ass. She wrote about our talks in the car, the stupid bet we made, the way she learned my workout routine and how what I ate still baffled her. She wrote about playing hooky, and going to Lake Tahoe, and how that trip was what truly sparked her. She wrote about how, at first, she was reluctant, but the moment her boots hit the dirt, she knew this was where she was supposed to be, and the fact that she was lucky enough to see it through my eyes as well helped her fall more in love with the sport than ever.

It wasn't just an article. It was a love letter.

By the time I was done reading the article, the noise of the world came back into my ears without me even noticing it was gone. And the first thing I heard was Wyatt Hartwell's voice over the speakers.

"—showing off the greatest sport on the dirt in the best way they know how. I know for a fact that Emersyn and Luca are around tonight and will be meandering all night with a special live—"

She's...*here.*

I dropped my phone, and without knowing exactly what was happening, I took off, my boots hitting the ground with a thump, the pain in my knee not even a blip on my radar. My knee could be iced, my knee could heal, but right now...I had three things on my mind.

Find her.

Apologize to her.

Love her.

She was here.

She *was* here.

Rounding the corner, I weaved in and out of cowboys, even getting a *'Hey, Ashford!'* from Ty as I sped past him. Horses whinnied as I darted past, my breath quickening as I rounded another corner...my heart stopping when she came into view coming from the stands. Her head was down, her hands gripping onto her camera, which only brought a smile to my face.

It was real...and she was *here*.

I slowed and stopped, and when her face rose, and her eyes met mine...all was right in the world again.

Her lips parted as she took a breath. "Oakes."

My shoulders rose with each breath I took as I forced the words to form in my head. *What do I say?* 'I'm sorry' didn't seem like it was strong enough. It didn't seem like it would fix everything, but what else was there to say?

"I'm sorry," she sighed, taking a step back. "I didn't know you would be here."

"Drew added it last minute," I admitted, taking another step toward her. Swallowing, I lifted my phone. "This...this is your article?"

Her eyes darted to my face, to my phone, then back to me. "What?"

"I..." I laughed. "I may have subscribed to your new blog...and I got the email...and I...I..." I was stammering now, looking down at the black phone screen as if it held the speech I needed to say. "I read it. And then I heard Hartwell talk about your blog and...you're here."

She tightened her lips, her eyebrows pinched, creating the most perfect little creases in her eyes. "I'm here..."

"What happened to *Rodeo Way*?" I asked, taking another step to close the distance between us.

"I quit. Luca quit. A lot of people quit. After what they did to my article," She drifted off, folding her arms over her chest, looking at her boots.

"What?"

"I told you," she whispered, her eyes catching mine for a second, "that wasn't my article. Sterling...he..." She scoffed and looked away, and I instantly wanted her to look at me again. I forgot how wonderful it felt to have her eyes on me. "It doesn't matter."

"It does, though." Another step forward. "Because if this..." I raised my phone again. "If this really is the article you wrote, that you gave them...I...I..." I dropped my arm and tapped my phone to life. "Emmy..." She shuddered. "*The man and the bull...*"

She closed her eyes. "You read it?"

"I read it. Fuck, Emmy—"

"I asked Drew," she stopped me, taking a step back, and I took a step forward. "He told me you gave the okay. You'll get a cut, of course, but—"

"I don't want a cut from it," I stopped her this time.

She blinked. "I'm sorry. I shouldn't have assumed."

"It's perfectly okay, and Emmy..."

"Can you"—she sighed—"not call me Emmy?"

"That's what I always call you," I said, lowering my voice once the gap between getting smaller. I was so close to her.

"Not since," Her eyes fluttered closed, her voice shaking.

"Seven weeks ago, when I fucked up. I trusted someone else and not you, and I was an asshole. You should have punched me in the gut, told me to listen, because, Emmy...I should have believed you." Ever so lightly, I reached up and moved a piece of hair from her shoulder. "I'm sorry I didn't listen to you. This is your article, isn't it? Not what I read in that magazine."

Meeting my eyes, she nodded. "Sterling added everything, claiming he found everything online, that it wasn't hard when he 'knew people.' But...turns out when you threaten to sue, they listen. I sent that to Drew before posting it, asking him for permission. He said you were okay with it and gave me the green light."

"I had no idea, but Emmy, I love that you published this." I sighed, feeling my lips tug into a smile. "I love that you did this. You took control, and look at you." I took her face in my palms. "You look so much better in an arena than you did in that building."

A sweet sigh left her lungs as her lips twisted. She wanted to smile; I could see it. I could practically taste it. "How did you find the blog?"

I shrugged a shoulder, lowering my hands to her neck. "I caved and Googled your name."

She bit her bottom lip, still hiding the smile I wanted to see. "You Googled me?"

I nodded. "It's been the worst seven weeks of my life." I finally closed the gap, our bodies now centimeters apart. All I had to do was lower my lips to hers, and she'd be mine again, but instead, my thumb lightly trailed her jawline, her soft skin sending flutters through my entire arm, my scar heating up. "I'm sorry I spoke to you like that. I'm sorry I hurt you. I'm sorry... I'm so fucking sorry."

"Oakes." She stopped me, placing a hand on my chest. I could feel my heart beating against her palm, and it filled me with warmth. "I forgive you, if you forgive me. I never wanted to hurt you."

"I love you. I tried not to, but it's impossible. No matter how hard I tried to focus on something else...it's you. It's always you. I love you, Emmy. I've missed you, and I...I'm just... God, I can't believe you're here."

Her camera bag hit the ground with a thump, and her hand cupped my face, pulling me down to her, kissing me for the first time in months. It felt like there was no time missing, like we had been together forever, and the time apart didn't even happen. I kissed her back, my fingers slipping into her hair. Her hat fell from her head, hitting the ground next to her camera bag, but she didn't stop kissing me. She just wrapped her arms around my neck and pulled me even closer. She was here. She was kissing me. She still loved me.

"I love you," she whispered against my lips once I broke the kiss. "I've missed you."

"I love you," I whispered back, pulling her body flush to mine.

"Well, that didn't take you long to find each other."

I raised my head, looking behind Emersyn. She twisted in my arms to see Luca and Drew standing a few feet away, their arms folded, both grinning at us.

"I win the bet." Drew held out a palm to Luca.

Luca shook his head, the devilish grin only growing as he scooted closer to Drew.

"Bet?" I repeated, my grip tightening on Emersyn's waist.

"I said you'd find her before the rodeo even started, and Luca said it would happen during their live and that the entire world would get to see that reunion." Drew smiled as Luca dug in his back pocket, pulling out a fifty and placing it in Drew's hand. "Thank you." Drew pulled his hand away, his eyes not once leaving us.

"They bet on us?" She turned to me but then spun back to her friend. "You weren't looking at the site. You were texting Drew."

Luca barked out a laugh. "Yeah. All of this"—he waved his hand toward us—"was totally planned by yours truly."

Drew furrowed his brow and looked at Luca. "I helped. I changed the schedule."

Luca's laugh got louder, and he reached up to grab Drew's shoulder, turning him away from us. "Let's give them a moment, yeah?"

Once their backs were turned, Luca looked over his shoulder, giving Emersyn a thumbs up and wink.

"Not sure if that thumbs up is for him...or us." She chuckled, turning back to me.

I kissed her. "I'm going to say it was for us."

"They bet on us," she repeated softly.

"They bet on us," I parroted, leaning in for one more kiss.

I pulled Emersyn up the metal stairs to the chute, Luca right behind her with the Instagram live going. We hadn't separated once since we found each other. She would get caught up in something for the blog, but I would search for her hand, kiss her lips lightly, and smile in her direction when we heard someone mention my name.

"Still got Jon Bon Jovi as the song?" she asked as I slipped on my gloves.

"I would never change that song." She gave me a look, telling me she damn well knew I had stopped playing it, but I just gave her a kiss and acted as if those seven weeks didn't exist. "Got my helmet?"

She lifted it and gestured to the phone Luca was holding. "Now, tell me...and everyone watching"—she smiled as I took my helmet from her, slipping it over my unruly hair—"what goes through your head when you get on that bull?"

I raised my brow and met her gaze through the metal bars. "I think of a time, sixteen years ago, when I met the love of my life. The time a horse stomped on my hand, and I almost quit, but she told me not to let one injury define me and that I could ride bulls one-handed. Her words go through my mind before every ride, and I know"—I raised the helmet, leaning in to give her a kiss—"those words and you are the reason I last the eight seconds every time. I love you."

Emersyn sighed, closing her eyes as she melted in front of me and all her Instagram followers. "I love you."

With one more kiss, I lowered my helmet and hoisted myself on the bull. I situated my hands and pulled my fingers through the rope. Jon Bon Jovi began to blast through the speakers as Wyatt Hartwell introduced me, his voice raised as he called out the million-dollar bull rider, the one to watch, the one who was going to reclaim his title. And then...I raised my hand and looked at the woman I loved.

I nodded, and the chute broke open, giving the best ride of my life. Eight seconds of thrill and wonder as the crowd cheered. And when my feet hit the ground, I removed my helmet and ran. Emersyn shouted, her body moving as she jumped over the metal gate, her feet landing in the dirt, and I met her halfway, just in time to wrap my arms around her and hoist her off the ground. With every 'I love you' I muttered into her hair, warmth filled me, and I was finally whole.

"Every ride needs to end this way." I raised my chin, resting my forehead against hers.

"I'll be here for every single one."

"Is that a promise?" I raised a brow.

"A bet?"

"Even better." Then I smiled and kissed her, and the crowd went even wilder.

EPILOGUE
Oakes

*E*ight months later

"You know this bet doesn't matter anymore, right?" I followed Emersyn up to the metal gates as she played with the protective vest that was way too big for her. "I didn't...couldn't...do a handstand, so you don't need to ride a bull."

"Trying to talk me out of it, Ashford?" She spun on her heel and raised a brow at me.

Damn, she was sexy.

"No," I deadpanned, knowing that no matter what I said, she would still follow through with it. "I just wanted to remind you that you don't have to."

"But they have everything ready for me. How could I say, 'Oh, never mind, my overprotective boyfriend has decided I can't do this.'"

"I'm not overprotective."

"Territorial?" she suggested, leaning in every so slightly.

"Now, that I can agree to. You are mine, but..."

"I'm getting on that bull."

"But I'm just saying you don't have to."

"There's no talking her out of it. She's been ready for this for months now," Luca commented, already at the gate, his hand stroking the back of the bull.

"You're petting it?" I looked at him like he was crazy.

Luca had been a constant now that he and Emersyn were business partners. Their blog and podcast had taken off, so much so that they were being requested at rodeos. Since the NFR in December—which I'm proud to say I reclaimed my title—we had been on the road constantly. Luca and Drew made sure Emersyn's and my schedules matched up, but there were times when I had to travel without her. When she had to be home to edit photos or record a podcast, she was always moving, always working, and she loved it. Those lags seemed longer without her, but knowing she would be home waiting for me when I got back made everything worth it. We wasted no time making her apartment our home base, turning that into our *home*. I loved going back to it at the end of a long sprint, loved curling up with her in our bed, and making love to her all night long. There was no way I'd ever get enough of her.

On the road, we booked Airbnbs, stayed at campsites, and had a standing reservation at my mom's farm, and none of it seemed to bother Emersyn or Luca, or Drew—since those two had somehow ended up in a relationship together. What started with emails and texts turned into more when Luca finally got the courage and asked Drew out. Drew was shocked, to say the least, but the look he gave Luca told me he was truly himself now. They complemented each other and were really fun to go on double dates with. Drew joked that when Emersyn and I finally tied the knot, he'd be my best man while Luca was her man of honor. The only thing with that was he didn't know how true that was.

Watching Emersyn listen to the man giving her instructions on climbing on the back of a bull, the small velvet box burned a hole in my chest pocket. My plan was to ask her the second she jumped off the bull.

"Of course I'm petting it," Luca chuckled. "It's nice and calm."

The bull jerked in the chute, and Luca's hand flew away just as fast.

"Don't hurt yourself!" Drew shouted from the center of the dirt, his arms folded, looking like he belonged there. He was more relaxed since becoming his true self, not hiding behind a suit or what was expected of him. Now, his once slicked back blonde hair was curly and free, flowing out in all directions; and instead of slacks and a button-down shirt, he was wearing jeans and a t-shirt—probably the first time I ever saw him in jeans. It was good to see him like this. "I just found you, so…"

"Ah, don't worry!" Luca shouted back. "He's contained."

"Not until the chute opens, and he comes after you," Drew deadpanned, looking at his new boyfriend with concern.

"Honestly"—I held out my palms—"the only ones I'm worried about right now are Emmy and your dumb ass for being on the dirt. Will you come up here please?"

Drew rolled his neck and dropped his arms before jogging toward the chutes, raising himself up on one of the metal grates close to Luca, pulling his arm away from the bull. The two exchanged a look before Luca gave him a quick kiss.

"I will be fine, and so will Drew. We are all going to be fine," Emersyn promised. "Now…I'm getting my ass on this bull." She rubbed her hands together and bounced in place, the fabric of her gloves sounding just as rough as they felt.

"Helmet," I reminded her, reaching for the black helmet Luca held and slipping it over her head. "Now, I really need you to last the eight seconds and jump off the bull and run back here as fast as you can."

"Why?" She smiled. "Worried the bull is gonna chase me down?"

I licked my lips. "Remember, I've seen you ride a mechanical bull and do a fucking handstand on a horse. I know you can do this."

"Then why are you trying to stop me?"

"Because I have a very important question to ask you when you're done, so I'm just as antsy as you are."

Her eyes widened. "Wait...what?"

"Remember what I taught you. Look at the bull." I kept my eyes on her but pointed to the bull. "Feel his body, feel his breath, don't squeeze too hard, and when you're ready, and your breathing is steady...nod."

"You can't tell me you have a very important question for me and then change the subject like that. Ask me now." She grabbed my hand and squeezed.

I laughed and grabbed the metal bars on the helmet, pulling her close to me. I touched my forehead to the helmet. "Trust me, you want me to wait. Now, get your pretty ass on that bull."

I could see Emersyn swallow, licking her lips, and she turned.

"Okay..." she breathed.

With me on one side and Luca on the other, Emersyn lowered herself on the bull. He jerked and bucked in the small space, and a yelp filled the air, quickly turning into a laugh as Emersyn raised her chin.

"Oh, I'm kind of regretting this now."

"No regrets!" Drew shouted. "Just nod!"

"He's mad," she said, a shake leaving her lungs.

"Yeah, he is," I chuckled, knocking on her helmet. "You holding on? You got your hand in the right place?"

She nodded. "What's your question?" she asked, looking up at me.

"Ride. Then I'll ask. Drew's off the dirt, you're holding on, keep that arm up. Ride."

Emersyn's blue eyes met mine as she shifted her weight once more on the bull. The question built up in my core...but waiting would be better.

She'd last the eight seconds, then she'd jump off, the adrenaline pumping through her entire body. I could feel my heart begin to race, not just for her ride, but for everything that came after. It was going to be the longest eight seconds of my life.

Emersyn took a breath through her lips, settled her body, raised her arm, and nodded.

ACKNOWLEDGEMENTS

I will try to keep this short and sweet, but that never really goes well for me. When it came to writing this book, I had...fun. So much fun. Never did I doubt the story during that first draft. I never had imposter syndrome. I never questioned it. I never drafted a story so fast. Never wanted to spend as much time in a document as I did with *Break the Chute*. This book reminded me why I loved to write. I often call it my heart book, and even though it took me a lot of drafts to get it just right...I still hole that. Break the Chute is my heart book, but I didn't do this alone. Books take more than one person to become a physical item you hold in your hand and as much as I would like to take all the credit for this particular book...I simply can't.

First and foremost, my husband and family. For putting up with me click, click, clicking well into the night and during movies, and for supporting me every step of the way—thank you! I may have dedicated this book to my past self...but it's for you four as well.

Jessee—damn this would not exist with you. Thank you for telling me to write a book for fun, to write a book for me and then cheering me on as I rewrote it basically from the ground up and reading it again and loving it again. Oakes will always be yours. I couldn't do this without you. Ever.

Tessa—the first one to get chapter by chapter and beg for more. Thank you for always being there and boosting my spirits. I'm not sure Oakes and Emersyn would be who they are without you.

Elizabeth—Emersyn's muse—thank you for being courageous and making your life what you wanted it to be. You took the bull by the horns and became a woman I look up too in more ways than one. You are simply amazing. Thank you so much for inspiring Emersyn and myself.

To all the gals at the Mountains and Manuscripts Retreat in 2025. Thank you for letting me cry—and not letting me give up.

To my amazing PA, Kayla. The best PA an indie author could ask for. Thank you for taking my scattered brain and keeping it all organized. Your encouragement and love for this story kept me going and without you...this book would still be sitting on my shelf waiting...and waiting...and waiting...to be published. THANK YOU!

My fabulous street team!! The hustle and bustle you guys did to help spread the word, the posts and reels and encouragement in the chat was exactly what I needed. I love each and every one of you!!!

My writing group, Grayson, MJ, India, Cindy, Jessee...thank you for listening to my broken record over and over again and giving me encouragement. Its been two years now and I still value you guys!!

All the beta readers who helped this book grow to what it is now, Quin, Kayla, Kate, Beth...you made this story what it is. Thank you!

My amazing cover designer, EverAfter Cover Design, for giving me the best cover possible. I still swoon when I see it.

The artist that helped bring Oakes and Emmy to life. Kloe and Erika – thank you for letter me see them every day.

To the editors who helped make this book what it is, Cait, Jenn, Vee...I love each and every one of you.

Oakes and Emmy—thank YOU for reminding me why I love to tell stories.

This was a year and half in the making, and I am so grateful to each and every one of you reading this now, for taking the chance on the book that changed my life and gave me myself back. Thank you for loving them, probably more than I do. I love you!

With love,
Stefanie

ALSO BY
Stefanie K Steck

The Moments of Us Series

That Right Moment

That Next Moment

That First Moment

The Hartwell Hills Series

Somebody Like Me

Never Left You

Fool For You

Book 4 — Coming Soon

Standalones

Break the Chute

About the Author

Stefanie K Steck is a romance writer, Army wife, mom of three crazy kids and curator of a small zoo. She currently lives in Utah and has recently found joy in camping. In the little spare time she has, you can find her reading, writing, cuddling her favorite Guinea pig, Nugget, or rewatching the *Back to the Future Trilogy* or the *Marvel Cinematic Universe (The Infinity Saga* obviously).

Follow her on Instagram @authorstefanieksteck
www.stefanieksteckbooks.com

www.ingramcontent.com/pod-product-compliance
Lightning Source LLC
Chambersburg PA
CBHW021842130726
47989CB00009B/3055